Ice

By Will Robbins

Compilation and Introduction copyright © 2009 by
Triple Crown Publications
PO Box 247378
Columbus, Ohio 43224
www.TripleCrownPublications.com

Library of Congress Control Number: 2009935877
ISBN 13: 978-0-9820996-8-1
Author: Will Robbins
Graphics Design: http://www.leapgraphics.com
Editor-in-Chief: Vickie Stringer
Editor: Alanna Boutin
Editorial Assistant: Christina Carter

First Trade Paperback Edition Printing 2009

10 9 8 7 6 5 4 3 2 1

Printed in the United States of America

DEDICATION

This work is dedicated in loving memory to people I've lost
and who have affected my life.

My cousins/godbrothers Evan and Ricky Graham, this book
wouldn't have been inspired without your sacrifices and
unexpected deaths.

My sister Alexandria "Xandy" Milan Robbins.
You showed me what true courage and strength really is.

My cousin Robert Simmons.
Thanks for believing in me.

My cousin Franklin Simmons.
You should've come home with me.

Taylik "Smokeface" Davis.
Thanks for being the key to me finding another family
and my first love.

Margaret "Grandma" Davis.
Thanks for treating me like a grandson and always
accepting me in your home.

My spiritual and martial arts brother Laquan "QB" Body.
Thanks for making me a better fighter.

Special dedication.
Calvis "Dobby Shemuel" Sykes.
A devoted husband, father, son, brother, uncle, and friend.
The world feels the loss.

MAY 27, 1976–JUNE 6, 2009

ACKNOWLEDGMENTS

It sounds cliché, but thanks to the Most High for giving me the patience and skills to complete this work under so many stresses and obstacles. Thank you, Vickie Stringer and the Triple Crown Family, for taking a chance on me. Thank you, Alanna, for your editing skills. Ellen Abdunafi, thanks for being the best mom you knew how to be. Thanks for being my backbone even though I was man enough to stand on my own. Pops, I hope you're proud! To my beautiful wife, Shavon, I am because of you. To my sons, Sadiel "Puddah" Gonzales, Lemar "Mar Mar" Davis, and William Ricky "LG" Robbins, continue to be strong men and look out for one another. To my daughter, Anisha "Boogie Bear" Robbins, you're beautiful but come harder than that. Life is hard on a young black woman. To my brother Yasin, continue to chase ya dreams. To my brother Amir, thanks for all the advice and showing me another example of a positive black man. To my brother Malik, I know you're still mad, but I know you're proud. This book is partly because of you, too. Thanks for the laptop, baby! To my brother Robert, continue to take care of your mother; quit being lazy! Life is out there. To my sister Dorinda, you are a rose that blossomed out of cracked concrete. I love you so much; stay strong! To my sister Sabourah, thanks for having my back when Mommy was riding it too hard. To my goddaughter Taleesa Scott, continue to keep ya legs closed and your heart and mind open; keep writing that poetry, baby! To my goddaughter Shamaryah "Mar Mar" Sykes, continue to make your father proud, and we can have some daddy-daughter days too, Lord willing. To my countless nieces and nephews, you know who you all are. Sorry I don't see y'all much, but you are all in my heart and on my mind. To my brothers from another mother with unconditional love:

Chris Pacheco, continue to strive to be the best father you can be.

Troy Scott, life has always been hard on you; toughen up and get back out there.

Calvis Sykes, gone but not forgotten; your kids are still

tearing things up like a cyclone down here.
Willis "Man" Rivera, thanks for always being a phone
call away. Your infectious laugh always made things
better for me.

Hammed Rivera, go back to college and do ya thing.
You always made me proud, and you inspired me; now
you know.

Terrance Lee, I was always proud of you going overseas.
I'm glad you're back home safe. Stay off my phone and
out of my closet!

Diamula and Pedro, I didn't forget y'all grimy asses, but
I love y'all anyway.

Lemar Davis, thanks for teaching me something that
no one can ever take away, Kenpo Karate. Thanks for
being a father figure and sorry for any disappointments
I may have caused you.

Anthony Davis, thanks for the countless hours in the
gym and teaching me. Thanks for opening the doors for
me to be accepted as family.

Tracey Johnson, I always admired your strength, gener-
ousity, and fighting skills; thanks for passing down the
teachings to me as well. To Aliesha Davis, my son's
mother, thanks for bringing my son through the
matrix. Thanks for being my first love. May you truly
find happiness one day on your own terms.

Shaun Small, bring my nieces around and check out
your boy and his family!

Marcus Harrison, thanks for holding me down with the
movies and DVDs.

To my mother- and father-in-law, Pam and Jr. Santiago,
I don't know how I would've conducted myself as a man
if you guys didn't show up.

Ramone Dashiell, I'm proud of you; keep writing.

Alonzo "Hamburger" Jones, a true Eastwick Hustler,
I'm coming for that 20-minute spot; you know what
I'm talking about!

To my countless aunts and uncles, I hope you guys are
proud, too.

To anyone not mentioned, it's not on purpose or that
you guys didn't mean anything to me, but it would take
another book just to thank you all. Peace and blessings
to all, and last but not least, thank you, readers, for the
support.

1

Oh Shit

Woo sat on the porcelain god cursing his father for buying the cheap hospital tissue, which seemed to leave a cut on your ass rather than the comfortable dingle berries of Charmin's tissue. He flushed the toilet and began to wash his hands and stare in the mirror. Woo was very light-skinned, a feature he inherited from his white mother. He looked more like a Puerto Rican than what most people would call a mulatto, but who could really tell the difference between the two? He stared at the red blemishes on his face and chiseled body, a few traits he also inherited from his mother.

His mother was tall and had the body of a fitness instructor. Woo continued to examine the blemishes and wondered why his father had to mess with a white woman. Woo loved his mother and was good looking despite the blemishes, but he felt like he could be a pretty boy without them. He dried his hands and thought of his dead mother he never had a chance to know.

Woo exited the bathroom and saw his father lying on the bed in his bedroom, which was right across from the bathroom. His father was a tall, medium-built black man with braids. The two men looked exactly alike with the exception of the dark skin and braids.

"Everything come out alright?" Tyson asked, as his son appeared in the doorway.

"Yeah, and why do you keep buying that cheap toilet paper? It feels like I'm wiping my ass with sandpaper," he said with his face curled up.

"Hey, we have to save money somewhere to get out of this shit hole," Tyson stated, looking around the room.

Woo smiled and said, "Yeah, but not at the expense of our asses." They both joined in on the laugh. "We would be out of this shit hole if I was out there working for Ice or running things with my cousins," Woo said, changing the subject with a little attitude.

"First of all, watch your mouth. We don't need Ice or your cousins. Those fools gonna wind up dead or in jail, and I refuse to see you there. You worked too hard since you got out of the detention center to throw it all away," Tyson said with the sincerity that only a loving father could have.

"Your brother threw his life away when he decided to kill someone who disrespected him. Your sister just had a baby and dropped out of school. Lord knows what she'll do now. I know you're not looking to go down any of those roads, are you?"

"No, Pop, I was just thinking," Woo said, lowering his voice and shaking his head to show he was sorry for mentioning it.

"Hey, *Cheers* is coming on," Woo said, trying to change the subject. He sat on his father's bed and began to watch *Cheers*, something the two of them did every night no matter what was going on. It was their way of spending quality time with each other. During the commercial break, Woo asked lightheartedly, "Pop, why did you mess with white women?"

Tyson looked at his son to see if he really wanted an answer.

"Well?" Woo said, as he looked back at his father.

"'Cause when the lights go out, they're all pink inside," Tyson stated, as they both laughed.

"What was it about my mother that you had to have her?" Woo asked.

"She had good credit. You know white people have good credit, and mine was messed up," Tyson said laughing.

"Come on, Pop, stop playing. You play too much," Woo stated as he lightly pushed his father.

Tyson sat up and leaned his back against the wall, his head tilting back, and took a deep breath. Slowly, he let the air out as he thought of what to tell his inquiring son.

"Well, son, your mother was a friend of your aunt and she used to come to the house all the time. At first, she was a pain in the ass, I guess 'cause she was young and had a crush on me." Tyson reached for his cigarettes and pulled one out. He lit it, took a drag, and blew the smoke out slowly. Then he waved the smoke away with his hands because he knew how much Woo hated cigarette smoke. He continued, "She came to the house a lot over the years, but I didn't look at her in any type of way until her prom."

Woo listened as if his life depended on what his father had to say next. Tyson's eyes were closed as he visualized his woman standing in front of him.

"What about the prom?" Woo asked excitedly, breaking Tyson's fantasy.

Opening his eyes and shaking his head, Tyson asked, "Oh shit, where was I?"

Woo laughed and said, "The prom. You a'ight?"

"Yeah, I'm a'ight," Tyson said, mocking his son's slang. "Your aunt was getting ready for the prom, and your grandmother was helping her. There was a knock at the door, so I had to answer it. I opened the door, and there she was standing there in all her glory," Tyson explained as his face brightened up at the thought of his woman.

"Who? My mother?" Woo asked, already knowing the answer.

"No, the tooth fairy," Tyson answered to let his son know it was a dumb question. "She wore this long champagne dress with matching open-toe shoes. She had long, beautiful hair, and a diamond necklace that ended at the cleavage of her dress," Tyson described. "The dress showed her body off better than anything else I ever saw her in," Tyson said. "The next day after the prom, we went out, and the rest is history."

"What about the dude she went to the prom with?" Woo asked curiously.

"He was a nobody. Besides, he couldn't compete with my looks and smooth lines anyway," Tyson said with a smile.

"You should be lucky that I was smooth enough to pull your mother. Otherwise, your white ass wouldn't be here," Tyson said teasing his son.

They talked right through the episode of *Cheers*. Woo rarely asked questions about his mother. He always felt cheated when people spoke about her around him. She passed away when he was only six months old, so he avoided stories and questions like the plague. He figured the less he knew, the less pain it would cause him. But there was something different about this night, something that made him feel comfortable talking about his mother. He knew his father felt the same as he did, so he figured they could comfort each other. It seemed strange to Tyson when Woo continued with the questions about his mother.

"Pop, how did Mom pass?" Woo asked with concern in his voice. Tyson looked down and let out a sigh before answering his son's question. They had this conversation years ago, and Tyson didn't think he would have to explain it again. It hurt him just as much as it did Woo to hear or speak of his dead woman, but he knew he had to go down memory lane, even if it was just for his son's sake.

"Hold on, I'll be right back." Tyson bolted out, trying to avoid the question. He walked into the kitchen to the refrigerator and grabbed a Budweiser. Opening it, he raised the bottle to his lips and began to gulp the beer down.

Woo, waiting for his father to enter the room, put two pillows behind his head and lay back.

Tyson threw the empty bottle in the trash and stepped back into his room. Seeing his son lying there, he smiled at his son like a proud father.

"What?" Woo asked as he caught his father's gaze.

"Nothing," Tyson replied as he sat back down on the bed.

"Pop, we don't have to talk about this if it bothers you," Woo said, feeling sorry that he brought the subject up.

"It's alright," Tyson replied smiling and slapping his son's foot.

"Well, your mother was supposed to take it easy after having you, but she never told me that," Tyson exclaimed with a sigh. "She didn't want to worry me.

"She was thoughtful like that," Tyson said, wiping a tear from the corner of his eye. "We went to a bowling alley, and as she lifted up a bowling ball to launch it down the lane, she caught a heart attack," Tyson told his son while trying to keep his composure.

Woo sat up and stared at his father and saw how much hurt was in his eyes. "Your mother was in a coma for months, fighting, but she never came out of it," Tyson recalled while looking into his son's eyes to see if he was okay.

"And finally she passed," Woo said with a raspy voice.

"Yeah," Tyson replied in a voice just above a whisper.

Woo perked up, trying to lighten the subject, and asked, "Pop, why did you mess with fat women?"

With a mischievous grin, Tyson said, "Well, when I realized how much pussy I was missing, I decided to give them a try."

"But that last one you messed with was fat as hell. She was so fat that if you hit her with a bus, she'd swear you threw a rock at her," Woo stated as they both began to laugh.

"Oh shit," Tyson said as he looked at the clock. It was 12 a.m., time for him to leave for work. Tyson worked late nights at his brother's bar to pay the bills. Woo always felt his uncle was a cheap, anal bastard. He loved his uncle, but hated that his uncle wouldn't let him step foot in his bar. He also thought his uncle could've paid his father more money.

"Pop, why don't you work for someone else?" Woo asked while stretching his back.

"Because your uncle is the only one who will pay me under the table," Tyson said, while lighting another cigarette. "If I get a regular job, my Veterans check will be terminated, and a regular job is not worth it," Tyson explained to his son as he turned off the TV.

"Why don't you get a job if you're so worried about me or the bills around here?" Tyson asked sarcastically.

"I ain't that worried," Woo exclaimed with a laugh.

Woo used to sell drugs for Ice with his cousins before the detention center and then his cousins helped reform him afterwards. But getting a regular job at McDonalds, Burger King, or Kentucky Fried Chicken wasn't in his plans. Tyson understood that Woo handled thousands of dollars working for Ice, so he knew his son wouldn't bust his ass at nobodies' fast-food restaurant. He was just happy and proud that his 17-year-old son was going to school and keeping his nose clean.

"Hey, why don't you go to bed? You have school in the morning," Tyson said as he put on his coat. The remark was more of a request than a question.

"A'ight, I'll see you in the morning, Pop," Woo said as he yawned. He walked his father to the door, and they embraced each other as Tyson said, "Don't forget to lock up."

Tyson walked down the dark, narrow, smelly hallway to meet the brisk night air. As he stepped outside, he lifted his collar to ward off the cool breeze. Tyson shook his head in despair as he looked at his surroundings. Between the drunks, crackheads, dealers, and decrepit buildings, the whole scene looked like Michael Jackson's "Thriller." He cursed himself for not having himself together enough to provide better for his son. "No wonder Ice has so many people working for him with the way shit is out here," Tyson said out loud to himself as he lit a cigarette.

Woo lay in his single bed listening to Robin Harris's "Bébé's Kids" on his 5-disc change CD player radio trying to fall asleep. "I wonder what Ice is doing?" he asked himself out loud. Woo worked for Ice for three years before getting caught and locked up. Ice was like a father to him and to all the kids whose fathers were locked up, or who were crackheads, or just nonexistent. Woo's father was locked up when he was seven years old. And after all of Woo's trials and tribulations, Ice seemed to come right on time. Ice really didn't give a fuck about the kids, only what they could do for him. Woo continued to remember the times he had working for Ice until he finally fell asleep.

Woo woke up to the smell of eggs and bacon. He walked out of his room, rubbing his eyes, to see his father standing over the stove in his black robe cooking. "Good morning, Pop," Woo said rubbing his soft, short curly hair that all the ladies loved.

"What's up? You hungry?" Tyson asked, showing his son a big plate of food.

"Always ... just let me use the bathroom first," Woo said as he headed down the hall. Tyson always made it home in time to cook breakfast for Woo before he went to school. Woo walked into the kitchen to see his food on the table and his father knocked out on his bed. He finished his breakfast and hurried into his room to get dressed.

Woo was meticulous when it came to dressing. He and his father didn't have much, but the best clothes were something he didn't do without. "I'll have to thank Ice later for these clothes," he spoke out loud as he grabbed a pair of Sean John dress pants and a Sean John sweater from his closet. "What am I talking about? I worked for these clothes," he said as he thought of his previous statement.

He put together his outfit and got dressed. Now his only dilemma was what to wear on his feet. He looked inside of his closet and saw his various sneakers and Timberland boots around his closet. Finally, he picked out a pair of dress shoes that matched his sweater, looked in his wall-mounted mirror, and said to himself, "Us light-skinned people makin' a comeback," and he laughed. Woo put on his black leather coat, grabbed his book bag, and headed for the door.

will robbins

2

SCHOOL BOYZ

Woo walked to his boy Taye's house, which was right next door to his building complex. Taye's house was one of the biggest houses on the block. Woo was greeted at the door by Taye's grandmother, who was short in stature but had a pit bull demeanor.

"Taye ready?" Woo asked as he kissed Grandma on her cheek.

"Upstairs, motherfucka," she said back as a term of endearment.

"You really gotta watch that mouth, Grandma," Woo said as they smiled at each other.

He walked up the steep steps into the attic thinking to himself that the steps seemed more like a ladder. Taye was putting on his black and white Nike's as Woo walked in. The attic had wall-to-wall carpet, two twin-sized beds, a big screen TV, VCR, DVD player, PlayStation with various games, and beautiful mahogany dressers. It even had a bathroom and a small refrigerator so Taye never had to go downstairs for anything. His attic was bigger than Woo's whole apartment.

Woo was a little envious, but it was quickly nullified by the fact that he spent most of his time over here, and Taye and his family were more than giving.

"What's up?" Taye asked as he stood up and gave Woo a pound. Taye was the same height as Woo and had a track star physique, since that's what he was.

"Hurry up, man, we're goin' be late for class," Woo said. "Your grandma is crazy, man. She keeps callin' me a motherfucka'," Woo told Taye as they walked down the stairs.

"She calls everybody that," Taye said, smacking Woo on the back of his neck. Taye kissed his grandma on the cheek and said, "Good morning," as he walked towards the door.

"Aren't you going to eat something before you go?" she asked.

"I don't have time," Taye said as he opened the door for himself and Woo.

With a warning in her voice, Grandma said, "You'd have time, motherfucka, if you woke up when I told you to." Taye ignored his grandma as they walked out the door. "Have a good day, you mother-fuckas," Grandma yelled as Taye closed the door.

The two young men hit the street and headed toward the bus stop. The cold air made it easy to see their breaths. It was times like these that Woo wished he had saved the money that he made hustling to buy a car. When he was making money, however, he was too young to buy a vehicle.

"Damn, it's cold out here," Taye complained, rubbing his hands together.

"You should have asked Grandma to use that big-ass Caddie," Woo said with his hands buried in his pockets.

"Where y'all goin'?" a voice from across the street asked.

"To school," Woo answered as he stepped up on the curb to address his boy Jab.

"Look at the school boyz," a caramel-complexioned teen with a lot of ice on said as he gave Woo and Taye a pound.

"What's up, E-Double?" Woo asked, greeting his cousin.

E-Double got his nickname because he was a Gemini and had two distinct personalities, but his government name was Khalil Watkins.

"Nothin' … me and Black makin' that money like you used to," E-Double said as Black walked up.

"What's up?" Black asked, giving his cousin Woo a punch in the chest.

"Ouch, faggot," Woo, said holding his chest. "You better count your money, Black. You know how Bruce is," Woo said looking at Bruce walk down the street. Black was real black, so black that his shadow was confused. Black's government name was Raheem Watkins. Black had a big Afro, the kind that all the women wanted to braid. People used to tease Black, E-Double, and Woo when they stood side by side. Everyone said that they looked like the three color stages that Michael Jackson went through to be white.

Black counted his money and noticed the dope fiend gave him a fake bill. "Yo, hold up, Bruce!" he yelled as he walked toward the fiend. The anger in Black's voice and the expression on his face caused the fiend to take flight.

Black took off after Bruce, but to no avail. Black's Timberlands and the fiend's speed made him impossible to catch. Black realized he couldn't catch Bruce, so he picked up a Snapple bottle and launched it like a baseball. The bottle seemed to fly through the air in slow motion as it connected to the back of Bruce's head. The bottle shattered, and blood burst from the impact. Bruce stumbled, but his fear and adrenaline helped him make it around the corner. Black thought to himself that his Little League skills were still intact after he tagged Bruce. He looked back to see his brother, cousin, and his boy, Jab, on the ground, laughing at what they had witnessed.

As Black crossed the street, a car stopped in front of him. "Let me get two," a white man with yellow teeth said, smiling at Black. Black looked both ways before digging into his pockets and inconspicuously handing him a small piece of paradise. Most dealers wouldn't sell to a white person just in case it's a cop or informer, but Black knew with whom he was dealing. He stepped onto the corner and said out of breath, "That fuckin' fiend is fast as hell."

"You ain't catchin' no fiend," Jab, a redbone-complexioned boy said, which caused the fellas to laugh.

Taye hoisted his book bag on his shoulders more comfortably and said, "Woo, let's get to the bus stop."

"Y'all don't have to catch a bus. I'll give y'all a ride," E-Double said as he threw dice against the wall.

"Hell, no! We ride with you with shit in the car, you get stopped, we all goin' to jail. I can't go back to jail. I have a fat ass and can't fight. That a recipe for rape," Woo said to entertain everyone.

"Fuck you, then," E-Double replied as a joke.

As Woo and Taye began to walk, a black Mercedes Benz SUV with tinted windows pulled up. Slowly, the window rolled down and Ice's face appeared.

"What's up, Ice?" the boys asked in chorus. Woo and Taye turned

around at the mention of Ice's name.

"Checkin' on my business," Ice said taking off his glasses, staring at the boys. Ice was a light-brown-skinned man with dreadlocks and a baby face. His cold stare and quick temper made up for his baby face, though. Everyone knew that Ice wasn't someone you could mess with. He was exiled out of his own country of Haiti for being too violent.

"Business can't be too bad, Ice," Woo said, leaning into the window.

"You still looking smooth I see," Ice replied, touching Woo's sweater.

"Some things just don't change," Woo said.

"Except you workin' for me," Ice responded with a sly grin. E-Double, Jab, and Black shot dice as the conversation between Woo and Ice lingered on.

"Woo, we gotta go," Taye said, shootin' rocks in Ice's direction. Taye hated Ice for what he did to his cousin. Taye's cousin Jamal used to open up shop for one of Ice's busiest blocks. Jamal made the mistake of coming to work late. Ice and his boys threw Jamal a beating so bad that he couldn't see out of his left eye or hear out of his left ear. They also made it so that Jamal would never walk upright again. And to humiliate Jamal a little further, Ice put Jamal back to work on the corner wearing a huge Flava Flav clock so he would never be late again.

Taye swore one day that he would pay Ice back for his indiscretions. Ice knew that Taye hated him, and he knew why. Ice actually liked Taye. He made a lot of money betting on Taye at the track meets, and that's why he didn't make Taye take an early retirement.

"I'll give you school boyz a ride if your boy could stop grillin' me long enough to get in," Ice said, pointing in Taye's directions. Woo turned and saw the look on Taye's face and thought to himself, "Ice would be dead if looks could kill." Woo knew that Taye would never accept a ride from Ice so he turned around and said, "Maybe some other time, Ice. And what is it with this school boyz shit?"

"You'll catch a ride with Ice but not me?" E-Double asked, overhearing the conversation.

"That's right, 'cause I got class and style, and you just a corner boy. Now stop by my spot later; I have a couple more packages that need handling," Ice said, giving E-Double the finger as he put his

will robbins

glasses back on.

E-Double wanted to tell Ice where he could go and what to do with his finger, but he didn't want to make waves. He simply waved him off, shook his head, and continued playing dice. E-Double and Black weren't punks by any means, but they wanted to keep Ice around because it was good for business.

"That was cold, Ice," Woo said, pointing his finger.

"That's why my name is Ice, now get to school," he said with a proud grin, rolling up his window.

"I hate that ma'fucka," Black said, giving Ice's car the finger as it drove off.

"Why?" Woo asked nonchalantly. He didn't understand the emotion since Ice put them in a position to eat for years.

"Everybody hate him 'cept you," Taye said with his face curled up.

"That ma'fucka just a snake. Let's leave it at that," E-Double said.

"Here comes the bus, Ritz," Jab said with a smile, knowing that the name irritated Woo.

"If I didn't have to catch the bus, I'd kick yo' ass," Woo said, smacking Jab lightly across the face. Then he ran towards the bus and almost tripped to his people's amusement.

"Ha, ha, that's why you almost bust yo' ass," Jab yelled before Woo and Taye jumped on the bus.

They walked to the back of the bus like every other black person. Woo thought it was strange that most black people rushed to sit at the back of the bus after all the struggles to sit in the front. He viewed it as you only wanted to do what you couldn't do. Most of the younger generation sat at the back of the bus because that's where all the gossip and fun began. They even sat in the back of the classroom for the same reason and to avoid questions from the teacher as much as possible.

Woo was looking at his notes for class when Taye asked, "Hey, why did Jab call you Ritz?"

"Because I'm half-white and -black, but I'm darker than a Saltine cracker. Plus, he knows that it pisses me off," Woo said as a few people on the bus began to laugh. He smiled and blushed when he noticed the passengers were listening to his conversation.

The bus ride up Elizabeth Avenue was uneventful until Woo looked out the window and saw two females fighting. A short, black, burly girl had another female by her extensions, connecting with uppercuts. Excited, he stood up and exclaimed, "Yo, look at these two girls fighting!" All the passengers on the left side moved to the right side to see the fight.

"Can't we all just get along?" Taye said, yelling out the window to the other passengers' amusement. The male passengers in chorus began to shout, "Titties, titties, titties." Everyone continued to watch the fight until the combatants were out of view.

The late bell had already sounded as Woo and Taye walked into the school. They quickly headed down the hall to their Black Studies class. Even though Woo was mixed, he identified with his black culture, especially since he grew up in the projects with nothing but Blacks and Puerto Ricans.

"You're late," a slim, brown-skinned man with glasses and an Afro said as Woo and Taye entered the classroom.

"Sorry," Taye replied as he put down his book bag and took a seat.

"Next time try not to be late. I don't go for that 'Colored People's Time.' We brothers and sisters need to be on time always," Mr. Taylor said, fixing his glasses.

"I'm half-white, so I'm only half-late," Woo said, trying to be a comedian. Mr. Taylor was one of the few teachers that had faith in Woo despite his games and lack of focus.

The bell rang, and Mr. Taylor dismissed his class. The hallways were more crowded than a bunch of Mexicans carpooling.

"I'll catch you after school," Taye said, giving Woo a pound. Black Studies was the only class that the two had together. Taye tried to make it through the crowd to catch up with Lisa. Lisa was a dark butter-pecan Puerto Rican, with shoulder-length raven hair, young firm breasts, thick thighs like a horse, with an ass to boot.

"Lisa, Lisa," Taye called out to get her attention. He moved through the crowd swiftly to catch her.

"What's up, poppi?" Lisa asked with a smile as Taye stood in front of her.

"Damn, you look good," Taye said, licking his lips like he was LL Cool J. Lisa wore a short skirt that showed off her thick thighs and a tight, black shirt which made her breasts look like they were about to pop out.

"Let's go somewhere and talk," Taye said, grabbing her by the

will robbins

waist and kissing her on the neck.

Giggling like a little girl, Lisa said, "You don't really want to talk."

"I *do* want to talk," Taye replied, lying through his teeth. "I know the perfect place," he said grabbing her by the hand.

Taye walked Lisa down the stairs to the lower part of the school.

"Where are we going?" she asked, already knowing the answer. Taye skipped class plenty of times to fuck Lisa behind the staircase. It was more fun for Lisa to pretend that she didn't know what was going on.

Taye grabbed her in his arms and began to kiss her. She darted her tongue in and out of his mouth, and fire seemed to shoot through his body. As he felt her breasts, his manhood began to rise. Feeling something poke her thigh, Lisa unzipped Taye's pants and fondled his dick. He quickly pulled up her skirt and pulled down her panties. Then he turned her around and bent her over slightly and penetrated her. She let out a moan as Taye's inches began to fill her velvet wet spot. Feeling his dick inside her caused her to moan louder and louder. "Get this pussy, poppi," she yelled and moaned.

"Keep it down before we get caught," Taye warned, stroking harder and faster to come quicker.

"Hurry up then," Lisa replied, throwing her ass back trying to make him climax faster. Taye's eyes and head went backwards from the tight, wet strokes of Lisa's pussy.

"I'm comin', I'm comin'," Taye moaned as he pulled his dick out to avoid getting her pregnant. It was his form of birth control, which seemed to be working for him. The bell rang for their next class as they fixed themselves.

"Can I tell you something?" Lisa asked with shame in her eyes.

"Yeah," Taye said with concern.

"You can't tell anyone, Taye, I swear," she said, looking at him with her big brown eyes. Taye didn't even answer. He just waited for Lisa to say what was on her mind. "Ice ... Ice ..." Lisa struggled to get her words out.

"Ice *what*?" he asked with fire and contempt in his voice.

Looking at the ground and fidgeting, she told Taye that Ice had her sister Vicky dancing and selling her ass.

"That ma'fucka," Taye yelled as he heard the news. Lisa was in tears but tried to calm him down. Taye loved Lisa and her family.

"One day, I'm gonna pay Ice back for all the shit he's done to people, I swear," Taye said as he hugged and kissed Lisa on the forehead. They embraced for a while, trying to console each other before the silence was broken.

"Yo, y'all gonna be late for your next class if you don't hurry up," Woo said, knowing exactly where to find his peoples. He'd used the same spot a time or two himself.

Finally, the last bell rang, and Woo rushed to get outside for some fresh air. The heat in school was killing him. He stood outside, talking to some of his associates, waiting for Taye to arrive. Taye walked out holding Lisa's hand.

"Bitch, you better get off my man," Woo said, snapping his fingers and acting effeminate.

"Fuck you," Taye said with a smile.

"That's what I'm hoping for later," Woo continued in an effeminate manner.

Taye kissed Lisa good-bye before she jumped in her mother's car to go to work.

"Stop playin' like that, bitch," Taye said as they crossed the street.

"Why was Lisa crying earlier? I know your dick ain't that big," Woo said looking at Taye to see any kind of emotion. Woo and Taye were more like brothers, and Woo loved Lisa like a sister.

"That bitch-ass Ice got Vicky selling her ass," Taye replied, knowing that Lisa didn't want anybody to know. Woo wasn't just anybody, though, he was his boy. Taye figured if the right person fucked Vicky, everyone would find out anyway. He figured the news would sound better coming from him.

"So what you wanna do?" Woo asked.

"I don't know yet, but before I die, I'm gonna see Ice's ass melt."

Taye's words stung Woo. Woo still cared about Ice, but he wanted his boy to know he felt his pain. He knew Taye couldn't make a move against Ice. Ice wasn't untouchable, but it would take more than Taye to get at him. Woo was a little angry at the news he heard too, because he had a thing for Vicky. He remembered the time he told her he was a virgin so she would fuck him. Woo figured he was still cool enough to talk to Ice on Vicky's behalf.

"It's goin' to be a'ight, Taye, let's go home," Woo said putting his arm around him.

3

SHOOTIN' THE BREEZE

Silk's pool hall was a safe haven for all the local drug dealers, hustlers, dropouts, and kids cutting classes. Silk was small in stature, but he commanded respect. He used to live the street life in his younger age, but his ambition to grow old, among other things, made him go straight. He let the degenerates hang out at his spot in hopes that his wisdom would rub off on them. Silk never looked down on anyone or felt he was better than anyone. And he sometimes felt like he was just one bill away from returning to the streets himself.

"So, how long do you plan on staying in the crack and dope game, young blood?" Silk asked E-Double, who was concentrating on his shot.

"As long as the crack and dope game is nice to me," E-Double replied, taking his shot.

"The dope game never been nice to no one," a dope fiend said, pulling up his sleeve, revealing tracks filled with yellow pus and blood.

Everyone turned and curled up their faces at the grotesque sight.

"The dope game been real nice to us," Jab said, lifting up his sleeve, revealing a gold Movado watch studded with diamonds around the band.

"And nobody forced you to put that shit in your arm anyway," Jab said with arrogance and contempt in his voice.

"The crack game been good to you, Silk," E-Double said matter-of-factly.

"Oh, so I guess I was born with this cane and limp? I was shot trying to make the biggest deal of my life. It was also a big opportunity for the guys I was dealing with. They were young, ambitious, and didn't have respect for the game. Back in the day, it was all about honor. People held a higher code of morals than you guys today. My guys wanted the money and the crack, so naturally, I had to go. Out came the guns. I was so filled with trust and honor I didn't carry a weapon. They shot my brother in the chest and head. He died where he fell. I got away with just a shot in the leg, which caused my limp today. And this pool hall ain't from drug money. It's an inheritance."

"Who's 'they'?" Black asked over his shoulder as he played Street Fighter.

"Another time, another story," Silk said as he walked towards the back of the pool hall and disappeared. E-Double and Jab continued to shoot pool as Woo and Taye walked in. Everyone said their usual greetings and began to mingle.

"Pop two quarters in so I can bus' yo' ass in, Street Fighter," Woo said, smacking Black on his ass.

"I would, honkey nigga, but I got some business to handle," Black replied jokingly.

"You almost make me sound like a ghetto superhero," Woo said, taking the joke in stride. He was used to hearing all of the mixed jokes.

Black walked over to E-Double and dug his hands in his pockets, removing keys.

"Get your hands out my pocket, nigga," E-Double yelled, mocking a scene from Malcolm X. Everyone laughed at the reenactment.

"Where's he going?" Woo asked, tapping E-Double.

"He leaves every day around this time, but he don't tell nobody where he's going," E-Double said, knocking the eight ball in the side pocket.

"Let me shoot the breeze with you outside for a minute," Woo said to E-Double, who simply responded by heading towards the door. Besides being cousins, Woo and E-Double were godbrothers. They couldn't be closer if they were born of the same mother. Ever since they were young, they attended the same schools and grew up across the street from each other in opposite housing projects.

"Word on the street is that you and Black got enough cake and soldiers to compete with Ice," Woo said as they watched two kids slap box.

"We got one more run to do for Ice, and then we're on our own. I'ma make him eat them words, callin' us 'corner boys,'" E-Double said with pride, and a little anger, in his voice.

"Just be careful. Ice ain't gonna like y'all takin' money out of his pocket," Woo said.

E-Double wondered why Woo cared so much about Ice. He figured either Woo didn't know or blinded himself to the fact that Ice fucked everybody, but he'd open his eyes once Ice fucked him over.

"What?" Woo asked, catching E-Double's gaze.

"Nothin' ... just thinkin'," E-Double said. "Listen, I got to get back inside and take Jab for some more money."

"Go 'head, I got some homework to knock off," Woo said and gave E-Double a pound. Both of them stepped off.

● ● ● ●

Woo walked in the house to find his father watching TV.

"What took you so long today?" Tyson asked as he noticed his son standing in front of his door.

"Me and the fellas were just shootin' the breeze. Hey, did any more college applications come in the mail today?"

"Yeah, that makes one from Yale to go with the ones from Harvard, Rutgers, Howard, and Kean University," Tyson said, shuffling through the letters.

"I know you're smart, but your grades aren't good enough for Harvard or Yale, so why even apply?"

"I thought it would be funny to make the people's job a little harder by sending me a letter of rejection," Woo said, taking the applications from his father.

"So you're going to pay thirty to fifty dollars to get something you already know the answer to?"

"Well, since you put it that way, it doesn't seem funny at all," Woo said, closing his father's door as his dad started to laugh.

Woo stepped into his small room and sat at his desk to fill out his applications. He opened the application to Howard University first. He wanted to go to Howard U. ever since he visited one of his cousins on campus. He thought it was funny that a few blocks away from the campus were housing projects. People go to college to get out of the hood, but attending Howard was like a home away from home.

As Woo filled out the application, he thought about all the beautiful black women he saw, how cool the fraternities looked, and how the campus and the surroundings didn't look too much different from some parts of his hometown, Elizabeth N.J.

Like most applications, this one asked, "Why do you want to attend college, and why should this university accept you?" Woo thought long and hard once he reached this portion of the application. He simply wrote how he would be the first of his father's kids to graduate high school and attend college. He also wanted to receive a degree and give back to the neighborhood to rebuild some of the bridges he burned while he was a juvenile delinquent. As he wrote about why Howard would be the best college for him, there was a knock at the door.

"Hey, are you hungry?" Tyson asked.

"I'm too deep in thought to think about food," Woo said, still writing.

"I remember picking you up at the boys' detention center, and now I'm going to be dropping you off at some college," Tyson said, taking a seat on Woo's bed.

"Your mother would be proud of you, son," Tyson said, patting Woo on his back.

"How about you, Pop?" Woo asked, turning to look at his father.

"How 'bout me what?"

"Are you proud?"

"Every day someone asks me how I'm doing, and every time I say I'm making it. I want to do more than just make it, but my time has passed. You leaving the streets and going to college, I know when someone asks you how you doing, you're going to be able to say more than 'just making it.' So I'm more than proud of you, son." Tyson left the room and Woo continued to fill out the applications.

The phone rang, breaking Woo's train of thought. He picked it up.

"Hello," he replied.

"What's up? It's Taye."

"I'm just tryin' to fill out these applications."

"Are you takin' the SAT test in the morning?" Taye asked.

"I'll be at your house first thing in the morning."

"A'ight, peace," Taye said as he hung up the phone.

"Peace."

Knock, knock, knock.

Tyson jumped up to answer the door.

"Who is it?" Tyson asked, walking closer to the hardwood door.

"It's Black, I mean, it's Raheem, Uncle Tyson."

Tyson opened the door for his nephew. He didn't approve of the way his nephews lived, but he always made his house available as a neutral zone for them. He also knew that they helped to keep Woo in line, and for that, he was grateful.

"Woo home?" Black asked, giving his uncle a hug.

"He's in his room; go check him out," Tyson said, moving to the side to let Black in.

"Boy, you getting so black the whites of your eyes are brown. They don't even make niggas like you anymore," Tyson said jokingly. He knew Black and everyone else teased Woo for being mixed, so he joked around too.

"What's up?" Black asked, opening Woo's door.

"Just finishing these college applications."

"I always knew you had some brains," Black said, knocking on Woo's head.

"Where did you apply to?"

"Kean, Rutgers, Howard University," Woo answered, showing Black the applications.

"Howard's the move," Black said.

"How would you know?" Woo asked, putting his applications away.

"I know more than you think I know. Never mind. I just came by to see if you wanted to go to the movies."

Woo loved hanging out with E-Double and Black. It was the only time that they weren't hustling. He could hang out on the corners with them, but he made it a point not to stay in one place too long on the streets. He felt it was too easy to get robbed, shot, or arrested.

"I'm down with the movies," Woo said, grabbing his coat and heading towards the door. He stopped in front of his father's door.

"I'm going to the movies, Pop."

"Alright, don't come back too late; you have the SAT test in the morning."

"No problem," Woo said as he and Black walked out the door.

4

WHAT ABOUT THE NIGGAS EATIN' OFF OF MOMMY?

Black and E-Double chilled in their fully loaded Escalade sitting on 22s, admiring their surroundings. Normally, two teenage boys would never get away with driving a brand-new shiny Escalade around town without being stopped by the cops, but Ice had many police officers *and* the mayor on his payroll. Black and E-Double even had a few of their own officers on payroll just in case Ice and his people got overzealous with power. Ice and the Port Au Prince Posse were virtually untouchable. Black and E-Double were enjoying the privileges that came with being in the organization.

Even though the hood was infested with drugs and violence, it still held a love and unity among the people that you couldn't find in a suburban area. It was the love and unity that never seemed to be depicted in the media. The hood held a love and respect for E-Double and Black, and that's one of the reasons why they didn't take their money and move to a more private area. They also figured the fiends and the people needed easy access to them and their drugs.

E-Double loved the drug game and all of its perks. He had an opportunity to leave the game when Woo's father took him in and hooked him up with a job after he was released from the detention center. But the money, power, and respect were too intoxicating for E-Double to leave alone. He went right back to work for Ice. He felt like Woo. After handling thousands of dollars, he couldn't work at

McDonald's or any other fast-food establishment for minimum wage.

Tyson made E-Double move right back with his mother since he didn't want to reform. It bothered Woo that E-Double had to leave, but he knew his father needed the house to be drug free, especially since he and his father weren't completely free from the government. E-Double wasn't completely cleared either, but the excitement of the drugs, money, and getting caught really motivated E-Double. He was especially elated that his new drug connects would make Ice regret calling him a "corner boy." The new connects and Escalade were just the beginning of big things to come.

Black didn't love the drug game like E-Double. He had a love/hate relationship with the game. He loved the fact that he would never see an eviction notice on his mother's door or wake up with only lint in his pockets and an empty refrigerator. But Black hated the game for what it did to his mother and his family. He knew in his heart of hearts that if his mother never became a fiend, E-Double, Woo, and he would never have resorted to dealing drugs. But when you're too young to work and too embarrassed to carry groceries, there aren't too many alternatives to do what your mother is too strung out to do—and that's pay rent, feed, and clothe you.

Black, E-Double, and Woo were tired and embarrassed of taking hand-me-downs from their boys. They were also tired of being chased away from the local liquor store for trying to make a couple of dollars. Stealing and chain snatching wasn't profitable or safe. The drug game made more sense to them—especially the way Ice presented the picture.

Black hated spinning the same vicious cycle of hooking mothers on crack and dope, the same dope that strung his mother out and caused the family so much pain. He figured sometimes you have to do bad to do good. This was one of those times, he told himself to ease his conscience. Black promised himself that one day he would go legit. He would rebuild the bridges in his community that he was tearing down with drugs. It was a promise that Black and Woo made together. However, Black knew that before he could carry out his promise with Woo, he would first have to get E-Double to understand the error of their ways.

Black rarely made any moves or decisions without consulting E-Double. He wasn't afraid or dumb by any means. They loved and respected each other too much to keep each other in the dark. They did everything together. They starved together, stole together, sold drugs together, went to jail together, and would go legit together. Black just didn't know how he was going to sell the "American Dream" of getting out of the ghetto and making it big to E-Double. E-Double dropped out of school and swore that as long as there was money on the streets to be made, he wasn't going to waste his time with school. He loved the streets more than life itself.

"What's on your mind?" E-Double asked Black, who seemed to be deep in thought.

"It's these kids. They see the money, cars, jewelry, women, respect, and they look up to us. They want to be us," Black said with sympathy in his voice.

"So?" E-Double replied with no concern at all.

"So ... if they knew what we were doin' to their moms, pops, aunts, and uncles, they would despise us," he said with heart.

"So, we ain't force them. And it's because of their moms, pops, and aunts that we eatin'," E-Double replied, waving big bills in front of Black in a mocking manner.

"What about the niggas eatin' off of Mommy?" Black asked sarcastically in response to E-Double's ignorant-ass comment.

E-Double sucked his teeth, waved his hand, and looked out of the window.

"Oh, now you don't have anything smart to say?" Black asked, irritated.

"Don't you realize we're in the position we're in right now 'cause someone strung Mommy out? And now we're doin' the same thing to these kids. Don't you wonder what life would be like if Mommy wasn't on drugs? What kind of life we would have?" Black asked with pure interest in his voice.

"No, I don't wonder. Those days are long gone. Mommy made her choice, and we got the life we got. And if any of these lil' niggas want a job later on, I'll give them one! The same way Ice gave us one. I just wouldn't fuck them over the way Ice fucked us and everybody else over," E-Double said with venom in his voice. "And speaking of Ice, you need to start this car so we can meet with our new connect," E-Double said with less sting in his voice.

"What does our new connect have to do with Ice?"

"After we make these new moves, we won't have to fuck with Ice no more."

The ride up Elizabeth Avenue seemed real slow to Black and E-Double, considering they had a lot on their minds. They rarely raised their voices or disagreed with each other. The tension seemed to build up between them as they started to have different mind-sets about the game. The more Black thought about going legit, the more E-Double found more creative ways to stay in the game.

Black's disappearing acts and lack of focus on the streets really bothered E-Double. Black couldn't understand E-Double's infatuation with the streets. Black was only in the game as a means to an end, and he thought that was how E-Double felt, especially after he talked Woo into staying in school.

Black turned off of Elizabeth Avenue onto Broad Street. Traffic was heavy since it was Saturday, one of Broad Street's famous shopping days. Black and E-Double, like every other man, loved the Broad Street scene for the scantily clad women prancing around. The jewelry stores, clothing stores, baby shops, and restaurants made Broad Street an oasis for women and men who loved to shop. Looking at the abundance of women in tight dresses and fitted clothes gave the two brothers the patience to deal with Broad Street traffic.

Black looked at his watch to see the time. He began to honk his horn as he realized that he and E-Double were a little behind schedule. All the scantily clad women in the world couldn't distract Black once his mind was on business.

"Calm down on the horn," E-Double said, removing Black's hand from the horn.

"We're going to miss the train if we don't hurry up, and we have to find parking. Not to mention that Bruce is suppose to meet us," Black said, honking the horn again.

"Knowing Bruce, he's probably there already, and we can park in the paying lot to save time, so stop beeping the horn," E-Double said, annoyed. Traffic seemed to pick up before the two young men could engage in a full-scale argument.

Black took E-Double's advice and headed towards the pay parking lot to save time. He pulled in, took the ticket from the attendant, and parked. The train station was only a block away from the lot. E-Double saw Bruce standing in the entrance of the train station.

"See? I told you Bruce would be here," E-Double said, pointing at Bruce, who was standing in front of the entrance with a dirty T-shirt, faded black jeans, run-down, filthy white sneakers, and a nappy 'fro.

Bruce was one of the famous neighborhood fiends. E-Double didn't like fiends or like to be around them. He only liked their money, but he knew Bruce would serve his purpose for their little trip.

Black and E-Double never had to go to New York before to cop drugs. They strictly dealt with Ice, who supplied them with everything for a percentage. Black and E-Double felt like Ice was rapping them for the cash. Ice put them on at a young age so they never questioned the money or his judgment. As Black and E-Double got older, their knowledge of the game began to grow. Once they realized how much money Ice was getting with minimum risk, they decided to break off their relationship with him. But they wanted to make sure that their new connect in New York was legit before they got too impetuous.

As Black and E-Double walked towards the station, they saw the train pulling in. Quickly, they took off like track stars, almost knocking people over as they took flight. Black, E-Double, and Bruce ran up the stairs as the smell of beer and piss invaded their nostrils. Black was happy to see no one was standing in front of the teller as he reached the top of the steps. E-Double and Bruce stepped onto the platform near the train as Black bought the tickets.

"Let me get three round-trip tickets to New York, please," Black said out of breath.

The woman behind the booth had café-au-lait skin with sea green eyes, long hair, and she was short. Black thought to himself that if he had more time, he would've tried to get her number. He hoped that she would still be working when he returned. She had all of the features that he was attracted to. She seemed to have been moving slowly, deliberately, to him. He hoped that she was looking at him in an admiring way and didn't have an attitude. Then he just figured it was all in his mind since he was so anxious to get on the train and make his appointment.

All three men boarded the train and took a seat.

"Sit your black, dirty ass somewhere else," E-Double said to Bruce, who sat down right next to Black and E-Double.

Some of the passengers boarding the train started to laugh at the spectacle E-Double was making. Bruce looked in Black's direction for

will robbins

assurance before moving to another seat.

The three guys arrived in Madison Square Garden twenty minutes later. The station was packed, and everyone seemed to be stuck together by elbows and assholes. Finally, the crowd loosened up and dispersed as everyone reached the upper level.

Bruce led the way around the station. Black and E-Double used Bruce because other dealers used Bruce to be their mule. Bruce dealt with the sellers and carried all the drugs on the train just in case there was any police trouble. That's why most dealers used the train instead of driving to New York. Driving was easier, but if the cops stop you, everyone goes to jail, but on the train, the cops couldn't connect the drugs or the mule to you. And Bruce, just like all the other mules, only wanted drugs in payment for his risk.

"Where do we have to go now?" E-Double asked Bruce, who was speed walking like he was on a mission.

"We have to walk to the path train and then get on the D-Train to get to Harlem if you want your stuff," Bruce said, walking even faster than before.

Once they boarded the train to Harlem, Black was silent the whole trip. He was always silent before a business transaction. The trip was all new to him, and he was taking it all in. He was also worried about the police, dirty, greedy niggas, and Ice. He knew if everything worked out with this new business venture, he would have a lot of problems with Ice. Neither he nor E-Double ever spoke about how they would handle Ice when the situation arose. With all of Black's concentration on these other issues, they arrived at 138th & Broadway before he knew it.

"We're here, man," Bruce said, breaking Black out of his trance.

Black tapped E-Double, who had fallen asleep during the smooth train ride.

"The building is right up the block. Let me talk to the man first. They know me, so they'll relax a little," Bruce said, leading the way.

Black and E-Double were a little nervous about being in Harlem. They had heard a story or two about how hard it was. But they started to calm down some as soon as a few Dominican brothers all started to greet them as they passed. Harlem looked just like most urban areas with the same dilapidated buildings, fiends, and drunks hanging around; and, of course, the hardworking members of the community were also visible, to add some sensibility and pride.

"We need to talk to that man right there to make sure every-thing's okay," Bruce said, pointing to an olive-complexioned man who was wearing black leather pants and a colorful dress shirt.

Black and E-Double kept looking around, making sure that they were safe as well as their money. They'd never been to Harlem, but they knew that they were in a drug-infested community. It only took one desperate fiend or greedy dealer and your life could be over. At this moment of uncertainty, they started to miss the comfort of dealing with Ice. But the need to be a separate entity from Ice was the only thing that kept them from leaving quickly.

"What's up, Rico?" Bruce asked, extending his hand.

Rico just looked at Bruce as if he were crazy. Rico was serious about his position and never fraternized with potential customers. Rico knew, just like Black and E-Double did, that if you get caught with your pants down, your dick could be cut off.

"What y'all need?" he asked, showing no facial expression.

"We need to do business with Tony," Bruce said.

"Your boys mute or are they just officers?" Rico asked, looking into Black's and E-Double's eyes.

"No, no, no, I would never bring the law to you or Tony," Bruce said with fear and desperation in his voice. He knew that Rico would-n't have a problem killing all three of them on the spot.

"Look, we ain't no cops. We just here to do a little business with your peoples," E-Double said looking back at Rico with the same seri-ous facial expression.

"Alright, tell me what you need, and I'll see if we can accommo-date you," Rico said lightening his hard demeanor.

"We got eleven thousand and we need half a bird. Two fifty cooked and two fifty raw, and possibly some dope," Black replied.

"You sure y'all ain't cops?" Rico asked one more time for assur-ance.

"Would the cops just walk away and do business with someone else?" E-Double asked.

Rico looked at E-Double and said something in Spanish in his lit-tle microphone that could barely be seen. After a few seconds, he told them to go into the run-down building across the street.

Black, E-Double, and Bruce walked across the street, and a few seconds later, Bruce was knocking on a silver door. Black looked around and noticed a surveillance camera on the building. It was the same type of camera Ice used to check for cops and unwanted company. Just then, the silver metal door slowly opened, putting the fellas on the opposite side of the door on notice. A tall, dark man with a bulletproof vest and a .45 Magnum opened the door, allowing Black, Bruce, and E-Double access into the building.

"Straight upstairs, make a left, and go to the door all the way down the hall," the big man instructed them. Black and his crew walked up the stairs cautiously. The hall was filled with crack pipes, trash, and other drug paraphernalia. But to Black's surprise, the area didn't smell like piss and shit.

As they reached the top of the stairs, they saw a woman sucking a man's dick in a vacant apartment. Black could only think about his own mother and how she supported her habit. He put it out of his mind that his mother sucked a few dicks to get her drugs.

As they continued down the corridor, they noticed numerous people getting high and performing sexual favors in the many vacant apartments. The scene looked like it was straight out of New Jack City.

Two guards stood left and right in front of the door to which Black and his crew were instructed to go. Both men wore bulletproof vests and were armed with the same weapon as the man downstairs.

"What's up?" Black asked as they reached the door.

The man to the left stepped forward and started to frisk Black as his partner kept his eyes on Bruce and E-Double to make sure that they didn't pull any weapons. Then Bruce and E-Double went through the same rites of passage as Black.

Once they were found without weapons, one of the men said, "Take off your boots." They looked at the man as if he were playing.

"He's serious. No one gets in with anything on their feet. Accept it or leave," his partner replied to the confused guys.

"Take your boots off. We've come this far. I'm not going to turn back 'cause of some foot rule," Black said, removing his boots. E-Double and Bruce followed suit once they realized it was the only way they were going to get in.

After they stepped inside of the apartment, they realized why they had to remove their boots. They stepped on the softest, deepest, whitest Persian rug they had ever seen. The matching white furniture around the room complemented the rug.

Black and his crew continued to scan their environment. A picture of Al Pacino from the movie *Scarface* was hanging above a white and gold desk with two additional bodyguards standing left to right in front of the desk. Those men were also holding all-white pit bulls at their sides. Two caramel-complexioned women were sitting on a white chair, French kissing, which distracted Bruce and E-Double. Black was more concerned about the dogs, guards, their contact, Tony, and getting out alive. He could only see portions of Tony's body because he was still sitting behind his desk. From what Black saw of Tony, he could tell that he was a stout man.

"What's your name, poppi?" Tony asked Black with a heavy accent.

"Black," Black replied, staring at the guards with the pit bulls.

"Don't worry about them. They're safe. If you want to worry about something, worry about those bitches over there," Tony said, pointing at the two females kissing, who were also pointing .38 Snub-nosed pistols in the newcomers' direction. The impressive thing was that the women never even stopped kissing as they pointed their guns in the boys' direction.

Tony and his men began to laugh once Black and his crew realized the women were holding pistols on them. Then Tony waved the women's guns down.

"Don't ever underestimate a woman. Sometimes they are more dangerous than men. Now, let's do business," Tony said, puffing on a Cuban cigar.

"Where's the money?" he asked Black.

"Where's the shit?" E-Double answered with all of the toughness a man could muster in his position. Tony pushed a button on his desk, said a few words, and in a matter of seconds, a midget appeared in the doorway holding a black bag. At the sight of the midget, the three newcomers wanted to laugh, but they valued their lives too much to explode in laughter at the present moment.

"Where's the money?" Tony asked again, smiling.

Black tapped Bruce, and Bruce pulled the money from his left pants pocket.

The midget walked over and exchanged items with him. Looking at the midget waddle made it more difficult for the young men not to laugh.

will robbins

"I know you want to laugh, but it would be most unwise. He's more dangerous than any man or bitch in this room. That's why I have him around," Tony said, taking the money from the midget. He quickly counted the money at his desk with a money counter. Once he knew the money was all there, he bid the boys safe passage.

"I appreciate your business, Black. I would shake your hands, but I don't do that. It's a safety precaution, you understand," Tony said, blowing more smoke from his cigar.

"By the way, Bruce, if you keep bringing me new clients, I'll have to set you out some shit for free," Tony said as the boys were walking out the door.

Black was relieved that the meeting went safely and they walked away with their lives. He hoped that the trip back would also be successful. They guys didn't speak until they reached the safety of the train.

"Did you see that fuckin' midget?" E-Double asked as they all took a seat on the train.

Finally they all laughed to ease the tension. Once the train began to rock smoothly back and forth, Black and E-Double began to relax. Bruce was nervous since he was holding all the weight. However, at the thought of how much dope he would receive, he quickly calmed down as well.

Before long, the conductor yelled over the loudspeaker, "Next stop, Elizabeth."

Black and E-Double were happy that their new business venture went off without any trouble, but they knew trouble was ahead because they would have to deal with Ice eventually.

5

WHAT'S THE RULES?

The furniture in Woo's apartment wasn't elaborate or expensive, but it was homey. Three of Woo's boys sat on the black sectional couch covered with plastic that Woo's father purchased from Ikea. Despite Woo's father's objection, they all slouched on the couch with their feet set on the glass coffee table.

They were watching music videos, waiting for Woo to get off of the computer. They cracked jokes about how Woo's father still had a small TV sitting on top of the large, broken TV, using it as a stand. That seemed to be the custom in many black homes. The only thing that was missing here was the traditional white Jesus that hung in most black folks' homes. Tyson and Woo read the Bible enough to know that Christ was black, and they didn't want to keep perpetuating a lie or stereotype. Woo always made the joke that black people couldn't go without their Christmas, pork chops, or white Jesus.

"Yo, go to Phat Azz.com," Damien, a dark-skinned boy with short hair and dimples said as he approached the computer.

"Hell no, my father would whoop my ass," Woo said, pushing Damien back from the computer.

"Who's gonna know?" Damien countered, smacking Woo in the back of the head in retaliation.

"It goes on your phone bill or credit card, dumb ass," Man said, throwing a couch pillow at Damien for his stupidity. Man was tall and mocha-colored with a big sense of humor. It was one of the reasons he and Woo clicked so well.

"Besides, if we wanted to go to Phat Azz.com, we'd just go to your mama's house," Calvin said as all the boys laughed in chorus.

Damien was the butt of everyone's jokes, but everyone loved and respected him. Woo became best friends with Damien, Man, and Calvin in his junior year of high school. He was closer to Man at the time than anyone else.

Woo's friends had similar backgrounds and the same type of lifestyle. Man's father was an ex-alcoholic, like Tyson, and Man bounced around between his father and mother, who was an addict. Calvin didn't know his father, and his mother was also an addict. Damien really didn't come with too many domestic issues. He lived at home with his mother and father, who both had professional jobs. The only verbal abuse he sustained was the abuse that Man, Woo, or Calvin gave him. Subconsciously, they all picked on him out of jealousy of his perfect existence. But it was all in good fun. They cracked jokes on one another from time to time. They only had one rule: never do it in front of females.

Even though Woo's friends came from dysfunctional homes, they remained positive. It was one of the reasons Woo surrounded himself with them. Taye, Man, Damien, and Calvin kept him grounded. In actuality, they kept each other grounded.

"Hey, what y'all got in the refrigerator?" Calvin asked as he walked toward the fridge.

"Nothin' cooked," Woo replied, looking up from the computer.

As Calvin searched the refrigerator, someone pounded on the door.

"Calvin, answer the door since you in there," Woo yelled once he heard the knock at the door.

Calvin opened the door without asking who it was.

"I could've been the cops, a killer, or your ugly-ass mama; you *always* suppose to ask who it is before you open the door. Didn't your mother teach you nothing?" Taye said to Calvin once he opened the door.

"One, if you were the cops, we ain't doin' nothin'; two, if you was a killer, I'd welcome it 'cause I'd be dead and wouldn't have to pay child support for your black ass; three, my mama ain't ugly," Calvin

capped off as they laughed and gave each other a pound.

"Is that my dawg?" Woo asked, stepping away from the computer. Woo also became friends with Taye in his junior year of high school. Woo's new friends made it easy to leave his old life behind.

"This house is gettin' too small for us. We need to get out of here," Woo said, waving his hands towards the door.

They all exited Woo's apartment and stood in front of the building. Woo didn't see E-Double and his crew on the corner, so he figured they must be doing business elsewhere. He did see the fiends, drunks, and usual people hanging around outside.

"What we gonna do?" Man asked, pulling out a cigarette and lighting it. Man was the only friend of Woo's that smoked.

"Let's go to the pool hall," Calvin suggested.

"I'm tired of that," Damien said.

"Nobody asked you," Man said, smacking Damien in the face like he was a pimp and Damien was his bitch. Damien attempted to chase Man, but he knew he was too slow.

Taye looked at his silver Citizen quartz watch and said, "It's almost five. We could go to the Youth at Risk meeting at the Presbyterian Center."

"I'm down for that," Woo said.

"Me too. They always got snacks," Man said, catching his breath from his short sprint.

They strolled from Third and Bond Street to First Street, which was where the center was located. It was a community-based center geared to help families and individuals in crisis and to provide intervention when needed. It had programs for alcoholics, substance abuse, counseling for youth, day camps, summer camps, and anything else that a community needed to thrive and grow. The center could have been called the heart of the ghetto, especially since it was located right across the street from the Pioneer Homes and Migliore Manor project high-rises.

Woo and his boys all approached the beige building on the corner. Then he opened the light metal door so his boys could enter. They stepped in the building and asked the receptionist if the meeting were still taking place. After being assured that the meeting was still on, they walked into the room on the right-hand side.

The room was huge. It was one of the rooms used as a daycare center in the mornings and afternoons. As usual, chairs were placed in a circle with a bulletin board reading, "What's The Rules?" with numerous rules written at the bottom of it.

The boys looked around for any signs of snacks. The table where snacks usually sat on was empty. They assumed Mr. Rhames or Mrs. Janice was going to bring them in when they arrived. As they began to take their seats, a beautiful, slender, dark mocha-skinned woman walked in holding a big bag that read Dunkin' Donuts on the front of it.

"Hello, gentlemen," she said with a bright smile, placing the donuts on the table next to the fish tank. Everyone said hello in chorus.

"*That's* what I'm talking about," Man said, walking over to the donuts before Mrs. Janice could take a seat.

Everyone except Mrs. Janice said, "Greedy ass," as Man walked over to the donuts.

"No, no, no. What are the rules?" Mrs. Janice asked, pointing at the bulletin board. All the boys ran down the list to Mrs. Janice at the same time as if they were in the military.

"No cursing."

"No fighting."

"No mother jokes or disrespect."

"One person holds the floor."

"Respect the rules."

"Now that we got that out of the way, who wants to go first?" Mrs. Janice asked.

Before anyone could answer, a skinny, brown-skinned brother with a light beard walked in wearing a shirt and tie, carrying sodas.

"What's up, Mr. Rhames?" the boys asked in unison, happy to see him. All the brothers respected his knowledge and wisdom. He helped Woo and his boys out many times in the community as well as with school. The center was a good place for everyone, but Woo and his boys only came because of Mr. Rhames and Mrs. Janice.

Black, E-Double, and their crew used to go to the center for the meetings as well. They were the ones who initially got Woo to attend. As their power, respect, and wealth began to grow, however, they came to the center less and less, until their visits became nonexistent. Woo, on the other hand, continued to attend the meetings and brought a new crew of people that Mr. Rhames and Mrs. Janice could work with.

"Am I late?" Mr. Rhames asked.

"No, we were just about to start," Mrs. Janice replied with a smile.

Mr. Rhames took his seat and smiled at the brothers, indicating that he was ready.

"Me and Taye took the SAT exams yesterday," Woo said.

"I hope you didn't write like you speak," Mr. Rhames said half jokingly.

"Nah, we didn't," Woo replied, speaking for both of them.

"I know I'm going to sound like Furious Styles from *Boyz N the Hood*, but you *do* know those exams are culturally biased. They weren't made up with minorities in mind. The only portion that's universal is the math," Mr. Rhames said, remembering when he took the exams many years ago.

He and Mrs. Janice asked a few more questions before Mr. Rhames finally said, "What are your cousins doing, Woo?" Woo hesitated for a few, but he knew he couldn't lie to Mr. Rhames, especially since the streets always talked.

"They livin' that street life," Woo said a little ashamed.

"Well, it's a good thing you smartened up," Mrs. Janice said.

"Remember this, fellas, never get caught up in the myth that you don't choose the game, the game chooses you. *Everyone* has a choice. Just like you guys choose to be here. Just remember when you get caught, the game doesn't suffer the consequences—*you* do," Mr. Rhames said.

"That's what we know," Man said munching on a donut.

"So what colleges did you guys apply to, and do you need help filling out any financial aid forms?" Mrs. Janice asked, crossing her beautiful black legs. Mrs. Janice had the dark complexion that Woo loved on his women. He knew he wanted a dark-skinned sister so his children would be darker than him. He didn't like the fact that people had to play the guessing game about his ethnicity, even though he still had a thing for Vicky who was a light-skinned Puerto Rican.

"The Financial Aid Department said that my parents make too much money so my father is going to have to pay for most of it," Damien said.

"No, I'm not," Woo said jokingly.

"Get the hell out of here. You not my father," Damien said.

will robbins

"Man, 99.999 says that I am," Woo continued.

Calvin and Man said in the mock tone of Maury Povich, "Woo, you are the father."

Woo jumped in Damien's face and began to yell, "I told you! I told you!"

Mr. Rhames and Mrs. Janice couldn't do anything but laugh, even though the rules were being violated. After the side show, the meeting lingered on for about a half hour before the boys ran out of things to talk about. Everyone agreed to meet with each other next week at the same time as usual before anyone left. Mrs. Janice gave each of the boys a hug before she departed. Mr. Rhames departed in the same fashion.

All the brothers stepped outside to decide what their next move was going to be. Woo started to walk away when Man asked, "Where you going?"

"I'm goin' to karate class, and then I'ma go see Anasia."

"You still chasing that girl?" Calvin asked, teasing Woo.

They all teased Woo about karate and Anasia. Anasia was one of Woo's best friends, like Calvin and Man. The only difference was Woo wanted to be with Anasia, but time and opportunity never presented itself. She either had a man or he was with someone or he was too busy chasing Vicky.

Woo met Anasia at the center when she walked in with her father, holding a 6-foot martial arts trophy she won in a tournament in Atlantic City. Woo was always attracted to women who knew how to defend themselves. From that moment, Woo wanted to join karate classes just to get close to her.

Anasia's father and family trained Woo and treated him like a family member. He tried to get with Anasia ever since. And even though Woo's boys teased him about karate, they respected him for studying the art and little did Woo know it would eventually get him out of a few sticky situations. Before Woo left, all his boys posed like Ralph Macchio from the movie *Karate Kid* to make one last joke.

"I'll catch y'all tomorrow," Woo said smiling, stepping off.

6

SHE TIRED

The corner bodega was devoid of any activity when Black, E-Double, and Bruce arrived. The bodega sold groceries, but it was really a front for drugs, drug dealers, and fiends. Black and E-Double thought it was strange that the corner was empty. They knew that Ice and his people dealt with the bodega, and Ice wouldn't go for any inactivity on any of his corners or businesses. Black and E-Double made sure that Jab and Booga stayed on Third and Bond Street just to make sure that Ice wouldn't miss any money and get wise to their plan ahead of time.

Black and his people walked into the bodega and saw José behind the counter. The bodega had some bread, snacks, lunchmeat, cereal, and coolers filled with drinks, but the aisles were practically empty. It rarely had any deliveries, none that were legal anyway.

José sat behind the counter looking nervous while he played with his gold chains. He always wore his shirt halfway open, revealing his hairy chest. He also always wore colorful shirts that looked like he was vacationing in Hawaii. José was a dark Cuban that, if you didn't hear him talk, you would swear that he was black.

"What happened?" Black asked José, knowing something was wrong.

"The fuckin' police came and raided the place," José replied with a heavy accent.

"Did they find anything?" E-Double asked with concern.

"Of course not, or I wouldn't fuckin' be here," José answered with frustration in his voice.

"They took some of Ice's people away. That's why nobody's outside," José said, still playing with his chains.

"Did you call Ice?" Black asked, walking closer to the counter.

"I'm not an amateur. He's going down to bail everyone out and have a delivery dropped off," José said a little annoyed that Black would question his professionalism.

"That's good. Let me get some bags," Black said as he took his money out and set it on the counter. José reached under the counter and pulled out what seemed like a thousand bags. Black took the bags and passed José the money, who passed the money right back, to Black's surprise.

"Your money is no good here as long as you're with Ice," José said with a smile.

"Cool. Let's go," Black said as he shook José's hand and headed for the door.

Black, E-Double, and Bruce walked down the block towards one of the vacant high-rises. The block had all sorts of cracks, rocks, and trash showing the devastation of what a lack of care could produce. The parking lot was empty and filled with trash, cracks, and rocks as well. The run-down buildings across the street held even less pride of the streets.

The high-rises were empty because of the new HUD project that the city was working on. They moved everyone out of one high-rise into another so they could tear down the vacant buildings and turn them into houses. It was an attempt to provide people with low income the ability to afford their first homes.

In order to get his dope, Bruce had to hang around Black and E-Double until they sorted out the dope. Black and E-Double used one of the vacant apartments in the high-rises to bag up their product. They all entered the courtyard of the high-rises where all the windows were boarded up and the red metal doors were all locked except one. Local bums, fiends, and kids managed to break open one of the doors for their personal use.

The three guys walked up the stairs to the third floor of the building. Surprisingly, the building was empty except for one bum who was clutching his wine bottle like a baby. The hallway smelled like piss, as usual. Black had the key to one of the apartments that was locked. Ice managed to finagle a key away from one of the maintenance men so that his boys would have a place to bag up their work.

Black took out the key and put it into the lock and in one swift turn of the key, the door was unlocked. The apartment smelled like Febreze, a smell that Black and E-Doubled welcomed after the stench in the hallway. The smell didn't bother Bruce, since he smelled like piss all the time because of a lack of bathing.

The apartment was furnished with a simple plush couch, a wooden dining table with matching chairs, and a radio to entertain the men while they bagged up their work. The apartment remained fresh and clean, even though other individuals used the apartment. Black and E-Double didn't believe in working in a dirty environment. They made sure everyone cleaned up their mess after they used the apartment.

E-Double pulled up his Akademik jeans and took a seat at the dining table, and Black followed right behind. Bruce sat on the couch opposite the table. Black and E-Double looked at Bruce with a glare of impatience in their eyes. Bruce, knowing exactly what the look meant, dug down his pants and grabbed the black bag out and threw it towards E-Double, who raised his hands and let the bag fall on the table. Black looked at E-Double like something was wrong with him.

"I ain't touching that shit after he had it down his pants," E-Double said to Black's amusement.

"I ain't touching it either," Black said as they both began to laugh. Previously, Black and E-Double were so nervous during the business transaction that they didn't notice, or care, where Bruce hid the drugs. It really didn't matter to them—until now.

"Bruce, come take this shit out of the bag and throw the bag away," E-Double demanded.

"I ain't that dirty, boys," Bruce said while laughing. He opened the bag and laid the crack/coke and small portion of dope on the table. Then he walked into the kitchen, which was connected to the front room area, and threw the black bag in the small white trash can.

Black and E-Double began to bag up the crack and dope, which was a long, tedious process. Most dealers didn't even bother with dope because it held a higher penalty than crack or coke if a person was caught with it. But Black and E-Double needed to get a leg up on Ice quick. Meanwhile, Bruce began to feel sick since it was a couple of

will robbins

hours since he got high. He began to scratch and pace in anticipation of getting his free high.

"Turn the radio on and stop pacing; you makin' me nervous," E-Double said with an attitude.

Bruce walked over to the radio and tried to hold his shaking hand steady to turn the knob. "Same Girl," by Usher and R. Kelly was blaring over the radio when he turned to Hot 97.

"I'm getting sick," Bruce said as he sat back down on the gray couch, shaking and sweating. His sickness came over him like a spell. Black and E-Double didn't even notice the symptoms until he finally told them how he was feeling.

Black, feeling sympathy for Bruce, threw a couple of dime bags of dope at him. Bruce was shaking so badly that he missed the bag and it hit the floor. He jumped to the floor as if someone were shooting a gun. Clumsily, he grabbed the bag and jumped back on the couch while Black and E-Double looked at him as a source of entertainment for the moment. Next, Bruce pulled a sturdy string and a syringe from his pocket.

"You carry that shit with you everywhere you go?" Black asked, amazed.

"Yeah, especially for occasions like this. Plus, I don't believe in sharing needles," Bruce said, pulling up his sleeve and tying the string around his arm.

"Oh, shit, a careful fiend," E-Double said, laughing at the irony of the situation.

Bruce kept bleeding and dripping pus as he tried to hit a vein. Black and E-Double began to get fed up with the whole scene and ordered Bruce into the bathroom.

"You a'ight?" Black asked E-Double, who seemed to have a lost look on his face.

"Yeah," E-Double said, barely raising his voice over a whisper.

Black knew his brother too well to know when something was wrong. "Come on, tell me what's on your mind," Black said, as he put the dope and the bag back on the table.

"Looking at Bruce and that conversation we had the other day about Mommy just brought up some bad memories is all," E-Double said, looking right into Black's eyes. E-Double looked like he was about to cry from looking back in the past.

E-Double walked into his mother's room just in time to see her blow smoke from her crack pipe.

"Mama, when you gonna stop doin' this shit? Can't you see what it's doin' to us?" E-Double yelled, shaking his mother who seemed oblivious to his presence.

"I, I, need this, baby, just for a little while to get over," Sandra said between cries once she realized what was going on.

E-Double couldn't understand what would make his mother stress out so much to continue to use. Especially since Black, Woo, and he made enough money with Ice to support her and the rest of the family. His young teenage mind couldn't fathom that it was a disease that couldn't be turned off like a light switch.

After that incident Sandra really did get herself together. She attended meetings, got a part-time job, she even tried to get her boys back in school and get Ice to leave them alone. She was clean for about six months before she relapsed, not to anyone's surprise. The only surprise was how she relapsed.

E-Double entered the project building and took the steps three at a time until he reached the third floor. He unlocked the door marked with the letter G and entered the small two-bedroom apartment that he shared with his brother, Woo, and their sister. Woo, Black, and E-Double usually slept on the floor when they spent time at home. E-Double stopped in the middle of the front-room floor because he couldn't figure out whether he heard someone crying, moaning, or sobbing in his mother's room.

As he walked toward his mother's room, he heard a man's voice saying, "Yeah, suck that dick; take all that dick." He walked in slow motion, hoping that his mother was only freaky enough to be watching porn and fell asleep with the TV on. But E-Double's hopes were shattered when he looked in the crack of his mother's door and saw her on her knees sucking Ice off. E-Double wanted to believe that his eyes were lying to him. He wanted to scream, run, do something besides stand there; but the sight had frozen him in time.

Ice moaned so loud as he reached an orgasm that it took E-Double out of his trance. Sandra stood up, wiped her mouth, and asked Ice for the rocks.

"All y'all fiends are the same; y'all do anything for the rocks," Ice said fixing his pants. He threw a few capped bottles on Sandra's queen-size bed, completing their business transaction.

Ice had a thing for Sandra but she never wanted anything to do with him or his business. Every time Ice tried to get at her, she refused. Even as a fiend, Sandra possessed a beauty and a quality that most men couldn't ignore. Ice wanted to control and own Sandra's beauty. He figured that one day, the drugs would take control and he would have his opportunity to pay her back for thinking that she was too good for him. Ice was proud that his prediction came true and that he had his chance to degrade Sandra. If Ice knew that E-Double had witnessed his success, it would have made the whole ordeal that much sweeter.

As Ice walked to make an exit, E-Double silently ran out of the house. He jumped down the stairs flight by flight as if he were in the Olympics. He pushed the green metal door open and continued to run out of the courtyard high-rises. E-Double continued to run just as fast as his mind was running. He couldn't believe that he witnessed Ice smutting his mother out. He couldn't believe that his mother lied to him again. He couldn't believe that Ice's insatiable sexual appetite would lead his mother down a road that she had promised to leave behind. He couldn't believe that he now had to kill Ice.

E-Double ran until he ran right into Black and almost knocked him down.

"What are you running for?" Black asked as he grabbed onto E-Double to catch his balance. Black was standing on the corner with Jab and Booga, conducting business as usual.

"I'll tell you in a minute," E-Double said, bending over with his hands on both of his knees, trying to catch his breath. Then he stood upright, sucked in as much air as possible, and let it all out. "Take a walk with me," E-Double said.

"I'll be right back," Black said to Booga, a short, stocky teen who looked a little like Mike Tyson.

As E-Double and Black walked together, tears began to roll down E-Double's eyes.

"What happened?" Black asked looking into Double's eyes and putting his hand on his shoulders. E-Double wiped the tears from his eyes, braced himself, and proceeded to tell Black everything that he had witnessed between his mother and Ice.

Black wasn't surprised about the story that he heard from E-

Double. He knew Ice had a thing for his mother, and he knew that one day Ice would exploit his mother's addiction. E-Double was so irate that he expressed his thoughts of killing Ice a little too loudly.

"Keep it down, Double. I don't want nobody running back to Ice," Black said as he hugged his brother to calm him down.

"Everything a'ight?" Booga asked, noticing the small commotion.

"Yeah," Black said, releasing his embrace on Double. Black talked E-Double out of his impetuous thinking. He explained to his brother that Ice was their only way of making money, but they would pay him back a hundredfold when the time was right. As far as their mother was concerned, all Black could say was "She tried."

Bruce exploded out of the bathroom, causing the door to hit the wall. The loud bang woke E-Double up out of his trance. Black laughed at the way his brother jumped at the noise.

"Welcome back from memory lane," Black said, amused. He knew that once his brother had a certain look in his eyes that he was day-dreaming or deep in thought.

Bruce stumbled and fell on the couch and began to nod.

"Let's just finish baggin' this shit up and get out of here," E-Double said as his voice began to waver off.

7

SOMEDAY YOU GONNA HAVE TO PAY

"*Whaa, whaa, whaa,*" Ice sat up in his oval bed as he heard his 6-month-old baby boy crying in the other room. An olive-toned hand touched his bare back and a silky voice murmured, "Lay back down. I'll get him."

The woman pulled back the satin sheets and the goose down comforter from over her smooth, olive-toned body. She stood up and stretched her 5-foot-2-inch frame as Ice looked upon her round, firm ass as she went to the closet to retrieve her robe. Nadeem was from India and was a devout Hindu with long, black, silky hair. She almost looked like the woman actress that played in the movie *Mississippi Masala* with Denzel Washington. She walked across the cherrywood floor and exited the bedroom.

Ice and Nadeem both grew up in the 400 Building on Irvington Avenue in Pierce Manor. Ice always liked her from the moment he first laid eyes on her, but her beauty made him afraid of rejection. And the fact that he was picked on and didn't have anything when he came to the States didn't help his problem. Even when Ice came into money and power, he still found it hard to step to this woman of beauty. It wasn't until fate intervened that caused Ice to even speak to her.

One day, Ice and one of his soldiers pulled up in a Cadillac SUV in front of the 400 Building to check on business and he saw Nadeem's father being beaten by some unfamiliar men while Nadeem looked on helplessly. Ice stepped out of the truck, grabbed the first man by his collar, spun him around, and threw a jab straight from his shoulder, connecting to the man's chin, knocking him backwards towards the gate. The attacker hit the gate with such impact that he bounced off and burst his forehead on the concrete.

When the other man drew his gun on Ice, Ice's soldier popped him in his leg with a shot from his revolver. His soldier could've killed the man, but he was curious to know who would be stupid enough to step on Ice's territory unchecked.

After the whole ordeal, Ice found out that the men he had thrown a beating to belonged to Fat King from Newark, a loan shark/everything else. Nadeem's father had been late with paying the big man a handsome loan that required quick payment. Ice, with all his wisdom and scheming ways, paid off Nadeem's father's dept and paid an additional fee for the confusion with his men. He didn't need any extra problems out of Fat King. Ice didn't care though. He now had a perfect reason, an icebreaker, to step to his future woman. Nadeem and her father wanted to show Ice some gratitude and had him over for some exotic Indian cuisine. From that point on, Ice and Nadeem were hooked on each other.

Ice stood up and adjusted his crotch. He walked over and pulled the cream drapes back and let the sunshine enter his room and shine on his golden-brown complexion. He stood in his tall, picturesque window in his silk boxers and wife-beater that looked like it was going to bust under his muscular frame. Ice worked out several times a week. He kept his thirty-two-year-old body in shape. He knew that there were plenty of young lions out there ready to take his position. If they wanted to throw hands, he would be more than ready, and if they wanted to pop those thangs, he had something for their asses too.

He looked out on the city with a pride that only a king could have. Ice took the city by force in the late '90s. He deceived, conned, and muscled all the players in the city right out of their positions. Anyone he couldn't get to roll with his new regime, he rolled right over.

Ice came to the States to live with his aunt in the early '80s when he was seventeen years old after he was exiled out of Haiti. He moved from one poor environment to the next. Ice was tired of being poverty stricken and promised himself that he would come out of the ashes of poverty.

will robbins

It was hard for him when he first moved to Pierce Manor in Elizabeth, N.J. No one seemed to be familiar with Haitians, so he was always picked on. People called him Haitian Body Odor (HBO) and teased him about voodoo and his accent.

Even though Ice was a killer and left a powerful position in Haiti, he realized he was in a different place and had to play by a different set of rules. It wasn't until he started working for Diamond Black that everyone respected him.

Diamond Black had the city on lock. Nothing moved or went down without his input. Once Diamond introduced Ice as one of his peoples, all the love, respect, and loyalty was thrown Ice's way. Ice knew the love was phony, and he told himself that one day, he would own the city and bring the people to their knees.

Over the years, Ice and Diamond became real close. Diamond showed Ice the ropes and taught him all about the daily operations of the business. Ice became Diamond's best protégé and after a while, he began to run most of the daily operations of the business. Diamond seemed to take a backseat to Ice, but everyone knew who really called the shots.

Ice convinced Diamond that it would be good for business if he hired refugees from Haiti as soldiers. Diamond seemed to think that his new right-hand man and best protégé had a good idea. Diamond figured the more poor and hungry soldiers he had, the less he would have to deal with competition from the younger lions. He thought that Ice had a genuine love for him and the organization. He never would've thought that Ice was just biding his time before he could enforce his hostile takeover. Ice only loved the riches that the organization brought in.

Ice started to bring in many Haitians from Haiti. He had them cross over into the Dominican Republic, where his contact Dominican Diablo would help them get into the States illegally. Ice started to train them and groom them under his rule and dictatorship. He never even let them meet with Diamond Black. All they knew was that Ice brought them into the States and freed them from a life of poverty and death. All their loyalty was extended to him. Before Diamond knew it, there were at least three Haitians to every one of his soldiers. Before he could stop the pipeline from Haiti to the Dominican Republic into the U.S., it was too late.

Ice went straight for the head of the dragon. He knew that once he took Diamond out, he wouldn't have to deal with any resistance. Ice and his loyal Haitians stormed Diamond Black's mansion and took out the guards and the many dogs that Diamond had for protection.

Ice was used to guns. He had killed many times in Haiti and killed many people for the very organization he was taking over. He really loved to use the machete for more "personal" occasions. He walked right in Diamond's purple and gold room and took his mentor's head for his collection.

Then Ice made his new regime felt in Pierce Manor, Migliore Manor, Pioneer Holmes, Mravlag Manor in Bayway, and anywhere else that Diamond Black held power. Everyone knew who the Port Au Prince Posse was. Ice took the deed to the mansion, cars, and other businesses that Diamond owned. He had no problems taking over since he had been running every aspect of Diamond's businesses. Ice's promise to himself finally came true. He rose from the ashes of poverty in a *big* way.

Even though Ice owned a mansion, he preferred the comfortable penthouse suite he shared with Nadeem and his son. He didn't believe in sleeping in the house of a man that he had killed. Too many bad vibes, and it was very disrespectful he thought.

However, he didn't let the mansion go to waste. Ice used it for hood parties for his peoples and political meetings. He protected himself and his organization very well. He had his hands in the mayor's office, police, and sheriff's department. Ice also used the mansion to house the many Haitians that he smuggled into the States.

Occasionally, his soldiers would be arrested and deported back to Haiti, so there was always room in the mansion. Ice bought a lot of police protection, but every once in a while, the police had to make an example out of the Port Au Prince Posse to satisfy the taxpayers.

Ice stepped out of the shower with a leopard towel wrapped around his waist. He almost slipped on the cherrywood floor and cursed for not buying the rugs that he wanted. Nadeem hated rugs. Her father had too many rugs in their house. Nadeem and her father made rugs for a living before coming to the States.

He stepped into his walk-in closet to set out his clothes for the day. Ice wore nothing but the best to show his status. After years of ripped jeans and dirty T-shirts, Ice wouldn't accept anything but the

will robbins

finest and most expensive. He pulled out a black, wool, two-button suit, white cotton shirt, and silk tie, all by Prada, and matching black loafers by Giorgio Armani. He made sure that he and Nadeem hit all the fashion shows to get up on the latest designs and designers.

Ice was meticulous when it came to getting dressed. He took plenty of time, like he was going to the prom. After he was dressed, he knew he needed some accessories, so he walked over to his cherry red nightstand and picked out one of his many watches. This one was a diamond-crusted watch that he bought from Jacob's in New York. In fact, it was one of the first watches he bought when he first started rolling with Diamond Black.

He was thinking of Diamond, which put him in a mood to wear the watch in the first place. Sometimes Ice wished that he hadn't had to kill Diamond for the power, but that was the way life was at times.

Next, he picked up a small bottle labeled "Come to Me." It was an oil fragrance that many brothers sold on the street. He had more than enough money to purchase colognes, but he wanted to keep some things simple, and the oils were more pure. Ice finally looked in his wall-mounted mirror and was satisfied with his attire.

He stepped out of his bedroom and headed down the crystal spiral stairs, through the long corridor past the living room, dining room, and walked into the kitchen where Nadeem was feeding their son.

"Good morning, Toussaint," she said, putting a spoonful of Gerber food into the baby's mouth. She was the only one who still called Ice by his government name. He didn't mind though. He liked the way his name rolled off her tongue with her beautiful, silky accent.

"Good morning, baby," Ice replied, sitting down on one of the crystal and platinum-rimmed glass chairs. Before him sat a large plate of food. Nadeem always made sure that Ice ate a healthy meal before he left the house in the morning.

"Toussaint, I was thinking about taking some classes at Union County College next semester," she said, looking at her man to see any facial expressions of disapproval.

"Why? I make enough money so you don't ever have to work."

"It's not the money. I just want to do something productive with my time. And eventually you have to go legit."

"Now the truth comes out. It's not about you, it's about me going legit," Ice said with a little sarcasm in his voice. Lately "going legit" became the topic of their everyday conversation, and Ice was growing tired of it. "You don't have any problems spending the money and living in the lap of luxury," he said a little testy.

"Yeah, that's before we had a son. What would we do if something happens to you?" Nadeem asked with a crack in her voice.

"There's enough life insurance on me that if anything happens, you and Junior will be well taken care of. And there's enough savings bonds and a healthy trust fund so that even Junior's kids won't have to work," Ice said, lightening his tone with assurance.

"You fool! It's not about the money, and it never has been. Don't talk to me like I'm one of those bitches that came to you because I wanted to have a baller representing me. I had dreams and aspirations before we met, and I still do. And let's not forget *you* chased *me, not* the other way around; remember that," Nadeem said, upset at Ice's ignorance about money.

"You wasn't poppin' all that shit when I paid ya' father's dept off to keep Fat King from killin' his ass, were you?" Ice asked, matching her temper.

"Who you foolin'? You did that shit so you could get in my pants."

"It worked, didn't it?" Ice replied with a smile to lighten up the mood.

"So?" she replied, trying not to smile.

"Look, I'm sorry, baby, I don't want to argue. All this time, you've been the only person who understood me. You are the only Indian/Hindu that grew up in Pierce Manor and came up poor and was picked on just like me for being different. Every time I saw people picking on you, my heart broke 'cause they did the same thing to me. Now this very game that gave us power and respect, you asking me to leave, and I can't accept that. I don't want our children to go through anything that we went through, so please, baby, understand that."

"I do, baby, but you have to understand that I need you, and these streets ain't playin'. All the murder, drugs, and violence … someday, you gonna have to pay. And I want you out before the streets claims their debt," Nadeem said, fighting back tears.

"I *am* the streets!" Ice yelled, like he couldn't be touched. Little did he know he was wrong. *Very* wrong.

"I still want to go to school," Nadeem said, feeling defeated and getting back to the original conversation.

"Okay," Ice said, knowing that he couldn't deny his one true love the simple request to attend school. Ice knew that once his lady had her mind made up, it would be difficult to sway her.

"Listen, I have a meeting with some cats soon," Ice said looking at his watch. "We'll talk more about this later." Then he kissed his son's forehead and kissed Nadeem before he left the suite.

In another part of New Jersey, Plainfield, that is, Black and E-Double were holding a meeting in Banks' foster grandmother's basement. It was the new meeting place for all the Eastwick Hustlers Inc. soldiers. It was one of many places in New Jersey that Ice didn't conduct business, which made the meeting a little more secure and private. Black and E-Double could've used their own apartment for the meeting, but they never believed in shitting where you sleep. They also didn't want to run the risk of their mother or sister walking in on them.

Many members that were present E-Double and Black were familiar with, while others were new faces. The work that Banks, Booga, and Jab put in outside of Ice's organization really made Eastwick Hustlers Inc. grow in numbers faster than E-Double and Black could count. They knew that they could count on the niggas that they grew up with to make the organization grow. E-Double and Black spent so much time making Ice and his organization grow that they neglected their own team, but all that was about to change. History was about to repeat itself.

"Yo, yo, yo, listen up!" Black yelled to get the attention of his men in the overcrowded basement.

Black and E-Double were holding a meeting to let their soldiers and boys know about the current situation with Ice and to talk about their new organization, Eastwick Hustlers Inc. Jab, Booga, and Banks were passing around a blunt, waiting anxiously to hear what their man Black had to say. Jab and Booga grew up in the same housing complex as Black and E-Double. All of their mothers fell victim to the white god. So, naturally, the situation brought the boys closer together. Jab was almost as black as Black, and he were known for his temper and even more famous for his trigger finger. At an early age, Jab's father taught him how to shoot and to fight before he got locked up for armed robbery. Jab's skills made him a perfect candidate for

Booga, on the other hand, hated guns. He saw his father shoot his mother for not fucking some men he brought over the house to support his habit. She figured she wasn't going to fuck any man if she wasn't getting drugs out of the deal. Booga preferred to use his mind as a weapon. He was what you would call an "intelligent thug." Or what the government might call a "prodigy child." He could plan a bank heist, a drug heist, or any illegal heist known to man. He never pulled any heist himself, but many criminals employed his services. Booga wasn't naïve about the streets either. He didn't like guns, but he did master Chinese throwing stars. He could hit his target from yards away *with his eyes closed.* He was too smart and too skilled for Black and E-Double to let slip away.

Banks was a light-skinned, sixteen-year-old teen, short, with pretty emerald green eyes. He always carried the pound on his side to make up for being short. Banks didn't have any family. He was raised in a placement facility for abandoned children. He was the neighborhood stickup kid. He didn't care who he robbed or what he did. He didn't care about his life, so anybody could get it as far as he was concerned. Banks' reputation grew in Newark, Linden, and Elizabeth as a stone-cold robber and killer. E-Double picked Banks to be in the crew before he did something stupid like rob Ice's people, or worse, rob him or Black. So he chose the young brother to make sure that he and Black would never have any issues with him.

"In a couple days we meetin' Ice. We got a couple of packages to finish off and then we're on our own," Black said slamming his fist into his hand for emphasis.

"I know Jab, Booga, and Banks been preparing y'all for this shit," Black continued.

"Anybody got any problems with that, there's the door," E-Double, said pointing to it.

"I ain't got no problem with it, but what we leavin' Ice for?" Bobby, a tall, brown-skinned brother with a Down South accent asked.

"Yo, who this nigga?" E-Double asked with his face curled up.

"Remember I told you I was getting robbed by some niggas from Newark and some nigga came through shootin' at them niggas like Billy the Kid, from the movie *Young Guns?*" Banks asked.

"Yeah and?" E-Double asked waiting impatiently.

"That was *this* nigga right here," Banks said, looking at Bobby and tapping him on the chest.

"How you know this nigga ain't set the whole thing up?" Black asked.

"Look, I know I just started earnin' with y'all niggas, but I ain't set shit up," Bobby said nervously. "Link and Tyrell from Newark, they robbed me a few times when I was slippin'. I live in Newark, but I got this shorty out in Elizabeth I was messin' with. I saw them niggas robbin' Banks so I shot him some bail. Banks asked did I want to be down, so here I am."

"A'ight, Banks, you responsible for that nigga," Black said.

"Once again, why we breakin' off from Ice?" another crew member asked.

"What if I paid y'all 500 dollars, and y'all found out that I owed y'all thousands?" Black asked.

"It would be some problems," Banks said, cocking the hammer back on his nine.

"Well, Ice been shorten' us since we been down with him. But we not goin' to touch him unless he makes a move first. We don't want to start no war if we don't have to," E-Double replied.

"We can't afford a war with that nigga right now anyway. That nigga got the mayor, chief of police, and the sheriff's department in his pockets!" Jab said excitedly.

"That's why we got Booga doin' the planning," Black said.

"How did Ice get the mayor in his pocket?" another crew member asked.

"I got this one," Jab said smiling. Jab liked telling stories and being a little bit of a historian.

"Ice had some of his men rape the mayor's daughter, and then he gave the police enough evidence to lock his men up. Once they were on trial, evidence somehow 'got lost' and some jury members were paid off for a not guilty verdict. Once they got off, the mayor was distraught and pissed. So Ice set up a meetin' with the mayor and told him that he could have all the men touched that raped his daughter if he would take care of a few immigration problems for him.

"The mayor was still grieving, so he decided to take Ice up on his offer. He didn't know that Ice was taping the whole conversation. The next day, the men who raped his daughter were all laid out on the front steps of City Hall with their heads cut off," Jab said, proud that he remembered the details.

"That's some cold, calculatin' shit," Bobby said shaking his head.

"So how we gonna take on Ice if he got all this protection?" an aggressive lesbian chick named Bricks asked. Bricks grew up with Black and E-Double. She was more like a cousin than a crew member. Bricks once saved E-Double's life from some niggas in Linden when he was messing with some chick off Chancellor Avenue. Bricks was chilling with one of her female companions on the porch when she saw E-Double exiting his so-called girl's house. In a fit of jealousy, some niggas stepped to him. Before E-Double could pull his gun out, he was hit over the head with a bottle. The three men proceeded to stomp him mercilessly.

Just as one of the boys pulled out his Berretta, Bricks leaped off the porch in superhero time with her twin .45s blazing. The hail of bullets ripped through two of the boys' upper torsos, while the other boy was hit tragically in the dick. E-Double was never happier to see anyone in his life than he was to see Bricks. Bricks also kicked any bitch's ass for Black and E-Double if they got out of pocket.

"Don't worry, we have some police protection of our own. And if any of those officers go down, they takin' a whole lot of the force down with them, and the city can't afford that. Most of the police, sheriffs, and the mayor have ties to Ice or Eastwick Hustlers Inc. So if Black, Ice, or E-Double goes down, this whole city goes down. Ice is goin' to keep his protection on us if he knows what's good for him," Booga replied bluntly.

"And that's why we got you around, Booga, 'cause you always thinkin' and planning," Black said with a mischievous smile.

"Now, we not sayin' that Ice ain't gonna try and touch us 'cause he is. All we're sayin' is we don't have to worry about Johnny Law or gettin' football number sentences. But we still got to be careful. So from now on, nobody go nowhere by yourself, not your mother's house, girl's house, boy's house, or my house. And make sure you always strapped. We got to tighten up ship for awhile," Black said seriously.

"In a couple of days, we gonna meet with Ice. Banks, you coming with us to the meeting; you, too, Bobby, since you like Blazin' Saddles out this bitch. We might need y'all at this meetin' just in case Ice gets

will robbins

funny. The rest of y'all go make this money and don't forget shit we said in here today," Black said.

"And keep ya' ma'fuckin' mouths shut," E-Double said with conviction.

Ice pulled up in a majestic baby blue Aston Martin Vanquish, one of two in the world. He stopped in front of his club Lady Luck. It used to be the Queen of Hearts before he killed Diamond Black and took it over. It was early morning, and the club was empty except for a couple of bouncers and bodyguards hanging around. Ice stepped into his club and was greeted by one of his bouncers.

"What's up, Mr. Ice?" a Warren Sapp-looking Haitian asked.

"Business, Slim, always business," Ice replied. He walked past the bar and the dance floor and made his way up the private elevator to reach his office. Ice's office had a loud and calm appeal to it. It had wall-to-wall red carpeting, a red mahogany desk, off-white Italian couches, waterfalls that came down the wall and emptied into a small pond with Japanese fish, a Jacuzzi that sat right next to a fireplace, and countless, priceless art pieces decorated the walls. His window overlooked the bar, stage, and dance floor.

As Ice stepped into his office, he noticed his business partner at his desk with the newspaper. "What's up?" Ice asked.

"You read the fuckin' paper?" a light-skinned man with a Haitian accent asked angrily.

"No, what's in it?" Ice asked, confused.

The one people called Six-ten because of his height stood up and tossed the paper to his partner. Ice looked at the front cover of the paper and read,

Rising levels of deadly political and gang violence in the capital; armed gangs loyal to the former president said to be responsible for the many killings.

Ice's father was killed in a political struggle to bring power back to the government rather than the army. Many army men raped and murdered his mother right in front of him when he was just 10 years old. Ice was determined to pay the men back who violated and killed his mother and father, so he joined the side of a rebel clique at the age of 11 in favor of the government.

Once Ice avenged his parents' death, he became a guerilla leader at the age of 16 and tried to name himself governor-general of Haiti.

He became so ruthless and hungry for power that he killed, tortured, and seized the property of anyone who opposed him. Ice was so powerful and wicked at a young age that the U.S. armed forces were sent in to give power back to the government. Ice gave up power and fled to the U.S. after his forces were defeated.

"Yo, how we know Ice ain't gonna check us for weapons?" Bobby asked from the backseat of the Escalade.

"'Cause we been dealin' with him ever since we were 12 years old. He taught us how to buy, distribute, and to kill. And never once did he check us or question our loyalty. He still thinks we some naïve lowlife corner boys. *That's* how I know," E-Double said with cockiness in his voice.

"I hope you right, 'cause these guns ain't gonna mean shit if he take 'em," Bobby replied a little nervous.

"Shut the fuck up and let the playas worry, nigga," E-Double said, irritated at his new soldier.

Black continued to ride up Elizabeth Avenue with his mind on the task at hand. He parked the SUV in front of the Lady Luck Club. Black was careful not to park too close to Ice's vehicle. Everyone stepped outside of the vehicle, and Black laid down the instructions.

"No matter what happens in there, everyone keep a cool head. *I* do all the talking," Black said. Everyone nodded their head simultaneously and tucked their guns in the back of their waist. Then Black opened the big white door and entered the club with his men on his heels.

"What's up, Slim?" Black asked as he extended his hand and gave Slim a one-arm hug.

"Nothin' but that bitch on the pole," Slim replied, pointing towards the stage where a thick chocolate woman was hanging upside down from the pole with her legs spread eagle and her pussy exposed for the world to see.

"*Damn!* You see her pussy?" E-Double asked practically panting.

"Nigga, do you see those titties?" Banks replied.

Noticing she had a bigger audience, the stripper slid down the pole into a full straddle split, took off her top, and exposed her voluptuous breasts for the men. She slowly licked her brown hard nipples in a tantalizing way, reached for a two-sided dildo that lay on the floor, and began to suck on it very slowly, like a pro. As her captivated audi-

will robbins

ence still looked on, she lay on her back and spread her legs as far as they would go, put the head and shaft of the dildo into her pussy, and took the other end and inserted it into her ass as she gyrated and moaned to the pleasure of the men.

"Damn, where did Ice get that one?" E-Double asked with his dick half-erect.

"Ice got her somewhere from Brazil last time he was out there," Slim replied, still watching the show.

"Damn that, where is Ice? We got business to handle," Black said, trying his hardest not to look at the Brazilian bombshell.

"Right this way, gentlemen," Slim said with his hand extended, guiding the way.

All the men took a closer look as they walked past the stage where the woman was freaking off with the dildo. She winked at E-Double as their eyes met.

"Why can't we take the elevator, Slim?" Banks asked as they reached the stairs.

"'Cause it's Ice's private entrance. You ma'fuckas get the stairs," Slim replied, pushing Banks.

Slim knocked on the door and waited for the command to enter. Then he opened the door and invited the guests in.

"That's one fine bitch I got down there, isn't it, boys?" Ice asked, looking out his window at the show.

"She damn sure is," E-Double said, feeling like he could bust at any minute.

Black tapped his brother for his lack of focus. He always told him that his tender dick would get him into trouble.

"She's going to make me mad money," Ice said as he turned around to face his guests.

"Grab a seat, boys. Let Six-ten check y'all before you do," Ice said, as he sat down in his black leather reclining office chair. Six-ten walked over to the boys and began to search. He pulled a .38 Special revolver from Bobby, a nine from Banks, and a .45 caliber from Black and E-Double.

"What's with the searches?" Black asked, surprised and confused.

"I gotta keep you lil' niggas on ya' feet, that's all," Ice said smiling as if he were concealing something. All four men sat on the off-white Italian sectional couch as Six-ten placed the weapons in front of Ice.

"Allow me to extend my hospitality and offer you boys a drink," Ice stated. Black and E-Double quickly declined. They never smoked or poisoned their bodies with alcohol; too many family addicts. Banks quickly ordered an Incredible Hulk and Bobby ordered the same. He didn't want to turn down Ice's offer and offend him the first time they met.

"We just here to do business, Ice," Black said with sincerity.

"Let your boys finish their drink and we'll do business. Besides, I got a little show for y'all," Ice said, standing up. He fixed his tie and walked towards a closet. He stood a moment, then opened the closet door and yanked a husky, rough type of black person out of the closet with short blonde hair wearing a Bulls jersey. At first sight, the boys thought it was just another man Ice was about to make an example out of.

"Pick that bitch up," Ice said with venom in his voice. As Six-ten picked up the body, the boys noticed that it was Bricks. They all stood up as they recognized her.

"Sit the fuck back down!" Six-ten yelled, pointing a gun in their direction to emphasize the seriousness of their situation.

"Now, I bet you ma'fuckas want to know what's goin' on," Ice said, pulling Bricks by the neck and slamming her face into the desk, causing blood to burst from her forehead.

"This bitch here fucks with one of my dancers. And since pussy and drugs beats a ma'fucka, she started runnin' her mouth about this new organization y'all got forming. What is it?" Ice asked no one in particular.

"Eastwick Hustlers Inc.," Six-ten replied.

"Right, Eastwick Hustlers Inc. Then she starts talkin' 'bout how y'all gonna take over for yourselves and shit," Ice said, as he smacked Bricks viciously across her face. E-Double and Black just grit their teeth, seeing one of their people helpless. Banks and Bobby wanted to do something but without their guns, they knew it was hopeless.

"But I knew this bitch must be talkin' outta the side of her neck 'cause I know you boys wouldn't try some stupid shit like that, right?" Ice said as he tapped his gun on the side of his desk.

"Ice, you been dealin' with us since we was 12 years old. You know we wouldn't do some dumb shit like that. Me and my brother we call ourselves Eastwick Hustlers, but we ain't no organization. And how we gonna take over with no connect to supply us? We know you got too much protection for us to take over anyway," Black explained, trying to control his nervousness and fear.

"We'd be some fools tryin' to take over. We don't know where this bitch is getting her information from," E-Double said, trying to keep cool after he felt like he just betrayed one of his closest people. Especially after she saved his life. Black and E-Double tried to ease their guilt by convincing themselves that she betrayed herself, and them, by running her mouth. Now it was all about self-preservation.

"So this bitch doesn't know what she talking 'bout, huh?" Ice asked as he threw Bricks to the floor.

"Hell, no," Black said as he looked at his friend helplessly lying on the floor with her hands and mouth duct taped. Black felt sorry that he had to be so cruel, but he wasn't about to die over stupidity.

"So it doesn't matter what we do to this lyin' bitch, does it?" Six-ten asked.

"I wouldn't go that far, Ice. She may have caused us some trouble, but she did save my life once. Let us take care of her in our own way," E-Double said.

"She saved ya' life, not mine. Besides, I can't have anyone coming to me with lies, causing friction in my organization. Now how would that make me look?" Ice asked, looking in E-Double's direction.

"I know where you're coming from, but let us take it from here, Ice, please," Black said in desperation to save his soldier.

"Either she's telling the truth or she's lyin'. If she's telling the truth, then all of y'all need to die, but y'all already said she wasn't, so she needs to die," Ice said coldly.

"*What?*" all the boys asked, dumbfounded.

"This lyin' bitch almost got y'all killed; so it shouldn't be a problem to kill her," Six-ten said, handing Black a gun.

"Wait! There has to be another way," Double jumped up in one last attempt to save Bricks. Six-ten patted E-Double on his shoulder to let him know he needed to sit down. Ice stood up and began to speak.

"I see we have a delicate situation. She saved ya' life back in the day, so naturally, you feel the need to return the favor. So I'll give you a shot. Your life for hers," Ice said smiling maliciously. All the boys looked back and forth at one another in fear, knowing what was coming next. Ice knew that Black would never point the gun in his brother's direction so he had them right where he wanted them. Black made his decision without a second thought.

Black pointed the gun in Bricks' direction, trying not to look at her. A sweat bead dropped into his eye, breaking his focus. Colors of rage and death danced inside of his head. He seemed to be filled with colors of red, gray, and black, while smoke seemed to consume his mind as he contemplated what he was about to do.

"I'll do it," Banks said, knowing that his man couldn't kill someone so close to him. Banks felt that in this business, you always had to kill someone you knew.

"I got this," Black said, trying to be strong and set an example for his boys.

Just as Black was ready to squeeze the trigger, Ice yelled, "Wait! Not with that. With *this*," he said as he handed Black a machete to make things harder on him.

Bobby, Banks, and E-Double stood there, helpless to change their current situation. Black, feeling that the situation was do or die, raised the machete high above his head and with one stroke of the blade, he took off Bricks' head. Ice and Six-ten clapped their hands and stood there laughing. Black looked surprised at the heinous act he just committed, while Banks, E-Double, and Bobby almost lost their lunches.

Ice walked over to Black, removed the machete from his hand, and said, "That's what we do to lyin' bitches that interfere with our organization.

"Now grab a seat," Ice said.

"Make sure you get Cleanup and his crew up here to erase this bitch and her shit out of my office when I leave," Ice said to Six-ten.

"I'll get right on it," Six-ten replied.

"Now that we got that piece of business outta the way, let's handle this piece of business," Ice said. He stood up, walked to his wall, and removed an African painting from the wall, exposing his safe. After opening the safe, he pulled five keys of crack cocaine from the safe and placed them in a duffle bag.

"Now you boys know what to do, so get it done. And Black, if you think about fuckin' me, don't forget that shit you just did is all on camera," Ice said, pointing to an aerial camera. "Now get the fuck

will robbins

outta my office."

E-Double, Bobby, and Banks jumped up from their seat and followed Black out the door. Before Banks stepped out, he asked, "Can we get our guns back?"

"Do ya' mother suck dick?" Six-ten asked.

"A little bit," Banks answered to agitate the big man.

As Six-ten walked in Banks' direction, Banks ran and slammed the door.

When the boys went down the stairs, Ice and Six-ten stepped towards the elevator, and Six-ten asked his boss, "You know that bitch was tellin' the truth, don't you?"

"I know," Ice said as he pushed the button in the elevator.

"So why you let those ma'fuckas walk outta here?" Six-ten asked, confused.

"Money. It all comes down to money," Ice replied as they entered the elevator.

As Ice stepped out of the elevator, he saw his Brazilian dancer drinking at the bar.

"Scandalous, you see those niggas that just left out of here?" Ice asked.

Scandalous just replied by nodding her head.

"The brown skin one with all the ice on I want you to give him your name and address," Ice said grabbing her ass as she jumped from the barstool.

Scandalous happily jumped off the bar stool to catch up with the young playa; she was feeling him from the moment she saw him.

"What you do that for?" Six-ten asked.

"I want my money from them, but I'm not stupid enough to let them live. I want to kill E-Double first and see how his brother Black plays his hand. I want to see if this nigga is a chess thinker and not a checker thinker. I haven't had a good war since Diamond Black," Ice said smiling.

"So you want to start somethin'?" Six-ten asked.

"In a couple of days round one will start."

The boys were sitting in the Escalade, silently going over what just happened in their mind as Scandalous approached the vehicle on E-Double's side.

"What's up, baby?" Scandalous asked, licking her full lips with the promise of paradise. The boys jumped as they were awaken back into reality.

E-Double, regaining his cool first, responded with a smile and said, "You, baby."

"I thought we had some kind of connection back there," Scandalous said, fixing her tight strapless shirt so that E-Double could get a better look at her heavy cleavage.

"Get the fuck away from the car, bitch," Black yelled once he realized what was going on.

"What's wrong with your man?" Scandalous asked with her face distorted.

"Nothing, look … just give me your number and we'll hook up later," E-Double responded.

"That's what's up, baby," Scandalous said as she handed E-Double her business card.

Exotic Dancer Sukanya "Scandalous" Wright
908-558-####

"What the fuck is wrong with you?" Black asked, looking at E-Double as if he lost his mind.

"What the fuck is wrong with *you*?" E-Double asked with the same conviction.

"We almost got our asses killed in there, and you thinkin' 'bout some bitch! Not to mention I just killed Bricks, who was like family! What the fuck we suppose to tell people? How did this shit all happen?" Black yelled furiously, banging his fist on the steering wheel, causing Banks, Bobby, and E-Double to jump.

"You know how all this happened!" E-Double yelled. "Bricks got drunk, high, and sprung on some stripper bitch that worked for Ice and ran her mouth! She almost got us killed and got herself killed! I loved Bricks just as much as you, but she asked for this! We tell everybody, don't run ya' fuckin' mouth about family business, and that's just what the fuck she did," E-Double yelled with glassy eyes.

"And that's exactly what you about to do with that stripper!" Black continued with the same tone of anger.

"Look, I'm not Bricks! I don't get drunk or high, and I definitely don't get sprung. All I'ma do is get some pussy, and I'm out. You actin' like I'm sayin' we gonna let this shit ride," E-Double said, trying to fight back the tears he felt for Bricks.

"Look!" Bobby interrupted coming out of his nervous haze. "What happened in that room stays in that room. We don't tell nobody shit!"

"Yeah, man. Black, that shit wasn't ya' fault. You did what you had to do so we would walk out of there alive. And as far as that bitch go, if she would've given me her number, I'd be tryin' to fuck, too," Banks said waving his hands around like he was smacking a fat ass.

"That's 'cause you'd fuck anything that moves," Black returned, trying to ease the tension in the truck.

"Everything 'cept ya' momma," Banks replied, smacking Black in the back of the head.

Black turned the key in the ignition, started up the truck, and pulled into the traffic while thanking the Lord that he had another day to try and pay Ice back.

8

WHO YOU REALLY GONNA ROLL WIT'?

It was a cool Saturday morning. Banks and Bobby were dressed in black army fatigue pants, black hoodies, black hats, and black boots, sitting on a stoop of an abandoned building chomping a Black and Mild cigar, watching the block. Business was light since it was the middle of the month and Mother's Day was always between the first and third of the month. That's when all the mothers and fiends receive their checks for those of you who don't know. It's a little project humor.

"So who you really gonna roll wit'?" Bobby asked.

"What you mean?" Banks said, confused about the question he was just asked.

"Between Black and Ice, who you gonna roll wit'?" Bobby asked again, pouring the contents from the Black and Mild into the plastic covering.

"Nigga, I'm rollin' wit' Eastwick Hustlers Inc."

"It seems like Ice holdin' all the power and the cards," Bobby said, opening up the Black and Mild cigar, removing the extra lining of paper, and licking the ends of the cigar.

"Ice ain't holdin' nothin' but my dick! Fuck Ice!" Banks said, grabbing his crotch, being confident in Eastwick Hustlers Inc.

"And hurry up with that Black and Mild," he added with irritation in his voice and pushing Bobby, almost making him drop the contents as he was placing them back inside the Black and Mild. Just as Bobby was about to respond, Woo and Taye stepped up.

Woo was dressed casually as always, and Taye was wearing a black tracksuit.

"What's up?" Banks asked as they stepped on the block.

"I can't call it," Woo said, giving Banks and Bobby a pound, and Taye doing the same.

"Yo, any of y'all seen or heard from Black or E-Double?" Woo asked being a little more serious.

"Nah, we ain't seen or heard from them in a couple of days," Banks and Bobby responded honestly.

"I guess I should tell you two niggas," Woo said, taking a seat on the stoop next to Banks.

"What's up, nigga?" Banks asked attentively.

"Word on the street is that Black killed Bricks and that you, Bobby, and E-Double was there," Woo said, looking back and forth at Bobby and Banks to see any facial changes.

"Who the fuck said some dumb shit like that?" Banks asked defensively, lighting his Black and Mild cigar.

"Ain't no word. It's a tape," Taye said matter-of-factly.

"*What?*" Bobby asked as his face turned bright red.

"At a private party, Ice was showing this tape of Black cuttin' off Bricks' head and y'all niggas was standing there watching. Now what the fuck happened?" Woo asked.

"I don't know what the fuck y'all talkin' 'bout," Banks replied, trying to act dumb.

"Look, just 'cause I'm not down wit' anyone in the streets don't mean I ain't plugged into the streets. If you see Black or E-Double, tell them to hit a nigga up," Woo said standing, giving Banks and Bobby a pound.

"Where you two niggas goin' early this mornin'?" Bobby asked.

"I got a track meet," Taye responded as he and Woo stepped off.

"We should roll wit' y'all. Them bitches from Plainfield got thighs like ma'fuckin' horses!" Banks said with a big smile on his face.

"They'll never kick me in the ass," Woo said jokingly.

"A'ight, we out," Taye said as they walked towards the bus stop.

"Yo, how many people you think saw that tape?" Bobby asked acting nervous.

"I don't know but we need to get Black and E-Double on the line to see what they wanna do," Banks replied, pulling out his cell phone.

"Why the fuck would Ice show that tape and his Haitian ass is on it too?" Banks asked while dialing a number.

"Man, it's all kinds of shit they could do with technology that could make it look like the president was there and not Ice; and Ice got the money and the resources to do it," Bobby said sounding like a cheerleader.

Black was sitting on his bed shifting through some books he checked out from the public library. After killing Bricks, he needed something other than the streets to occupy his time. He tossed around *From NIGGAS to GODS,* part one & two by Akil, *Breaking the Curse of Willie Lynch: The Science Of Slave Psychology* by Alvin Morrow, *Street Dreams* by K'Wan, *Whoreson* by Donald Goines, and a GED book. Black decided on the GED book when his phone rang. He picked up the phone, lifted the flap, and said, "Eastwick, what's up, baby?"

"Yo, we need to talk but not on the phone," Banks said quickly with urgency in his voice.

"Calm down, nigga," Black said shifting through the pages of the book.

"Look, get ya' brotha and Booga and meet us at the spot in one hour," Banks commanded like he was in charge.

"A'ight, I'll call my brotha and Booga, and we'll meet y'all at the spot in an hour," Black said, laughing at how Banks acted like he was in charge.

♦ ♦ ♦ ♦

E-Double grabbed onto the wooden headboard with his ass in the air and said, "You a freaky bitch," as Scandalous sucked his dick from the back. As soon as he felt her finger near his ass, he jumped off the bed and said, "Hey, bitch, I ain't that freaky."

"I'm sorry, baby," Scandalous said, as she crawled on the bed towards him like a cat in heat. As she reached him, she put his manhood back in her hot, wet mouth and began to work. E-Double closed his eyes in a state of bliss. Scandalous worked his dick with both of her hands as she spit on it to provide more lubrication like a real porno star.

E-Double grabbed her hair and pulled her head down as far as it would go, and he thrust his dick deeper in her mouth causing her to choke. He knew he was well hung for his age, and he enjoyed the fact that this older, fine bitch could barely handle him. Then he laid Scandalous on her back to admire her frame. Her breasts were so perfect that when she lay down, they still stood up like mountains.

He climbed up on Scandalous' stomach and poured Body Butter lotion on her chest. After that, he used his firm hands to squeeze her breasts together and placed his dick between those firm, voluptuous mountains and began to stroke. Scandalous sucked the head of his dick to make him cum faster. Just as E-Double was about to let his million men march all over Scandalous' face, his cell phone rang. He reached for it on the nightstand and answered.

"This shit better be good," E-Double said halfway out of breath.

"What the fuck you doing?" Black asked.

"It's not what I'm doin', it's who I'm doin' and how I'm doin' it to her, nigga. Now this shit better be good," E-Double repeated as Scandalous still sucked on his dick.

"I need to pick you up for a meetin' at the spot right now. Where you at?"

"Pick me up on Catherine Street, 300 block," E-Double replied. He had been spending his days at Scandalous' crib to occupy his time since the murder of Bricks.

"I'm on it," Black replied as he hung up the phone.

❧ ❧ ❧ ❧

"Look, Prince, if this shit gonna work for you and ya' boys, y'all gotta be there exactly at 12 pm. I'ma shut the alarm system, phones, and the computers down. And the doors are goin' to lock for two minutes. So no one gets in or out. So y'all have *two minutes* to get the shit done," Booga said, looking at Prince to make sure he was paying attention.

"Let me get this straight. The doors are goin' to lock for two minutes, the phones and the alarms goin' to be off, and all you want is $10,000 for your trouble?" Prince asked, surprised.

"How you gonna do all that shit with just this computer?" Prince asked another question before he got the answer to the first one. It must have been rhetorical.

"A magician never reveals his secrets," Booga replied smugly, closing his laptop.

"Since you can do this shit, why you fuck around with Black and

E-Double? You could do ya' own shit with less problems of getting caught," Prince stated.

"'Cause Black and E-Double my boys, and one day, they gonna run the city, and I'ma be right there with them. Now go get our money, nigga," Booga said. As Prince exited the apartment, Booga's cell phone rang.

"Talk to me," Booga said, answering his cell phone.

"It's Black. Get ya'self together. We got to meet with Banks and Bobby at the spot in a few. I'm on my way to pick up my brother, and I'll be right there to get you," Black said on the other line.

"Cool. I'm ready now," Booga shot back.

"Cool," Black said and hung up the line.

❦ ❦ ❦ ❦

Woo stepped off the 24 bus and made his way to the Lady Luck Club to speak to Ice. He hadn't been to the club since he stopped working for Ice. He loved the man, but he also kept his distance so he wouldn't be tempted to work for his former mentor. Just riding the bus and living in a dump was enough persuasion for him to go back and work for Ice. If it weren't for the fact that Woo wanted to major in early childhood education with a minor in psychology and possibly run his own martial arts academy, he might have gone back to work for Ice. But he didn't want to let himself, his cousins, or his father down. He didn't want to see Ice this time, but the thought of Vicky working for him was weighing heavy on his mind and heart. He hoped that his mentor still had enough love for him to grant him the request to let Vicky go, but he had another thing coming.

Woo entered the club and was greeted by the Haitian known as Slim. The club had a few dancers rehearsing to get their money up for the upcoming night—one of which happened to be Vicky. The sight of Vicky swinging from the pole turned a fire on in Woo's belly that could be seen in his eyes. Slim, noticing the look, asked, "Is that ya' girl, sister, or something?"

"Nah, just a girl I know," Woo answered as his fire turned to sorrow, wondering how many men she sucked and fucked. He wished that he could save this girl, and he hoped that he was doing the right thing by speaking to Ice on her behalf. But he would soon find out that every woman wasn't meant to be saved.

"Ice in his office?" Woo asked.

will robbins

"Yeah, let's go," Slim said, always happy to see Woo. He led the young man into Ice's private elevator, which caused Woo to ask, "I thought this was Ice's private entrance."

"It is, but I think we could make an exception for an old friend and ex-biggest moneymaker," Slim replied with a smile.

He pressed the 3rd-floor button to Ice's office. The first floor was the dance floor, stage, bar, and sitting area. The 2nd floor was the VIP section, and the 3rd floor was Ice's office.

The elevator opened and surprised Ice and Six-ten, who were watching a recording on the flat screen TV. Woo saw an Indian man tied to a chair, being beaten by Ice before Ice cut the TV off. If Ice had known that that recording was going to be his downfall, he would have burned the tape.

"What's up there, playa?" Ice asked, surprised to see Woo.

"Who was that on the TV?" Woo asked, feeling that the person he saw looked familiar.

"That's none of your business, now sit down and tell me what I can do for you," Ice said politely. Woo took a seat and sighed heavily.

"Let me get right to it," Woo said. "I need a favor."

"Go 'head, son," Ice replied a little curious.

"I love you, respect you, and I would never question your judgment, but I need you to let Vicky go," Woo said sincerely with glassy eyes.

Ice and Six-ten laughed at the request to Woo's surprise.

"What's so funny?" Woo asked, feeling his temper was about to boil over.

Seeing the anger and hurt in his ex-pupil's eyes made Ice more considerate about the situation at hand. He knew for Woo to come to his office and ask such a request, the boy had to have some serious feelings for the girl.

"Look, man, Vicky doesn't owe me anything. She's free to come and go as she pleases. She came to me, asking for work, and I just obliged her. She's happy doin' what she's doin'. If I were you, I'd focus on that badass karate chick you been diggin'," Ice said, trying to give Woo sound advice before he got his feelings hurt.

Woo continued to look at Ice as if every word he said was a lie. He knew Vicky, and he knew she would never put herself out there like that. Or so he thought. Ice, knowing that Woo thought he was being deceived, said, "I'll call her up here, and you can ask her yourself." He stood up, turned around, and faced his window. He tapped on the glass to get Slim's attention, who was enjoying the preshow. As Slim looked up, Ice pointed in Vicky's direction and he knew exactly what that meant.

Vicky walked in, standing next to Slim, wearing a white feathery thong and matching top. Her hair was just as long as her sister Lisa's, but she was a little lighter in her complexion. No other dancer in the club could match Vicky's breasts and ass. She also had a six-pack that Beyonce would kill for. No doubt, Vicky was a masterpiece. She even used the word "Masterpiece" for her stage name.

"What the hell you doin' here, Woo?" she asked at the sight of her would-be man if he weren't wide open for Anasia, the karate chick. She still was a little hurt and salty about Anasia. She couldn't stand competition, but if she gave Woo the chance, she would've played second to none.

"I'm here to talk to you about what you're doin'."

"Woo seems to think that I'm forcing you into this lifestyle, so I called you up here to tell him otherwise," Ice said, still sitting behind his expensive desk like the kingpin he was.

"Ice is tellin' the truth. I came to him, and I'm lovin' it," Vicky said with an attitude at Woo's audacity to check her and her lifestyle.

"What is this, fuckin' McDonald's?" Woo asked, as Ice, Six-ten, and Slim laughed at his question. Vicky and Woo were less amused.

"This shit ain't for you, Vicky," Woo said heated.

"Oh, and I guess you are?" Vicky yelled.

"I could be."

"Bullshit! You still got ya' nose wide open for that bitch Anasia," Vicky continued to yell.

"Let's just get the fuck outta here and talk about this. This shit ain't for you," Woo repeated, lightening his tone.

"I'll prove this shit *is* for me," Vicky shot back as she walked towards Slim. As she reached him, she pushed him backwards towards the wall. Then she dropped to her knees, unzipped his pants, and went to work on his dick in front of everyone. Vicky really didn't want to do it, but she wanted Woo to hurt just like she did, and she needed to convince him that she was happy working for Ice.

Woo ran out of the office like a bat out of hell before he let his emotions go overboard. He felt like he could snap that bitch's neck. All the love, respect, and admiration for Vicky was left right where she was sucking dick as far as Woo was concerned. Ice enjoyed the drama right before Woo got hurt.

He walked over to Vicky, who was wiping her mouth, and smacked her hard across her face for her indiscretion. She fell to the floor and wiped the blood from her mouth. As she lay there, Ice yelled, "Get the fuck outta my office." Seeing the fire in his eyes, Vicky quickly gathered herself together and ran out of his office.

Ice then turned his fiery stare on Slim, who started to sweat at his boss's gaze. Ice snapped his fingers, and Six-ten was quickly on the move. Six-ten walked up to Slim and started to choke him with one of his bearlike hands. Slim was a big man himself, but he knew he was no match for the ruthless Six-ten.

As Slim started to drop to his knees, Ice began to speak. "First of all, don't ever bring anyone into my office unannounced; second of all, don't ever use my elevator; and last but not least, don't ever let some shit like that *ever* go down in my office again or ya' fat ass is dead. Now get the fuck outta my office," Ice said, kicking Slim in the ass as he stumbled to get up. Seething, Slim knew he would find a way to pay Ice and Six-ten back for their dirty deed, and whether big or small, it didn't matter.

Ice sat back down in his chair and reflected on the young man that ran out of his office with his feelings hurt. Out of all his runners, he truly cared about Woo. Six-ten was also thinking of the young man, but in a totally different manner. Six-ten fixed himself, stood in front of the off-white Italian sofa, and took a seat in front of Ice.

"So what do you want to do about Woo?" Six-ten asked inquisitively.

"What do you mean?" Ice shot back, not knowing the meaning of the question.

"Well, once we start takin' out his cousins and peoples, he ain't gonna sit idly by and watch."

"Leave him be; we'll be alright."

"I know you care about that boy, but he got mad fightin' and shootin' skills. That shit don't just go away 'cause a ma'fucka go square. I think we ne—"

That was as far as Six-ten got before Ice slammed his fist on his desk and yelled, "I said, leave the ma'fucka alone!" Ice gave Six-ten a stare that he had never seen in his partner before. Ice knew Six-ten was right. He knew that Woo was very dangerous, even at such a young age. But he couldn't bring himself to have the young man touched. His heart and mind conflicted with what he should do. There was something about the boy that reminded him of himself in his days in Haiti. Woo's spirit, strength, and courage was something that Ice admired. He couldn't kill someone with all that Woo had to offer.

Finally Ice stood up and looked out of his window down on the club.

"I didn't mean to upset you, man. I just wanted to know how you want to play this shit out."

"Don't worry about it, General," Ice said. General was the rank that Six-ten had when he fought alongside Ice in their days in Haiti.

"We have to meet with the chief of police and the mayor at the mansion in a couple of days. So be prepared for any of their shit," Ice reminded him.

"As for now, I need to go home to Nadeem. She's still grieving over her father. Apparently, he didn't pay off his debt to some kingpin and had to pay the piper," Ice said as he and Six-ten enjoyed a laugh at their cleverness—so they thought.

❧ ❧ ❧ ❧

Banks and Bobby were passing around a blunt and sipping on Henny when Black, Booga, and E-Double walked down the wooden stairs into the basement. The basement had wall-to-wall black carpet, a flat, wall-mounted 25-inch TV screen, and various football jerseys that were framed with other sports paraphernalia. The pool tables were an added attraction to kill time whenever necessary. It also had a stripper pole for the nights when the crew wanted to unwind with some freaks. The Eastwick Hustlers had their new base of operation hooked up like a little oasis.

Black, Booga, and E-Double pulled out their chairs and took a seat at the huge round table. Sometimes the crew would call Black, "King Arthur," and say that they were his "Knights of the Round Table." As Black sat down, Banks pushed the bottle of Henny across the table to him, who immediately pushed it back towards Banks.

"You know I don't drink that shit. Now what's got you callin' me, actin' all nutty?" Black asked.

"Ice showin' that tape of Bricks to people," Bobby blurted out a little drunk.

"How y'all know?" E-Double asked.

"Ya' cousin Woo and Taye said Ice was havin' a private party and was showin' the tape," Banks said.

"So, Ice always tapin' some shit and showin' it. Ain't nobody gonna run they mouth," E-Double said with too much confidence.

"Nah, but with this shit about to blow up with us and Ice, those tapes give him more leverage than us," Black said.

"So what you want to do?" Bobby asked.

"Get the ma'fuckin' tapes," Black said.

"How? Ice got that club locked and watched like Fort Knox, and we don't even know if the tapes are in that club. We all know that Ice got other businesses," E-Double said.

"Well, people keep their possessions close to them. Ice wouldn't bring the tapes to his house 'cause his woman could find them. He wouldn't keep them at his other business places 'cause he spends too much time at the Lady Luck Club. So our first look should be there," Booga said, opening his mouth for the first time since he took a seat.

"Sounds like a plan, but we still don't know how we gonna get into his office," E-Double said.

"That's easy. We have all of Ice's money, so we have to go there soon anyway. Before we go, we'll stop at the pet shop and buy all of their rats, mice, and some cheap snakes and let them loose in the club. My cousin is a health inspector for City Hall, and he could have the club closed for days. Once the club is closed, we'll get in and find the tapes easy," Booga said with a smile at his genius plan.

"You still didn't tell us how we getting' in," E-Double said.

"We get the keys from Slim," Black said, taking over.

"H⌐ ain't just gonna give us the keys," Banks stated.

"Everybody got a price, and if he doesn't give us the keys, we'll kill his ass and take 'em," E-Double replied.

"So when do we do this shit?" Bobby asked.

"Tomorrow," Black said.

"Y'all gotta do that shit without me. I got some business to take care of in Trenton tomorrow," Bobby said.

"What business is more important than Eastwick business?" Banks asked.

"I gotta take care of some child support shit," Bobby lied.

"By all means, take care of that shit. The man don't play any games with child support," Black said.

"So tomorrow we'll meet at my house in the afternoon to get this shit done," Black said. Everyone was in agreement.

Black stood up and said, "Bobby and Banks, y'all niggas sleep that Henny and weed off before y'all hit the block. I don't want y'all out there blitzed with the way shit goin'. I need y'all niggas sober," Black said.

"A'ight, King Arthur," Banks said, coasting.

"That's right, friends don't let friends drink and drive," Bobby said, feeling the same way Banks was feeling.

Black, Booga, and E-Double laughed at their two friends and headed up the stairs.

"Tomorrow," Black yelled.

"Tomorrow," Banks yelled, putting the bottle of Henny in the air, laughing.

9

Federal Agent

Bobby walked down the long corridor of the federal courthouse building, being escorted by two white men dressed in black suits. Bobby wore some of his usual attire. He wore his blue Sean John jeans halfway off his ass. His boxers would have been exposed if it weren't for the long white T-shirt he wore. He also had on a fresh pair of "trees."

The men brought him into the office of a man known as Mr. Darius Dawkins. Some even called him Director Dawkins, or "Da' Man." He was the head of Operations in the Drug Enforcement Administration (DEA) office.

Mr. Dawkins started as a beat cop and worked his way up to the top of the ranks on the police force. He made a career tracking Ice, but he knew his efforts were futile because Ice had too much police protection, not to mention his community and political ties. Every time Dawkins had a solid arrest, some ass-backwards boardroom deal would be made to set him free, or he would be let off on some bullshit courtroom technicality. It pissed him off to the core of his soul. Men that swore to protect and uphold the law were taking dirty money and his cases at the same time.

So when the opportunity arrived for Dawkins to join the DEA, he did so with no hesitation. The same ambition and tenacity that made Dawkins a good detective, he incorporated that into becoming the

head of Operations in the DEA office.

As head of Operations, he could pull resources from state to state. He could get people he knew didn't work for Ice to infiltrate the organization to bring Ice down. And that's exactly what he did. He recruited a young hotshot cop from Atlanta to infiltrate Ice's organization, along with a couple of good men he could trust.

The two agents on either side of Bobby tossed him into the office, causing him to stumble to his knees. Bobby straightened himself up and gave the two agents the middle finger as they turned and left.

Bobby looked up, and the first thing he saw was Mr. Dawkins sitting behind his desk. Even sitting behind the desk, "Da' Man" had an intimidating look. His massive black frame could rival any power lifter's. His eyes held a fire that couldn't be extinguished without the presence of sleep or death. Even though Mr. Dawkins was relatively young, he looked well beyond his years. Ice, stress, and politics of the job really stole his youth. But with the help of his new protégé, he was going to recapture some of his youth.

"Sorry my men got so rough," Mr. Dawkins said, standing up to offer Bobby a seat in his burgundy leather recliner that was imported from Greece. As Bobby walked toward his chair, Mr. Dawkins looked Bobby over and said, "Damn, Agent Simms, you *really* look the part!"

"Well, I'm not trying to get killed undercover, sir. And next time Ren and Stimpy push me, I'm kickin' their asses," James Simms, better known as Bobby to the Eastwick Hustlers Inc., shot back.

Agent Simms was a great detective in his own right. He resented the fact that he had to drop his cases in Atlanta to work undercover in New Jersey, and the fact that he almost got killed the other day didn't help matters any.

"So, how were the last couple of days, Agent?"

"Besides the fact that I almost got killed and was involved in a homicide, everything's been alright," Agent Simms said sarcastically.

"What happened?" Mr. Dawkins asked with genuine concern for his agent.

"There's a split in the Port Au Prince Posse. Two members, Black and E-Double, are breaking away, and they formed their own organization known as Eastwick Hustlers Inc. One of Black's members ran off at the mouth to the wrong person, and Ice forced Black to kill her with a machete to prove his loyalty. We were all lucky to get out alive.

But the crazy ma'fucka recorded the whole thing."

"*What?*"

"Yeah, seems like recording his escapades is Ice's little hobby. Look, I could bring in Black and a few of his members and put the squeeze on them to give up Ice. The only problem is they all have some kind of police protection or political connections just like Ice. I recently found out how Ice had the mayor's daughter raped just so he could take revenge on the mayor's behalf in order to own him. And he has the police chief in a few compromising positions as well."

"We know all those stories already," Dawkins replied.

"So if y'all know all this shit, why did you recruit me? And why didn't y'all arrest his ass, as well as everyone else involved?" Simms asked, annoyed.

"You know as well as I do, Agent, that we need proof. And without it, this is all just stories. Now, fuck squeezing anybody. You get your hands on that tape and any others and I will personally swoop down on the mayor, police chief, Ice, and the whole Eastwick Hustlers like a thousand legions of angels from heaven!" Dawkins said, raising his voice a little.

"Alright, alright. Black and his crew should be working on getting those tapes right now as we speak. Once they get them and I know where they're located, I'll call it in, and your so-called Dream Team better be there to collect the evidence without compromising my cover or my life," Simms said, still not changing his attitude.

"I never let you down yet, Agent. I still don't see your rush to get back to the ATL. You get to sell drugs, bang the finest bitches, you have a bangin' ride and crib, and it's all in the name of justice. Personally, I don't see what the problem is," Dawkins said slyly.

"Just like you have a hard-on for Ice and the Port Au Prince Posse, I have a hard-on for similar individuals back in Atlanta. I also made many promises to a lot of people, and I always keep my promises."

"I apologize. I didn't realize how passionate you were about your job. The sooner we nail Ice, the sooner you can go back to the ATL. This could be your career bust, so when you return home, you could write your own ticket, Agent."

"I'm not going to collect any evidence or make any bust hangin' around staring at your ugly mug, so I'm out," Agent Simms said as he stood up and shook Dawkins' hand.

"You're right, so get my evidence and be safe out there," Dawkins said matching Simms' grip.

Agent Simms stepped out of the office, leaving Dawkins to his own thoughts.

❦ ❦ ❦ ❦

Black and E-Double sat on the couch in silence as they waited for Jab, Banks, and Booga to show up. The apartment was usually silent since their mother was almost always on a mission and their sister was always chasing a baller. That's another reason that they didn't get another place, because the space was practically theirs, but they also wanted their mother and sister to have a safe and comfortable place to dwell. Black broke the silence and asked, "Do you ever think about Daddy or what it would be like if he were here?"

"No. He don't think about me, and I don't think about his ma'-fuckin' ass," E-Double responded.

"But if Dad was here, Ma might not be strung out, we might not be here doin' what we doin', and Ma might be a singer," Black rambled on.

"And you might have a bigger dick. What's your point?" E-Double asked, a little annoyed at Black's *what-if* games.

"I'm just sayin' it's got to be more to life than what we are doin'," Black stated.

"All I know is I have you and the game and neither of you are going anywhere," E-Double said.

"That's what I'm talking about. With the way things are going, I don't want to lose the only person I got to this game. That's why I want us out," Black said with sincerity. Before Double could get upset and give his opinion, a knock sounded on the door.

"We'll talk about this shit later," E said with seriousness in his voice as he rose up from his seat and grabbed his 9mm with the ivory grip and yelled, "Who the hell is it?"

"The police. Open up. I know you got that young girl in there, R. Kelly," Jab said with a snicker on the opposite side of the door.

E opened the door and said, "That's how ma'fuckas get shot."

Jab, Banks, and Booga all walked in and gave E-Double a pound. Jab sat down next to Black and asked, "How you want to do this play, boy?"

"Easy. E, Banks, Booga, and me gonna bring Ice his money. Slim is the only one at the door, so when he brings us up, it'll leave the door free. Give us a couple of minutes, then you come in with the box of animals and let those shits loose in the bathroom."

"How am I gonna get past the bouncers?" Jab asked.

"The bouncers are going to be too busy lookin' at ass to even notice you," Double said laughing.

"A'ight, let's do it," Jab said, standing up and giving Black a pound.

"Let's do it," Black repeated.

E-Double opened the door and everyone exited the apartment.

♥ ♥ ♥ ♥

Woo was in the karate school, punishing a heavy bag with kicks and punches, relieving the stress from the other day with Vicky. He continued to hit the bag even when he saw Taye in the doorway with a loud green tracksuit on. Taye took off his white Air Force Ones before he entered the school as a sign of respect.

"I ran into Anasia. She said I might find you down here. She also said she might come down here and work out with you."

"So, good for her," Woo said, still focusing on the bag.

Taye stepped up and began to hold the heavy bag and asked, "What's wrong?"

Woo hesitated and then began to speak. "I went to talk to Ice about Vicky. Turns out he doesn't have nothin' on her. She came to him for a job."

"That ma'fucka a liar!" Taye said, raising his voice.

"That's what I thought until she told me herself. She said she lovin' it."

"What is that, McDonald's?"

"That's what I said. I still didn't believe her until she started to suck Slim off right in front of me, Ice, and Six-ten," Woo said as he hit the bag so hard that Taye had to let go. Taye stood there in a state of shock at Woo's words.

"That's how I felt."

Coming out of his trance, Taye yelled, "FUCK VICKY!!!"

"YEAH, FUCK VICKY!!!" Woo yelled as he smashed the bag and caused it to explode and drop sand all over the floor. Taye, seeing the small explosion, said, "Damn, nigga you need some pussy."

"And you need to take that loud-ass tracksuit off, Green Hornet,"

Woo responded as they both shared a laugh.

"Listen, I need to get to practice. Where are you going to be at later?" Taye asked.

"I'll probably be with Man and them."

As Taye was putting on his sneakers, Anasia walked in. She was dressed in full karate gear. Even in her suit, her body was well complemented. She was wearing her hair shoulder-level with an off-center part. Her crème de cacao silky skin seemed to make the room shine.

"What's up, fellas?" she asked.

"You," Taye said as he ran out of the gym.

"What's he in a rush for?"

"He has track practice."

"Did you do that?" she asked as she saw Woo sweeping up the sand.

"Yeah," Woo said nonchalantly.

"Nigga, you need some pussy," she said as she laughed.

"Ha, ha, ha, is that an invitation?" Woo asked.

"Nigga, *pleeezz*, you can't handle this," Anasia teased.

"I'll handle it like I handled this heavy bag. I'll be beat'n that pussy up."

They both began to laugh. They always teased each other about sex, but Woo was always serious. He realized how much he loved Anasia as he looked at her beautiful smile and full lips. And now that Vicky was completely out of his life, he could focus more on her and his feelings.

"Come here and let me stretch you," Woo said.

Anasia walked over and placed her back against the wall and raised her leg as far as it would go. Woo pushed her leg up even higher. She was so flexible that her foot almost touched the wall. He began to stare in Anasia's beautiful brown eyes as he stretched her leg.

"What?" Anasia asked, noticing Woo staring at her. Many men got lost in her eyes.

"What? What?" Woo asked, not aware of his staring.

"What are you thinkin' 'bout nasty?"

"I was just thinking about us."

"Us what?"

"What it would be like if we were together."

"Please, you can't be serious. Don't think I don't know about that bitch Vicky. Not to mention any other hoes you might be messin' with."

"It's never been about Vicky or any other bitches. It's always been about you. That's why me and Vicky never got together. And you never saw me with any other bitch."

"Is that right?"

"Yeah, that's right. Anasia, I love you," Woo said with glassy eyes.

"But I—" that was as far as Anasia got before Woo kissed her with his soft lips. Anasia wanted to stop Woo, but his tongue sent shivers through her body. She began to kiss him back to let him know the feelings were mutual.

Woo loosened her belt and took off her top. Her sports bra held her breasts perfectly in place. He stopped his actions long enough to pull out a blue workout mat. As he lay the mat down, Anasia pulled her pants down. Woo lost his breath when he saw that there was barely anything covering her soft playground. She walked over to Woo, and they began to kiss again. He stepped behind her and kissed her neck, then he began to fondle her breasts.

Anasia began to moan slowly as Woo slid one of his hands down her barely legal covering and began to finger fuck her. He felt his inches raise as he touched her sugar walls. Then he pushed her forward slightly, and Anasia placed her hands on the mirrors to gain balance. Woo dropped to his knees, pulled the tread aside, and placed his tongue inside Anasia to both of their pleasure.

He eagerly licked in and out of her pussy and played with her clit.

"Uh, ooh, eat this pussy, ma'fucka," Anasia said between yells and moans. When she couldn't take the pleasure any more, she fell on the mat and began to shake in ecstasy.

Woo smiled and thought to himself that he was glad that he placed the mat down. Then he took off his clothes and climbed on top of her as she shook. He placed his dick in her as she shook in a state of bliss. Woo stroked long, hard, and fast. He slowed up his pace to tease her at times.

"Don't slow down. Faster! Faster!" she yelled, slapping Woo on his ass. He grabbed her ass and thrust his dick faster and deeper into her womanhood. He wanted to make sure that his first time with Anasia wouldn't be his last.

Anasia's moans made Woo begin to come. He pulled his dick out and came all over her flat stomach. As Woo let off, he said, "Sorry." To ease the embarrassing situation, Anasia quickly said, "Better on me than in me."

The situation wouldn't have been embarrassing if Anasia was just some bitch off the street, but Woo really loved her. He cleaned Anasia off with his white wifebeater. Then they lay in each other's arms and relished in what had just transpired between them.

❦ ❦ ❦ ❦

"Give us a couple of minutes, then bring those animals in and dump 'em," Black said, giving Jab instructions.

As they exited the SUV, Banks yelled, "Wait!" as if he forgot something.

"What?" E-Double asked impatiently.

"We need to leave the burners in the truck. Last time, we didn't get those shits back," Banks replied, missing his personalized heat. All the boys removed their weapons from their waist and placed them under the seats of the truck. Then they headed for the doors of the club, and once again, they were greeted by Slim. To Black and his crew's surprise, the club was fairly empty. That would make their task go over more easily.

Slim escorted the crew into Ice's office, knocked, and waited for the response to enter. He remembered the small ass whopping he received the last time he stepped in unannounced.

The boys walked in, and Six-ten stood up from his desk.

"Did you check these clowns before you let them in?" Six-ten asked, looking at the boys with a cold stare.

"They ain't got shit. I checked them myself," Slim lied.

"Then get the fuck out of my office, and the rest of you grab a seat." Before Slim made his way back downstairs, Jab had already successfully emptied over one hundred rats, sixty mice, and at least a dozen garden snakes to make sure the club would be closed for weeks.

The boys sat nervously, waiting for their business transaction to conclude before anyone noticed the animals were loose. Six-ten would never let them leave alive if he had found out their plot.

"You boys look a little nervous. I hope you got all our money," Six-ten barked.

"It's all there," Black said as he stood up and dropped stacks of

will robbins

paper on the desk.

Six-ten pulled the paper close to him and began to speak. "I know Ice will be pleased to hear you ma'fuckas was smart enough to bring our money. Now that y'all are on ya' own, I better not see y'all in the streets. Now get the fuck out of my office, you cockroaches," Six-ten ordered.

Once again, the crew was happy to walk out of the office alive. Not many people walked in that office and walked out alive to tell about it.

Black and his boys rushed back to the truck to get the hell out of Dodge. As Black put the key in the ignition, he turned to Jab and asked, "Did you handle ya' business?"

"No doubt."

"Booga, call ya' cousin and get him over here to close the club. We'll get the keys from Slim tonight and conduct our business."

As Black pulled away, Booga was right on the phone call.

Slim sat on the barstool manning the door. As he looked, he saw a rat run across the floor. He thought his eyes were deceiving him— until he saw more running across the stage and sitting area. As he stood up to investigate, a snake slithered across his foot. He was so terrified that he pulled out his Beretta Bobcat .25 and started to bust shots. Upon hearing the gunplay, Six-ten ran down the stairs with his silver and black Ruger P345.

"What the hell is wrong with you?" Six-ten asked, not aware that the club had become a jungle with all the small animals and snakes running around.

Slim let off a couple more shots and one hit a rat, causing his head to explode upon impact. Six-ten, now realizing what was going on, started to use the rats, mice, and snakes as target practice as well. But the animals and snakes seemed to multiply every time they killed one. Once they figured their efforts were futile, they decided to leave the club and call Ice. Just as they were leaving, Booga's cousin, Health Inspector Haas Briggs, showed up. They nearly knocked him down as he tried to enter the club.

Haas was a slender, brown-skinned guy with a bald head. The gray suit he wore made him look more like a tax collector than a health inspector. Haas knew exactly what he was there to do, but nothing prepared him for what he was about to see.

"Someone called in some complaints about rats, snakes, and mice

running around," Haas said as he looked at the two men who looked like scared little bitches.

"Take a look for yourself," Six-ten said, pushing past the man to get outside. Slim also followed.

As Haas made his rounds, he saw that the premises looked like something out of *Wild Kingdom*. He had no idea that his cousin had let that many animals loose in one building. A couple of rats would have gotten the job done.

He walked out, laughing, as he saw Six-ten and Slim losing their lunch. He never saw two big men act so scared in his life, especially, at the sight of rats and mice.

"Look, fellas, it looks like they had one big orgy up in there. We have to close the place down and fumigate it."

"How long will the club be closed for?" Six-ten asked, standing upright.

"Well, we have to make sure everything in there is dead. Then we have to come back and reinspect the place to make sure that those things didn't procreate. Then you have to be cleared by the board before you can conduct business," Haas said to Six-ten's disappointment.

"I'll have someone come by and put locks and chains on the door so if there is anything that you need out of there, you need to get it now." Haas handed Six-ten a business card of the company that would handle the situation and left.

"How the fuck did this happen?" Six-ten asked Slim.

"How should I know? The only ma'fuckas that was here was Black and his crew. Those fuckin' animals weren't there until after I brought them up to the office."

"So they had someone bring them in when you came upstairs. Ma'fuckas!!!" Six-ten yelled at the top of his lungs.

❧ ❧ ❧ ❧

Ice was on the gold silk couch consoling his woman who was upset about her father's disappearance. Nadeem and her father, along with her sister, always had it tough, and the fact that her father had a serious gambling problem didn't help matters. Her father was almost murdered for outstanding debts many times. He had been missing for days before she filed an official police report. Ice made sure that the officers were on their jobs and making reports to Nadeem every day to inform her of any new developments. Unfortunately, the officers kept coming up short to the point that she gave up all hope. She felt in her heart that her father had been murdered and the motive was gambling debts.

Nadeem lay in her pink robe with her head buried in Ice's chiseled chest. Her eyes were red and puffy from the many tears that she shed over the last few days. It would have helped ease her pain if Ice were home more often to support and console her. But his many business ventures curbed that plan. Suddenly, she sat up and said, "I know he's dead, Toussaint. I can feel it."

"Don't talk like that, baby," Ice said, stroking her silky hair. "The police will find him. He's probably hiding from his bookies. Once he has the money to pay, he'll turn up again," he said, trying to console his woman.

"He could have come to us for the money, so why hide?" Nadeem asked, confused.

"A man has a certain level of pride, baby. We bailed your father out so many times that it's not even funny. He probably was too embarrassed and felt like his well has run dry with us, and it practically has."

"How can you say that?" Nadeem asked, getting more upset.

"We couldn't keep paying his debts, or should I say *I* couldn't keep paying his debts. He would never get help or learn his lesson. And I tried to get him help several times, but he refused."

"My father was not a child that he needed to 'learn a lesson.' We should've been there for him!"

"You know how much debt he was into? Well over a million dollars! How the fuck a Hindu from the projects goes into a million-dollar debt? I don't care if it was my own father, I ain't paying no grown-ass man's debt."

"Well, my father is missing, or should I say dead. So now you don't have to worry about it any more!"

"Baby, I didn't mean it like that," Ice said, trying to pull Nadeem close to him. As she pulled away his phone rang.

"What's up?" Ice asked as he answered the phone.

"It's me, Six-ten. Listen ... the club is about to be shut down."

"What the fuck you talking 'bout?"

"Those ma'fuckas Black and his crew let a whole lot of rats, snakes, and mice loose in the club today when they came to pay us our

84

money," Six-ten said barely taking a breath. "The inspector from City Hall is here to shut us down for a couple of weeks until they fumigate and shit. You want me to get the shit outta the safe before they lock us out?"

"No, it's too hot right now. Besides it's not like they have a warrant to search the place. Besides, the safe is well hidden. It can stay in there until all is clean and clear. It ain't like we don't have money and product in other places," Ice said, trying to keep his cool.

"So you're not coming down here?" Six-ten asked.

"I had enough with the rodents and snakes in Haiti. Put someone on the job to make sure we open back up properly," Ice said.

If Six-ten and Ice weren't so close, Six-ten would have been afraid to tell him about the day's event. But they were equals in the game.

"Listen … meet me at the mansion. Bring our people. We need to get our affairs in order. We'll let them think that they got this one off. Then they'll think shit is sweet. Once the club reopens, we'll hit them hard," Ice said with conviction, and then hung up the phone before Six-ten could reply.

"Baby, I have to go. I'll be back in a couple of hours."

"You always have to go lately. You're never here for me like you used to be. My father is missing or dead, and you still rippin' and runnin'!"

"Look, it's business!" Ice yelled to avoid the bullshit.

"It's *always* business! God forbid I go out and find some business of my own," Nadeem yelled out of frustration.

"Your only business is my son, that funky-ass school you go to, and me. Any other business is no concern of yours," Ice said calmly, but feeling like he was about to explode.

"Fuck you, Ice. I hate yo—"

That was as far as she got before Ice backhanded her. The force of the blow made her stumble back and hit her head on the wall. As she sat on the floor, embarrassed and shocked, she tasted blood in her mouth.

Ice never hit Nadeem before, but he felt like she needed to be knocked back in line. He wanted to apologize to her as he saw her hurt look on the ground, but his pride got in the way. Under normal circumstances, he knew that his woman would never disrespect him, but the thought of her father being dead really weighed heavy on her

will robbins

mind. And he never would have raised a hand against her, but the club being closed down and the frustration that the Eastwick Hustlers were causing him made him step outside himself. He thought to himself that he would buy her a gift or take her on an expensive vacation to make her forget about what happened. But now, Ice walked out of the door and left Nadeem to her thoughts.

♦ ♦ ♦ ♦

Black, E-Double, Jab, Booga, Banks, and Bobby sat at the round table of their base of operation in Plainfield, talking about the day's events.

"So how those child support things go today?" Black asked Bobby.

"It went a'ight. Fuck that. How did shit go at the club?" Bobby asked enthusiastically.

"Shit went as smoothly as we planned," Banks said.

"So what now?" Bobby asked.

"In a few minutes, we go to my cousin Haas's house and get the keys for the chains and locks that are on the doors of the club. Then we go see Slim and see if we can get the other keys from him," Booga replied.

"That's cool," Bobby said.

"What we gonna do with the tapes if they are in there, and how we gonna get into the safe?" Banks asked.

"I got the safe, Banks, don't worry about that," Booga said.

"Once we get the tapes, Ice is going to try his hardest to get them back. Banks, you'll keep one or two in your safe. I'll keep some with me. That way, it'll be difficult to track them down all at once. Someone else will have a tape or two, but only me and E will know who," Black explained.

"If no one else has any questions, that means y'all ready to roll," E-Double said. Everyone adjusted their clothes and weapons and headed up the stairs.

♦ ♦ ♦ ♦

Slim lay in his oval bed wearing his boxers, entranced by the woman who was giving him a striptease act. He was resisting the urge to masturbate while the woman danced for him. The woman was Portuguese, and her florescent skin was smooth and bright. She was down to her thong and only had gold stars covering her pink nipples. Then she bent over and pulled her thong to the side, exposing her soft, moist, hot vagina to get Slim more aroused. She put three fingers in her mouth and then placed them in her hot spot.

Just as Slim thought he couldn't take it any more, a knock at his door broke through his lustful thoughts. The knock startled him as well as the dancer. He jumped from his bed and grabbed the Beretta from the nightstand and said, "Stay here."

The knocks became increasingly louder by the time Slim reached the door. As he looked through the peephole, the tension began to drop. Black was standing in front of the door. Slim had always liked Black. Black, in return, admired and respected Slim, so much so that he wanted Slim on his team. He hoped that Slim would give up the keys and keep his mouth shut. He really didn't want to kill him.

Slim opened the door and smiled. The smile soon disappeared as the door exploded wide open, smashing into his face, causing him to hit the floor hard. Slim tried to raise his Beretta out of fear but to no avail. Jab quickly kicked the weapon out of his hand. Black retrieved a mini .380 Cobra Patriot pistol and pointed it in Slim's face. Dazed and confused, Slim asked, "What the fuck is goin' on?"

"We want the keys to the club," E-Double said.

"For what?" Slim asked.

"We want the ma'fuckin' tapes," Jab said, punching Slim in the face.

"Is that it?" Slim asked, laughing to the crew's confusion.

"Yeah, that's it. What the fuck is so funny?" E-Double asked.

"All y'all had to do was ask. The way Ice and Six-ten played me like a chump the other day, I was looking for a way to pay them ma'fuckas back."

"So are the tapes there?" Black asked, helping Slim to his feet and putting his .380 away.

"He keeps everything in the safe. I'll go with y'all and let y'all in and show you how to get in the safe."

"If you know all this shit, why didn't you take them yourself and blackmail everybody?" E-Double asked.

"I couldn't without some kind of protection. I knew if I took those tapes, Ice would have deaded my ass," Slim explained.

"What makes you think he won't do it now that you helping us?" Black asked.

"I don't see anything wrong with being an Eastwick Hustler,"

Slim said to see if Black would take him on as a crew member.

"So I guess you down with us now," E-Double said.

"You know you a dead man for helping us," Jab said.

"No more dead than y'all," Slim replied.

"Let's roll," E-Double said.

"Let me get dressed and calm this bitch down. I'll be right out," Slim said.

"That wasn't as hard as I thought it would be," Black said, happy that Slim was finally on his team.

It was cool, dark, and quiet as Black pulled in front of the Lady Luck Club with Slim behind him in a red Cadillac truck with suede interior and gold 24-inch rims. Booga walked straight to the door and began unchaining the locks with the keys he received from Haas. Slim was right behind him to open the doors and enter the pass codes.

As they entered the club, they all ran and jumped around in a panic. They had forgotten about the loose animals. They quickly rushed to Ice's office. Slim removed a painting of Toussaint L'Ouverture riding on an elephant with his right hand raised high holding a machete. Once the painting was removed, Slim worked the safe. With a couple of twists and turns of the knob, the safe was opened. It contained over a dozen VHS tapes and a few audiocassettes, not to mention countless drugs and money. The VHS tapes were labeled with names such as Da Mayor, Police Chief, Bricks, a killing at the park, and a few others.

Black quickly put all the contents in a black duffle bag. Slim took the money and left the drugs. He didn't feel the need to deal drugs; he also didn't want to leave his former boss totally pissed. He knew that Ice wouldn't find out about the burglary until the club reopened in a couple of weeks, especially since he was the one in charge of opening the club back up. His reports to Ice would be that everything was coming along fine. By then, he would be knee-deep in the protection of the Eastwick Hustlers. He would soon find out that it didn't matter what clique you ran with. You could always be touched.

"Look, everybody at my crib tomorrow. We gonna check these tapes and find out how much information we workin' with. Then we gonna split them up between us. You, too, Slim, you one of us now, so fall in line," Black said like a true leader. Black didn't realize the power he held in his hands. He had enough information to be the King of

Elizabeth. He held the mayor's, chief of police's, and most importantly, he held Ice's life in his hands. Those tapes were about to rock
everyone's world.

10

SNITCHES

Weeks passed and the Eastwick Hustlers proved to be prosperous. Black and E-Double's new connect in New York helped them flood the streets with the best shit that fiends had ever tasted. They opened up shop in a few locations in Jersey. Newark, Jersey City, Plainfield, and Asbury Park had showed much love to the Eastwick Hustlers. Jab headed up operations in Newark and continued to recruit soldiers. Banks robbed any- and everyone who wasn't down with the Eastwick Hustlers without any problems of retaliation. Booga's paper seemed to overflow from all the ends he received from his planned bank heist. Bobby remained under the radar for obvious reasons. Even though everyone was maintaining, the Eastwick Hustlers knew that once the Lady Luck Club reopened, the shit would hit the fan.

Bobby sat in his lavish apartment that was funded compliments of the federal government. He pulled out his cell phone and nervously dialed Mr. Dawkins. Even though Bobby had a fine crib, expensive jewelry, a cool ride, and stacks of paper, his conscience was eating at his core. He knew the war between the Eastwick Hustlers and the Port Au Prince Posse would cause more bloodshed than a Roman war. He hoped that his next attempt would alleviate some of the bloodshed that was coming.

"Hello," Dawkins said into the receiver.

"Dawkins … it's me, Simms. I need you to call some people you trust in the Elizabeth Police Department (EPD) and have them go down to the First National Bank on Broad Street," Bobby said rushing through his words.

"Slow down, Simms. What's going on?"

"Booga, one of the Eastwick Hustlers, has a few men going down there to rob the bank. He's helping them from his laptop at home. He's shutting down their alarms, phones, and computer systems. He's even locking the doors for two full minutes," Simms continued to rush through his words, knowing that there wasn't a lot of time left.

"So what does that have to do with this case?" Dawkins asked, feeling like his time was being wasted. "I'm only interested in busting Ice, not some common bank robbers. That shits for local law enforcement," Dawkins continued.

"Black and E-Double retrieved the tapes weeks ago. I didn't say anything because I needed more time to locate them all. I'm pretty sure their man Booga knows where the tapes are. So if you bust these robbers and put the squeeze on them to give up Booga, Booga may, in turn, give up the location to the tapes to get his ass out of the fire."

"Where does this Booga live so we can bust him right along with his robbing buddies?"

"I'm not exactly sure. I never had the opportunity to go to his residence. We usually only conduct business at the spot in Plainfield. That's why it's important that your men get down there at 12 pm, make the arrest, and make sure that they give up Booga."

"I see your point. I'm on it. Stay clear and safe. I'll let you know how this plays out," Dawkins said hanging up the line.

❧ ❧ ❧ ❧

Sgt. Ernesto Cruz sat in his office with his "Jump Out Boys," which was a name that the hood gave them since they always rode around in a black van and jumped out on the corner boys. Sgt. Cruz had been on the force for years. He was middle age and very dedicated. Mr. Dawkins trained him well. Dawkins tried to recruit Cruz, but Cruz declined. He felt like he could be more effective in the department.

Sgt. Cruz ran the only Puerto Rican squad in the department, and they were all loyal and dedicated to each other. They refused to have their good names and heritage tarnished. Even though they were bad-

will robbins

mouthed and disrespected by their colleagues, they were very effective on the streets. That's why Dawkins had used their services more than once. They were part of his "Dream Team." Just as everyone in the office started to get antsy from a lack of action, Cruz's phone rang.

"Hit Squad, Sgt. Cruz speaking. How may I help you?"

"What happened to the 'Jump Out Boys'?" Dawkins asked, laughing.

"Man, you know that's just a name them corner boys gave us. Dawkins, is that you?" Cruz asked, joining in on the laugh.

"Yeah, you and your boys ready to work?"

"You know it. What do you got?"

"There's a bank robbery going down at 12 pm today."

"That doesn't leave us much time."

"Listen ... this is not an ordinary bank robbery. Someone is going to be helping them from a laptop. He's a member of the Eastwick Hustlers. The doors are going to lock at 12 pm. The alarms and phones are going to be down. I suggest that you post your men outside and take them down after the commission of the robbery. That way, there won't be any hostage situation. Make sure that someone lives because we need them to give up this Eastwick Hustler punk, understand? I'll be down there personally to interrogate those assholes."

"You know I always got you, Dawkins. I look forward to seeing you."

"On your feet, gentlemen. The shit is about to go down," Cruz said, standing up, showing his tall frame.

"About time. I was beginning to have fun watching the paint dry," Detective Julio Mendes said. Mendes served on the Hit Squad for only a year. He pulled many undercover jobs as a gangbanger since he once was a Latin king in his younger years. His tattoos and scars made him fit right in, and his love for action and drama made him a valuable asset to the team. He also respected and loved Sgt. Cruz for helping him get out of the gang in his teenage years, as well as helping him get into the academy. Cruz helped to erase his juvenile file so he could have a fresh start.

"We need to be in full gear. There's a bank robbery going down on Broad Street," Cruz said.

"I'll go get the van and check the weapons," Det. Antonio Mateo said. Mateo was a renegade type of officer with a hothead. He was the type to put everyone in danger with his impulsive behavior. Cruz pulled him under his wing after no one wanted to work with him. Cruz felt like the man just needed some guidance.

"You sure you want to take him on this mission?" Officer Ace Garcia asked, tying his long hair back with a rubber band. Garcia was the oldest on the team, and he always ventured on the side of caution. Mateo made him nervous.

"He'll be alright," Cruz said, passing his men Kevlar vests.

Everyone put their full gear on and headed out of the precinct. As the men left, some officers asked, "Hey, what's going on? Where are you going?"

"It's a practice drill," Cruz lied. He didn't trust anyone in the precinct except his loyal Puerto Rican brothers. And since he ran his own unit, he rarely answered to anyone.

♦ ♦ ♦ ♦

Prince pulled up in his personalized purple Denali truck. He always liked the color of purple—royalty—just like his name. He turned off the truck and gave instructions to his crew.

"Look, we gonna do this shit just like last time. Booga shit don't be missin'. Check your weapons, we got a minute left."

Prince pulled the mask over his brown acne-pocked skin. He was tall and fat, which made him intimidating to his four-man crew. Prince was far from attractive or intelligent. The only reason he pulled women was because of his money. He loaded up his sawed-off shotgun while his crew members loaded the "Choppers" and "Street Sweepers."

As Prince and his men stepped out of the truck, Sgt. Cruz and his men were on the opposite side of the street watching everything unfold. "There they are," Mateo said, pointing in the direction of the men.

"Be easy," Garcia warned.

"Everyone put your hands up!" Prince and his crew yelled, waving their weapons. A guard standing to the left of the door tried to grab his gun as he saw the assailants. Dizzy, one of Prince's men, saw the actions of the guard and responded by hitting him with the end of his "Chopper," knocking the man out cold.

"Next ma'fucka tries some stupid shit and I'm splattering brain matter all over the walls in here!" Prince yelled. The teller behind the window tried to press the alarm as if she was saving her money. Prince noticed her disregarding his warning and started to laugh.

"Ha, ha, ha, that shit ain't workin' for you, is it?" Prince asked, still laughing. "I should shoot your ass for trying anyway!" he yelled.

"Peewee, get the money, you, too, Lem!" Prince yelled stupidly shouting out names.

Peewee jumped over the counter and punched the white woman in her face who had pushed the alarm button. Her eyes were glazed over from the blow and blood trickled down her nose and mouth. Lem grabbed the pearl necklace from around her neck before he started to bag the cash. Ox, a big, burly Dominican guy, worked the floor taking watches and jewelry from the occupants sprawled all over it.

"Thirty seconds before our two minutes is up!" Prince yelled, still monitoring their surroundings. Peewee and Lem jumped over the counter and said, "We hit the jackpot; let's go!"

Prince and his crew backed out the door still facing the customers to make sure that there wouldn't be any sudden movements. Suddenly, they heard, "Freeze, assholes!"

Mateo spoke, pointing his Spa 12 gauge shotgun in their direction.

Garcia was a little pissed at Mateo's actions because he wanted to get Prince and his men in a more compromising position. Peewee raised the "Street Sweeper" and sprayed at Cruz and his men, but they leaped behind a few cars before they could get hit. Tires flattened and the windows on the cars shattered with debris falling on the police officers.

Prince, Ox, and Lem followed suit, and the "Choppers" and the sawed-off shotgun ripped through the parked cars as well as passing vehicles. They all tried to gain entry back into the bank, but the security guard had already locked the doors and called for additional officers. Prince and his crew took cover on the side of the bank wall.

"Give me cover while I get a better angle," Cruz told his men. Quickly, he stood up and ran to the other side of the bank to cover the sidewalk better. As Cruz ran, Ox started to fire off his matching Glock 17s. Mateo, Garcia, and Mendes fired their weapons. Mateo's SPA 12 gauge shotgun blew off Ox's right leg. Garcia's rounds from his AR 15 ripped through Ox's body like butter, and Mendes' Wilson Combat pump action shotgun took Ox right out of his "trees." Ox's blood splattered all over Prince and his men.

Lem, seeing the horror unfold before him, decided to make a run for the getaway vehicle. He let out wild shots that caused Garcia, Mendes, and Mateo to slouch back behind the car for cover. Lem forgot about Sgt. Cruz, who positioned himself on the opposite side of the bank. Cruz let out three shots from his Witness Elite walnut grip .38 Super. The first shot hit Lem in his abdomen, which caused him to buckle and drop his weapon. The second hit him in his shoulder and knocked him backwards just in time for the third shot to hit him in his throat. Lem hit the pavement and held his throat and kicked as he gargled and choked on his own blood.

Prince and Peewee, seeing that their boys were both down, tried to make it to the getaway truck. Out of desperation, Prince fired in the direction of Mateo, Garcia, and Mendes while Peewee fired at Sgt. Cruz to keep him at bay. Once the two men successfully made it to the truck without being hit, Peewee began to spray the "Chopper" while opening the truck window and yelling, "Fuck y'all! Suck my dick, bitches."

But before he could pull himself back into the vehicle, Mateo let out a round from his shotgun. The pellets exploded and shattered the rearview mirror, as well as hit Peewee in his shoulder.

"Oh shit, I'm hit!" Peewee yelled as he held his shoulder.

"Calm down, bitch!" Prince yelled as he pulled wildly in the middle of traffic. Sgt. Cruz and his men continued to fire at the vehicle to incapacitate it, but to no avail. Prince was an expert wheelman. However, his skills were no match for the three squad cars that blocked his path.

Prince turned the wheel and began to skid. Once again, Peewee aimed his Chopper out the window and let loose on the three squad cars. The officers quickly jumped out of the vehicles and took cover. Just as Prince tried to turn the truck around and go the opposite way, three more squad cars blocked the road. Those officers jumped out of their vehicles and aimed shotguns in Prince and Peewee's direction. Then Sgt. Cruz quickly began to talk on the megaphone.

"Throw all your weapons out of the vehicle and put your hands out the windows where I can see them."

Peewee tried to raise his weapon again, but Prince grabbed his hands and said in a defeated tone, "We caught. We gotta do what they say."

"No! Fuck that," Peewee said as he stepped from the truck, raised his weapon, and the officers let out countless rounds from their shotguns.

As the bullets went flying, Prince ducked down and prayed that he wouldn't get hit. One round hit Peewee in his chest and made him fly backwards. His body flew back against the truck. However, his adrenaline allowed him to let off a final round that ripped through an officer's body. That officer hurtled backwards and hit the street hard.

Anger rushed through all the officers' veins as they saw their fellow man dead on the pavement. One officer took aim with his police .38 Special revolver and let off a shot. The shot hit Peewee right in his left eye and blood, flesh, and bone fragments exploded in the air as Peewee hit the ground, his essence spilling on the cold dark ground. All the officers rushed the truck and had their weapons drawn on Prince.

"Don't move, asshole!" Mateo said, hoping that Prince would give him a reason to pull the trigger. Prince was cuffed and given a "tune-up" by the boys in blue before the officers tried to take him to the squad car.

"He's ours," Sgt. Cruz said, pulling Prince away from one of the officers.

"Fuck you, spic, he's our collar. If we hadn't saved you and the Chiquita Bananas over there, they would've gotten away," Officer Swank said, pulling at Prince.

"It's so nice to be wanted," Prince said laughing.

"Shut the fuck up," all the officers said. Swank did one even better and punched Prince in the face.

"Who the fuck you callin' spic, honkey?" Mateo fired back, jumping into Swank's face.

"Calm down, cowboy," Cruz said as he pulled Mateo back.

"Alright, you take him in. But we'll be right behind you," Cruz said with a smile.

"Why you let those racist crackers get away with shit like that?" Mateo asked.

"Because once Dawkins gets down here, he's going to turn a lot of shit upside down for some of those boys," Cruz said as a matter-of-fact.

Back at the station, Captain Blake Johnson was tearing Sgt. Cruz a new asshole. Captain Johnson was a tough officer who was born and raised in Migliore Manor Projects. He was just as passionate about cleaning up the streets as Dawkins, Simms, and Cruz. He knew that his precinct was dirty and that some of his men were on Ice's payroll. But keeping his precinct clean was like pushing a boulder up a steep mountain.

"Why the fuck didn't you wait for backup?" Captain Johnson yelled with his brown eyes widening.

"We got a tip and had to move fast! There wasn't any time to request backup … sir," Cruz said, lowering his voice as he recognized that he was talking to a superior officer.

"I don't care what type of tip you got. I got a dead officer and three dead assholes, and I don't know how much city damage you and your boys caused out there. Not to mention I got the chief of police up my ass!" Captain Johnson continued to yell as the vein in his left temple looked like it was going to bust out of his black skin.

"You and I both know that there are some dirty officers in this house, and we don't know which ones either. I couldn't take the chance that those assholes would be tipped off and blow my whole operation."

"What operation you running that I don't know about?"

"Director Dawkins called me and told me to make the arrest on these bank robbers for an investigation that he's running."

"Director *who*?" Johnson asked, not believing the name that was just uttered in his presence.

"Director Dawkins," Dawkins said walking into Captain Johnson's office wearing a dark blue Brook Brothers suit.

"Holy shit! Dawkins … how long has it been?" Johnson asked, smiling with his skinny hand extended.

"Too long," Dawkins replied as Johnson's hand seemed to disappear in his vice grip.

"So what's this investigation you got running, and what brings you this way?" Captain Johnson asked as he offered Dawkins a seat.

"The man your reliable Hit Squad captured has information on one of the Eastwick Hustlers. I need him to tell me everything he knows because it should help with my investigation," Dawkins explained.

will robbins

"Once again, *what* investigation?" Captain Johnson asked, knowing that his original question was being ignored.

"No disrespect to you, Captain, but you and I both know that you have some loose lips in this department, so I'd rather not say."

"Understood. But what can I do to help?"

"Just lead me to the prisoner and give me a private room so we can talk. I'll need Cruz's assistance as well."

"No problem. Let's go."

● ● ● ●

Prince sat chained to a desk blowing smoke, trying to look cool. But he was nervous as hell sitting chained in front of Officer Swank, who walked his white, fat, balding ass toward Prince and said, "Don't even *think* about opening your mouth about who helped you. 'Cause if Booga gets knocked and he opens his mouth about anything, you might as well start writing your eulogy, nigga. You, Ice, and those fuckin' Eastwick Hustlers pay my mortgage and put my kids through college. If you open up your rat-ass mouth and fuck that up, I'll rip your fuckin' balls out through your throat," Swank said, wiping sweat beads from his forehead.

"Fuck you, ya mortgage, and ya ugly-ass kids," Prince said, trying to be tough.

With no reply, Swank walked up and belted Prince again for his stupidity. Just as he lifted his fist again to knock some sense into Prince, Dawkins, Cruz, and Johnson walked in.

"That'll be enough, Officer," Dawkins barked.

"This is *my* interrogation, Captain. What the hell is *he* doing here?" Swank started the force at the same time as Dawkins and Johnson. He hated the fact that Dawkins and Johnson were his superiors. He couldn't wrap his racist mind around the fact that most brothers were more intelligent than him.

"This is *my* investigation and *my* interrogation. So, thanks for your minor help, Officer," Dawkins said. He purposely kept calling Swank "officer" to piss him off.

As Swank headed toward the door, Cruz said with a taunting smile, "See you later, *Officer*." Captain Johnson left the room as well to give Dawkins and Cruz some privacy with Prince.

"Well, well, well. Look what we got here. The Great Prince. You went from a no-whore-having-pimp to a stupid-ass bank robber,"

98

Dawkins said as he took a seat in front of Prince. Cruz posted himself at the door to ensure that the privacy level was secure.

"Fuck you, Dawkins. I ain't got shit to say," Prince said as he spit blood from his mouth.

"I'm glad to see that you remember me from your pimp days, but I think you have *a lot* to say. Right now, you're facing the death of a police officer and at least a hundred other charges. You're looking at life in prison without the possibility of parole, young brother. Since I'm the head of Operations for the DEA, I could move the case to a different state where you could get the death penalty," Dawkins said slyly.

Prince sat quietly, soaking in all that Dawkins had to say while he weighed his options. Then he wiped his bloody mouth and began to speak.

"If I talk, I'm a dead man anyway," Prince said with a stern look on his face.

"Not necessarily," Cruz said, stepping forward and speaking for the first time. Dawkins and Prince both looked at the detective curiously.

"What's he talking about?" Prince asked Dawkins, who was just as curious to know what Cruz meant.

Cruz pulled up a seat and sat down in front of Prince and Dawkins. Prince stared at him, looking for a lifeline to somehow get him out of his sea of troubles. He knew there were too many dirty cops to make it on the inside and too many niggas on the outside who would kill him.

"My team could protect you better than the Pope if you give us what we need to help out in this case," Cruz explained as he looked at Dawkins for a sign of approval.

"How about the Witness Protection Program and I walk? You the head of Operations for the DEA, so I know you got pull, houses, money, and shit."

"Fuck you. You're responsible for the death of a police officer. You don't get shit. You're lucky if I let Cruz and his men protect your silly ass!" Dawkins yelled as he gripped Prince by his collar.

"Right now, I'm all you got. 'Cause if I wasn't, you wouldn't be sweating me so hard. So I think you gonna do everything to protect my black ass, or I'll just take my chances on the inside," Prince said trying to look hard and sound even more cocky. Dawkins let his grip go as he came to terms with reality. He knew he had a man on the inside but he needed Prince to give up Booga so he could get a wire on the tapes.

"Alright, alright," Dawkins said as he calmed down. "What do you have to tell us?" he asked.

"You got something to tell me before I open my mouth."

Dawkins and Cruz were both losing their patience, but they knew what was at risk if they didn't keep their cool. Slowly, Dawkins sat back down, rubbed his huge hands together, and began to speak.

"Witness protection, but you can't just walk. The family of that officer you killed and the people in the community won't go for it. You'll have to do some time. We'll work out other particulars if your info leads to the arrest we want."

"And what arrest is that?" Prince asked.

"Ice," Dawkins answered.

At the mention of Ice's name, the hair on the back of Prince's neck stood up.

"You must be talkin' 'bout some serious-ass witness protection and a limited amount of time if you want Ice," Prince stated.

"Right now, all we want is some punk named Booga. We'll talk about Ice afterwards. If we like what we hear, we'll set everything up in writing," Dawkins said.

"That's easy," Prince said with a smile.

"Well, let's have it," Cruz said losing his patience again.

"Check out 514 Court Street, apartment 3, Midtown," Prince replied.

Dawkins looked at Cruz, and Cruz replied, "I'm on it."

As Cruz hurried out of the door, Dawkins turned to Prince and said, "For your sake, this better not be bullshit."

Cruz opened the door to his office and saw his men sitting idle. To brighten up their day, he said, "Let's go, boys, we got a wire on the other bank robber suspect."

At the sound of the news, his men were on their feet.

Booga sat at his desk, working out the kinks for his next heist. He had no idea that the Hit Squad was on his tail. If he did, he would have taken his ends and headed somewhere off the map. Instead, he stepped from his laptop and headed for the bathroom to take a piss. He pulled his dick out of the hole of his boxers and began to piss, enjoying the pleasure of relieving himself. But he jumped and pissed on the walls, the toilet, and himself when he heard his front door crash open. As he tried to pull his nerves together, all he heard was the voice of Cruz and his men say, "Get down on the ground and don't move, bitch!" As he complied with the officers, he wished that he had enough piss left to let loose on them. He wanted them to feel exactly how he felt. Pissed on.

In no time, Cruz and his men got Booga under control. Before they walked out with him, they took the laptop and various disks for more evidence.

Booga sat in the back of the squad car relaxed. He knew they didn't have anything on him. He never kept his info stored in his laptop. And the disks were just various games. He knew someone had opened their mouth about something, but he figured it was just some fiend looking for a quick fix from the officers. Little did he know Prince was about to ruin all his thoughts.

Before Booga could complete all of his thoughts, Cruz had pulled the black van into the parking lot of the precinct. Normally, Mateo would strike a suspect on the way in the precinct, but Booga was very calm about his shit, which also caused Mateo to be calm.

Cruz walked Booga into the same room that Prince was questioned in. Booga sat in the room, and it seemed like hours before Dawkins walked in on him. Booga seemed real cool as Dawkins entered the room. He seemed a little too cool for Dawkins' taste. He knew the kid had a lot of money for the best lawyers and he had deep connections. He knew it would be a little difficult to crack this nut.

"What's up, young brutha? I'm Darius Dawkins, director of Operations for the DEA," Dawkins said as he extended his hand out to Booga, who looked at Dawkins as if he were a leper. Undeterred, Dawkins pulled his hand back and sat down across from Booga.

"Well, I hope you have something to tell me since you didn't shake my hand."

"Yeah, I have good news, and I have bad news," Booga said.

"Tell me the bad news," Dawkins replied, willing to play Booga's game.

"The bad news is I don't have shit to tell you. The good news is I

will robbins

just saved a lot of money on my car insurance by switching to Geico," Booga said as he burst out laughing. Dawkins joined in on the laughter as well.

"You like that one?" Booga asked, still laughing.

"Yeah, I do," Dawkins replied, continuing to laugh. Then without warning, he jumped up, grabbed Booga by the back of his head, and slammed it into the desk, causing blood to pour from his broken nose and split lip.

"Oh, shit," Booga groaned as he held his nose.

"Did you like my joke? Now that we both realize that we're not comedians, let's get down to business."

"Fuck you! Suck my dick!" Booga retorted as he spat at Dawkins, who quickly moved out of the way.

Then Dawkins quietly walked out of the room without saying a word. He purposely left the door cracked open. Booga sat there nervous, unsure of what the big man was going to do. Before his imagination went wild, he saw Dawkins standing in front of the door with Prince. At the sight of Prince, Booga's heart dropped and his blood pressure rose. Dawkins said real loud, "Thanks for all of your info, Prince. I'll see you at the trial."

"Fuck you, Dawkins, we had a deal. I gave you Booga, and I'll give you any info on Ice that I got. You *have* to protect me. You *promised*."

"You bitch-ass nigga, you *fuckin'* snitch. I'll take ya' fuckin' life!" Booga yelled after he heard the conversation unfold. He would have tried to kill Prince if he weren't chained to the table.

"Thank you, Prince," Dawkins said again to an incoherent Prince.

Prince was too shocked to hear anything as he saw Booga staring at him with hell in his eyes. Cruz pulled Prince back to the holding cell since he had served his purpose. Dawkins walked back into the room with Booga, hoping that his sneaky tactic had worked.

"Now, I don't care about you or some dumb-ass bank robbery. I know how you did it, and Prince is all the evidence that we need. You are right now an accessory to the murder of a police officer. I'm pretty sure you know you won't be hittin' the bricks for a long time with that one. All I want to know is where are the ma'fuckin' tapes and don't play dumb with me, bitch. You play ball, and you could walk. I'll even leave you here for a few days so your boys won't get suspicious."

Booga knew he wasn't a snitch, but he also knew once Prince

started to talk, he wasn't walking on any charge. Booga decided that it was best to feed Dawkins something just so he could walk. He knew that the info he would give to Dawkins would blow up in somebody's face, literally.

"I know where a couple of the tapes are. But if I tell you, I walk out of here smelling like roses. And I want the shit in *writing*. I know how y'all ma'fuckin' asses are."

"Start talking."

"Fuck you. You think I'm stupid? I want my lawyer to go over the paperwork and you and your superiors to sign it." Without any words, Dawkins left out of the room. It was hours before he returned with the legal documents. Booga's lawyer was more than angry at the precinct's antics. His lawyer read over the documents and gave Booga the okay to speak.

"My man Banks has some of the tapes in a safe. He lives Uptown, right up the street from Jefferson Park. The house is at 515 Madison Ave. It's a big yellow aluminum-covered house. You can't miss it. And if you're fast, you may even catch him there."

"Now that that's settled, I'll be leaving with my client," said Mr. Ripstein, the lawyer. "That is, if he's not under arrest." He was old but very well versed in the art of law.

"How do I know that the info that your client gave me is true?" Dawkins asked.

"I'm pretty sure that my client told you the truth, but you have the right to arrest him. However, it will make things very difficult for your case against Ice, and I doubt that you want that," Ripstein answered.

Dawkins looked at Mr. Ripstein in surprise. He knew that he had to let up on Booga now that Ripstein was onto his game plan. But he would exercise his right to arrest Booga if push came to shove. Ripstein walked out of the precinct with his client in tow.

Dawkins was so pissed that he had to let Booga go. He wanted to hold Booga until he found out if the tip were true. He knew that if he put pressure on Booga that Ripstein would blow any and all chances he would have to get Ice through Booga or any of the Eastwick Hustlers. Dawkins immediately dispatched the Hit Squad to pick Banks up.

❦ ❦ ❦ ❦

Ice and Six-ten were both happy as they walked into the Lady Luck Club. It was the first time that it was open in weeks. But their happiness would soon turn sour when they both realized that they had been robbed. Ice and Six-ten stepped into the private elevator and headed to the office. As they stepped off the elevator, Ice took in a deep breath of relief as he stood in his office for the first time in weeks. They both walked around and took in the scenery as if they had never been in the office before. Suddenly, Ice's eyes landed on his painting laying on the floor and saw his safe exposed. He knew something was terribly wrong.

He walked to his safe and opened it up. Then he hit the roof, cursing and throwing things around the office. "Fuck! Fuck! Fuck! Who took my ma'fuckin' tapes and money?"

As he continued to yell, Six-ten looked into the safe as if Ice were mistaken. Quickly thinking, Six-ten said, "That fat ma'fucka Slim had the keys. He's the only one who could have pulled this shit off. They left the damn drugs, though. Who the fuck does some dumb shit like that?"

"Then we takin' a ma'fuckin' ride," Ice said, cocking back his hammer on his Desert Eagle.

♥ ♥ ♥ ♥

Slim, once again, was being entertained by his Portuguese friend when his door caved in. He saw Ice's Desert Eagle aimed at him, and he quickly pushed his vanilla deluxe lover in Ice's sight. Ice pulled the trigger, and the bullet seemed to soar through the air in Matrix-like speed and caught the woman right in her forehead. The force of the bullet made her fly backwards and guaranteed her a closed-casket funeral.

Slim tried to reach for his weapon that lay on his nightstand. This time, Six-ten smoothly pulled the trigger on his cannon and shot Slim's hand. Slim screamed in pain as he grabbed his wrist, to see most of his hand was shot off. He knew exactly why Ice and Six-ten were at his spot, but he figured he could play dumb to save his life. "What the fuck is goin' on?" he asked, fighting back tears.

"Where are my tapes and money, bitch?" Ice asked coldly.

"I don't know what the hell you talking 'bout, Ice," Slim lied.

Irritated with Slim's lies, Six-ten decided Slim would look good with his Stacey Adam shoes in his mouth. He aimed and knocked out

Slim's two front teeth. As Slim fell backwards on the bed, Ice grabbed him by the throat and shoved his Desert Eagle into his temple and said, "I'll let your punk ass live if you just tell me where my money and tapes are."

Ice squeezed a little tighter until Slim began to choke out the words, "Okay, okay." Ice let go, and Slim sat up on the bed and rubbed his throat and began to speak.

"Banks has your tapes. I spent the money already." Six-ten moved in a little closer and put Slim's lights out permanently.

Ice pulled out his cell phone and called one of his soldier boys.

"Speedy ... this is Ice. I need for you to handle a job for me."

"No problem ... what is it?" Speedy, a rough young Haitian, asked, waiting for instructions.

"I need you to go and take out the boy Banks and get my tapes back. He's right there at 515 Madison Avenue. It's a house. Don't fuck up."

"I'm in Jefferson Park. The house is just up the road. I'll handle that shit right now," Speedy said as he hung up the cell phone.

"We got work up the road," Speedy said as he tapped his boy Razor. Speedy and Razor were both in their twenties and both have been putting in work for Ice for years. They came to the States dirt-poor with their parents and Ice sold them on the "American Dream," but they had no idea the price they would pay for working for Ice.

They both checked their hammers and headed up the block. As Banks was walking down the steps of his porch, Speedy and Razor approached him.

"What's up, nigga?" Speedy asked as he lifted up his shirt revealing the pound to show Banks that the situation was sensitive and serious. Razor lifted up his shirt as well to stop any superman bullshit that might have been floating around in Banks' head.

"What y'all want?" Banks asked. He knew he robbed too many people not to get robbed in return, but he never thought he would get robbed on his front porch.

"Turn your ass around and walk back in the house slowly and quietly," Razor demanded.

Banks wanted to reach for his gun, but he knew it was useless. They had two guns to his one, and they would have a quicker draw than him. He simply walked in the house and waited for further

will robbins

instructions. He felt that if he were given a chance, he would show them how to rob someone for real.

As soon as Banks walked into the house, Speedy knocked him in the back of the head with the butt of his 9mm Beretta, causing him to hit the floor. Banks held the back of his head and without thinking, he jumped up, turned, and kicked Speedy to the ground out of sheer anger. Then he tried to reach for his gun, but the explosion of Razor's Beretta Cheetah .22 quickly cut him down. The shot hit Banks in his shoulder, and it would've hurt like hell if it hadn't exited his body just as fast as it entered.

Speedy jumped up and started to stomp Banks with his "trees," and he would've killed him on the spot if Razor hadn't intervened.

"Yo! Don't forget what we came here for, Speed," Razor said as he pulled him off Banks.

Once Speedy caught his breath, he yelled, "Where's the ma'-fuckin' safe?"

Banks knew that he wasn't going to walk out of his house again alive so he was more than willing to lead them to his safe. As he stood on his feet, he looked both men in the eyes and said, "Right this way, bitch." Then Banks let out an eerie laugh that threw Speedy and Razor for a loop. He led the men up the carpeted stairs and walked right into his bedroom.

"This is a nice fuckin' room," Razor said in admiration as he looked around the room that was decorated lavishly with a king-sized bed, an oak bed frame and headboard. The bed was decorated with the most expensive bedding that Ikea had to offer. The rest of his shit looked like it could have been on *MTV Cribs*.

"Yeah, this is a nice room. Too bad you gonna die in it," Speedy said as he laughed. "Now get the safe, bitch, and stop playing," Speedy said as he pushed Banks. Banks stepped into his closet and pushed a button. The safe magically appeared from the hardwood floor panels.

"Let me find out that this ma'fucka got some Batman shit," Razor said to Speed's amusement.

"And then some," Banks said at the wisecrack as he pushed the buttons on the safe. Out of nowhere, it seemed like Banks felt a blow to his eye that caused it to swell up with blood.

"Shut the fuck up and open the safe," Razor said after he hit Banks in the eye with his gun. As Banks was opening the safe, he was happy that he had Booga install the explosive device inside it.

Banks knew that anyone who robbed him would never let him live. So he had the explosives installed so that anyone who robbed him would die too. No one was going to kill him and enjoy his money. As Banks was entering the code for the safe to explode, he was laughing hysterically.

"Stop fucking laughing and open the safe!" Speedy yelled as Banks continued to laugh. The two killers weren't aware that they were only two buttons away from being blown to kingdom come.

The Hit Squad was rolling down Madison Avenue, only seconds away from pulling in front of Banks' house.

"Okay, men. We know that Banks is young, but he's dangerous. So nobody go in half-cocked on this one, alright?" Cruz said concerned for the safety of his men. They all had too many close calls for the week dealing with this case to last them a lifetime. Meanwhile, Banks was in the closet and was seconds away from pressing the last button.

"This will be the last blow job any of us will have, ma'fuckas," Banks said as he pressed the button. Cruz and his men were running towards the house with their guns drawn when they were knocked backwards by an enormous explosion. When they came to their senses, they saw three, crispy-creamed bodies lying on the ground near them, lifeless and burning.

will robbins

11

DEATH OF A PRINCE

Summer was approaching fast. It was going to be a hot and torturous one on the streets. The deaths of Bricks, Slim, and Banks only added more fuel to the fire that was already heating up between the Port Au Prince Posse and the Eastwick Hustlers. Although some of their strongest members were killed, Black and E-Double continued to hold onto Ice's tapes, much to his dismay, and their business still continued to flourish. But the Eastwick Hustlers knew that their business wouldn't continue to thrive without facing Ice and his crew head-on.

Black, E-Double, Booga, and Jab sat at the dining-room table silently, thinking of their fallen soldiers. They all sat quietly not wanting to reveal their fear. Black and E-Double started to think that they had bitten off more than they could chew. They knew that they would have problems with the Port Au Prince Posse, but now that they were seeing the reality of it all, they wished that they could take it all back for the sake of their lost people. After several minutes of silence, the beast in E-Double seemed to erupt.

"Man, fuck this! Banks is dead, Bricks is dead, and so is Slim! So why the fuck is Ice and Six-ten still walkin' around like shit is sweet? And what the fuck are we scared for? We knew what we were getting into before we started this shit. We killed for Ice to make his shit grow, now we need to kill for ourselves to make our shit grow," E-Double

said before Booga, Black, or Jab could respond.

Black continued to sit with his head in his hands, feeling defeated. E-Double's comments didn't move him one bit. He never wanted to be this tied to the drug game. He only wanted it as a means to an end, not a means to other people's end.

E-Double would never admit that he was enjoying what was going on even a little bit, but he knew he would enjoy it a little more once he engaged in some payback. Booga was just thankful that his little conversation with Dawkins and Cruz didn't get back to anyone. But he was more than willing to strike back and represent for the Eastwick Hustlers Inc.

Black stood up from his chair and headed for the front door without saying a word. This was usually the time that he disappeared for a few hours without telling anyone where he was going. Most times, no one ever questioned him, but with everything that was going on and Black's rule, E-Double decided that he should inquire about his brother.

"Yo! Where you goin' by yourself?" Double asked.

"Same place I go this time every day," Black answered as he continued toward the door. Double stood up and followed him. His answers just weren't good enough.

"You still ain't tell me where you goin'," Double said, raising his voice a little.

"I'm safe, don't worry," Black said as he put his hand on his brother's chest to keep him from following any further. Double knew that Black was serious, so he decided to let it go. Double closed the door, shook his head, and sighed. He felt like he was losing his brother and everything around him was falling apart. But he knew with his plan some things would be put back in perspective.

"Yo, what's up with ya' brutha?" Jab asked.

"I don't know, but I don't like it. I'm goin' to make a move on Ice with or without him," Double said defiantly as he sat back down at the table.

"What's the plan?" Booga asked for the first time since he was the master planner for the organization.

"Just stick around and you'll find out," E-Double responded slyly.

❦ ❦ ❦ ❦

Ice was holding a meeting in his mansion with his partner, Six-

will robbins

ten, and some of their generals. He was happy that the Eastwick Hustlers didn't retaliate for the deaths of Slim, Banks, or Bricks, but it also made him a little uneasy. He knew that the organization didn't consist of punks, so he was wondering when and where they were going to hit. He needed to prepare his men for the unexpected.

He stood up, tied his locks in a rubber band, and fixed his all-white Armani suit. Then he casually leaned forward and put his hands on the onyx table for support and looked all his men in the eyes before he spoke. His men were nervous because it was times like this that Ice was so unpredictable.

"Listen, we've killed men from the Eastwick Hustlers, and they haven't hit back. And I *still* don't have my tapes or money. The only reason some of you men are still alive right now is because I know Black isn't going to the police with those tapes that I've asked some of you to get back," Ice said, coldly glaring at some of his generals. The heads of his men dropped out of fear and disappointment in themselves. They couldn't stand the cold fire in Ice's eyes.

"We tried to get those tapes back, boss, but Black and his boys ain't some bitch-ass kids," Stringer, a portly Haitian, stated, trying to save face in front of his own men. The words seemed to rush from his mouth, and the look on Ice's face made him wish that he could take them back.

Like magic, Ice's pearl handle, gold-plated machete appeared in his hand and with one swift motion, Stringer's head flew in the air. Blood spattered all over Ice's white suit, and Stringer's head fell neatly onto the onyx table. No one dared move or said another word.

"Anyone else got some bitchin' up to do?" Six-ten asked.

No one answered out of fear for their lives. Before Ice continued to talk, a slim, beautiful, dark cocoa-brown woman walked in carrying a blue silk shirt and handed it to Ice, who was removing his blood-stained shirt and jacket.

"Listen ... since nothing major has happened yet, I'm going to take the opportunity to leave town for a few weeks. You will all report to Six-ten about anything, *especially* if you get a wire on my tapes. Now get out and get my money," Ice said.

"Wait! Get this pussy out of here before you leave."

His men picked up the body and carried it out the back door to feed to the dogs. One of his men took the head off the table and tried to bounce it like a ball.

"What the fuck is wrong with you?" Six-ten asked as he looked at the young teen's act of play.

"Since his head had a lot of air in it, I thought it would bounce," the youngster said, laughing.

"That's why I like you. You don't let shit bother you," Ice said, joining in on the laugh.

"Where are you going?" Six-ten asked, confused.

Ice hadn't spoken to him about leaving, especially now when they needed to be focused on taking out Black and E-Double.

"I need to get away with Nadeem. When I get back, we are going full throttle against the Eastwick Hustlers. Just keep business running smooth as usual until I get back," he said with his hands on Six-ten's massive shoulders.

As Six-ten started to respond, he was interrupted by a beautiful, young, café-au-lait-complexioned Haitian woman who said, "Sorry to interrupt, but you guys have some visitors." Her voice was a little shaken because she wasn't sure if she should have interrupted or not.

Sensing her fear, Ice said with a smile, "Send them in please, Sheila."

His smile, that many women loved, put her at ease as well as made her wet between her thighs just a little. She walked out of the dining room switching her healthy ass, hoping to impress the king-pin.

Sheila walked back into the room with the mayor, chief of police, and Officer Swank on her heels. The three men skipped the formalities and took a seat at the huge onyx table.

"Nice to see you boys, too," Ice said sarcastically, knowing that he had all three men snug in his pocket.

"Have those tapes resurfaced back into your hands?" the mayor asked, trying to hold back his fear and frustration.

"Not as of yet," Ice replied.

"What the fuck do you mean 'not as of yet'?" Chief Williams asked, not afraid to show his anger. He was a tough, strong black man almost as big as Dawkins. He only got into bed with Ice because he was blackmailed into doing it. He also knew Ice could keep the violence down in the city as well as make him look good as the chief of police, all while filling his pockets up. He actually held a deep hatred for

Haitians in general because they were tearing up his city with all their violence. After all, some Haitians even raped the mayor's daughter, and he almost thought that Ice had something to do with it, but he didn't. At least, that's what the evidence showed.

"Look! Just like he said, not as of yet. If you boys are so worried about it, then why don't you bust a few heads and make some arrests to stir up the tapes?" Six-ten asked.

"You know damn well we can't do that. Everybody is connected to everybody. If we do that, ain't no tellin' who's goin' to rat who out. That dirty bastard Prince gave up info, and we still don't know how much. Booga was in the precinct, and he walked, so he gave info, too," Swank said, sweating like a pig.

"Neither one of them gave up too much info 'cause ya' white ass ain't locked up. Look, we don't have to worry about anyone giving up info 'cause don't nobody want to go to prison. When I get back, we'll get the tapes and everyone can rest easy," Ice calmly explained.

"We are all sweating bullets over these tapes, and you're talking about when you 'get back'? What if that bitch-ass Prince does talk, or Booga? Then what, huh?" Chief Williams asked.

"Prince is somewhere in your custody, so handle him if you so scared. And don't worry about Booga or the Eastwick Hustlers. They'll be handled," Six-ten said with confidence.

"They damn well better be 'cause we are all running out of time with Dawkins and the goddamn Hit Squad breathing down everyone's neck," Mayor Cross said as he stood up, preparing to leave.

"Ha, ha, ha," Ice laughed.

"What the hell is so funny?" Mayor Cross asked.

"You actually worried about Dawkins? He's been after me for 10 years and ain't been able to pin shit on me yet."

"That's why you shouldn't be so damn cocky. He's got a hard-on for you like you ain't gonna believe. The fact that he ain't caught you in ten years makes him more dangerous now than ever before," Chief Williams said with warning. He actually would've wanted Dawkins to bust Ice if he knew that he wouldn't go down as well.

"I'm tired of playing cat and mouse with you boys. Get those god-damn tapes!" Swank yelled as he was headed for the door.

"Hey, Swank! Maybe you should do some push-aways. It would help with some of that stress," Six-ten said.

"Push-aways?"

"Yeah, push away from the table, you fat bastard, now get the fuck outta here," Six-ten said.

"Fuck you," Swank replied, his voice laced with venom, as he followed Sheila to the door.

"Look, don't worry about a thing. Everything is under control, gentlemen," Ice said trying to reassure the men.

"Good. You let me know when those tapes are back in your possession," the mayor said. Ice walked both men to the door. Mayor Cross and Chief Williams stepped inside the limousine where Swank was already waiting, with steam pouring from his ears.

"One day, that nig—" was all that Swank got out of his mouth before Williams gave him an I-dare-you-to-say-it look.

"One day, that dirty Haitian is going to pay," he uttered.

"He's right about Prince, though. He's in our custody, so we need to take care of him—and soon. If he breathes anything, it could be detrimental to all of our careers," the mayor said.

"I'm on it. He's in my precinct, waiting on a deal from Dawkins that ain't never gonna come through. He's dead, no doubt," Swank said, happy that he was going to responsible for another black man's death.

♦ ♦ ♦ ♦

"Yo! Cruz, get Dawkins' bitch ass down here. I need to talk to his ass," Prince yelled from his holding cell. Cruz continued to walk past Prince's cell, ignoring him. The officers laughed at Prince, and his blood began to boil.

"Cruz, you better come back here, or I'll rat out every dirty fuckin' pig in here."

Cruz started to entertain Prince's outburst, but he knew that that was all they were. He and his men were clean, and Internal Affairs would never take a cop killer's word about dirty officers. But one officer didn't take to the threat too kindly.

"Listen, boy, you better keep your black-ass mouth shut before someone closes it *permanently*," the officer threatened, standing close to the cell.

Out of anger and frustration, Prince grabbed the officer by the collar and pulled him into the cell bars repeatedly. The officer's head connected with the bars, and blood splattered in Prince's face. The officer was out cold on his feet. He didn't even get a chance to regret what he said to Prince before he passed out.

Cruz rushed over to the cell and grabbed Prince by the collar and gave him the same treatment that he gave to the officer. Cruz knew that the officer was racist and he deserved what he got, but he was still an officer, and Prince was a low-down, dirty cop-killer. The force of the blow knocked Prince backwards, and he fell against the wall. Once he hit the floor, he covered his face to ease the pain.

"Open this fucking cell," Cruz said to an officer nearby. The turnkey hurried and opened the door as other officers rushed in and gave Prince a hell of a beating. Prince felt like Rodney King, but the only difference was Prince wasn't going to see any money from the state.

♦ ♦ ♦ ♦

Swank was taken to his car by his associates. His money-green, fully loaded, customized Lexus was paid for with drug money and the many dealers he muscled. Swank was also living fat off the despair of the people in the community. As a career police officer, the only things that he protected and served were his family, money, and himself. Swank was dirty for a very long time, and that's why he never excelled in his career. The rate Swank was going, he would soon be arrested or dead the way he played the streets and the force.

Swank rolled slowly down First Street, looking at all the players and the black females he could possibly hit later on in the night. No matter how racist Swank was, he could never turn down the mighty power of the black woman and her pussy. The scenario was all too familiar to the people in the community. Swank was like a slave master checking on his field hands and stealing some black pussy while he was at it. In the end, no white man could resist the power of the black woman and her soft spot.

Swank pulled in front of the 201 Building on First Street and stepped out. Everyone on the corner would normally run, but they knew it would be bad for business to run from Swank. He was the devil incarnate. He stood on the corner cool, calm, and collected as he lit his Camel cigarette, slowly blew the smoke out, and said, "JD, come here and let me talk to you a few ticks."

JD was a young black hustler independent of the Port Au Prince Posse and the Eastwick Hustlers. He paid them high rent to operate on First Street. Swank kept him and his boys protected, and he owed Swank a lot of favors. Swank was now going to cash in on *all* the favors.

"What's up, Swank?" JD asked. He towered over Swank by a few inches, which wasn't much since Swank was only 5'8". JD's 'fro also made him look taller than he really was.

"I need you to take a ride with me Uptown to the precinct."

"What for? I got business to handle."

"You ain't got no business but the business I tell you, nigger," Swank said, feeling good that he had some type of power over someone.

"Now get ya' black ass in the car before I give you an old-fashioned whippin'."

JD sucked his teeth, turned around, and said, "Big Keith, take care of things. I'll be back."

As they entered the car, Swank said, "Damn, JD, you suck ya' teeth almost as good as you suck dick." Swank thought the comment was humorous and started to laugh.

"Man, I don't play that gay shit. What the fuck do you want?" JD asked forcefully, trying to maintain his manhood that Swank tried to dent with his comment. Swank unbuttoned his pants so that his gut would be more comfortable. He fixed himself behind the wheel and pulled off as he began to speak.

"I need you to kill someone in the holding cell of the precinct," Swank said easily and unflinching.

At the mention of murder, JD looked over at Swank as if he were crazy.

"You're *serious*?" JD asked in disbelief.

"What's wrong? Don't I look serious?" Swank asked as he concentrated on the road.

"You say that shit like you asking me to take your daughter to the prom or something."

"I could never fix my mouth to ask no nigger to take my daughter to the prom. I'd kill her and myself for even thinking about it. Now listen, you know Prince, the bank-robbing pimp, don't you?"

"Yeah and?"

"We have him down at the station, and he's going to run his mouth, so I need him dead."

will robbins

"What does that have to do with me and my crew?"

"Because if he runs his mouth, I go down, Port Au Prince Posse goes down, and the Eastwick Hustlers go down ..."

Before Swank could finish his statement, JD started to see the possibilities of running Jersey. Before he could fantasize any longer, Swank said loudly, "And YOU go down, bitch!!"

JD broke out of his fantasy and started to realize the seriousness of what Swank was asking him to do.

"I can't do that shit! I'll go down for life!" JD yelled.

"Calm down, bitch, you won't do life. I'll give you a few names to drop, you'll cut a deal, and I'll make sure that all you'll do is a year in county and five years probation. You can do a year on your head, and you already have probation. A little more ain't gonna hurt you. Besides, if you don't do it, you won't have a life."

JD knew that Swank would make good on his words and kill him, so he figured the alternative was his best bet.

"All right, Swank, you got me," JD said, defeated.

Swank pulled into the station parking lot and let JD out. He gave JD clear instructions on what was suppose to go down. "Listen, I'm putting you in handcuffs, and I'll say I picked you up for robbing a store while I was off duty. When you're in the cell, take him out."

"With what? I ain't got bad breath like you," JD said sarcastically.

Ignoring JD's comment, Swank pulled out a small Kershaw knife and said, "This should do the trick."

❦ ❦ ❦ ❦

"I need to go to the fuckin' hospital," Prince said, coughing, as pain shot through his body from the ass whipping he received.

"Shut the fuck up already. They ain't sendin' you nowhere," a short, white man said who was sharing the cell with Prince. Normally, the white man would have kept his mouth shut, but he knew that Prince was too weak to fight.

"Fuck you, honkey," Prince said, holding his ribs, wishing that he had the strength to fuck the white man up.

"Shut the fuck up, both of you, before I come back there and start thumping skulls!" an officer yelled from his desk. He wasn't annoyed at their bickering. He was just mad that they were interrupting his jelly doughnut fix.

Swank walked in with JD in tow, pushing and shoving, putting on an act. He walked in and stepped to the desk sergeant.

"I'm booking him for gun possession and robbery," Swank said. As Swank walked by with JD in hand, a fellow officer said, "I'll handle this punk for you, Swank."

"That's okay. I got it, Keens," Swank said as he walked back to the holding cell and said, "Open this cell." Once again, the turnkey walked and opened the cell. Swank pushed JD inside the cell and said, "Don't fuck up."

JD and Prince hung out at the same clubs and partied together. They even shared a few women together. So it was difficult for JD to wrap his mind around the fact that he was about to kill a friend. But he thought to himself, better him than me. It was survival of the fittest. Prince was much bigger than JD, who was afraid of Prince because of his massive size. At first, he was nervous and unsure if he would be able to take Prince out, but after entering the cell and seeing Prince's condition, he regained his heart.

JD walked in and took a seat on the cold steel. He looked over and saw Prince battered, lying on the piss-filled floor. He almost felt sorry for his friend, but he couldn't stand snitches, and that's what Prince had become. He wasn't about to lose his ends and his life over Prince's bitch ass.

"What's up, Prince?" JD asked.

Prince tried his hardest to sit up as he asked, "Who the fuck is you?"

"It's ya' man, JD, baby."

"Oh shit. Help me up, my nigga, and show me some love." JD stood up and pulled Prince to his feet. In agony, Prince rose from the filthy floor.

"Aagh, be easy with me, my nigga," Prince moaned as he stood up.

JD looked Prince over and said, "Damn, nigga, they fucked you up good."

"Yeah, but you know they can't hold ya' man down. You feel me?" Prince asked as he laughed and shook JD's hand and gave him a hug for the first time. JD gripped Prince's right hand and pulled the knife out with his left hand.

"I guess they can't hold you down, you fuckin' snitch," JD said as he plunged the knife in the back of Prince's neck.

Prince's body jerked, but he had enough strength to grab JD by his throat. JD pulled the knife out of Prince's neck and blood shot out like cherry Kool-Aid. JD became frightened of Prince's strength, and he began to plunge the knife deep into Prince's heavy gut several times. He didn't stop until Prince's body fell and the piss-filled floor was replaced with his bright, crimson blood.

By the time the officers noticed Prince's dead body, they weren't sure which man in the holding cell was responsible. It went over as well as Swank hoped it would. "Reasonable Doubt" if there ever was one.

12

FRONT STREET PIER

It was a hot, sunny day and the Front Street basketball court was filled with players. The Eastwick Hustlers were out in full force, breaking the monotony of dealing. Woo and his boys were out on the court as well. Woo was just keeping his mind occupied as he waited on his SAT results and acceptance letters. The ladies were out in full force as well, scheming on which drug dealer or playas were going to be their new baby daddy.

"I guess this is the Eastwick Hustlers vs. the School Boyz," Black said as he stood opposite of Woo as they were about to jump for the ball.

Woo's five-man team consisted of his boys Man, Taye, Calvin, and Damien. The Eastwick Hustlers on court were Black, E-Double, Booga, Jab, and Flex. Flex was Jab's right-hand man in Newark. He represented Hawthorne Avenue to the fullest. He was also Fat King's nephew. He was almost as dangerous and ruthless as Banks. He sold drugs and soldiered just as well as he played basketball. He would've gone pro if he hadn't got shot in his knee one night while hanging on the corner.

Woo tipped the ball to Man, who quickly made it up the court with the ball. Booga stood in his path and was quickly made a fool of when Man crossed over, breaking Booga's ankle and slamming the ball down in the rim.

"Look at this nigga tryin' to be like Allen Iverson," Booga said, trying to ease his embarrassment.

"More like Allen Jiverson. Let me post him up," Flex said, pushing Booga out of the way. As the ball game went on, a honey-colored Hummer with tinted windows pulled up unnoticed.

"Let me blast all these fools," Mark said as he sat in the passenger seat, anxious to commit a few 187s. Mark was one of Six-ten and Ice's respected generals. He wasn't of Haitian descent, but he was black, strong, ruthless, and grew up and lived in Pierce Manor all his life. He went through many struggles with Ice until they were both put on by Diamond. Mark helped plan the whole hostile takeover with Ice and Six-ten.

Six-ten sat in the vehicle with his eyes fixated on the ball game. He envied the young men playing ball. He grew up too fast and had seen too many things at their age to even think about sports. His sport was killing and surviving. He didn't know the pleasure of fun and leisure time at their age.

As Six-ten daydreamed, Mark rolled down the window and pointed his MP5 at the defenseless and unsuspecting crowd. He started to pull the trigger, but a few seconds before he could do it, Six-ten pulled his arm as he realized what was about to happen.

"What's up? Don't you want to blast these niggas?" Mark asked as he pulled the weapon back in the window.

"Yeah, but not right now. I have to drop you off and meet Ice and his woman. They need a lift to the port for their vacation," Six-ten explained, still a little disgusted with his man for taking a vacation on such a short notice and in the middle of a small war.

"I also got something goin' on with that stripper Kasha from the club," Six-ten said, shifting his mood with a smile.

"You mean Suga Walls?" Mark asked in disbelief. "I thought she didn't fuck with hustlers or Haitians?"

"Something or someone got her to change her mind, son." Six-ten was excited and was only thinking with his dick to consider any foul play right now. Mark thought that things were a little out of order.

"Why all of a sudden out of nowhere does this bitch want to start fuckin' with *you*?" Mark asked, trying to raise a red flag on the program.

"I don't know, nigga, but I ain't turnin' a fine bitch down like that. I'll figure all this shit out later on tonight."

"Later on tonight might be a little too late. Let me at least follow you to see how things play out," Mark said with a little authority, acting like the strong general he was.

"Nigga, get the fuck outta here. You'd fuck up a wet dream," Sixten said, as he pulled off to head Uptown to drop Mark off. No one on the court had realized how close he or she was to meeting the Grim Reaper only seconds before.

♦ ♦ ♦ ♦

Nadeem was passing her son to her sister, all excited about her trip with Ice. It had been a long time since they had spent any real time alone with each other. With Ice's criminal activity, the baby, school, and her father's mysterious disappearance, things had been rough for both of them. Now it was time to relax.

"You have my cell phone number, Toussaint's number, and the hotel's number that we'll be staying at, right?" Nadeem asked her sister Samantha. Samantha was younger than Nadeem but just as beautiful.

"I have everything, big sis', don't worry about it," Samantha said, flashing her pearly white smile. "You just forget about school, Daddy, and everything else and have fun."

"Thank you so much, I love you," Nadeem said as she kissed her sister on the cheek. "And be a good baby for your aunt, Lil' Toussaint," Nadeem finished as she kissed her son on his lips.

"Earl, please take these bags down to the car. Six-ten should be here soon."

Earl was a quiet man, but he was a dangerous bodyguard. Six-ten wouldn't even fuck with Earl. Earl was short in stature, but he was a powerhouse that acquired his skills in the U.S. Marine Corps. He had been with the Special Elite Forces. He protected Ice's penthouse and his lady like they were his own.

"Toussaint, hurry, baby, before we miss our plane," Nadeem yelled anxiously.

Ice was making his way down the stairs when his cell phone rang.

"What's up? This better be good," Ice said answering the phone.

"It's Mark. I think we may have a little problem, boss."

"Well, take it up with Six-ten."

"It's about Six-ten. Supposedly he's going to meet up with Suga Walls from the club tonight."

will robbins

"All of a sudden?"

"That's what I'm talking 'bout. So I told him let me follow him to make sure shit is all right, but he told me no. You know how he is."

"Look, just follow his ass tonight, but don't let him know you're around. It might not be anything, but I want to make sure that my man is taken care of. I'm holding you personally responsible for him, so if anything happens to him, I'm coming for you. Got it?"

"Yeah."

Whether Six-ten knew it or not, he was going to have an escort as far as Mark was concerned.

Ice pulled his woman in his arms and kissed her passionately for the first time in a while as he waited for his ride.

* * * *

The basketball court was clearing out as the School Boyz took the win home with them. Many sisters picked their man out for the night to get right. Many sisters wanted to choose Woo, but they weren't trying to have a karate foot way up their ass, and he wasn't even in the game no more.

"Yo, we rented a house at the Jersey Shore for a party. Y'all niggas don't forget," Black yelled as the crowd dispersed.

"We'll be there," the crowd said in unison.

"Hold up, Woo!" Black yelled.

E-Double grabbed Booga by his arm and waited until Black and everyone else was out of earshot.

"Yo, you ready for tonight?"

"Yeah, but what about the party at the beach?"

"We just gonna show up late. Besides, that'll be our alibi."

"Cool. Is Kasha ready?"

"You know she love Black. I told her he would deal with her if she did him this favor. So shorty is more than ready."

"OK, 9 o'clock tonight at the pier, right?"

"You got it, baby," Double said as he and Booga gave each other a pound.

* * * *

Six-ten made his way to the Newark Airport as Ice sat next to him in uncomfortable silence. Six-ten knew when his partner had something on his mind, so he decided to break the silence. "Say what's on ya' mind, man."

"You know I don't like to talk business in front of my woman, but I guess I have to this time."

"What's up?"

"I'm not feeling this whole thing with you and Kasha."

"Mark ran his mouth. What is wrong with you two? When have I not handled business or myself properly? Last I checked, I was my own man," Six-ten said weaving in and out of traffic.

"With everything that's goin' down, you haven't stopped to ask yourself why all of a sudden she wants to mess with you. I mean, this is the same woman who swore off hustlers and Haitians in the same breath. Out of all the women you could have, why do you have to mess with *this* one?" Ice continued to try to sway his friend away from Kasha, but Six-ten had made his mind up.

"I want what I can't have. Forbidden fruit, I guess. I'm not turnin' down this fine-ass woman for no one or nothing," Six-ten said as he pulled up in front of the 'port gate.

"Look, we don't have time to argue, brotha, 'cause y'all here already. Now get the fuck outta my car and enjoy y'all vacation," Six-ten said with a smile.

"Be careful of what you ask for. You just might get it," Nadeem said as she put her small, feminine hand on the massive shoulder of Six-ten. Then she kissed Six-ten on the cheek and exited the vehicle.

"I love you, too," Six-ten replied to Nadeem.

Ice turned to Six-ten and said, "Look, be real careful while I'm gone."

"I got you."

"No! I'm serious. Be careful while I'm gone. I love ya', bruh'."

"I love ya', too. Be safe."

As Nadeem and Ice walked into the 'port, Six-ten pulled off.

❧ ❧ ❧ ❧

Bobby—a.k.a. Agent Simms—sat in Dawkins' office waiting for him to return. He didn't know what to expect from Dawkins since the investigation wasn't running as smoothly as possible. Simms didn't locate the tapes or get any closer to any information that would send the Port Au Prince Posse or the Eastwick Hustlers away for life, except for the murder of Bricks, which Dawkins was willing to give a pass to until he got more substantial evidence against Ice.

Dawkins stepped into the office drinking coffee as he walked past

Simms, walked around his desk, and took a seat. Simms stood up as Dawkins walked into the room. His slim, muscular cut legs almost collapsed as he waited for Dawkins to tell him to sit back down. Simms took a seat upon Dawkins' request and exhaled. But his comfort wouldn't last for long.

Dawkins put his coffee down, looked Simms in the eyes, and asked, "What do you have for me?"

Inhaling deeply to stall, Simms replied, "Nothing too useful, sir."

"So no wire on the rest of those tapes?"

"It's not like it's the topic of conversation, sir. And if I ask about them, it might raise suspicion," Simms answered, trying to keep his cool. He knew Dawkins would start in with the time and money issue of the case as well as the case being time sensitive. He resented the fact that Dawkins wasn't on the street and hadn't been for years. He felt that Dawkins had lost his touch a little and forgotten the mechanics of undercover work. He wasn't going to rush things, blow his cover and his life because Dawkins was anxious and had a personal vendetta against Ice.

"Well, you might have to arouse some suspicion to get this thing done."

"I have enough surveillance and info so you could lock up Black, his brother, and his crew. You start giving out football numbers, and I guarantee that they'll talk," Simms said with frustration in his voice.

"You don't get it! I don't want to lock some young black boys up. We have enough of them in our fucked-up system. They don't need our prison system. They need strong black men to guide them down the *right* path. But we can't accomplish that with guys like Ice seducing them into the life of drugs, money, and violence.

"I'm in a power position as a black man, and I'm going to use my power to help our people and our community. And locking up our young brothers and sisters doesn't help the community. It only breaks it down. Once we knock out the Ice's in the community, we may be able to get our younger brothers back. So do your job," Dawkins finished his small sermon. He knew that Black and his team had to be taken down, but he also knew it wasn't too late for them to make a difference.

"Look, I understand where you are coming from. I don't like seeing our people locked up any more than you do. But we know it's only a matter of time before Black and E-Double become the new Ice.

124

Listen, I'll try a new angle on the case," Simms said, perking up as he entertained a new idea.

"What is it?" Dawkins asked attentively.

"How about I switch teams?"

"What are you talking about?"

"I have no bad blood with Ice. Why not give him some phony info on the Eastwick Hustlers and profess my loyalty to him."

"Because that loyalty is going to be tested. And we both know how sick and twisted Ice and his crew can be. It's too dangerous, and I can't let you do it."

"I'm telling you it will work, sir."

"Legally, for the case, you can sell drugs and live the life of a hustler, but you can't kill anyone, and we both know that's how your loyalty will be tested."

"Well, I have to do something to speed up this case. I'm tired of seeing the drug deals, killings, and all this other shit go unanswered," Simms said as he stood up and paced around the office to let out some energy.

"I know you're angry and frustrated, man, but this all comes with the territory and the oath you swore," Dawkins said as he stood up and placed his hands on Simms' shoulders. He looked him dead in the eyes and spoke to him like a brother rather than a superior.

"The only way that we are going to break this case is with those tapes. If we have them, they *can't* be disputed."

"I don't know how to get them, and we're running out of time, sir."

"Try this. We have enough men and the right tools to break in and search Black's house and the rest of the Eastwick Hustlers' houses until we find those tapes."

"If we do that and find the tapes, they won't be admissible in court. It would be a violation of their civil rights and due process!" Simms said, concerned about his boss's antics.

"Calm down, man; let's sit back down and work this out. Suppose some kids break into the houses and steal money, jewelry, as well as the tapes. It wouldn't be a violation of anybody's rights if some concerned parent of one of the thieves find the tapes and turn them in," Dawkins explained, happy with his tactics.

"I guess that would fly in court, and this whole thing would be over."

will robbins

"Sometimes to catch a criminal you have to act and think like one, Simms. Remember, justice isn't blind when it comes to black people. So we have to be eye surgeons for justice. It's just unfortunate that justice is determined by a bunch of biased criminals in the first place. So we, as black law enforcement officers, have to be a constant balance for our people. And with that being said, call Cruz and set something up soon. Only do it when the opportunity presents itself. I don't want to blow this. It might be our last chance at getting those tapes," Dawkins said.

Simms stood up, shook Dawkins' hand, and walked out of the office. He was a little relieved that Dawkins came up with a contingency plan. He felt like he was at the end of his rope. Months had gone by with little progress. But he hoped that Dawkins' plan would produce the tapes and get the ball rolling.

♦ ♦ ♦ ♦

Kasha stood up from her queen-sized bed and pulled the yellow thong up her thick, unmarked, smooth, light-skinned legs. Her body was flawless and brought many men to their knees. Her personality plus her body were a lethal combination. She was the best stripper that Ice had ever employed. Even he tried to crack her legs once or twice but gave up after he found out her little bio. Kasha's father was a hustling Haitian man that left her and her mother dirt-poor in Haiti for a better life in the U.S. Kasha's mother sold her body and saved up enough money to leave Haiti, and it landed them in Elizabeth, N.J.

Kasha's friend Melinda put Ice down to the fact that Kasha wouldn't mess with Haitian men or hustlers after what her father did, and Ice backed off. Six-ten, on the other hand, found her beauty irresistible and mystic. Her standoffish attitude had him open, and every chance he had to crack on her, he did, despite all of the rejections. Tonight, however, would be the last time she would hear his dumb one-liners. She definitely hated, "You have a kind chin, the kind I like to rest my balls on."

Kasha put on a long, light-blue summer dress by Versace for her short evening with Six-ten. She looked in the mirror to see her coppery, brick-red hair was precisely cut in a long, curved bob. The dress had complemented her curves very well. She looked so fine that if she were attracted to women, she would have made her own self wet. Satisfied with her attire, she walked out of her room decorated with

Chinese décor.

Black and E-Double were in their apartment getting ready for the party at the shore. Black was putting on a stare-worthy player's white suit that he copped from Forever Image for Men on Broad and East Jersey Street. E-Double walked into Black's room as he got dressed, wearing an all-black Rocawear sweat suit to Black's surprise.

"Brotha, I know damn well you ain't wearing that to the party," Black said as he turned from the mirror.

"No. I got something to handle first, and then I'll be at the party."

"What do you have to take care of without me?"

"Just some business, Dapper Don. Don't worry about it," Double said flashing a smile, revealing his dimples that women loved.

"*Should* I be worried, little brotha? I hope it ain't nothin' stupid. I don't have time to argue 'cause the girls are settin' up shop at the house and we already late." Black knew his little brother was up to something, but he knew at this point there would be no stopping him. And he was tired of all the arguing and disagreeing that they had been going through lately. He knew that as soon as things calmed down, they would have to take a trip together or do something special just to remember the good times.

"So who you rollin' with? You know I don't want anybody traveling alone," Black said as he grabbed his keys off the dresser.

"Booga and Jab are on the way, and soon as we finish, we'll be at the party. Who you rollin with?"

"Bobby is already downstairs waiting for me," Black replied. "You know I love you, right?" Black asked as he held Double's face in his hands, looking him directly in the eyes for truth and emphasis.

"I know, I love you, too, now get out of here and warm them bitches up for me." As Black was going down the stairs, Booga was on his way up dressed in similar clothing as Double.

"What's up, Black? You look sharp."

"Thanks. Yo, what are you and my brotha up to tonight?"

"Just some business that's gonna help us grow. Nothin' to worry about, Black."

"If it's nothin' to worry about, then tell me what it is. I mean, I *am* boss dawg, nigga."

Feeling like the interrogation was getting too deep, Booga said, "Talk to Double. We already behind schedule. Jab is waiting in the car.

Go holla at him." Then Booga pushed past Black and ran up the stairs before Black could press the issue.

• • • •

Kasha sat on her plush sky blue love seat sipping on Henny and Coke, trying to ease her nerves. She knew she was about to set up a dangerous and important man. If anyone found out about it, it would mean certain death. But the way E-Double and Booga laid the plan out, it was flawless. The only reason that she was participating was because the money that Double had offered was too sweet to pass up. Black was also offered up as an added bonus.

She swore off hustlers, but the strength and sensitivity in Black's deep hazel eyes melted her. His voice sent chills through her body. They spoke on many occasions, and it was always about life, spirituality, and changing the hearts and minds of black people. Most times in his company, she forgot that he was a hustler. He always treated her like a lady and never made any bad references to her being a stripper. The fact that he never pushed up on her like most men turned her on even more.

Her cell phone rang, causing her to jump. She almost spilled her drink on her dress, but she was a professional when it came to holding on to her drinks, especially since she worked at a club where people bumped into her all the time.

"Hello," Kasha answered with her sensuous voice.

"It's Double ... you ready for tonight?"

"I've been ready, but if this nigga don't show up soon, I might change my mind," Kasha said, trying to find a reason to back out of the deal.

"He's supposed to be there at 9. It's only 8:30 pm, so calm down. I'm just makin' sure you alright with this."

"I'm not alright with this, but you better have my money and your brother better be on standby for a sista," Kasha replied with her street attitude.

"I got you, Suga Walls," Double said laughing, trying to antagonize her even more.

Just as she was about to tell Double where to go, her doorbell rang.

"Look, it's Six-ten. I gotta go."

"Just make sure you get his ass at the pier," Double warned and hung up.

"Everything's a go?" Booga asked.

"Who are you, Memphis Bleek now? Yeah, everything's a go."

Booga pulled off and headed toward their destination.

❧ ❧ ❧ ❧

Black and Bobby were in the Escalade headed down the highway for the shore. It was one of the first times that they actually were ever alone. Black usually only rolled with Double and Bobby with Banks. Since Banks' death, Bobby felt a little out of place on the team. But he would now use this opportunity to get closer to Black and, hopefully, find out where the tapes were.

"Hey, Bobby, what do you want to get out of all of this?"

"All of what?"

"This hustling and shit."

"I never thought about it. I mean, I got cars, money, and bitches. I guess I got everything I want right now," Bobby replied.

"What about you? Why are you hustling?"

"At first, I hustled out of sense of necessity. Now I hustle as a means to an end," Black said as he realized he was close to the beach and house he rented.

"A means to end what?" Bobby asked.

"A means to my family's financial suffering and the advancement of our people once I get my shit together," Black replied sincerely.

"Your family ain't suffering financially no more than a lot of other people are suffering from what you do," Bobby said, wishing he could take his words back because he sounded more like a cop than a hustler.

"What you mean 'from what I do'? Nigga, you doing the same thing, let's not forget. And I'm not just talking about my brother, mother, and sister. I'm talking about taking care of our kids' kids. The white man has set up his family for generations and generations illegally, and they still are. And they did it off the backs of our people. They did it then, and they doin' it now. I do feel bad that I'm exploiting and profiting off the misery of our people in the hood, but it's just temporary. Eventually, I'm going to exploit the white man's system and make it work for our people and me. I just need a little more time and education, baby," Black said finishing his small sermon.

"You just got a little deep on me, brotha; slow down," Bobby said thinking that there was more to Black than a ruthless, heartless drug dealer.

"I'm a little tired of hustling, too, kid. I bet whatever is on those tapes we got from Ice could end this whole shit, huh?" Bobby asked.

"If I didn't know better, I swear you was acting like a cop," Black said, suddenly suspicious of Bobby's comments.

"You know damn well I ain't no cop. I just feel what you sayin', and I figured if you were tired of the game, those tapes could get you out," Bobby explained, hoping that he wouldn't start to sweat.

"Those tapes are mine, yours, and the rest of the Eastwick Hustlers' leverage against the cops, Ice, and the Port Au Prince Posse. As long as we have them, we don't have to worry too much," Black explained.

"We? I don't even know where the tapes are—let alone what's on them," Bobby said with frustration in his voice, trying to pump info out of Black as subtly as possible.

"The tapes are safe, and as long as they're safe, we're safe. The less you know, the better it is for you," Black said as he pulled into the driveway of the rented house where people were dancing on the porch, in the house, and on the beach. The DJ was bumping Ludacris' "Pimping All Over the World."

Bobby let the conversation about the tapes alone. He knew that if he were persistent about them, it would only arouse suspicion in Black. Besides, the women were hitting for something, and Bobby wanted to get loose and forget about the case—at least for tonight.

❦ ❦ ❦ ❦

Six-ten drove his Hummer to the Front Street Pier reluctantly. He hated hanging around downtown, even though most of his cash flow derived from there. But he couldn't turn down the request of Kasha, especially after he saw her heavy cleavage bounce in her dress as he hit all the potholes and bumps in the road as he headed towards the pier. Kasha felt uneasy and nervous, but Six-ten was too horny to be concerned with her feelings. She was quiet most of the night, but Six-ten assumed that was just her personality.

"What made you go out with me tonight?" Six-ten asked as he put his hand on Kasha's thick, light-skinned thigh.

Kasha jumped a little and removed Six-ten's hand, letting him know that she wasn't ready for the touchy feely yet.

"I know I swore off hustlers and Haitians, but lately, that seems to be all that I run into, or that's all that approaches me. I have needs, too, and if I'm going to mess with anyone, I might as well have one of the best Haitians that there is," Kasha said, licking her lips, playing her role a little too well.

Six-ten knew that everyone played him as second to Ice, so Kasha's comment upset him a little bit. He shrugged the comment off, though, and relished in the fact that he was finally with her.

The conversation between Kasha and Six-ten went into sex mode as they reached the pier. Six-ten was so distracted that he didn't even notice the black Acura Legend following him as he pulled into the parking area of the pier.

"Yo, drive around the block one good time before we do our thing," Double told Booga as he looked out of the rearview mirror.

"Why? What's up?" Jab asked, looking around nervously.

"I think a car might be following us."

Booga looked around and saw a dark blue Infiniti G35 in the rearview mirror. He drove past the pier and made a left on Magnolia. Booga, Jab, and Double looked for the Infiniti, but it was out of sight.

Mark pulled over and parked his vehicle on the side of the road where Six-ten couldn't see him. Booga turned on First Street and made his way back down Front Street to the pier. As they drove by, they saw the Infiniti again.

"There's that damn car again," Double said a little annoyed. Usually no one was at the pier, so this car was throwing him for a loop.

"We could do this shit another time," Booga said, feeling the bad vibe.

"We gotta do this shit right now! We don't have another time. Besides, what are we gonna do about Kasha?"

"Fuck it then. We got a party to hurry up and get to," Booga said, turning off his lights and pulling over.

❦ ❦ ❦ ❦

Mark's cell phone rang, causing him to be distracted. He didn't even realize that another car had pulled up on the scene.

"You all over here braggin' about ya head game, so what's up?" Six-ten asked, grabbing at his almost erect dick.

Kasha thought to herself, *Where these niggas at?*

"My head game is sick, but you not worthy of this head yet," she said teasingly, trying to stall for time.

"So what makes a brotha deserving of having your juicy lips on his

will robbins

dick?"

"I need to see if a brotha can eat this pussy like he at a buffet."

"Get the fuck outta here. I do you first, and I won't get done at all," Six-ten said laughing.

Kasha saw Double, Jab, and Booga moving up the rear on Six-ten's side of the car and lifted her leg over the seat and said, "If you eat this pussy right, I'll swallow all your kids' daddy."

Six-ten licked his thick lips and started to put his tongue in her velvet walls when Double opened up the car door and pulled a startled Six-ten out. Booga, Jab, and Double pulled the big man on the ground. Six-ten tried to get up, but Jab, who kicked him in the face with his steel-toed "trees," quickly knocked him back down.

After the blow he received, Six-ten's lips started swell up like Jimmie Walker's from *Good Times*. Double pulled out a Baby Desert Eagle to strike fear in Six-ten, who, by now, wished that he had taken Mark along to be his muscle, but he had been thinking with his dick and not his head.

Mark's cell phone rang again, and he didn't notice the action across the street.

"Hello ... yeah everything alright, boss. I got you," Mark answered.

"You better make sure nothing happens to my brother 'cause like I said, I'm holding you personally responsible. If something does happen, you might as well write your eulogy," Ice said with a heavy accent.

"He's cool, boss. He's probably getting his dick sucked as we speak."

Mark couldn't be further from the truth if he'd tried.

Double, Jab, and Booga were busy stomping a mud hole in Six-ten as Kasha nervously looked on.

"This is for Banks, this is for Bricks, and this is for Slim," Double yelled as he stomped on Six-ten, fighting back tears of hurt and anger.

"Just shoot his Haitian ass," Kasha yelled, as she feared that the display would bring unwanted attention. Just as Kasha yelled, Mark was alerted.

"Are you sure my boy is a'ight?" Ice asked. Mark didn't even have the chance to answer. He dropped the phone on the car floor, leaving Ice to wonder what was going on.

Double, Jab, and Booga stopped their Rodney King beating on Six-ten. Double raised his gun, took a deep breath, and pointed it at Six-ten. He felt like a big man towering over the helpless Six-ten.

"When you get to hell, tell Banks, Slim, and Bricks that I sent you," he said with heat in his eyes and venom in his voice. Double was a second away from ending Six-ten's life, but he was distracted by a loud bang and glass shattering on the Hummer.

Mark was running in Double, Jab, and Booga's direction, shooting wildly. Once the three men and Kasha realized what was going on, they all took cover alongside the Hummer. Mark was running full force, still shooting.

Double let off a blind shot that made Mark stumble. Mark decided that it would be wise to take cover rather than run up on his targets, half-cocked. He started to run for a utility pole for cover. As he ran, Booga took aim and threw two Chinese stars in his direction. Before Mark reached the pole, he felt something penetrate his shoulder and his calf. He knew he wasn't hit with a bullet because he didn't hear a gunshot.

Blood trickled down Mark's back and calf. Once he reached the pole, he investigated his wounds, pulled the stars from his body, and found it humorous that he was hit with throwing stars.

"I heard you were good with these shits, but I thought people were bullshittin'. Who the fuck uses stars in the hood, bitch-ass ma'fucka," Mark said halfway laughing and groaning in pain.

"It worked, didn't it?" Booga responded, trying to get inside of Mark's head.

Mark almost threw the stars back at Booga, but decided it would be against his best interest. During the verbal jabs, Six-ten rose to his feet without being noticed. He pulled his gun from the back of his waist, raised his weapon, and took aim at Double. Kasha yelled as she saw Double's life about to be taken. Double turned around, only to see the hot flash of Six-ten's gun.

Jab, quick on his feet, was able to dive and get him and Double out of the way. As they were hitting the ground, Booga was able to throw one last star in Six-ten's direction. The Chinese star landed right in his eye socket. The shock and force of the blow knocked the big man off his feet in excruciating agony. As he lay screaming on the ground, Jab released two bullets in Six-ten's chest to make sure that they wouldn't have any more problems out of the big man again.

Mark made a mad run to his car as he busts shots to hold Booga,

will robbins

Jab, and Double at bay. The three men started to pursue after the so-called hit man, but the sound of sirens and the thought of jail made everyone wise up.

Mark sped off like a thief in the night. He was wondering what went wrong. He felt like his life was slowly being drained, like the blood from Six-ten's eye socket. He wasn't sure if he should skip town or warn Ice about what happened to his fallen soldier. He decided that it would be best to take a few days and get his affairs in order before he would tell Ice about what went down. He wasn't sure if Ice would take his life or not, but he wasn't going to give it up easily.

Kasha sat in the backseat of the car in silence. She wasn't sure how to respond to what she just witnessed. She knew it was going to happen, but it was still too much for her to take in at one time.

Booga, Jab, and Double were silent as well, but for different reasons. They all had bodies over their heads, so taking a life wasn't much to them. But the life they had taken this time would bring a shit storm over the city like never before. They were trying to figure out how they would tell Black about what they did once the streets started to talk. They felt like Black was losing his edge because of the way he handled the whole situation. They didn't realize that the way he handled things kept most people alive, including—innocent people. The three men felt vindicated after taking Six-ten's life, so they were willing to take any consequence that came their way.

The men dropped Kasha off with a suitcase filled with stacks of paper to ease her conscience for her involvement in killing Six-ten. They also assured her that she would be hearing from Black soon, which made her a little wet in the panties. Then they headed to Double's house to change for the party. They wore sleek, casual outfits with a thug twist added in, then hit the highway ready to get up in some new pussy to ease their minds about what they had done. They would deal with Black and the consequences later.

13

TROUBLE IN PARADISE

Ice and Nadeem were enjoying peace and tranquility on the beautiful island of Anguilla while all hell was breaking loose in Eastwick. They had no idea that Six-ten was dead and gone. The private villa in Cap Juluca provided them with the escape that they needed to rekindle their romance and leave the bullshit of the hood behind. Too bad that one phone call and an act of indiscretion were going to bring trouble in paradise.

Ice and Nadeem walked hand in hand on the white, sandy beach looking like royalty. The clear turquoise water brushed up against their feet as they took in the sultry atmosphere, pleased with their Caribbean vacation. Normally, they would have stayed in their villa exploring each other's body, but their surroundings were much more enticing. Although Ice traveled a lot, this, however, was the first time he did so without the intention of creating more drug and other illegal business.

Nadeem was the opposite of Ice. She spent too much time worrying about other people to take time to travel and enjoy herself. So now that the opportunity arrived to leave the hood alone for a while, Ice jumped on it. It was his way of apologizing to Nadeem for striking her, and it cost him a pretty penny.

As Ice and Nadeem continued to walk, they noticed that many couples and stragglers had stopped. "Why did everyone stop, baby?"

Nadeem asked as she held Ice by his thick muscular waist.

Ice simply held Nadeem and pointed at the sky. The sun was setting and everyone stood around to see the blue sky turn pink while the remainder of the sun shined down on the clear water, making it appear golden.

"That's beautiful, baby. The sky and sun never looks that way in the hood," Nadeem said, still looking towards the sky.

"I know you're amazed at what you're seeing right now, and I understand, because that's how I feel every time I look at you, baby," Ice said, as he looked his woman deep in her eyes.

Nadeem wanted her man right then and there as her spot became moist with his romantic comment. She was a freak but not freaky enough to have sex on the beach with everyone watching. But she had something waiting for his ass once they got back to their private villa. Nadeem was too wrapped up in the beauty of Ice's eyes to see that another woman was admiring her man. When that lady heard Ice's comment, she became wet. And she was going to find out what Ice was all about at any cost.

Ice and Nadeem started to walk away as Ice's newest admirer burned a hole through Nadeem. They never even noticed the woman who followed them.

"Are you hungry, baby? We've been on the beach all day," Ice said.

"A little. Where do you want to go?"

"We could go back to the villa and have a catered surfside candle-light dinner," Ice suggested with more than food on his mind.

"That would be nice, but I heard that Uncle Ernie's Snack Bar was the spot. I know what you want to do once we get back to the villa, and it's not eating food either," Nadeem answered, giving Ice a little pinch on his side.

"I'm pretty sure you don't mind me eatin' you, baby," Ice said as he leaned over and lightly bit on her neck.

"You know what?" Nadeem asked.

"What?"

"Let's skip dinner and go straight for dessert," Nadeem replied with a devilish grin.

Ice's comment and the way he bit her neck turned her on in the worst way. The walk to the villa was short, especially since it was located right on the beach. The happy couple walked into the whitewashed

Moorish-styled building like teenagers in love. People who observed them would have never guessed that they had a serious fight and almost spilt up weeks ago.

Ice and Nadeem walked into their lavishly decorated villa, kissing passionately, like the world was going to end tomorrow and this was their last night on earth. They both began to strip their clothes off as if they were on fire. They were so into each other that they didn't notice the fact that the door was open. Ice laid Nadeem on the plush sheepskin rug and ate what he promised to eat. He pushed her legs up and stuck his tongue deep inside of her love canal. Then he took his thumb and rubbed it around in circles over her clitoris, his tongue moving around in circles in sync with his thumb.

Just as Nadeem thought she couldn't handle any more, Ice opened her lips, exposing her clitoris more and began to suck and lick it simultaneously. Nadeem began to shake and gyrate her hips in motion with Ice's rhythm.

"Damn, baby, lick this kitty kat," she said as she played with Ice's ears. "Ooh, ooh, aah, shit, I'm about to come, daddy, suck this pussy," Nadeem said as she played with her hard nipples.

As Ice was getting down, his new admirer, who just so happened to follow them, appeared in the doorway. When Ice looked up to see the ecstasy on his woman's face, he saw his admirer watching him perform. She winked at him, licked her luscious lips seductively, and closed the door silently.

Ice was a little surprised to see someone looking at him, but it wasn't the first time someone saw him giving oral pleasure. He didn't mind the act of voyeurism. But he knew that if Nadeem had seen the woman, the mood would have been dropped for hours. He couldn't wait any longer to put his long rod in his woman's tight, wet pussy. He put her short legs on his wide, strong shoulders and placed himself inside of her.

Nadeem tensed up as she felt her man enter her. Ice was large, and it had been awhile since they had lain together. He stroked her slow to ease the pain and tension. He wanted her pussy to conform to his dick. After a few minutes of slow strokes, Nadeem began to beg for his dick.

"Faster, baby, fuck this pussy hard and good, nigga," Nadeem screamed. She only referred to Ice as a "nigga" during their lovemak-

will robbins

ing sessions. It turned him on and made him stroke harder. In turn, he only called her a bitch to bring out the freak in her during sex.

"Take this dick, freak-ass bitch," Ice taunted his woman to bring out the best in her. Nadeem and Ice fucked long and hard and had rug burns to show for it. Afterward, they lay in each other's arms, too tired to move.

"Damn, my ass feels like it's on fire," Nadeem said as she turned on her side.

"I know, I just smoked it," Ice said, laughing.

"No. I'm talking about the rug burns, bitch," Nadeem said playfully.

"My knees feel the same way, baby. Next time, I'm taking your freaky ass to the bedroom."

"Well, I'm going in the shower to cool off and take care of these burns," Nadeem said.

"I would, but I have a little more energy to burn, so I'll hit the gym downstairs."

"I thought *I* was your gym," Nadeem said with a smile as she opened her legs wide, revealing her clean-shaven promised land.

Ice stood up and lifted Nadeem to her feet and kissed her again. Their naked bodies pressed together looked like a perfect piece of art.

"Go take that shower and I'll be up in a few, baby."

Nadeem walked away, and Ice patted her on her phat ass.

"Watch the burns, baby," Nadeem said as she threw him his clothes.

Ice walked into the room and changed into some Phat Farm sweat pants, a tight black wifebeater, and a fresh pair of Air Force Ones. As he put on his sweat pants, he was a little regretful that he had made love on a rug, even though it was plush.

Nadeem let the cool water run down her backside. It eased the rug burn, but not the memory she would hold of her sex session with Ice. They had made love many times before, obviously, but never in a lover's paradise such as Anguilla.

Meanwhile, Ice walked into the barely occupied gym and went straight for what he loved the most, the bench press. He put two 45 plates on each side of the bar and lay on the bench, took a deep breath, and lifted the 225 lb weight. He completed his reps, and by then, his chest was pulsating. After that, he slowly walked over to the free weights, picked up the 65 lb dumbbells, and began to curl them slow-ly. His arms seemed to swell like magic as he lifted each bell. Ice worked out for about an hour before he called it quits and headed to the showers. He stripped down to his birthday suit and entered the shower area.

As the water flowed and hit his body, he said, "Aahh, shit." The water seemed to punish his knees even more. He lathered up with cocoa nut soap and began to sing Earth, Wind & Fire's "Reasons." As he turned around to let the water attack his back, he was surprised to see an exotic half-Black and Chinese woman admiring his body.

"You sing as well as you look," the woman said with lust filling her eyes.

Ice stood still and let the woman get an eyeful of his body. He knew he had nothing to be ashamed of. He turned the water off, grabbed his towel, and wrapped it around his waist. Then he stepped toward the woman who should have been the poster girl for Apple Bottoms Jeans. Her chest was like that of a Chinese woman, but her ass was sure enough fit for a black woman. Her eyes and hair were a dead giveaway that she was of Asian descent, but her thick, full lips spoke volumes of the motherland. Once Ice gave her the lookover, he said, "You're the woman that stood in front of my door."

"That's funny. I was hoping that I was the woman in your dreams," she said as she took her pointer finger and rubbed it down Ice's six-pack, stopping just before she reached his manhood.

"You're kind of bold. I like that," Ice said as the woman briefly explored his body.

"I just know what I want, and I want you right now."

"What's your name and room number, and we can hook up later."

"My name is Malaya. We don't need a room. Why put off later what we can do right now?" she asked as she ripped the towel from Ice's waist.

She groped Ice's piece and said, "I have my work cut out for me, don't I?"

"Looking at ya body, it looks like we both have our work cut out for us."

Malaya dropped to her knees and grabbed Ice's manhood with both hands and put his head in her mouth. She began to go up and down on his dick like her neck was broke.

"Damn, baby, suck this dick. Lick my balls, too, shit. I hope your pussy is as tight as your head game, baby."

"I hope so, too, ma'fucka 'cause you ain't never gonna get this pussy again, bitch," Nadeem said standing in front of her man who was receiving lip service from anther bitch. Ice and the woman jumped out of fear at Nadeem's presence.

"I, I, I," Malaya stammered on her words, too shocked and surprised to articulate anything else.

"I, I, *what*, bitch?" Nadeem threw a right and a left cross that connected to both of Malaya's eyes. If anyone had any problems wondering if Malaya was half Chinese, they wouldn't for a while the way Nadeem slanted her eyes.

"What the fuck is wrong with you? What the fuck are you doing down here?" Ice began to ask questions in succession, trying to buy time for a good excuse that would never come.

"I came down here to work out with you and surprise you! But *I'm* the one getting the surprise."

As Nadeem spoke, Malaya tried to get up, only to be kicked back down by Nadeem's Baby Phat sneakers.

"Nadeem, I'm—" that was as far as Ice got before Nadeem cut him off.

"—You're sorry! Is *that* what you were about to say? Sorry you got caught, that's about it! You *are* a sorry ma'fucka, and I'm off this island. You can have that beat down, broke-ass, chinky-ass bitch!" Nadeem yelled as she turned and left Ice standing with his face on the ground. As she left, Malaya started to get up.

Once she stood on her feet, Ice said, "I'm caught, and you got fucked up, so we might as well finish what we started."

Malaya started to slap Ice for his comment, but she figured one beat down was enough. She lightly pushed Ice aside and left almost as fast as Nadeem.

"I guess that's a no!" Ice yelled, trying to make light of the situation.

Nadeem was in the villa packing and crying hysterically. *This vacation was suppose to bring us closer together,* was all that kept popping up in her head.

Ice walked in for round two as Nadeem was packing. At first he didn't say anything because he believed that she was fronting. This wasn't the first time that she caught him in the act, and she always cried, yelled, and made threats, but she never did leave.

Just as Nadeem headed for the door, Ice grabbed her arm and asked, "Where the fuck do you think you're going?"

"I'm getting the fuck out of here and away from you, now let me go," Nadeem said, snatching her arm away from his grip.

"Baby, I said I was sorry," Ice explained as if he only drank the last bit of Kool-Aid in the house.

Nadeem burned inside so bad she felt like a phoenix. Without warning, she began to throw hooks left and right at Ice. She connected a few times, but Ice grabbed her arms and threw her on the bed.

"Baby, stop this shit. She didn't mean anything to me!"

"I don't mean shit to you either, ma'fucka!" Once again Nadeem launched at Ice with fury. Normally, Ice would have backhanded her and called it a day, but he knew he was dead wrong.

He grabbed Nadeem again to stop her actions. She simply fell in his arms, crying.

"I can't let you leave me, baby," Ice said. Nadeem, feeling that fire, pushed Ice again and headed for the door. Ice was too tired from his sexcapades and workout to keep fighting with Nadeem. As she exited the door, he yelled, "How the fuck are you going to get off the island?"

"Don't worry about me and don't bring ya bitch ass home either," Nadeem yelled over her shoulder.

Ice was about to chase after her, but his cell phone rang for the first time since he hit ground on the island.

"Who the fuck is this?" Ice asked with the attitude of a man who just lost his woman.

"It's me, boss," Mark answered, trying to control his voice and keep his hands from shaking. He knew calling Ice meant that he was signing his death warrant.

"Speak," was the only word that Ice could say. He knew that whatever Mark had to say he really didn't want to hear.

Mark knew there was no easy way to tell Ice what he had to tell him, so he just opened up his mouth and said, "Six-ten is gone."

"You better mean that he's with that bitch out of town somewhere and you can't reach him."

Ice knew what Mark meant, but he was holding on to a small thread that his best man was still alive.

will robbins

"I wish. But he's dead," Mark said on the other line, trembling.

"What the fuck happened?"

"That bitch, Suga Walls, led Six-ten to the pier, and everything was fine. Next thing I knew, I heard her yelling, 'Shoot that ma'fucka.'"

"What the fuck were you doin' that somebody got the drop on my brother?"

"I was on the phone with *you*," Mark said, trying to find a Hail Mary at the end of the quarter.

"You saying it's *my* fault that you weren't on ya' job?" Ice asked, getting more furious by the moment.

"No! I'm just saying—"

"—What else happened and quit the bullshit!" Ice yelled in a deafening tone.

"I ran toward E-Double and that bitch Booga, shootin'. But they got the drop on me. Next thing I know, I hear the cops coming and everybody took off."

"So you left my brother to die by himself on the fuckin' streets?"

"What else was I suppose to do—get booked?"

"You were suppose to make sure that nothing happened to 'ten. Now the ma'fuckas responsible for this shit life ain't worth shit, *and neither is yours!*" Ice threw the phone up against the wall, and it shattered into pieces like his heart. He sat on the bed and for the first time since his parents died he cried. Six-ten saved his life many times in Haiti without thought of his own, and now when his brother needed him the most, he was partying. Now that Six-ten was dead and gone, Ice was determined to turn the heat up on the Eastwick Hustlers.

14

Nigga Done Started Somethin'

Ice sat in his office with his capos, patiently waiting for his new right-hand man Dunois Dubois. Dubois ran things in Canada for Ice. Now that Six-ten was dead and gone, Ice needed Dunois close by as an advisor and personal pit bull. Dubois was a 50-something-year-old mulatto of Haitian descent. He was small in stature, but what he lacked in size and youth, he more than made up for with wisdom and fierceness.

Candy, one of Ice's strippers, escorted Dubois into the office. Dubois was wearing an all-white dashiki and handmade leather sandals. He didn't look his age, with the exception of his thinning hair. His features were mesmerizing. His cobalt blue eyes and light skin seemed to illuminate the whole room. At first and last glance, Dubois didn't seem like much, but those who knew him knew better. Not only was he a swift and tough fighter, he was a voodoo physician and only the great Francois "Papa Doc" Duvalier rivaled his skills.

At first sight of Dubois, Ice's whole demeanor of melancholy changed to elation. He knew the great man would help him straighten out the mess he was in. No one spoke a word as Ice walked around his desk to greet Dubois. Ice embraced him and seemed to tower over the small man. They greeted each other in their native tongue.

Then Ice stood back and took in the radiance of Dubois. He hadn't seen the man in years. He usually always sent word to Dubois by his capos, phone, or through Six-ten. Six-ten traveled to Canada on many occasions with instructions for the man, so much so that Six-ten and Dubois had developed a close relationship. Dubois was in Elizabeth for business, but more importantly, he had a personal vendetta against Six-ten's killers.

"It's so good to see you, Dangerous D," Ice said with a smile, giving the old man the once-over.

Two of Ice's generals looked at one another in confusion as one said, "Dangerous D?" They both snickered a little, making the grave mistake of judging the man by his appearance.

"Likewise, son," Dubois replied in a raspy voice.

"Have a seat," Ice said as he pointed to the leather Italian recliner.

Dubois sat in the seat and crossed his legs as he got comfortable.

"Let me offer you a drink, sir," Ice said, showing the man the respect that should be given to an elder.

"Grey Goose, straight," Dubois said as he looked around at the other men in the room, discerning their spirits. He wanted to make sure that he was in a room full of warriors, rather than bitches and snitches. It wouldn't be too long before the men would show their worth.

Ice walked over and handed Dubois his drink and sat back behind his desk.

"It's unfortunate what happened to our brother Six-ten. A tragedy indeed," Dubois said before he took a sip of his drink.

Ice sighed at the mention of Six-ten's name and said, "True. But not compared to the tragedy that's going to come to the ma'fuckas that did this shit."

"Relax, son," Dubois said as he reached across the desk and put his hand on top of Ice's.

"That's why I'm glad you're here. I always loved your calm demeanor."

"First of all, what are all these men doing here, rather than being out on the streets taking care of the people responsible?"

"I felt it was important for my capos to meet the man that was going to be by my side and instructing them," Ice said, sounding like a little boy looking for his father's approval. For the first time, Ice's men saw him uncomfortable and unsure of himself.

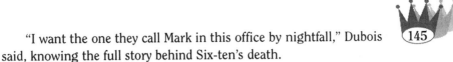

"I want the one they call Mark in this office by nightfall," Dubois said, knowing the full story behind Six-ten's death.

"How the fuck we gonna do that? Them Eastwick Hustler ma'-fuckas keep hittin' our dope houses, robbin' us, shootin' at us. Ice, you been on vacation, and you just got here, ma'fucka!" yelled a defiant Trip, a middle-aged black man with a beard thicker and longer than Freeway's.

Ice stood up and slammed both of his fists into his desk, creating dents. Dubois quickly stood up and waved the big man down. Ice sat down. His chest heaved up and down as he breathed heavily. Dubois laughed eerily to the dismay of everyone in the room. Then he stopped laughing and raised his hand in Trip's direction, who was looking at him with his lazy dark brown eyes. Dubois began to chant in Creole for a few moments as Trip's body went numb in the chair.

The other men were looking on in astonishment and fear as they took in the scene. Dubois seemed to have a euphoric look on his face. He reached out towards Trip's chest, and in one fast motion, he ripped his still-pulsating heart out and held it up high in the air for everyone to see.

"Oh, shit, oh, shit," the other men yelled as they ran and put their backs to the wall. They all covered their mouths with their hands as if they were holding in their lunch for the last six months. They had all heard about voodoo practitioners, but this was their first time witnessing it firsthand. Ice sat back and enjoyed the show. He was no stranger to voodoo or Dubois' methods.

"Bunch of bitches," Ice said as he stood up, clapping and laughing.

"Next man want to show me he don't have no heart, I will rip it out and show you, you have no heart! Now get the fuck out of here," Dubois said as he threw the heart in the men's direction. As the still-beating organ spattered against the wall, the men ran out of the office.

"Yo, did y'all see that shit?" Kareem asked once they were outside of the office. He was down with the Port Au Prince Posse for years. He made it as a capo because he had mad connections outside of the Port Au Prince Posse, connections that Ice needed.

"*Did I see it?* I almost *felt* that shit!" Raymond said touching his heart.

"I heard about Haitians and that fucking voodoo shit, but, damn.

will robbins

Those fuckin' Haitians are crazy with that shit," Donald said.

"Watch ya' fuckin mouth," Annex, a Haitian brother warned. He was shocked at what he saw, too, but he wasn't going to be disrespected.

"I didn't mean any disrespect, Annex, but that shit was crazy," Donald said, trying to redeem himself. Donald, Kareem, and Raymond were all capos, but they were underdogs compared to Annex, especially since they weren't Haitian.

"I don't give a fuck were Mark is at, but he's gonna be in front of Dubois by nightfall, I bet you that shit," Kareem said. They all headed out of the club in hopes of finding Mark.

❦ ❦ ❦ ❦

Black paced up and down the carpet in his apartment, fuming at his brother's decision to kill Six-ten. He would now have to focus all his energy in the streets to assure the Eastwick Hustlers' longevity—not in the drug game, but in the game of life. The streets were the last place he wanted to be. He had other plans in mind, plans that would now be put on hold because of his brother's impetuous actions.

"Yo, you need to calm down before you burn a hole in the rug," E-Double said as he sat on the couch, watching his brother lose his mind.

"Calm down? You hit Ice's dope houses, robbed his peoples, and killed Six-ten! You know what you three ma'fuckas started? Y'all started a *war*!" Black yelled at E-Double, Jab, and Booga.

"The war was started when Ice started cheating us! The war started when he killed Bricks and helped caused the death of Banks! You said we wasn't gonna let that shit slide, but you did! Where the fuck have you been lately, and where is ya' head at, bruh'?" E-Double stood a few feet away as he threw his verbal jabs at Black.

"First of all, we need to calm down. Your brother is right, Black. This war started a long time ago. We just hit back and turned up the heat a little bit. Instead of fighting and arguing with each other, what do you want us to do now?" Booga asked as he stood in between his two longtime boys.

Black walked off and took a seat in a matching recliner opposite the couch. He sat down, rubbed his head, and sighed. E-Double and Booga took their cue and sat back down as well.

"Now what?" Double asked, a little irritated. If it were completely up to him, he would storm the hell out of Ice's club and kill anything that moved.

"We have to lay low and see what Ice is going to do next," Black said, holding his head down.

"You want us to hide like bitches?" Double asked.

"No! I want us to be chess players, not checker players. We have enough men out there to make sure shit is running smoothly. We built this shit, so we wouldn't have to be on the front lines. When Ice hits back, he gunnin' for you, Jab, Booga, Flex, and me. He's not going after our street team. I'm not going to allow us to be easy targets or sitting ducks for Ice. If he wants us, he's going to have to work for it."

"I feel where you're coming from, Black, but how long are we going to hide from Ice and let him pick our boys off to get to us?" Jab asked.

"As long as it takes to come up with a plan to kill Ice without getting locked up or killed ourselves."

"Fuck this punk-ass bullshit! I'm out," Double said as he headed for the front door. Black jumped up from his seat to stop his brother.

"Don't try and stop me, Black," Double said with warning.

"You're still my little brother, and I can still kick ya' ass," Black said. They stood face to face and neither man looked like he was ready to back down. Booga jumped up and stood in between his boys one more time.

"Nobody in here is an enemy. Black, let it go, please."

"Alright. At least tell me where you are going."

"I'll be at Sukanya's, if you want to get at Ice. If you don't, don't holla," Double said, still staring his brother in the eye. He knew he couldn't beat Black, so he was glad that his brother stood down. He opened the door and left his brother standing there, hurt and fuming. Once he cooled down, he would call his brother and straighten things out.

Black closed the door and sat back down, feeling overwhelmed and defeated. He spoke to Booga and Jab with the hopes that they would at least understand his motives.

"I know y'all think that my decision is a punk move but—"

"—It ain't no punk move," Booga cut in.

"I just don't want to lose my best boys to the streets. We didn't sign on this shit to die. We signed on to make money and live. Now we play a cat and mouse game with Ice and everybody playing for keeps." Black seemed like he was on the verge of tears from frustration.

"It's like you said, we got soldiers on the front lines so we don't have to be. We were on the front lines since we were twelve. Now we nineteen. We have money, power, and respect. Let them other ma'-fuckas prove them worthy of us. You didn't make a punk decision; you made a wise decision."

Booga's words healed Black a little. He would have felt a lot better if the words had come from his own brother.

"Call Flex and have him wrap shit up in Newark. Leave Jab with instructions here in Elizabeth, call Naim in Jersey City and let him know what's up. And last but not least, call Noah in Asbury Park. I want everyone to meet at the spot."

"Banks' adopted grandmother's house? I thought—"

Black jumped in and said, "I pay her taxes and help take care of her in place of Banks. I told her the basement had sentimental value and I would still like to use it from time to time. So it's cool. Have them meet us there in a few hours so we can get shit straight," Black concluded.

"What about Double?" Booga inquired.

"He'll be with that chick Sukanya. After he gets his dick sucked a few times, he'll calm down and call. And when he does, I'll have him meet us at the spot today or tomorrow. Whichever one comes first."

"Alright. I'll get on them calls right now," Booga said as Black left him standing in the front room.

♦ ♦ ♦ ♦

Annex, Donald, Kareem, and Raymond drove down E. Elizabeth Avenue in Linden in search of Mark. They knew he was involved with a woman that lived on Chancellor Avenue, a woman that he thought no one knew about.

They took a right on Chancellor, headed down the block, and turned the music down in the Black Yukon to avoid attention. Soon, they pulled in front of a brick house that had a Southern-style appeal to it. The neighborhood was quiet, and the clock was ticking on the men to catch up with Mark.

They exited the vehicle as quietly as possible. The porch light was on and the bright lights of the house shined through the curtains and blinds, giving the appearance that someone was home.

"Donald and Raymond, y'all hit the back, just in case," Annex said. The two men ran around the back of the house as they were told. Annex and Kareem stepped onto the porch with their firearms at their sides, just in case Mark answered the door with larceny in his heart. Cautiously, Annex opened the screen door and knocked a few times.

A light-skinned woman with dark blemishes and matted hair answered the door. Everyone slept with an ugly woman once or twice, but she took the cake. She was a "butta head" girl. Everything looked good but her head. Then she flashed a smile, revealing yellow, decaying teeth. Probably if she drank water, she could easily turn it into lemonade. Annex wished that he had taken the back once he saw this woman. Now he realized why Mark kept this one hidden.

"Hello," the mysterious, ugly woman said as she looked Annex up and down like he was a Hershey Kiss.

"We looking for Mark," Annex said as he tried not to laugh in her face.

Kareem wasn't any help as he stood off to the side, laughing his ass off. The comic view came to a short end as Annex's and Mark's eyes connected when Mark walked out of the bathroom, fixing his pants. Before Miss Ugly could reply, Annex pushed her aside and bum rushed through her door with Kareem hot on his tail.

Mark rushed to the back door just as Annex thought he would. Mark would have pulled his gun, but he left it on the coffee table in the front room. Annex and Kareem would have ended the chase early with a bullet in Mark's back, but Dubois wanted him alive. But the way Dubois handled things, Mark would have been better off with a bullet in his back.

Mark crashed through the back door and was greeted with a blow to his forehead that knocked him down, stopping his forward motion. Donald and Raymond stood over him, laughing.

Adrenaline, fear, and anger fueled Mark's every emotion. He leaned forward and with all his might, punched Donald in his balls. Donald was hit with so much force that he hit the ground and threw up. Annex and Kareem once again thought that it was a comic sight while Raymond jumped out of the way to make sure that he wasn't next. Finally, Mark stood up and blood was slowly leaking from his forehead.

"Listen, man ... it ain't my fault what happened to Six-ten. I, I

will robbins

tried to save him. Come on, man, y'all know me!" Mark yelled, looking at his fellow capos. They all hung out together and did much dirt together. He was appealing to their friendship. But once again, no one wanted to put their life on the line. They all knew the consequences of the game, and sympathy wasn't part of it. Survival of the fittest.

Donald finally got his bearings together and walked over to Mark. With one fast motion, he threw a punch and knocked Mark on his ass. Then Donald stood over him and said, "Punk-ass bitch, explain that shit to Ice—if he let you live long enough to tell it."

Mark's stash screamed at the mention of her man being killed. She ran to the front room to retrieve Mark's gun, but the men didn't pay her any mind.

Annex pulled Mark to his feet and said, "You shouldn't have fucked up."

"You ma'fuckas," Miss Ugly yelled as she pulled the trigger. The bullet zipped through the air like it was cotton and exploded in Kareem's chest, knocking him into some trash cans. Using the distraction, Mark punched Donald, knocking him halfway unconscious as he headed out the gate. Before Miss Ugly could get off another round, Annex pulled his piece and fired. He made it so everyone could see her thoughts. Then he helped Donald up and ran out the gate in search of Mark while Donald stumbled behind.

To Annex and Donald's relief, Raymond already had Mark in the backseat of the Yukon, holding him at bay with his Beretta. Annex was sure that someone had called the cops with all the yelling, noise, and gunshots, so he jumped in the driver's seat and sped off.

♥ ♥ ♥ ♥

Black, Jab, Booga, Flex, Na'im, and Noah sat at the round table in their spot in Plainfield. Black was extremely quiet for the occasion. Jab, Booga, Flex, and Na'im passed around a blunt and a bottle of Henny, waiting for Black to speak. They knew they were there to talk business, but they wanted their minds to coast before they got into some serious talk.

"Yo, Black. Did you hear from Double yet?" Booga asked.

"Not yet, but if I don't hear from him by tomorrow, I'ma stop by the girl's house."

"So what else do you want us to do, Black?" Na'im asked. Na'im was tall and chocolate-colored with dreads and a goatee. He was twen-

150

ty-three, and he was that nigga in Jersey City. Black and the Eastwick Hustlers stepped to him with an offer he couldn't refuse, mob style. Rather than lose his life and business, Na'im decided to coexist with Black.

"I just want us to be clear and on one accord before we step to Ice again. I know he's going to hit us, so I don't want us out on front street. He's not going to come out for us himself. He's going to send his soldiers to do his dirty work, and we're going to do the same. The more soldiers he loses, the more it'll force him to do the work himself, and when he does, that's when we'll come out in full force," Black concluded.

The men fell silent after Black's explanation, taking in all he said. Actually, they were fighting through the weed and Henny to comprehend everything they heard. Finally, after a few minutes went by, Noah said, "That sounds like a plan."

Black and E-Double met Noah a few summers back at a basketball function in Asbury Park. Woo's boys, Man, and Calvin, played on the ball team for Elizabeth, and Noah's boys were representing Asbury Park. During the game, Black started to talk shit about who would win the game, and one of Noah's boys got in over his head and bet Black $100,000.

At the time, Black was only seventeen, and the large amount attracted Noah. He wanted to know how a seventeen-year-old kid could come up with that type of money. Noah was a Puerto Rican brother, and he was the man standing next to the man that ran shit in Asbury Park. Noah was looking for other connections to break off all ties with his boss, and Black presented him with the opportunity that he needed. They kept their business transactions a secret until it was time for Noah to take out his boss.

He was in a situation similar to what Black found himself in with Ice. Even though Noah had boss status, he was nothing compared to Ice and his entourage, even with the rest of the Eastwick Hustlers and the brothers from Newark and Jersey City.

"Once I hear from E, we all going somewhere to relax and get our heads together," Black said with a sigh.

"Bobby is always talking about the ATL. Why don't we go down there?" Booga asked.

"Speaking of Bobby, where that nigga been?" Flex asked.

will robbins

"I seen him on Third and Bond a few times, but that's about it," Jab said.

"Who that nigga report to?" Noah asked.

"He reports to me, but he said he was going back home to the ATL. He'll be back soon, but I might as well tell him to stay there until we get there now," Black said.

"That's cool with me," Jab said, almost choking on smoke.

Black pulled out his cell phone and tried to call his brother.

"Damn, no answer," Black said, frustrated. He turned on the wall-mounted TV and let BET consume his mind.

♥ ♥ ♥ ♥

Ice and Dubois sat in the office, reminiscing on their times in Haiti and how the drug game brought them power and respect beyond their wildest dreams.

Although it was rare for mulattos to get along with fellow Haitians in Haiti, Ice and Dubois seemed to make it work. Dubois turned the conversation back to business as he asked, "How do you want to handle the boy, E-Double?"

"I'll tell you right now," Ice said as he pushed the speakerphone button and dialed Sukanya.

Sukanya lay in her bed with her arms wrapped around Double like she was holding on for dear life. Both of them were asleep after a long afternoon and night of freaky fucking.

"Ring, ring, ring," Sukanya's phone was blaring.

Lucky for her, Double was a sound sleeper. That's one of the reasons he didn't answer his cell phone when Black dialed.

"Hello," she said as she picked up the phone.

"It's Ice, baby."

"Who?" she asked, struggling to hear Ice through the speakerphone.

Ice picked up the phone and repeated himself. Sukanya sat up in her bed with her eyes planted on Double to make sure he didn't wake up. She spoke in a whispered tone.

"What is it, Ice? And why are you calling so late?" she asked.

"Make sure that boy E-Double is at your spot tomorrow. I'm sending some people by there to take care of business."

"He's here right now."

"Make sure he stays there. It's on at 12 o'clock!" Ice hung up the phone.

Sukanya cared about Double, but she was a hood bitch. Money always took precedence over anything for a hood bitch, and she represented to the fullest.

"What's the plan?" Dubois asked, once Ice hung up the phone.

"I'm sending the 'Dirty Birds' to take care of E-Double."

"Who are they, and are they reliable?"

"They are paternal twins, and they are very reliable and dangerous. They're called the 'Dirty Birds' because they would kill their own kids for a price. They are my personal assassins, and they never miss," Ice explained to Dubois' delight.

"If they are reliable like the clowns we sent out to get Mark, than we are in big trouble, son," Dubois said, standing up, finally taking the time to admire his surroundings.

"Well, in the beginning they were hungry. Now they have gotten lazy and think the street is sweet. We held it down for years with no opposition. The Eastwick Hustlers are a strong network, and now I know they are not to be underestimated. Our men are savages, and I promise, they will be back on point," Ice explained like he was the man standing next to the man.

"I hope so."

Ice's door burst open violently, causing him to jump as Mark stumbled into the room. Dubois kept his composure and simply turned around to see Mark hit the floor.

"Sorry about that, Ice, but this ma'fucka was fightin' all the way here. We didn't want to shoot him 'cause I know you wanted him alive," Annex said, out of breath. Then he and Donald threw Mark into a chair, Ice tossed some duct tape to his men, and they tied Mark up. Mark still struggled to get loose, but his efforts were futile.

"Stop struggling, little bitch," Dubois said, poised.

"Where is Kareem?" Ice asked, noticing he was one soldier short.

"Mark's ugly-ass bitch shot him when we were dealing with his ass. We didn't even see her ass coming," Raymond said, hoping that they wouldn't suffer the same fate as Mark. They would have if Ice cared about Kareem the way he cared about Six-ten.

"I hope she didn't live to tell the story," Dubois said.

"We left the bitch thoughtless," Annex said, trying to hold his attitude towards Dubois. He didn't like Dubois, and he didn't respect his

will robbins

presence. He didn't realize all the work Dubois put into building the Port Au Prince Posse with Ice. And he could care less that Dubois was a voodoo priest. To Annex, all that voodoo shit could be stopped with a bullet. And if Dubois pushed him, they would both find out.

Ice stepped toward Mark, trying to cool the fury that burned inside him as he looked at his former capo.

"Well, well, well, the chicken has come home to roost."

"Come on, Ice, that shit wasn't my fault. That bitch set us up. I told him not to fuck with her," Mark replied, squirming in his seat, close to tears.

"That bitch and everyone else involved is going to get it, but you first," Ice said, pulling his weapon from his shoulder holster and raising it to Mark's head.

"Wait," Dubois said just before Ice pulled the trigger.

"*What?*" Ice yelled, unable to hold his temper any longer.

"That's the easy way for this bitch. Make him suffer just like you're suffering. Make him wish that you *had* pulled that trigger," Dubois said, instructing Ice.

Ice put his weapon back into the holster and watched as Dubois raised his hand toward Mark and chanted something in Creole. Mark squirmed and yelled in his seat as Dubois chanted. A few seconds passed, and then Mark's eyes busted right out of his eye sockets. Once again, Ice's men were shocked and almost lost their stomachs. Mark screamed in agony and kicked vigorously from the pain.

"Oh, shit, what the fuck was that?" Raymond asked in disbelief of what he just witnessed.

"Pain and power," Dubois answered nonchalantly.

As Mark sat in the chair writhing in pain, blood pouring down his face, Annex had some sympathy for his boy and said, "Ice ... just let me shoot him. You made your point."

Ice looked at Dubois for confirmation. Dubois seemed unmoved and pleased at the young man's agony. He simply smiled and once again raised his hand and chanted. Annex saw the pleasure on Dubois' face and wanted to shoot him to end his pleasure and end Mark's misery. Mark wished he would pass out from the pain, but he wasn't that lucky. His body seemed to burn from the inside out every second that Dubois chanted.

Sick, Annex left the room. He didn't want to see the unnecessary torture that Mark was going through. Raymond and Donald wanted to leave as well, but they also wanted to see what other supernatural shit Dubois could perform.

As Mark twisted and turned in the chair, Dubois said his last words and Mark's body spontaneously combusted into flames. The men in the room watched as Mark's flesh turned charcoal black. Dubois and Ice enjoyed the nauseating smell of Mark's roasting flesh. Raymond and Donald couldn't take the hideous sight or revolting smell any longer, so they fled from the room.

Annex sat at the bar downstairs, away from the action. No one deserved to die like that was all Annex could think about as he drank straight shots of Captain Morgan. Raymond and Donald ran down the stairs as if the whole room were on fire. In their rush, they almost fell down the stairs like a white chick in a horror movie. They grabbed a seat next to Annex very agitated about what they saw. They didn't have any remorse or sympathy like Annex. What they saw was too fascinating for them to have any thoughts of guilt.

Donald grabbed the bottle of Captain Morgan and poured himself a shot. He said, "Yo, Annex, you should have seen that shit upstairs, boy!"

"Hell, yeah, that shit was crazy, bruh'," Raymond said, seizing the bottle.

Annex sucked his teeth and looked at his boys with disgust before he replied, "I didn't see shit, because I didn't want to see shit. Don't you two ma'fuckas realize that that could have been any one of us? As soon as we fuck up or get out of pocket, that ma'fucka Dubois gonna do some freaky shit to us too."

Angry, he threw the bottle of Captain Morgan against the wall and stalked out of the club. But Donald and Raymond just laughed and kept talking about the voodoo shit they had witnessed.

"E-Double is next," Ice said as he looked over at Mark's blackened bones and ashes on the floor.

"That bitch Suga Walls is up for it, too," Dubois said with a diabolical look on his face. Both men seemed to be possessed with vengeance and death.

Ice and Dubois were going to take out the Eastwick Hustlers domino style, one by one, or so they thought.

❧ ❧ ❧ ❧

Twelve o' clock was coming faster than a man getting his dick sucked by a prostitute, and E-Double was trying to get away from Sukanya's clutches. Double was putting on his clothes as Sukanya tried to lure him back into bed. She continued to pull at his belt, making it hard for him to leave.

The "Dirty Birds" pulled in front of her home on Catherine Street. Chris and Christine were paternal twins, and they were efficient killers. Christine stepped out of the sky blue Ford Explorer armed with a sawed-off shotgun. She was wearing white leather Gucci pants and a blue halter top with knee-high Gucci boots. Her hair was in short spikes that complemented her slender face. Even though her body was sizzling, no man had ever tasted her goods. She was a beautiful, feminine lesbian. Her sexiness was only matched by her skill as an assassin.

Chris looked liked the Grim Reaper, dressed in all-black attire and black shades. He was just as slender as his sister, but he had a muscular build and sported a baldy. They stood side by side as they approached the house.

"Take the back, Chris," Christine said, taking charge of the situation. Chris took the back like he was told. Christine rang the doorbell in hopes that Double would open the door. She raised her shotgun as she waited for the door to open. The door slowly opened as Christine slowly squeezed the trigger. Once Sukanya appeared, Christine lowered her death weapon and her panties became wet. Sukanya answered the door in her thong and matching top. Christine saw Sukanya dance plenty of times and hit on her even more, but Sukanya let her know that she was strictly dickly.

Chris tried to open the back door, but it was locked. He started to blow the lock but decided it would be a bad idea to warn Double, especially if his sister wasn't in the house yet.

"Damn, it's a beautiful day in the neighborhood," Christine said as she looked Sukanya up and down. Sukanya had many men and women look at her like that, but she had never before felt degraded in her own home. Now she wished that she would've gotten dressed before answering the door.

"He's upstairs, first room to the left," Sukanya said, trying to ignore her admirer's lustful stares.

"Alright," was all that Christine replied as she continued to stare with hungry eyes at the nearly naked body before her as she headed up the stairs. Before the gunplay, started Sukanya got dressed in her front room and headed out of the house before the drama unfolded. She figured she'd hear what happened later on.

E-Double sat on the bed hunched over, putting on his "trees." He finally called Black to pick him up from Sukanya's house. Even though he was mad at Black, he still respected the rule of never traveling alone, at least this time anyway.

The door slowly creaked open and Double said, "I told you I have to go already, bitch." Then he turned around to look at Sukanya, who he thought was behind him. He was surprised to see another woman standing in the doorway pointing a sawed-off shotgun in his direction. As she pulled the trigger, Double dived to the floor. The pellets ripped through the bed, missing him by a second.

Without looking, Double lay on the floor, raised his gun over the bed, and shot desperately in Christine's direction. She quickly backed out of the room before she could get hit. Double was happy to see that Sukanya's bed had wheels. He kicked the bed towards the door, causing a distraction as he ran towards the adjoining bathroom.

Christine tried to get a shot off at Double before he could make it into the bathroom, but he got a blind shot off first that made her change her mind.

Double panicked as he stood in the small bathroom. He knew it would only be a few seconds before Christine would shoot the bathroom up with her shotgun.

"Come on out and make this shit easy, nigga," Christine said as she blew off a round into the bathroom. Double would have been hit if he weren't taking cover in the bathtub.

Getting brave, Double yelled, "Fuck you, bitch." He shot a few rounds off as well, and he was lucky enough to hit his victim in the shoulder.

"Aagh ... shit!" she screamed as she felt the heat of the bullet burn right through her shoulder. She would have fired back, but she dropped the shotgun when she fell from the force of the bullet.

Double looked at the open window and saw his second chance to get away. He knew the window wasn't too far from the ground, and he decided to take his chances. He lifted his left leg out the window, ducked his head as he put both hands on the ledge, lifted his right leg

will robbins

out, and started to hang with both hands from the window. He took a deep breath and let his grip go.

He landed on his feet and looked up to see Christine pointing her shotgun at him again. Once again, she shot at him, but he was too quick as he took off running. Double ran around the house and bumped right into Chris.

Black and Jab pulled up in front of the house in time to see the gunplay. They rushed to get to the side of the house, but they were too late.

The last thing Double saw was the flash of a gun as he was hit twice. The first bullet burned fire in his six-pack stomach. He tried to raise his gun to take Chris with him, but it was too late as the second shot made it to his heart, immediately stopping all his motion.

"Noooo," Black yelled as he saw his brother falling to the ground. The sound alerted Chris, who turned around just in time to catch a full clip of Black's nine.

Raging death was in Christine's eyes as she saw her brother get gunned down right in front of her. She took aim carelessly in Black's direction, abandoning all her skills. She was so hurt and unfocused that she didn't even realize that Jab had her in his sights. Before she could get a shot off, Jab loaded her up with some hot shit. Then he and Black ran over to see E-Double's status.

Black knelt down and lifted his brother's head and body and pulled him close to his chest. Black was wailing so profusely that he didn't hear the police sirens in the background or Jab warning him.

"Black! Black! Black!" Jab continued to yell. Black looked up without saying a word. "The cops are coming. He's dead. We can't do anything for him, and we damn sure can't do anything from jail. Let ya' mother claim the body and let's get the fuck out of here," Jab said with tears in his eyes and sympathy in his voice.

Black knew that Jab was right even though he didn't want to accept it. He lightly let E-Double's body go and kissed him on the cheek as his warm, salty tears dropped onto Double's face. Quickly, the two men escaped the no small carnage that they left behind.

15

DA' FUNERAL

S mith's Funeral Home was packed like a club on ladies' night. Once again, everyone showed up to pay his or her last respects for a young ghetto superstar. Unfortunately for the black community, Smith's Funeral Home was putting out too many ghetto superstars for the summer. Like most funerals, a lot of the mourners wore T-shirts of the fallen soldier in memory. People were milling around crying, smoking, and consoling one another. The funeral parlor was too packed to accommodate the many people that showed up. Besides having a big family, E-Double and Black seemed to have an even bigger entourage.

Although Woo saw Double dead at the hospital, he couldn't bring himself to step inside the funeral home. As long as he stood outside, he could pretend that it was someone else. The reality of his cousin being dead was too much for him to handle. Taye, Man, Calvin, and Damien stood with their boy outside, waiting for him to make the decision to go inside. They knew there was nothing that they could say or do to alleviate Woo's pain. They did know that if the topic of revenge came up, they would be right there.

"I'm going in," Woo finally said with bloodshot eyes and a clogged nose. His legs seemed to shake as he climbed the steps. The closer Woo got to the top of the steps, the more he heard wailing and screaming inside. The more that he tried to fight his tears, the more they seemed to fall. Woo walked in, and the first thing he saw was his aunt leaned over in the casket, holding onto her son, screaming.

"Aaagh, they took my baby! Why did they have to take my baby?"

Black stood over his mother and attempted to pry her away from the golden casket with red velvet lining to no avail. She was like a woman possessed. Jab and Flex walked over to assist Black with his mother. They were able to sit her in the front pew just in time for Woo to get a clear view of his cousin's lifeless body.

Woo stood in front of the casket staring down at Double. Just like everyone else, he couldn't help but to think that Double was in a peaceful sleep. He leaned in and kissed Double on his forehead. It felt like he had just kissed a block of ice. He stepped off and hugged and kissed his aunt and took a seat next to his sister.

Black was sitting down, refusing to cry. He thought that Double would be looking down on him, thinking that his fearless brother was a punk for crying. He cracked a smile as he thought about what his brother would say, "What ya' bitch ass crying for?"

A tall, slender, redbone man wearing a sleek black suit walked up and stood in front of the casket. As he viewed the body, most of the people in the room fell silent. Black squinted his eyes a little to focus on the individual before him. As memories flashed through Black, he looked and thought, *I know that's NOT my father.* He hadn't seen or heard from his father in years.

All doubt was removed when Sandra jumped from her seat and asked sternly, "All these years and *now* you show up? Where were you when we needed you? You sorry ma'fucka! My baby would still be here if it wasn't for you!" Sandra yelled as she beat on Black's father's chest. Tyson walked over and pulled his sister into his arms. She turned around and embraced him.

"Maybe you should leave, Nate," Tyson said as he gripped his sister.

"Nice to see you, too, Tyson," Nate responded. Then Nate walked over and looked his son in the eye.

"I'm sorry, son. I should have been there for you all."

Black just looked at his father with stone-cold eyes. Nate reached into his pocket and pulled out a business card and passed it to Black. "Call me. I'll be in town for a few days." Black took the card and ripped it in half. It hit the floor right in front of his father. Nate received the message well and headed for the door.

Just when everyone thought that the drama was over, Ice and Dubois walked in, looking like *Men in Black*. Most of the people looked and held their breath. Black and his family couldn't believe their eyes. Black turned around and was infuriated by the sight. *How dare this ma'fucka have the audacity to show up?* was all that ran through his mind. He started to approach the unwanted guests, but his mother quickly pulled him back down by his arm.

Although Sandra was angry as well, she knew her son wouldn't get away with disrespecting Ice in public, or anywhere else for that matter. She wanted to get at him as well, but Ice wouldn't have been as cool as Nate and just walk away. Everyone took their cue from Sandra and Black and calmed down. No one made a move, to the disappointment of Dubois and Ice.

The service commenced without further delay or drama. Everyone said their last good-bye to the hood prince and headed outside. Black continued to stay after everyone stepped out. He wanted to spend a few more minutes alone with his brother. As he knelt down and looked upon his brother, his vision became blurry and he couldn't fight the tears anymore.

"What the fuck am I going to do without you, lil' nigga? What am I suppose to do now?" Black continued to ask between sobs. "I know one thing. Wherever you are, you gonna have company real soon. I promise you that." As Black continued to speak, he was notified that he only had a few more seconds before he must move on. Black, Woo, Jab, Booga, Noah, and Flex were hauling out their slain warrior, trying to remain strong. They placed the body in the hearse and closed the door.

❦ ❦ ❦ ❦

The funeral presented the perfect opportunity for Agent Simms, Sgt. Cruz, and his men to hit up the Eastwick Hustlers' cribs. Sgt. Cruz pulled up in the black Chevy van, and Simms and the rest of the Hit Squad jumped out, ready to handle business. The men ran through the courts of Bayway like storm troopers dressed in all-black bearing their guns. The courts were empty like a cemetery at nighttime, just like the men hoped. There would be no witnesses to their unlawful entry, and the break-in would look legit.

They ran to Building 39 and made their way up to the third floor in record time. Det. Mendes stepped up to the plate when it came time to jimmy the lock. That was one of his specialties when he was a gang member/hustler.

"Just a few more seconds," Mendes said, trying to ease the men's impatience. The lock snapped, and all the men let out a sigh of relief. They slowly walked in with their guns pointed, walking on the side of caution. They knew that occasionally some members of the family would stay home, even at funerals. Sometimes it was easier to deny death than face the reality of it. The men were once again lucky, because they found the apartment empty.

"Ace, you get the kitchen. Julio and Antonio, get the front area. Simms and I will get the bedrooms," Cruz barked. Ace went to work on the kitchen like a sick heroin addict desperately searching for a needle full of paradise. He emptied the cabinets and all the contents on the floor as well as everything in the refrigerator. He made the kitchen look like a dirty cereal factory once he was through.

Julio and Antonio tossed the front room like a couple of Tasmanian devils. They cut into all the furniture like sushi and broke the large TV for effect. Anything that looked like it could contain audio or videocassettes was broken with malice.

Meanwhile, Agent Simms—a.k.a. Bobby—was in Black and Double's room, tearing it a new asshole. He knocked all their posters and artwork on the floor looking for hidden safes. He cut and flipped their beds and also broke the TV. He spared nothing. Had he had a drill, he would have checked the floors.

Cruz checked Sandra's room but only won the constellation prize of finding minimum amounts of drugs and paraphernalia. These things were untouchable since the search was illegal. All the men gathered in the front room angrier than a fag that found out the gay parade was cancelled.

"What the fuck am I going to do now?" Agent Simms demanded.

"Right now, we are all going to get out of here and try another angle later," Cruz said calmly. They all understood Simms' plight. He was undercover way too long and was almost at his breaking point. If something didn't give in the case soon, he was going to fully lose it. The men took their cue and exited just as swiftly as they arrived.

♥ ♥ ♥ ♥

Black had rented out Club Cache on Third Street to accommodate the many guests that would gather after the burial of E-Double. There were so many people that they must have broken the fire code several times over. But money always went a long way, and Black was pulling out all the stops. The top caterers in town catered the food, and the DJ was none other than the legendary Kid Capri. The entire guests had to wear all-white for the occasion. It was more like a party than a sad gathering, and that's the way Black wanted it. He was pretty sure that would have been the way his brother would have wanted it.

Although the music was bumping, the mood in the room was solemn. Black walked up to the bar and for the first time in his life he took a drink. His chest burned from the first shot of scotch. He wanted to be in a place and time where the death of his brother didn't exist, and he knew that the alcohol would help him achieve his goal.

As he ordered another shot, he felt a light touch on his shoulder and a cool whisper in his ear as Kasha said, "I'm really sorry for your loss, Black." He turned around to see whom the voice belonged to and was pleasantly surprised. Kasha displayed a figure to envy as she was dressed in an all-white, skin-tight, sexy, classy gown.

"Kasha, you look … *damn*, you look—"

"—good," Kasha cut in as she saw Black was at a loss for words.

"Yeah, you look good. Damn good." That was one of the first times that Black had looked at her in that way, and she couldn't help but wonder if it was the alcohol talking. She knew that he didn't drink, so she realized that he was looking for a way to soothe his pain. She knew it was wrong to take advantage of him in this state of mind, but he was too beautiful of a man to let go.

"I saw your mom over at the table. She looked like she was about to leave with your uncle," Kasha informed him.

"Alright, don't go nowhere. I'll be right back."

Black walked over to his mother's table as Tyson was helping her stand.

"Ma, are you getting ready to leave?" Black asked.

"You put something together real nice, son, but I need to be alone. I know your brother is looking down and is real proud of what you put together for him." She walked up and embraced her son so tightly that she squeezed the wind right out of him. He didn't mind though. He just wished that he could have squeezed his brother before he died the same way that she was squeezing him.

Woo looked at the embrace and decided that he didn't want it to end. He walked up to the DJ booth and said, "Yo, Kid Capri, could you play Al Green's 'Let's Stay Together,' please."

DJ Kid Capri obliged and as the beat was cued up, Black looked at his mother and said, "You can't leave now, Mama. You got to dance off this." Black had a huge smile on his face and for the first time in days, Sandra was smiling ear to ear. She couldn't resist her son's smile, and they both stepped to the dance floor.

Woo smiled ear to ear as well, knowing that his plan had worked. He gave Kid Capri a pound of acceptance. DJ Kid Capri handed Woo the mike, and he said loudly, "A'ight, y'all, we got a party now!" Everyone followed suit of Black and Sandra and joined them on the dance floor.

Kid Capri kept playing hit after hit as Sandra and Black continued to dance off of every song, forgetting the day's events momentarily. Kid Capri switched up the tempo and played Mad Cobra's "Flex." Kasha arrived just in time to ask, "May I take it from here, Miss Sandra?"

"Go ahead, baby, I damn sure wasn't gonna grind on him. You won't catch me on *Jerry Springer*," Sandra replied jokingly as she kissed her son on the cheek.

"I love you too, Ma," Black replied as they both laughed.

"Your uncle is going to take me home. I'll see you later," Sandra said as she disappeared into the many horny guests that were grinding on one another.

Black and Kasha blended in with the crowd as she turned around and pressed her healthy ass against his manhood. Black's hands roamed her body as their thighs moved rhythmically together. She felt Black rise, and she was just as turned on as he was. When she turned her head around, her eyes met with Black's. Their eyes held a hunger in them that only they could understand. The months of anticipation of fucking Black had her insides on fire. Black was never with a woman, and the only person who knew this info was his brother. They shared many secrets, and this was one thing that Black was going to miss.

Kasha reached in with her full, succulent lips and boldly kissed Black on his soft lips. As their tongues intertwined, the music seemed to stop and the people disappeared. Time stood still. Black had kissed many women before, but Kasha sent shock waves through his body. She seemed to melt in his arms, and his kiss gave her an itch between her thighs that only he could scratch.

"*Damn*, girl ... if I knew it was like that, we would have done that a long time ago," Black said, feeling dizzy from the alcohol and the intoxicating kiss.

"Back at you, baby."

"Let me get Flex and Woo so they can drop us off at my crib," Black said.

Woo was still getting his grind on with Anasia when Black tapped him on the shoulder. "Yo, I need you and Flex to drop me and Kasha off at my spot. I'll meet y'all outside."

Woo put his hand on Black's shoulder to pull him near as he whispered in his ear, "You finally gonna get you some with ya' bitch ass."

Black just looked at Woo with a small smile of denial. "Don't think Double was the only one who knew ya' little secret, baby."

"Fuck you, nigga. Just meet me outside, bitch," Black replied with a smile.

Black and Kasha waited outside patiently for Woo and Flex as they enjoyed the nighttime summer breeze.

"What's up, Black?" a few brothers responded as they walked by.

"I'm a'ight, baby."

"Stay up, baby. Fuck Ice."

Shortly, Flex and Woo appeared, and Black tossed Woo the keys to the Escalade.

The ride to Bayway was short and sweet as Woo pulled up in front of the building.

"Pick me up sometime tomorrow," Black told Woo as he exited the vehicle. Black was a real gentleman as he helped Kasha out of the SUV.

He grabbed her hand ever so slightly as they walked through the court like royalty. Black put the key in the door and entered the apartment with his new friend. The apartment was pitch-black, and Black thought that that was strange. He pulled his piece out and said, "Wait outside for a second, Kasha." He was more than cautious now, and he had good reason to be after the death of his brother.

He turned on the lights, and to his surprise, he saw his mother sitting on the couch, crying, and the apartment looked like Hiroshima.

"Ma, what happened? Did you do this?"

Before she could answer, Kasha walked in and said, "Oh my god, what happened?" She was surprised to see the rubble that was left after the Hit Squad was through.

"I don't know who did this, baby. Your uncle dropped me off, and this was the way I found the place."

"Damn," was all that Black could say as he further looked at the apartment.

"First my baby, now this shit," Sandra said.

Kasha walked up and hugged Sandra. The sight of her embracing his mother gave him a feeling of comfort. He was happy that he had chosen to deal with her after all the time of swearing her off.

"Don't worry, Ma. Tomorrow we'll be looking for a new place. It's about time that we get out of here anyway," Black said to his mother's delight.

❦ ❦ ❦ ❦

Once again, Ice was in his mansion having dinner with Mayor Cross, the chief of police, and Officer Swank. With all the violence that was going down in the city, they needed to iron out some serious details.

"I realize your position, Mayor, and the city's outcry to stop this violence, but you must understand our position as well," Dubois said.

"And what exactly *is* your position, Mr. Dubois?" the mayor asked.

"In a lucrative business such as ours, there is always some competition. And to make sure that our business continues to be lucrative, we must gain respect as well as eliminate any competition. Now we have been disrespected, and the competition continues to grow so, naturally, more violence *will* occur," Dubois explained.

"That's unacceptable!" the chief yelled.

"Calm down in my home," Ice said politely.

The chief really hated seeing his city go to waste right in front of his eyes. But to go against Ice would be career suicide, to say the least.

"The elections are going to be coming up, whether you realize it or not, and with all the violence you are creating, that doesn't give me a leg to stand on, Mr. Ice," Mayor Cross explained.

"So what does that have to do with me?" Ice asked.

Officer Swank was happy to answer his question. This gave him the opportunity to bust his bubble, especially since he thought all black people were niggers.

"Well, sir," Swank said sarcastically, "if the mayor doesn't get reelected based on the violence in the city, than the next mayor could choose a new chief of police and clean up the city of all the violence. That would make business very hard for you and the Port Au Prince Posse. Not only that, you wouldn't have too much to hold over our heads either," Swank explained smugly.

"So I guess that it would be in the best interest of business to calm the violence down then, huh?" Ice asked.

"If you want to continue your sweet ride and have police protection, it would be wise to make sure that I'm reelected as mayor. And that will *not* happen if this violence continues," Mayor Cross said.

"It is wise to stop the violence for awhile. But before we do, we must handle one more person and then we will stop all violence until after the elections," Dubois said.

"I don't mind compromising. Take care of your business and make sure the streets are safe until after the elections," the mayor instructed.

"So we reached an agreement?" Dubois asked.

"We sure have," the chief answered.

"Now that *that* is settled, let's enjoy this meal," Ice said.

The table was filled with curry goat, black rice, fish, salad, and bread. It was food fit for a king. Although Swank hated black people, he sure enjoyed the food and women that the culture had to offer. He ate until he felt like he was going to bust.

❦ ❦ ❦ ❦

Black lay in bed only covered by his boxers with Kasha right by his side. She was covered with Black's Chicago Bulls jersey. It was one of the things that the two of them had in common, a love for the Chicago Bulls.

"What are you thinking about?" Kasha asked as she rubbed on Black's chest.

"Life."

"What about it?" she asked, confused.

"The way we abuse it and take it for granted, and how our actions affect others," Black explained.

will robbins

"How do you mean?"

"Someone hooked my mother on drugs to get what they wanted while they were taking from us. So me and Double, in turn, hooked other mothers on drugs to get what we wanted. Me and Double were so into hustling that we rarely spent time with our mother or other family members, and now Double is gone. We had an argument before he died. We almost had a fight, and we never patched it up. Now he's gone, and I didn't tell him good-bye. And if it wasn't for my mother abusing her life, Double might still be here," Black said with tears falling silently down his cheek.

Water welled up in Kasha's eyes as she listened to him. She took her soft hand and wiped the tears from his cheek. Then she pulled his face closer to hers and once again tasted his lips. Black was a little stiff in motion for a man about to get some so Kasha asked, "Is everything alright?"

Black sat up in bed and for a few moments he was silent. Kasha sat up as well and just stared at him, not comprehending.

"If I tell you something, you have to promise you won't laugh," Black said seriously.

Kasha looked at him strangely and said, "I promise."

Black was still hesitant and shy about telling his secret to her. Kasha rubbed his back and said, "You can tell me, baby. I promise I won't laugh or tell anyone."

"You swear?" Black asked, still reluctant to tell his secret.

"I swear, baby. What is it?"

Black looked away and whispered, "I'm a virgin."

"What?"

"I'm a virgin," Black continued to whisper.

"*What?*" Kasha asked again, still struggling to hear what he had said.

"I've never been with a woman before," Black said looking Kasha right in the eye.

She was taken aback momentarily at the revelation that she was in bed with a virgin. She had seen Black with many women and assumed that he had slept with at least half of them. She just continued to look at him in disbelief until she heard, "You don't believe me?"

"I do believe you. I'm just shocked. I thought that you, Double, and the rest of your boys had the ladies open."

"I didn't want to fuck with just anybody."

"So I'm not *just anybody*?"

"No. If you were, you wouldn't be here. Besides, I never said we were fucking," Black said teasing.

"Oh really?"

"Really."

Black and Kasha began to kiss again, and he loosened up with every electrifying kiss. Kasha took total control of the situation, making Black more comfortable. She laid him on his back and began to nibble on his ears as he caressed her back. She made her way down to his neck and sent chills throughout his body. Then she sat up and removed the jersey, revealing her precious mountains to Black.

Black had seen them before as she danced but never up close and personal like this. He sat up and took a mouth full of her left breast, sucking and licking them like a pro. Kasha exhaled in a state of passion as she grabbed his head. As Black sucked on her breasts, she reached down in his boxers and was pleasantly surprised. Actually, she was shocked as she stopped all of her motion.

"You alright? Did I do something wrong?" Black asked a little nervous.

"No, but did you steal ya' dick from a horse, nigga?"

Both of them laughed at the comment. Black always knew he was blessed, but he never made much of it.

Kasha's comment gave him the confidence he needed. Now he laid her on her back and returned her kisses passionately. By now, Kasha was moist and hot. Black could feel the heat coming from her vagina before he even removed her panties. He continued to explore her body with his hands and tongue and gave her chills in places that she didn't know she had. Smoothly, he removed her panties like a pro.

Kasha pulled Black down and fondled with the hole in his boxers until she pulled his dick through the hole. She guided Black in and said, "Be careful." She didn't want him to get overexcited his first time and tear her up with his "Mandingo pole."

Black was stroking Kasha and thinking to himself, *So this is what pussy feels like?* Kasha was matching his strokes, trying to take him all in with every stroke. "Take this pussy, baby. Damn, this dick is big as hell; fuck me, baby." She grabbed the back of Black's neck and wrapped her legs around his waist and stroked harder and faster as she

will robbins

came closer to climatic ecstasy. Black threw his dick in her harder and faster with her feverish strokes. "I'm comin', don't stop, I'm comin', oooh, shit, damn!" Kasha yelled. Black bust in her as her screams of passion made him explode.

"So, was it everything you thought it would be?" Kasha asked when she finally gathered her breath again.

"It was *better* than I thought it would be. Actually, I didn't think about it too hard. How was it, fuckin' a virgin?"

"Shit. It didn't feel like I was fuckin' no virgin."

They both laughed at the comment.

"So, why did you give me your virginity? You could have had anyone you wanted."

"I couldn't judge you because you're a stripper. I'm a damn drug dealer. But I don't want to do this my whole life. I have goals. I also know that you don't want to be a stripper your whole life. You have a good head on ya' shoulders and carry yourself like a woman, and I respect that. I feel like I could build with you. And seeing you with my mother and being here for me when you could be somewhere else says a lot about you," Black explained.

"That's special, so I guess I'm your woman now?"

"I guess so."

"Well, since I'm your woman, I need to be honest with you, Black," Kasha said, sitting up in the bed.

"Don't tell me you have a fuckin' disease, Kasha," Black said seriously.

"No, stupid. But whatever I tell you, you have to promise not to ill out on me."

"A'ight, I promise."

"When Six-ten was killed, I was there with E-Double and Booga. They offered me a lot of money and they said they would hook us up. The money really didn't mean anything to me, but the promise of hooking up with you I couldn't resist. So I put myself out there," Kasha explained timidly. She didn't want to lose Black because of a bad deal.

"I know," Black said coolly.

"You *know*? Here I am sweating bullets, and you know already?!" Kasha asked a little upset.

"Now, I told you why I gave you my virginity, but I never told you why I love you," Black said.

Kasha did a double take as if she didn't hear correctly.

"Did you just say that you *loved* me?"

"Any woman willing to risk her life just to get at me is worth loving. I knew for a while now. I thought it was stupid on your part, but I also thought that it was cute."

"I love you, too, as corny as it sounds, Black," Kasha said as she lay back in his arms.

They woke up to the smell of home cooked breakfast. Black walked out of the room first as Kasha was getting dressed. Sandra managed to clean the kitchen up well enough to whip something together. It would be the first time in a long time that she and Black would be in the apartment together. Once again, Black's sister was missing in action amid everything that was going on.

"Good morning, baby," Sandra replied, seeing her son in the kitchen doorway.

"Good morning, Ma. Is Danika here?"

"You know ya sister. Nothing is going to stop her flow. After the funeral, she disappeared."

Kasha stood in the back of Black and said, "Good morning, Miss Sandra."

"Good morning, girl. I heard that you two had a good time last night."

Kasha blushed at the comment while Black just said, "Come on, Ma."

"I'm just teasing, baby. Go sit at the table and I'll bring y'all some breakfast."

Sandra leaned over and poured eggs on Black's and Kasha's plates, and Black couldn't help but notice his mother's beauty, especially when she wasn't high. He missed the days when they would all sit at the table like a family, with the exception of his father.

After serving the plates, Sandra joined her son and his new woman.

"I shouldn't tell you, but your father came by while you were asleep," Sandra said as she watched her son jam his mouth full of eggs.

"Yeah, what did he want after all this time?" Black asked as he chewed his food.

will robbins

"You know your father and I have never been much for words, but he said he lost one son to the street and he doesn't want to lose another one."

"It's a little too late now."

"I know how you feel, but you can still learn a lot from your father, baby."

"Excuse my language but fuck him," Black said leaving the table.

"I know he's stubborn but try to talk to him, Kasha."

"I will, Miss Sandra," Kasha said as she followed Black to his room.

"I know you don't want to hear this, but he is the only father you are ever going to have, baby," Kasha said as she sat on the bed next to Black.

"I mean, you lost your brother, but maybe you could gain a father. Maybe you might learn something about yourself as well as Double."

The mention of Double had Black thinking a little. Maybe he should get to know his father. Or at least make him feel the pain of rejection like he made him, Double, and Danika feel.

"I don't even have his number," Black said regretfully.

"Hold on, baby," Kasha said as she stood up and retrieved her purse. She searched in the bag for a few moments and then pulled out a taped business card.

"Here you go, baby."

Black took the business card and recognized it immediately. "This is the card that my father gave me at the funeral," he said, surprised.

"Yeah. I saw the whole interaction between you and your father. I thought that you might eventually need it, so I picked it up and saved it," Kasha explained.

"Damn. You're fine, smart, thoughtful, and you're all about me. I knew I fell in love with the right woman."

"You damn sure did, Black."

They engaged in a passionate kiss.

"I got to get out of here, baby. I have an appointment to keep. Let me know when you call your father. I want to know how everything went," Kasha said as she fixed her hair and clothes.

"You don't need a ride or cab fare?"

"No. I have to stop at the store, and then I'll call a cab from there. Don't you want to know where I'm going at least?"

"No. I figured if you wanted me to know you would have said something. You're my woman, but I don't own you," Black said. "You must be used to them other cats stressing ya' whereabouts and shit," he said teasingly.

"Kiss my ass," Kasha said as she walked over and planted a wet one on her man's face. Black escorted her out the front door, and she said good-bye to Sandra on her way out.

Then Black took a seat next to his mother on the soft love seat.

"You know you picked a good woman," Sandra said.

"I know. Can you believe that she saved the card Daddy gave me that I ripped up?"

"She did?" Sandra asked surprised.

"Yeah. I think I'ma call Daddy."

"*What?* What did that girl say to you that I couldn't to make you change your mind? Don't tell me you whipped already," Sandra said, teasing her son.

"No. She basically said that I would never know myself or Double without knowing my father," Black explained. "I'd like to think that I know myself and Double pretty well, but if you don't know from whence you came, you don't know where you're going."

"I told you you picked a good woman."

Black stared at his mother, enjoying the time that they were spending together. Sandra, noticing her son's stare, asked, "What?"

"I like you better like this, Ma."

"Like what?"

"No disrespect, Ma, but I like you better when you're not high."

"Well, get used to it, 'cause I'm leaving that shit alone."

Black just looked at his mother with a blank stare.

"What? You don't believe me? Check my room." Black walked in his mother's room and saw a few brochures and plane tickets for a rehab center in Colorado. He picked up the pamphlets and tickets and walked back out to his mother.

"Are you serious?" Black asked, trying not to get too excited. He had been let down before, and he didn't want it to happen again.

"Yes, I'm serious," Sandra replied.

"Where did you get the tickets and the information?"

"When your father came by last night we had a long talk. We talk about my problems with addiction, what you have been doing in these

will robbins

streets, why he hasn't been around, and what he intends to do now. And after all the talking, he came by this morning with the info and tickets," Sandra explained.

"Why didn't y'all wake me up?"

"Your father thought that it would be best if you reached out to him. He didn't want to force himself on you."

"So now everything is cool with you and my father?"

"Just because we had a long talk and he gave me some tickets doesn't mean that we're cool. It just means that your father and I have both made mistakes with you kids, and I can't stand in judgment of him, and neither can you. It's time to start the healing process."

"I know. I'm just going to take it day by day as far as y'all are concerned, but I do love you, Ma."

"I love you too, baby."

♦ ♦ ♦ ♦

Kasha was sitting in the Dunkin' Doughnuts waiting for her cab, drinking her coffee, and thinking about her new relationship. She finished her coffee just in time to hear the cab driver blow the horn. When she walked out the door, she bumped into two men on her way to the cab.

"Watch where y'all goin', ma'fuckas," she said as she tried to maneuver around them.

"You should watch where you're goin', bitch," Donald said.

"Yeah, this is for Six-ten," Annex added. He raised his .45, and Kasha's eyes opened wider than Jay Z's at a surprise party. She was frozen in time as Annex squeezed the trigger three times. The first bullet shattered her skull as brain matter squirted on the two men as well as the Dunkin' Doughnut's window. The other two gave her chest two new airholes as she hit the ground. The cab driver pulled off faster than Jeff Gordon on the racetrack, trying to avoid being a witness.

Annex and Donald jumped in their car, ready to report their deed to Dubois and Ice.

16

RECONCILIATION/RETALIATION

Black and Sandra were still sitting on the couch deep in conversation as they heard police sirens and an ambulance in the distance. They thought they heard gunshots but figured that it might be kids shooting for fun or some other nonsense. But when they looked out their third-floor window, they saw the commotion in the distance.

"I wonder what happened this time?" Sandra asked, upset at the thought that someone else's child was killed.

"I don't know, Ma. Someone else just got caught slippin' is all."

Then they looked at each other for a brief second as they were thinking the same thing.

"Oh, shit! Kasha!" Black yelled as he ran straight for the front door.

He made it through the courtyard and across the street just in time to see the medic pull a white sheet over Kasha's body. Black pushed through the officers and the medics and pulled the sheet from over her body. As he saw her head and face dismembered, he screamed with rage, his face distorted like a demon from hell. "I'm gonna kill that ma'fucka!!!" Black yelled.

"Wait! You know who did this?" an officer asked as he grabbed Black by the arm.

"Get the fuck off me," Black said snatching his arm back from the officer. As Black walked away, the officer tried to detain him once more.

"Let him go," a familiar voice said. The officer turned around and immediately recognized Officer Swank.

"We'll catch up with him another time," Swank said, smiling.

Black burst into his apartment like a raging bull.

"What happened out there?" Sandra asked as she followed her son into his room.

"That ma'fucka Ice just killed Kasha. He did Double and I was going to wait to kill his ass, but now he took the woman I loved and he's going to pay!!!" Black was in his closet throwing everything until he found a locked box. He unlocked it and pulled out two twin onyx-plated Baby Desert Eagles. At the sight of the guns, Sandra was reduced to tears.

"Please, baby, not like this. This isn't right. I know you're hurt, but not like this."

"What he did isn't right, and he's gonna pay," Black said crying and spitting as he talked. He was out of control as his mother tried to block his path.

"Move out my way, Ma, please."

Sandra held onto her son like he was being ripped away by a slave master.

"Ma, please get off of me." The rage inside Black couldn't be contained as he pulled away from his mother's vice grip. Sandra fell to the floor and cried out, "Please, son, please don't go." As the door slammed a moment later, she jumped up.

Then Sandra sank back on the floor for a few seconds crying until it dawned on her that Nate, Black's father, was still in town. She called the hotel that he was staying in. As the phone rang she said to herself, "Please, Nate, please, pick up."

"Hello," Nate said as he picked up the phone.

"Thank God you're there," Sandra said hysterically and crying.

"Hello ... hello, who is this?" Nate asked, not able to recognize the voice.

"It's me, Sandra ..."

"What is it? Calm down and tell me."

"Ice ... Ice had Raheem's girlfriend killed, he took two guns out of here, and I think he's going after him," Sandra explained a little more calmly.

"Where does Ice stay?"

"Check the Lady Luck Club on Elizabeth Avenue."

"I know where it's at. I'll call you soon."

"Nate ..."

"What?"

"Don't let them take my baby."

"You mean *our* baby. I'll call you soon." Nate headed out of the hotel en route to stop Black from ending his life.

Black was driving in a Land Cruiser that he borrowed from one of his corner boys. The only thing that stopped him from driving like a bat out of hell was traffic. Nate was more successful maneuvering in and out of traffic. He knew exactly where his son was headed, and he wanted to beat him there for obvious reasons. Black took the route past the Elizabeth High School, hoping that he would hit less traffic once he got to Elizabeth Avenue. He found no success on Elizabeth Avenue either. Nate took the back streets like a professional cab driver and pulled in front of the Lady Luck Club. There was no sign of Black anywhere. He stepped out of his Navigator and paced up and down the block in anticipation of seeing his son.

Shortly, Black pulled up in front of the club and hopped out of the vehicle, brandishing both of his weapons of mass destruction. He started to sprint in the club and ran right into the arms of his father. He was in such a rage that he didn't have any idea of who gripped him. Nate had Black in a bear hug from the back. When Black finally managed to turn around with fire smoldering in his eyes, he noticed his father. As they made eye contact, his anger charged into madness.

"Get the fuck off of me, nigga!" Black said shaking and pulling like he was having a seizure.

Nate only made his grip tighter.

Black continued to curse and tried to jerk away from his father, but to no avail. Soon, his rage turned into uncontrollable tears of hurt and frustration. Nate released Black and took the guns out of his son's hands and put them in his SUV. Then he grabbed his son back into his arms as Black wept.

"I know, son, I know," Nate said, rubbing Black's head as he held him tightly in his arms. It was the first time that he hugged his son in years. They stood in the middle of the block embracing each other and crying as pedestrians looked on curiously.

will robbins

Meanwhile, Sandra was pacing back and forth in her front room, chain-smoking. She was more than worried about her son—she was nearly losing her mind. She was fighting the need to get high to forget about her troubles. Just as she was thinking she should leave to get right, her phone rang. She raced towards the phone like it was the Second Coming of Jesus.

"Hello, hello," she answered desperately.

"It's Nate … I got him here with me."

"Thank God. Let me talk to him."

Nate looked at Black and passed him the cell phone.

"Hello," Black said.

"Baby, are you okay?"

"Yeah, I'm a'ight," Black answered, sniffling and wiping his tears. Then he handed his father the phone.

"I'll have him home in a few. I need to talk to my son for a few first," Nate told Sandra.

"Okay. I'll see y'all when you get back."

"Sandra …"

"What, Nate?"

"Don't do anything stupid. Hang in there, please," Nate said with concern.

"I will." Now that she knew her son was safe, it was easier to fight her gorilla.

Black sat in his father's SUV and pulled out his cell phone to dial Booga. He didn't care if his father heard what he had to say. If his father had been there from the beginning, none of the things that were transpiring would be going on, or so Black thought. Black prayed that Booga would answer his phone. After a few rings, Booga finally picked up the phone.

"Eastwick Hustlers' finest, Booga speaking, baby."

"Booga … it's Black. Listen. Ice just had Kasha killed," Black said.

"*What? When?* Where you at?" Booga asked, agitated.

"Never mind that. Double's dead, Kasha's dead, and you bound to be next. It seems like Ice is trying to take out everyone who killed Sixten, and you and Jab are the last ones," Black explained.

"So what you wanna do?"

"Call Flex and Jab, have everyone meet at the spot. I'll be there in a few. I just need to tie things up with my father," Black said, looking in Nate's direction.

"A'ight, Black, I'm on it. They won't catch me slipping," Booga said, passing a throwing star through his fingers.

"Peace."

"Peace, bruh'."

Black and Nate looked at each other for moments without saying a word. Each man was consumed with his own thoughts. Neither man knew how to express himself at the moment.

Then Nate pulled into traffic as both men continued to ride in silence. Black continued to glance over at his father without saying a word. He did it so many times that Nate finally became uncomfortable and said, "What?"

Black just sucked his teeth and said, "Nothing."

"I know we don't know each other that well, but I know that your nothing is something," Nate replied.

"You tell me what my nothing is," Black said with attitude. He was angry with Nate, but more importantly, he was past anger where his dead girlfriend was concerned, and Nate was going to get the brunt of it. Nate didn't reply right away. He just continued with his aimless driving, which landed him and Black in the parking lot of the Olympian Diner off the highway.

"What the hell are we doing here?" Black asked, still continuing with his attitude. He wanted to know his father, but he wasn't going to let his guard down that fast.

"I haven't eaten all day, and if I don't get something, soon my diabetes will be acting up," Nate said. He also wanted a public place, thinking that it would keep Black from causing a scene if their conversation got too heated.

Father and son walked in the diner and were seated by a beautiful, middle-aged waitress. "Hi, I'm Tracey. Would you like something to drink, sir?" she asked looking at the older man.

"I would like some coffee, please," Nate said.

"How would you like that, sir?"

"I would like it like I like my women … black."

Tracey smiled and said, "It's nice to know we still have some brothers out here that appreciate the sisters. What would the young man be having?"

"I'll take a sprite."

She walked off to retrieve their drinks. After she brought their drinks back, she took their orders, and Nate flirted a little bit as Black looked on.

Maybe that's where Double got his skills from, Black thought to himself. As they were seated, Black asked, "So you a pimp, huh?"

"No. I just know what a woman needs to hear."

"Do you know what I need to hear?"

"Yeah. I do."

"What is it then?"

"You need to hear where I been all this time. You need to hear how much I love you, your brother, and your sister, as well as your mother, believe it or not. You want to know if I loved y'all so much, how could I have left y'all lonely without a father."

Black tilted his head and gave his father a look that said, *Exactly—now talk.*

Nate saw Black's expression and said, "This isn't going to be easy."

"It wasn't easy for us, either," Black chimed in.

Nate sipped on his coffee to stall in order to get his thoughts together. He knew this day would come, but he never prepared himself.

"Well, Black, I've come a long way from the man you are seeing today. Right now, I run a business in Cali, and it's doing very well. That's where I've been for so many years. But before that, I was a junky, a fiend, a heroin addict. And I'm not down talking your mother, but she turned me out."

Black listened intently and hung on to his father's every word.

"A good friend of mine recommended the facility in Colorado to me. I tried to get your mother to come with me but she refused. She said she wasn't going to nobody's facility. She was happy in the hood."

"So you blaming everything on my mother?" Black asked, getting infuriated.

"I'm not blaming your mother. I'm just giving you answers, and it is what it is. You have to decipher the difference. Now please, let me finish."

"Go ahead."

Just as Nate began to speak, Tracey brought over their food.

"Enjoy your meal, men," she said and walked off.

Nate continued after the waitress was passed earshot.

"Your mother told me that if I left, I might as well not come back. I asked what about the kids, but she said 'They're my kids if you leave.' It was a personal choice for me. Be a no-good junky father or be a father that my kids would be proud of, so I left. I was hoping that your mother was bluffing and over time she would change her mind. I came back in six months to be there for all of y'all, but she wasn't having it. I tried for visitation rights, but those white-ass judges don't give a fuck about a brother trying to take care of his kids. After a while, I tried to get custody because I knew your mother was still out there, but once again, I was told that you guys were better off with your mother, and I was furious."

At this time, Tracey walked over and asked, "Is everything okay?"

Nate and Black both nodded. As she walked away, Black couldn't help but look at her healthy ass. Nate noticed Black looking and just smiled.

"What?" Black asked as he caught his father's gaze.

"Nothing, just smiling at your good taste, baby boy."

"So what happened after the courts didn't step in?" Black asked.

"I left."

"Just like that. You left?"

"I couldn't kidnap y'all. There was nothing else for me to do, especially after your mother had a restraining order against me. Look, I had to get out and get myself together or I probably would still be out in the streets. The same friend who told me about Colorado offered me a job in Cali. Now we're partners in a magazine company. A week turned into months, and months turned into years, and that was my fault. I should have been there and for that, I have no excuse, but it is what it is," Nate explained as he fought back tears.

"I'm not saying I forgive you or that I'll forget, but I can try to understand," Black said, fighting tears as well.

Tracey walked over and noticed that the food had barely been touch and the men were a little emotional so she almost walked away until she heard, "It's okay, I'll take the check."

"Is something wrong?" Tracey asked concerned.

"Yeah, something is definitely wrong. I'm sitting here having lunch with my son when I could be having lunch with you," Nate said, smiling. Nate was tall with broad shoulders and had a precious smile.

Tracey just smiled and said, "Well, we'll have to work something out next time, Mr. ..." She was reaching for his name.

Nate caught on and said, "Just call me Nate."

"Okay, Nate. Leave me with your number so we can make arrangements."

Nate pulled out one of his business cards and handed it to Tracey. Black walked away, smiling at his father's actions. Nate paid the bill and left Tracey a substantial tip and then made his way to his SUV.

♥ ♥ ♥ ♥

Booga, Jab, Flex, Noah, Na'im, and a few other young men were in the basement waiting on Black. They were passing the time smoking, drinking, and playing Madden 2007.

"The thirty, the twenty, the ten, *touchdown*, bitch!" Jab yelled, taunting Booga.

"Nigga, you got that by luck," Booga said.

"Nigga, I been scoring on ya' bitch ass all day."

"Who's next?" Jab asked.

No one answered the challenge. They knew Jab was a cold Madden fiend. Black finally entered the basement with Bobby trailing behind him. The room fell silent.

"My brother is dead, and my girl just got killed, and y'all down here playing video games, smoking, drinking, partying, and shit," Black said as he looked at all his men with disgust.

"Black, it ain't even like that," Booga said, trying to explain.

"Fuck that! Throw the fuckin alcohol out and get rid of the blunts. Turn the game off and get ya black asses to the table!" Black yelled loud enough to bust an eardrum.

Everyone scrambled like roaches when the lights go on to follow his orders. They quickly took a seat at the table and waited for Black to begin.

"I'm glad to see we can still be in play mode after all the things that have been going down," Black addressed the group. "Especially *you*, Booga, when you next on Ice's hit list. Obviously Ice is killing everyone who was involved in Six-ten's murder."

"I'm not in play mode, but I'm not going to act scared either," Booga said with a brave front.

"What do you want us to do, Black? I mean, we could storm his businesses and get at him," Jab said.

"Right now, we not goin' to do anything. It's too hot right now, and we'll be the first ones looked at," Black said.

"So what's the plan?" Flex asked.

"Right now, we continue to lay low, and it's business as usual. When the time is right, we gonna attack the head of the dragon," Black said slyly.

"What you mean, Black?" Booga asked.

"We gonna do some training while we lay low, and when the time is right, we gonna strike the mansion."

"Are you fuckin' crazy? That's suicide!" Jab said.

"No, it's not," Noah said in a heavy Puerto Rican accent.

"That's how I took my boss out and gained power in Asbury Park. Once you take the man out, you *become* the man. Take Ice out and they won't have a savior except the one you give them, which would be Black. And we all know that Black is fair, so we would all reap the benefits," Noah explained proudly.

"That sounds good but how many men we gonna have? I mean, that mansion got to have mad men, security, and shit," Na'im said.

"Money talks and for the right price, we can find out how many men, how to get past security, and what time Ice will be there so we won't be striking for nothing," Black explained.

As the conversation lingered, Woo, Man, Calvin, Damien, and Taye walked down the steps into the basement. "What the hell are y'all doing down here?" Black asked.

"I stopped by your crib to check on you. Aunt Sandra told me what happened with you and Kasha and that Ice's men killed her. I figured enough was enough, so I came looking for you," Woo said.

"Looking for me for what?" Black asked.

"Ice finally barked up the wrong tree when he took E-Double, and now it's time for payback, and we in on it," Woo said, waving his hand toward his small entourage.

"Hell, no. Y'all niggas doing too good to get caught up in this shit. Fuck that!" Black said sincerely looking at each man as if he were crazy.

"No disrespect, Black, but Ice disfigured my cousin and still got him out on the block. He got my girl's sister shak'n her ass, and he hurt Woo, which is like my brother. And me and Double wasn't that close, but he was good people," Taye said.

"I'm pretty sure that each man here has a legitimate reason to be here. Ice has done something to every man in here, but I can't have y'all deaths on my conscience. This is war! It's a lot of people in this room, and every man in here ain't comin' back alive. I'll be damn if I get some innocent ma'fuckas to die for this shit!" Black's voice was rising like a kite on a cool summer breeze.

"If this is war, don't you think you need us? You think that you can just run down on Ice with limited soldiers?" Woo asked.

"We don't need y'all—period," Black responded firmly.

"When did I ever have to ask your permission, cousin? If I remember correctly, we started workin' at the same time, and I was damn good at it, too. Better than you and Double put together. I could outshoot, outsmart, and outhustle you any day of the week. So why don't you want my help? And don't give me the school boy shit, either," Woo finished.

Black was steaming at Woo's breakdown, but it happened to be the truth. Woo was a conning, convincing con artist, and an evil, calculating person when he wanted to be.

Black grabbed a seat to calm down before he showed his smart-ass cousin who could outbox who. He didn't care that Woo had a black belt in Kenpo Karate. He remembered that he and Double almost came to blows, and that was the last time that they saw each other alive. He wasn't going to make the same mistake twice, especially since he knew Woo wasn't going to change his mind about taking Ice out.

"Look, Woo, I know you good, real good. You and ya boys gonna do what y'all want to do anyway. You don't need my permission. But you not makin' a move before we do. We doin' this shit together," Black explained. Woo smiled like he was given the secret to eternal life.

"What the fuck are you smiling for?" Black asked.

"This is goin' to be like old times, with the exception of Double missing," Woo said.

Woo and his boys grabbed a seat and mingled with the rest of the men in the basement. When everyone started to get restless, Jab asked, "Black, what's the plan now?"

"The plan is we keep working and as for Woo and his boys, y'all keep goin' to school like everyone expects. Booga and me gonna work out all the other details and when we need to fill y'all in, we'll fill y'all in."

"Wait! What do you mean you and Booga gonna plan everything?" Woo asked with attitude.

"Just what the fuck I said. Don't push ya' luck, Woo. We family and all, but I'm not about to take too much disrespect. Just be happy you a part of this shit," Black responded matching Woo's attitude.

"Be happy? Be happy? Why the fuck would I be happy when I'm only doin' this shit 'cause Double is dead? If Ice didn't cross the line, I wouldn't even be here. And I also know that you plan on attacking Ice's mansion, and I know the whole layout of the place, and I know you need my info to get the job done. So *you* need *me* more than *I* need *you*," Woo explained defiantly.

"A'ight, looks like I'm gonna need you after all," Black said smoothly.

"I thought you'd see it my way," Woo stated.

"Everyone else get out except Bobby, Booga, and Woo, and get on ya' grind," Black said.

Everyone left the men to lay out the plans and figured they'd get the details later. Before Taye left, he turned to Woo and asked, "You want me to come back later to pick you up?"

"Nah, he'll be a'ight," Booga answered.

Once the room was empty, the men began to put together a fool-proof scam.

17

CHANCE MEETINGS

The summer proved to be a scorcher with the death rate rising in Jersey due to the war between the Port Au Prince Posse and the Eastwick Hustlers. Winter was coming fast, and if Black had it his way, it was going to be the coldest winter ever for the Port Au Prince Posse. Vengeance was on his mind, and death rested in his heart. Ice didn't know it yet, but he had awakened a sleeping dragon. If it was a chess game of war Ice was looking for, he found the Bobby Fisher he needed.

Black and Woo sat at the kitchen table mapping out a plan of attack.

Woo was showing his artistic skills as he drew the blueprints of the mansion from the inside out. He stuck to every detail down to the diamond, crystal, and gold chandeliers that hung high above the Italian marble floors. Black looked on in amazement as Woo continued to draw.

"Yo, how do you know so much about the mansion?" Black asked.

Still in deep concentration on the task at hand, Woo replied, "After I brought in so much money and put in work, Ice started to trust me and he brought me around the mansion a lot.

"He said that I made a lot of improvements and showed a lot of skills for my age. He was thinking about letting me work as a guard in the mansion, so he figured I would need to know the layout of the place."

"So what happened?"

"Well, I was in the mansion for weeks, and that's when I told everyone I was going to Boston to visit my people. Ice wanted it to be a little secret. He didn't want any other soldiers to get envious. But after he realized that no one could pick up my slack, he put me back out on the block. That's how I know the layout, about the men, the dogs, and the security. I even know where he keeps his money and what time he makes pickups and drop-offs," Woo explained proudly.

"Now the trust that he put in you is goin' to be his downfall," Black said.

"So when do you want to get the boys together and start workin' this shit?"

"Soon, real soon. Look, I'ma get out of here and take care of some business."

"Black, every day around this time you keep disappearing. What's up?"

"Just business, baby, just business. I'll let you and everyone else know when the time is right," Black said as he stood up from the table with a smile. The walk from the table to the door was short as Black exited Woo's apartment.

● ● ● ●

Ice and Dubois once again sat in the office talking business over with his capos. "Once again, I'm glad we have this opportunity to meet," Ice said. He was in better spirits since most of his revenge had been exacted and his business was still thriving despite the war. "We still running the streets, and them bitch-ass Eastwick Hustlers can't do shit about it," Ice boasted.

At the mention of Ice's words, the small crowd erupted into cheers. Dubois stood and raised his hands to motion the men to silence. Everyone closed their mouths faster than an Arab closing shop on 9/11.

"Right now, we have the elections coming up for the mayor and his people. So for now, all the attacks on the Eastwick Hustlers and anybody else we have beefs with must stop temporarily," Ice said.

The men looked around at one another as if they heard wrong. They were close to wiping out all of their competition, and now Ice was saying give it a rest. They thought that he was crazy. Annex was the only member in the room brave enough to speak his mind. He wanted to stir Dubois up.

"Ice, why would we stop now since we almost have the Eastwick Hustlers on their knees and we're moving swiftly into other territory? If we rest now, we leave everybody time to rebuild as well as move in on *our* territory."

Dubois might have been upset with the man, but he had a valid point. Ice gulped his shot of Henny down and let the alcohol cool his throat.

"Annex, you are very wise and have a valid point, and that's why you're one of my favorite capos. But don't ever think that you're that smart to question my judgment," Ice warned.

"What Ice is trying to say is we need to support the mayor and his associates in their endeavors. There has been a lot of blood shed since he's been in office, and the people are very unhappy. If the people are unhappy and think that the mayor can't control the streets, then they will elect a mayor who can. And we can't have that. He and his people are our protection," Dubois explained.

"What if they attack us?" Donald asked.

"If you are attacked, then handle business, but under no circumstances do we start anything until after the mayor is reelected into office," Ice said as seriously as a heart attack.

"Do you men understand that?" Dubois asked.

"Yeah," the men all answered in unison.

"Then get out there and get our paper," Ice said, ending the late-night session.

❢ ❢ ❢ ❢

The alarm sounded, waking Woo up from his sound sleep. It was warning him that it was time to get up and face the first day of school as a senior. Most seniors were ecstatic about the first day of school. It meant that they were close to independence and the turn of a new life. Woo, however, was unfazed by all this. He had lost his cousin and some valuable friends over the summer and instead of planning to go to college, he was plotting murder. And he didn't score as high as he would have liked to on his SAT, which meant he would have to take it all over again. It also meant that he would have to bust his ass to get his GPA up if he had any hopes of Montclair, Rutgers, or Howard U. hollering at him.

Two houses down, Taye motivated himself out of the bed before his grandmother could yell, "Get up, you motherfucka." Taye was a little more excited about the first day of school because he knew it wouldn't be long before he could resume his passion—track and women. Even though he had a beautiful woman, like most men, he found a side-chick. Track was also second nature to him, just like women. And just like all the women that vied for his attention, he also had college coaches all over his nuts.

Woo walked down the steps and started to head to Taye's house, but he stopped his motion when he saw Taye closing his fence and heading in his direction.

"I see you not dressed for the first day of school, playboy," Taye said, giving Woo a pound.

"You either, son," Woo said.

"With smooth lines and a big dick, I don't have to impress the women with gear," Taye said boastfully.

"Whatever, nigga."

The block wasn't filled with the usual players, such as Black, Jab, Bobby, or Flex. All the top dogs were still laying low and were replaced by some low-rent hustlers.

"What's up, Taye and Woo?" a young, light-skinned cat said as Woo and Taye approached the corner.

"Yo, Dontae, shouldn't ya' yellow ass be in school some goddamn where?" Taye asked.

"Me and my boys out here makin' that crazy paper. We can't make this kind of money in school," the kid said, flashing wads of paper.

The kid's ignorance reminded Woo of himself, Black, and Double when they were his age. Light-skin and his boys couldn't be older than 14. The question that burned in Woo's mind was, were they working for Black, and if so, what the fuck was wrong with Black?

"Man, who the hell y'all out here workin' for?" Woo asked angrily.

"Man, we out here workin' for the king of Eastwick," a dark-skinned, pudgy boy answered, stepping a little closer to Woo.

"Back up, lil' man. Who's the king of Eastwick?"

The young boys laughed at Woo's question. Slowly, Woo's anger was emerging and Taye saw it in his eyes.

"What the fuck is so funny?" Taye asked, not amused at the three stooges.

"Y'all lookin' at us like we need to be in school, and y'all don't even know who the king of Eastwick is," the tallest of the three boys answered.

"Well, tell us, dickhead," Woo said, restraining the urge to knock the hell out of all three boys for their mockery.

"We out here for Ice, baby," they all said in chorus as if they had been practicing the line all day.

Woo's and Taye's faces curled up at the mention of Ice's name.

"Well, let me give you three ma'fuckas a little advice since y'all too stupid to know ya mouths from the hole in ya' asses. This here corner belongs to the Eastwick Hustlers, and I suggest that y'all take ya' work somewhere else before somebody comes and body ya' asses," Woo said feeling a little sympathy that the boys had to be on the corner to feed themselves. If he could have, he would have given them money to take their asses off the corner.

"If y'all still out here when I get back, I'ma fuck y'all up my damn self," Taye said as he and Woo stepped off. He hoped his threat was well received, but he knew that the boys were well protected by Ice. And that in itself made the boys cocky and ignorant.

♥ ♥ ♥ ♥

Nadeem sat on her expensive imported couch that was handmade in Africa, rocking her son to sleep. She was wondering what Ice was up to. They hadn't spoken or seen each other since she left him hanging in the villa in Anguilla. He hadn't even bothered to stop by the house to attempt to give her an apology or make up with her. With her broken heart and stubbornness, she wasn't going to sweat him either. Child or no child, king of the city or not, she wasn't going to chase no man—period. She would have to put her worrying aside for the moment. Like many others, she was going back to Union County College to start and finish her last semester.

As she began to gather her books, there was a knock at her door. She briefly jumped as the knocked surprised her. Part of her was hoping that Ice would be on the other side of the door while another part hoped that he had forgotten about her. On her way to the door, she saw the gold and platinum antique clock on the wall and noticed it was about the time that her sister needed to arrive to babysit. Nadeem answered the door and her sister quickly teased, "I bet you thought I was Ice."

"Shut up and come in."

Samantha and Nadeem made their way back to the couch. They both sat down lightly as not to wake up the baby.

"So what's up with you and Ice? I know he cheated, but I thought you would have forgiven him by now. I mean, shit, all the money and power he got and he fine. I wouldn't care how many bitches he fucked, I just wouldn't let no other bitch have him full time," Samantha said. Samantha was straight hood. She abandoned her culture and the traditional ways of a Hindu woman and adopted the ways of a hood rat.

Nadeem just sighed and said, "I love Ice and all, but I love myself much more to be used. A man can only do what you allow him to do, and I'm not allowing Ice to hurt me any more."

"I don't believe you just said some dumb shit like that. You actually gonna let him go so he could take care of some other bitch? You worked too hard. You had his baby, had his back—that shit got to count for something."

"Obviously not, because he never stopped by here yet or called," Nadeem said, getting up and grabbing her books.

"Well, at least he didn't come and put you out of the house. That's a good thing, right?"

"Toussaint may have cheated and that was stupid in itself. He's not crazy though. He wouldn't try to put me and his son out. It would bring to much trouble to his life. Besides, I know he has other property, and I know more than likely he's probably lying with some bitch right now. I am *too* through," Nadeem said as she kissed her sleeping son and hugged her sister.

She headed for the door while Samantha shook her head, wishing she had a portion of her sister's lifestyle. Samantha was just as pretty as Nadeem, but she carried herself with less style and maturity. She always came off as a money-hungry hood rat, and that's how she was treated.

♦ ♦ ♦ ♦

JD lay in his county cell, wondering what he got himself into. He trusted a snake and felt like he got bit. Swank never came in to see him or drop word to him on what was going on. The only thing that gave him comfort for the moment was that he knew Big Keith was handling business right and he had money in his commissary and phone privileges. A noise interrupted his thoughts as he heard foot-steps coming in his direction. A tall, dark officer appeared and calmly said, "You have a visitor."

JD stood up and headed down the tier in the direction of the vis-itation area. The whole way he couldn't figure out who would be there to see him. He ruled out his mother because she said she would never visit any of her kids in prison. He knew it wasn't his baby mama because he already heard about her messing with another nigga. Big Keith was holding it down in the streets, and anyone else could care less.

He sat in the booth and was surprised to see Swank on the oppo-site side of the glass. JD slowly picked up the receiver, and Swank fol-lowed suit.

"Looking good, JD. How you doing?" Swank asked with a conde-scending smile.

"Fuck that! What's going on?"

"Calm that temper down and save it for the showers," Swank said half-joking with a pinch of anger added to it. He didn't like some two-bit nigga talking down to him. JD sucked his teeth and took a deep breath to calm down. Once again, JD asked, "What's going on?"

"Right now as we speak, I have someone paying the prosecutor off and greasing a judge's palm," Swank said, lying through his yellow, stained teeth.

"Is that supposed to make me feel comfortable? When is someone going to cut me a deal?"

"Soon, baby, soon. Just keep ya mouth shut and everything will be gravy. I got to go," Swank said as he struggled to pick his fat body up from the chair.

JD was fuming. He felt in his gut that Swank was lying. If Swank didn't come through like he promised, JD was going to drop his own name—Swank's. One dirty cop is more precious to the DA than ten corner boys. He would be hitting the streets soon, and his cell would be replaced with Swank's fat ass.

❦ ❦ ❦ ❦

Nadeem sat in her psychology class as her stomach pangs started to take control. Luckily, it was only a few more minutes before class would end and she could take care of herself. But the minutes seemed to be hours as the professor went on about learned behaviors in different environments.

She was ecstatic once the professor completed her lecture and dismissed the class. She quickly gathered her belongings and headed for the first available elevator as she hurried out of the revolving door in a rush to answer her stomach's call. Nadeem ran so fast that she bumped into a man, which caused her to drop her books on the ground. She quickly bent down to retrieve her books and apologized without even looking at the person she bumped into. The man bent down to offer his assistance.

"Here, let me give you a hand," the man said.

The voice sounded smooth and silky but not familiar to Nadeem. As she looked up to see who the smooth voice belonged to, she was by far not disappointed except that he looked a little young.

Nadeem looked into the man's eyes and was captivated by their beauty. Those eyes held passion and pain in them, something that she had never seen before. His smooth, dark skin made her forget all about her hunger pangs.

"Are you okay? I mean, I didn't even see you coming," Black said giving Nadeem the once over. He was so concerned about her safety that he didn't even notice her exotic beauty.

Nadeem smiled and said, "No, it was my fault. I was moving like a bat out of hell and didn't notice you."

"It's okay. So I guess you go to this school?"

"Yeah, it's my last semester."

"I guess there's going to be a lot of disappointed brothas after this semester, huh?"

Nadeem just smiled at the man's attempt to flirt. She was a little impressed because most young guys would yell, "Hey, Ma" or "Yo bitch, come here." Normally she would have politely told the man to step but she needed to have her spirits lifted after what Ice put her through. She wasn't even sure if she had a man any more, so there was no harm in letting this fella talk to her.

"You have a pretty smile. I'm glad I had the opportunity to see it," Black said.

"Thank you."

"I'm sorry, I'm going on and on, but I don't even know your name," Black said.

"It's Nadeem, and yours?"

will robbins

"Black."

"And that's your real name?"

"That's what everyone calls me. I don't know you well enough to give you my government yet."

"Well, how does one get to know you better?" Nadeem couldn't believe that those words had just come out of her mouth. She couldn't help herself. Black had her a little intrigued. She also knew that he was younger than her, but he reminded her of Ice at his age.

Black was still hurting over Kasha, but Nadeem piqued his interest. Up until he saw her, he really didn't have anything to smile about. Many women wanted to comfort him in his time of loss, but he really didn't want to lose his focus. Nadeem seemed like a woman he could build with. She seemed to have the same style and flow as Kasha. She didn't have the presence of a hood rat or a gold digger or a fame chaser, for that matter. He also liked the fact that she didn't know who he was. So he knew her interest was genuine.

Various students passed by as Black and Nadeem were locked in their own world.

"Listen, why don't I walk you to ya ride and we can exchange info and hook up later, if that's alright with you?"

"Aren't you a little young to be hooking up with me?"

"I'm not jail bait, if that's what you're asking."

Nadeem smiled at the response.

"Walking me to my ride seems like a plan, but all that hooking up stuff, I'm not too sure about," Nadeem said.

"I'll walk you to your car, and we can figure out details later."

"Follow me," Nadeem said smiling.

Black gladly complied and was surprised as Nadeem stopped in front of a '06 black Envoy.

"Seems like you're pretty paid, Nadeem," Black said.

"I'm not hurting."

Black and Nadeem exchanged numbers. As she opened her front door, Black felt compelled to try to spend more time with her ASAP.

"Hey, why don't we stop and get something to eat?" Black suggested.

Nadeem turned around and gave him a look that seemed to ask, are you serious?

194

Black, catching on to the look, quickly responded and said,

"Nothing fancy. I mean, we could go to Hollywood Chicken, McDonald's, the Chinese Spot. I just want to spend a little more time with you."

Nadeem seemed to be letting down her guard, so Black continued to pull her in.

"I don't mean no harm, but it's been awhile since I've seen a woman as beautiful as you, and you seem to carry yourself very well. You don't see too much of that out here, you know."

"I'm very flattered, but I'm kind of in a complicated situation right now."

"So what was all the flirting and exchanging numbers?" Black asked, hoping he didn't prematurely judge the woman. She was coming off as a play fiend.

Noticing Black's frustration, Nadeem felt she had to explain herself before he got the wrong impression. She closed her car door, looked Black directly in his eyes, and said, "Look, I am in a complicated situation right now, but complicated situations also become uncomplicated. You seem to be like a breath of fresh air, and I would hate to just pass you off. But I don't know whether I'm coming or going, and I don't think it's right for me to pull you into my crazy situation. So I figure once I know what's going down, I could put you down, understand?"

"I understand, but don't be surprised if I don't mind being pulled in your crazy situation. I mean, it can't be anymore crazier than mine. I assume you have a man, and I respect your position. But you, too, are like a breath of fresh air, and I want to continue this feeling. Look, I'll leave you with that thought. You have a pleasant day," Black said as he lightly kissed her hand and stepped off.

Nadeem jumped in her car and sat for a few seconds as she relished in the moment that had just transpired. She thought to herself, *chance meeting*.

will robbins

18

CLEANING THE STREETS

The streets seemed to have a no-violence policy with the elections coming up. But the drug epidemic was running rampant in the streets. The Port Au Prince Posse forced their way in and took over a small portion of downtown Elizabeth with the absence of Black and his strong capos. The Eastwick Hustlers weren't hurting financially. They continued to receive their work from Tony in New York. They even had a small business venture in the city that was very prosperous with less peril.

Black heard of the reports of Ice taking over First and Magnolia and Third and Bond Street. But he wasn't greedy and didn't want to lose more soldiers before the actual war began. He simply moved some of his men into Linden and parts of New York with the cooperation of Tony. So neither he nor his team were hurting.

Mayor Cross, Chief Williams, and Officer Swank sat in a quiet, private booth in Manolo's Restaurant on the corner of First Street and Elizabeth Avenue. They were making plans for the election.

"Seems like Ice kept his word and made sure the violence stopped," Mayor Cross said proudly.

"Don't trust that nig—" Swank abruptly stopped his mouth in its track once he remembered he was in the company of a strong black man.

"Look, don't get so happy. Ice could change his mind at any time and botch things up for us," Swank continued.

"He won't. He needs our protection, just like we need him to keep his mouth shut," Williams said, speaking up for the first time.

"Which leads me to my next question. How much money do you think he's going to contribute to our election endeavors?" the mayor asked.

Chief Williams sighed and said, "I was hoping that we could pull our resources and do this thing properly and sever all ties with Ice eventually. I don't know about you two gentlemen, but I'm finding it harder to bend over each day that passes."

Swank wanted to knock the chief of police on his ass for his comment but opted to voice his opinion instead. He took a deep breath and said, "That's easy for you to say, Chief. You're at the top of the food chain and at the rate you're going, it won't be long before you make commissioner. Unlike you, I'm not moving up any faster, and neither is my pay. But my mortgage and bills keep increasing, so I need the money that Ice sends my way. So if it means that I have to bend for a little while longer, then so be it. At least it's better than bending over for the department."

The mayor and the chief were both appalled at Swank's statements, but both of them knew that he was right. The truth hurts all people. The mayor wanted to be free of Ice's grip, but without destroying the evidence that Ice held over the men, he felt like his hands were tied. But that didn't stop him from entertaining the thought, so he quickly asked, "How *do* we sever ties with Ice without making an unbearable enemy?"

"We're all in a complicated situation that needs to be handled with kid gloves. If we have Ice killed, that doesn't kill the evidence, and it will only ensure that someone else will take the throne," Williams said.

"But the tapes were stolen and for all we know, he doesn't have anything else on us," the mayor said, perking up.

"But we can't take the chance," Williams replied.

Swank looked from left to right in the mayor and the chief's direction, trying to fathom what he was hearing. He couldn't believe that they were trying to plot a conspiracy against the man that helped pay his mortgage and put his daughters through college. He hated the fact that he was taking handouts from a nigga, but shit, Ice was that

will robbins

nigga. Before Swank blew a gasket he said, "I can't believe I'm hearing what I'm hearing from you two."

Both men stopped their chatter and looked at their associate strangely. Williams spoke up and asked, "What's the problem now, Swank?"

"Do you guys forget that this man has us by the balls because of the info he has on us? Not to mention some of his shit was stolen so someone else has us by the balls as well, and you're talking about taking him out? That's career and life suicide!" Swank yelled, unable to contain his anger. Even though they were in a private booth, Swank's octaves were loud enough to disturb the patrons.

A young Portuguese waitress walked over to the table to check on the men. As she reached the table, she quietly asked, "Is everything alright, gentlemen?"

The men looked the woman over to admire her beauty, but it didn't last long as Swank coldly replied, "If something was wrong, I would have called you over here, bitch, but since I didn't, go somewhere and write on your tablet."

The waitress was nearly reduced to tears as she walked away.

"Asshole," was all that Williams could say once he witnessed Swank's rude display.

"Look … Swank, eventually we have to detach ourselves from this whole situation. If not, we're leaving our lives and our careers in the hands of a criminal instead of the people we took an oath to protect and provide for," the mayor said sincerely.

What the mayor had said struck a chord in Swank that was long overdue to be played. He remembered when he first graduated out of the academy and how he took an oath to serve, protect, and uphold the law. It didn't matter what nationality you were, if you needed his service, he would be there like Superman. But somewhere between the academy and where he was now, the line between loyalty and money was crossed. Seeing young blacks and Puerto Ricans drive Bentleys, Benzes, and all types of SUVs hardened Swank's heart to the plight of the people in the hood. He was tired of driving a piece of shit car and returning home to a low-rent apartment with his pregnant wife. Swank abandoned all his morals and loyalty for the almighty dollar. He definitely didn't care about defending the "Blue Wall."

"Swank, if it's money that you want, then money you shall have.

Once the mayor is reelected and I become commissioner, I'm pretty sure we can bump your salary as well as your rank. How does lieutenant sound? Before you answer, you have to be with us on taking Ice out. And I know that Ice isn't your only source of income. I know about JD and Big Keith, and I suggest that you do something about JD before that comes back and bites all of us in the ass," Williams said.

Swank couldn't answer because he was still tripping off the fact that he could be made a lieutenant. He had been waiting for this opportunity for years, and now it was in front of his face to grab. The mayor, noticing that Swank was in a daze, asked, "Swank, did you just hear the offer that was laid out for you?"

Swank came out of his daze and for the first time in a long time, the mayor and the chief saw a huge smile that was across the fat man's face.

"Uh, uh, yeah, I heard what he said."

"So what do you think?" the mayor asked.

"I'm with you guys. I'll handle JD. As for Ice, I think I know how to handle our complicated situation."

The mayor and the chief moved in closer to hear the plan of their wicked associate.

♥   ♥   ♥   ♥

Black walked in his apartment and was surprised to see his sister sitting on the couch. "What brings you home?" he asked unenthusiastically.

Danika put her drink down and with the same attitude said, "Nice to see you, too."

"I'm sorry, big sis. I just had a long day, that's all," he lied as he sat next to her. He actually was floating after meeting Nadeem, but seeing his sister put him on guard. He knew most times that she came home, she came home with drama or she wanted something. It wouldn't be too long before he found out her real motives for being there.

"That's all right, but I did come home to talk to you."

Black looked at his sister and braced himself for her bullshit. He was younger but definitely more mature.

"What is it now, Danika?" he asked as he sighed.

"*Damn*, I didn't even say anything and you trippin'. Nigga get a little power on the streets and don't know how to act," she said as she sucked on her perfect teeth and rolled her pretty brown eyes that all the hustlers fell for.

"Whatever, say what you got to say so I can do what I got to do," Black said, not hiding his frustration. They loved each other, but this was their typical interaction with one another.

Danika lit a 'Port as Black moved away from her. She lit up the cigarette on purpose to work his nerves. After she blew smoke, she said, "Big Keith needs to talk to you. He said it's real important."

"So that's who you fuck with now?"

"None of your business. But like I said, he needs to talk to you."

"About what?"

"Damn, you ask a lot of questions, nigga."

"Well?"

"I don't know. Some stupid shit about ending some street war."

"It ain't bullshit. That's why E was killed, and why you need to be safer."

"I'm safe, baby brother. So are you going to call him?"

"I'll call him later and see what's up."

Black started to walk toward his room when Danika said, "Hey, I figured with Mommy gone in Colorado, you might need someone to cook a good meal."

Black turned around and said, "Yeah, that would be cool." He started to walk away again, but he was stopped once more by Danika's voice.

"Black, Daddy called. He said the invitation to go to L.A. is still open whenever we're ready." Black wasn't going to L.A. without handling his business, but he was glad to hear that their father called.

"I'll let you know, and some fried chicken would be nice ugly," he teased.

"Just for that, I ain't makin' you shit," Danika replied as they shared a laugh for the first time in a long time.

❦ ❦ ❦ ❦

JD sat on his bunk, salivating as he thought about the day he could stick his big black foot up Swank's white, racist, cracker ass. Swank ripped him off, lied, and broke many promises, and if he broke his promise to get him off easy, Swank was going to burn with him. An officer interrupted JD's thoughts when he was told that he had a visitor. *Think about the devil and he appears* was what ran through

JD's mind.

JD sat down and was thoroughly surprised to see Big Keith on the other side of the glass.

The huge smiles that both men wore proved that they were more than happy to see one another. "What's up, big dawg?" Big Keith spoke into the receiver.

"I'm alright. What's up on the streets, baby?"

"Money is coming in like a gravy train. Black stopped charging us rent for whatever reason. He's also hittin' us off with better quality shit at a cheaper price. Ice doesn't know shit, and he's happy as long as he gets his rent money for the corner," Keith explained.

"So that's what's up. What is Swank talkin' about?"

"I'm glad you asked. Swank talking 'bout doin' some business with Black and us. He said he knows a way that we could get at Ice."

"You mean take Ice out? Is that ma'fucka crazy? What do we get out of this shit, and what did Black say?" JD became irate at the thought of taking Ice out. Swank couldn't be trusted, and he proved that because JD was *still* in the county and Black was cool, but JD wasn't sure if Black had enough manpower to take on Ice.

"Calm down, baby," Keith said. "I know you don't trust Swank, but he's offering his team of experts to help out in this situation to make sure the job gets done. He said he has some specially trained Marine boys on the force that's down with him, and they are more than happy to help out. I don't know about Black yet. I had his sister talk to him, so hopefully, he'll call soon. And when he does, I'll present him with the info. It works out for everyone. Swank is offering us the city once Ice is out of the picture," Keith explained.

JD took a few seconds to take in all that he heard.

"So what's up?" Keith asked once he didn't get a response from JD.

JD took a deep breath and unloaded his concerns on Keith. "Things sound good, but we have a few problems. One, I'm still in here, and Swank ain't saying nothing on how I'ma get out. Number two, even if we take out Ice with the Eastwick Hustlers and Swank's boys, how is Swank gonna offer us the city? It ain't like Black and the Eastwick Hustlers just gonna lay it down for us. And we damn sure don't have the manpower to take on their crew 'cause if we did, we wouldn't be getting our work from them," JD said.

will robbins

"Man, the Port Au Prince Posse and the Eastwick Hustlers only exist because Swank, the chief, and the mayor let them exist. If Swank say you the man, then you the man. I know you not afraid of success, are you?"

"Be smart, Keith. Ice has something on all those niggas, and that's why Swank wants us to help take out Ice. They have no choice but to let that man loose. And the word on the street is Black got something on them too. That's why they didn't touch him. If Ice or the mayor could have Black killed, they would have, but they can't without exposing themselves. And if we kill Ice, I'm pretty sure that they'll want us to kill Black, and I ain't with that," JD said with conviction.

"I feel you. Black is cool people. You still got heart enough to go at it with Ice, though, right?"

"No doubt."

JD and Keith were going to continue to talk business until they heard a scruffy voice say, "Time's up." A heavyset black guard ended the visit. JD would usually have been upset, but he and Keith had covered all their bases.

❦ ❦ ❦ ❦

Most of the officers in the Elizabeth Police Department were uneasy while Dawkins was in one of the back rooms with Sgt. Cruz and his Hit Squad. Dawkins wasn't Internal Affairs Division (IAD), but he definitely had the power to take away some badges.

Dawkins stood in the middle of the room talking to the Hit Squad and a few trusted uniformed officers. The streets were too quiet for Dawkins' taste, and with the war between the Port Au Prince Posse and the Eastwick Hustlers, he knew something wasn't right. It was the quiet before the storm that bothered him. He figured he'd stir things up on the streets to see what birds would sing if their cages were rattled a little.

"Alright, things are quiet on the streets right now, and I don't like it. I want you men ripping up those corners and find out what's going on. Use any type of tactics to get people to talk. This shit has been going on for too long," Dawkins said out of frustration.

Sgt. Cruz stood up and spoke for the first time. "We'll shake things up on the streets for you 'cause that's what we do. However, we're going strictly by the book. I don't want any asshole getting off because we rough them up or they get off because of some technical-ity on our part."

As the men spoke, there were many crooked officers outside the room straining to hear what was being said. Before the men could walk away from their childish eavesdropping, the door suddenly opened and the Hit Squad bumped into several officers. Gaining his composure and trying to avoid embarrassment, one of the officers said, "I'm sorry, Cruz, just wanted to see if we could offer our assis-tance." Sgt. Cruz just looked at the man and his eyes said it all—hell, no!

On First, Second, and Third Street, money was coming through like Wall Street. The Port Au Prince Posse and the Eastwick Hustlers' spots were flowing with money and drug-hungry fiends. Since the vio-lence stopped, both teams were more prosperous. Too bad the Hit Squad and various officers were going to fuck up the game. The Port Au Prince Posse was serving fiends on First and Second Street, while the Eastwick Hustlers held onto Midtown like it was Fort Knox. With the money they were making, it might as well have been Fort Knox.

Greg, T-Money, and Bird were holding down the block on Court Street, representing hard for the Eastwick Hustlers. All three men had been putting in work for a year now and had proven themselves as a good street team. Plenty of times they held their ground against the attacks of the Port Au Prince Posse. Gregg was about 6'2", weighing about 300 pounds, and was a few years older than Black. He resided and made his bones in Linden. When he heard about a ruthless young brother by the name of Black that was making money and was willing to do battle with Ice, he had to get down. T-Money and Bird had been loyal soldiers, so naturally, they rolled with their man.

It was business as usual when Sgt. Cruz and his Hit Squad rolled up on the three-man crew. The van pulled up inconspicuously and several men jumped out like the A-Team. Gregg and his team were taken totally by surprise, which was rare. Since they weren't attacked in quite a while, they had become a little too relaxed. Now it was too late to remove their guns or move from the stash spot.

"Damn," was all Gregg could say as he put his hands in the air before Cruz could bark any demands.

T-Money followed suit with Gregg, while Bird was a little more defiant. Bird was short and had a temper to match his height. He

will robbins

wanted to go down like a real street legend, and he didn't care how he did it.

Det. Mateo was happy to see some resistance. It gave him the type of excuse he needed to let out some frustration. With one swift motion, the detective knocked Bird on the right side of his forehead with the butt of his service revolver.

"Ma'fucka," was all Bird could say as he felt the force of the blow. With catlike reflexes, Bird threw a right hook and connected to Mateo's face. The sucker punch barely fazed Mateo as he laughed at the young man.

"Stupid-ass nigga," Gregg replied as he saw the side show go down.

T-Money continued to hold his position and just shake his head at the young man. Mateo liked the fire in the little man, so he just pushed him up against the wall while the rest of the Hit Squad started to search T-Money and Gregg.

Sgt. Cruz ran his hands around Gregg's waist and stopped at the small of his back when he felt a piece of steel. Gregg knew he was hit, and his mind started to race on what he should do. He knew he was too big and slow to run, and fighting was definitely out of the question.

"What do we have here, Gregg? Looks like we're looking at a couple of years on this one," Sgt. Cruz stated.

"We got another one, Sergeant," Mateo said with the same cocky attitude as Cruz.

"The fun doesn't stop here. This asshole has one too," Det. Mendes said as he finished his search on T-Money.

Det. Garcia was busy doing recon work, and he wasn't disappointed when he found the stash spot between a rooming house and a bodega. Garcia found bags and bags of drugs snugly placed between a huge tire and a rusty garbage can.

The three-man crew knew that they were hit, the only question was—how bad. Each man wanted to talk his way out of it, but they wouldn't dare snitch in each other's presence. Bird was the only man that had enough heart not to talk. He didn't care how he would get his street credentials as long as he was written in the books as thorough.

"Alright. Either we have some caged birds or some singing birds. Which one will it be?" Cruz asked, looking in Bird's direction, hoping that the little man lost his heart in fear of being locked up.

"I don't know why you lookin' my way. I ain't got shit to say to you bitch-ass niggas. You might as well lock me up right now," Bird stated as he spat on the ground.

The Hit Squad all got a big laugh at the man acting tough. Bird felt like they took him for a joke, so he decided to give them something to laugh about. He cocked back and threw a huge haymaker from the shoulder that connected to the left side of Mateo's face again. All the men thought that Mateo was going to go ape shit because of his attitude. Surprisingly, all Mateo did was laugh the young man's blow off and pulled out the cuffs.

As Mateo cuffed Bird, Sgt. Cruz started his interrogation. "What's the matter? Don't you teach ya' dogs any manners, Gregg?" Cruz asked.

Still with his hands on his head, Gregg answered, "He's his own man, sir." Gregg and Cruz had a lot of run-ins with each other since Gregg started to work for Black. They sort of had a rapport and mutual respect for one another.

"So, where are Black and the rest of the higher-ups in the Eastwick Hustlers?" Cruz asked to no one in particular.

The three-man crew were silent for a few seconds. Growing tired of the street mentality of never snitch, Cruz said, "Alright, round them up, boys."

Gregg wanted to let out just a little information to get him and his boys off the hook. "Alright, look, we ain't seen Black or his other people in weeks. They been laying low and letting us foot soldiers handle all the dirty work to prove ourselves during this time of war."

Cruz and his men just looked at each other once they heard Gregg's explanation. Det. Mendes decided to speak up and ask questions, which really wasn't his style. "There hasn't been any killings out here in a few months, so what war are you talking about?"

"Man, their ain't been no killin' out here for awhile because of the elections. Ice ain't been comin' at us like that 'cause he got the mayor in his pockets and he wants to keep it that way, Sherlock," Bird stated sarcastically.

"So I guess we got ourselves a shit storm to look forward to after the elections, huh?" Cruz asked.

"You goddamn right, bitch," Bird said.

will robbins

Cruz and his men were growing tired of the young man and the whole situation.

"Alright, T-Money, Gregg, y'all got a pass on this one, but ya' little friend gonna take a hit for his mouth. Now we're gonna come back, and I expect a little more cooperation from you, baby," Cruz stated.

Cruz and his fellow officers hit First, Second, Third Street, Midtown, Uptown, and received the same results—little to no information at all. But they were being real street sweepers. Anyone who didn't want to cooperate received the same treatment as Bird, handcuffed from elbow to asshole. The blocks got cold as an old woman's bed.

♥ ♥ ♥ ♥

Back at the station, Dawkins waited in the Hit Squad's clubhouse to see what type of results they would produce. Also keeping him company was Agent Simms. Simms was familiar with the squad and was keeping a very low profile with the Eastwick Hustlers. He knew the streets being quiet was just the quiet before the storm, and he wanted to be very helpful to the Hit Squad and provide any and all information so he could close the case and go home faster. Just as the men started to become restless, Sgt. Cruz and his men walked in the room, tossing Bird in front of them.

Bird caught himself from stumbling and was totally shocked to see Dawkins standing over Agent Simms—a.k.a. Bobby. Dawkins and Simms were caught totally by surprise by their guest. Quickly gaining his composure, Bird asked, "Yo, Bobby, what the fuck you doin' here?"

Thinking on his toes and not wanting to lose his only inside man on the case, Dawkins balled up his apelike fist and punched Simms in his face. Simms fell out of the chair and held the left side of his face, which seemed to swell instantly.

Simms fell right into character and said, "Fuck you, Dawkins! I ain't got shit to tell you! I don't know where Black is, and even if I did, I wouldn't tell ya' bitch ass shit!"

"That's right, don't tell that ma'fucka shit," Bird blabbered out.

Mateo just pushed him deeper into the room. The shove put Bird inches away from Dawkins' face. Bird looked like a little child standing next to the massive man. Bird's big heart and dreams of being a street legend wouldn't allow him to be intimidated by the big man.

Cruz and his men took a seat to watch the sideshow. They wanted to see how Dawkins would handle the brave-hearted Bird. They were thoroughly impressed with how Dawkins and Simms acted to throw Bird off, and they wanted to see more.

Standing face to chest, Bird said, "What?" He wanted to show Dawkins that he had no fear.

Dawkins shoved the young man, and he fell back into a seat. Bird started to jump back up, but Dawkins lifted his pointer finger and shook it as if to say, "Don't get yourself fucked up." So Bird sat still and listened to the big man.

"Now, Marcus Higgins, that *is* your name, isn't it?" Dawkins asked, putting his hands behind his back to look less combative.

Bird just looked at him like he was crazy.

"You don't have to answer that. I already know the answer," Dawkins said.

Simms finally lifted himself off the floor and took a seat to listen to the interrogation.

The room fell silent for a few seconds as Dawkins paced the floor. His Stacey Adams shoes seemed to have a light jazz sound as they clicked against the white tile floor. Bird started to get nervous as the seconds passed. He wished that Dawkins would get on with the questioning and just put his black ass in a cell. Before Bird knew it, he got his wish when Dawkins said, "You're going to tell me what I want to know whether you like it or not. I don't care about your street credibility."

"And if I don't tell you, what you gonna do? Put me in a squad car and drive me around the city of Elizabeth lockin' niggas up saying I ratted. That's that Hollywood bullshit. And I know y'all ain't gonna whoop my ass 'cause y'all don't want to mess up ya' case. So what the hell you gonna do, bitch?"

Dawkins chuckled at the kid's attempt to be diplomatic. "Smart boy, isn't he?" Dawkins asked, looking at Cruz.

"Smart indeed," Cruz replied.

"They ain't gonna do shit, Bird!" Simms yelled out still in character.

"You guys really don't know who you're fuckin' with," Dawkins said. Dawkins took a seat right in front of Bird and put his game face on. Slowly, he took a deep breath and asked, "Does the name Paulette Higgins mean anything to you?"

"Yeah. That's my ma'fuckin' mother, why?" Bird asked with his face all distorted and confused.

Dawkins smiled, knowing he got a rise out of Bird.

"Well, you know that ride you thought I was going to take you on?"

"Yeah, what about it?"

"Well, how about I take your mother on that ride and make Ice, Black, and any other hustler out there think that *she's* a rat? It wouldn't take too long for them to kill her, and you."

"Fuck you, you can't do that!" Bird yelled, jumping from his seat.

After Bird's outburst, Dawkins' whole body illuminated with joy. "I'm DEA, lil' nigga. I can do what the fuck I want and as soon as you realize that I ain't no joke, the better off you'll be. I don't give a fuck about you, your mother, or any other person in your family. All I care about is breaking my case, and you're holding my shit up, so talk, bitch!" Dawkins voice and attitude scared and broke Bird's hardcore attitude.

"Yo, Bird, that's ya' mom, dawg. You gotta do what you gotta do. I ain't gonna say shit, baby," Simms replied, playing the sympathetic role.

Tears started to well up in Bird's eyes as he realized he was stuck between a rock and a hard times place. Sweating and panting, Bird was going to break the code of the street and snitch. Being a street legend wasn't as important as keeping his mother alive.

"A'ight, Dawkins, you got it," Bird said in a defeated tone.

Dawkins and the rest of the men started to perk up at the thought of breaking the case. Bird whipped the tears from his eyes, took a deep breath, and started to speak. "After the elections ..." Bird's voice cracked as he tried to speak.

"You need some water, a soda, or something?" Dawkins asked, feeling friendly.

"Yeah," was all that Bird said. Dawkins looked at Mateo as if to tell him to fetch the young boy a drink.

"This fucker throws punches in bunches at me, and I'm supposed to get him a drink? He's lucky I don't catch him a foot in the ass," Mateo said defiantly.

Dawkins shot him a look that didn't need any explanation. Mateo quickly left the room. Just as fast, as he left he returned with a Sprite soda. He was more than anxious to hear the boy speak. Bird cracked the can, took a gulp, and proceeded to talk.

"A'ight, Black and his men plan on attacking Ice's mansion a few days after the elections. I don't know what day yet, but I know niggas from Newark, Elizabeth, Linden, Jersey City, Asbury Park, and New York is going to be involved. Black wants to take Ice out the same way Ice took out Diamond Black back in the day," Bird explained.

"That's it?" Dawkins asked, hoping that there would be more information.

"That's all I know. I'm one of the lowest men in rank. I won't know until the day it's going down," Bird explained pleadingly. He hoped it was enough information so that Dawkins would leave his mother out of the equation.

"So what about the tapes that Black stole from Ice? Where are they?" Dawkins asked.

"I already told you I'm the lowest man. You already know that shit. If there are any tapes, I don't know anything about them," Bird said annoyed.

Dawkins gripped the boy up and lifted him off his feet and yelled, "Look here, you ma'fucka, I'm through playing games with ya' bitch ass. Tell me something else I can use. I'm pretty sure I can run that little gun of yours out there and find a body on it, so talk!"

"Come on, man, you think I'm gonna hold out on you after you threatened to put my mom's life in danger? I don't care if I die in the streets, but that's not for my moms."

Dawkins shoved the kid back in his seat, knowing full well he was telling the truth.

"So what does ya' boy, Bobby, here know? Does he know more than you?" Dawkins asked.

Bird looked in Bobby's direction and said, "I don't know what he knows. We don't even work the same blocks. I just know he works for Black, that's it."

"Get him out of here and when my boys hit the block, you better have more info for me or start spending quality time with your mother," Dawkins said as threatening as he could be. Bird stood on his feet, and Mendes led him out the door.

"So what do you think, Agent Simms?" Dawkins asked.

"I think you hit like a bitch," Simms replied as the men laughed.

will robbins

"I know it was a close one, but we pulled through. Good police work, Agent."

"I know Bird is telling the truth. Black has been holding off on when he wants to attack Ice, but he does want to hit the mansion. I'll know when we're close to the date because Black wants all of his men training and planning for it. So I'll continue to stay close to Black. We've gotten closer since his brother's death, and he trusts me a little bit," Simms explained.

"Good. We'll let the hit on Ice and his crew take place, and we'll arrest everyone on the premises for weapons charges, assault, and anything else we can pin on them, but Ice has to be on the premises. Simms, you need to find out when the hit is going to take place and let the Hit Squad and myself know so we can back you up and get this thing done. It's time to clean up these streets," Dawkins said.

will robbins

19

First Date

Ice sat idly in his office, reminiscing about the good times he shared with Nadeem and how he really messed things up. He couldn't figure out why he needed so many women when Nadeem was more than a woman. He was even more perplexed about why he had to tape his sexcapades and dirty deeds. As a leader, Ice was tough on the surface, but he was more than worried about his current situation. He was unsure what Black would do with the tapes, and the streets were talking about how strong and enormous Black's army was growing.

In an attempt to clear his conscience, Ice picked up his office phone and dialed home for the first time in months. Nadeem picked up the phone in hopes that it would be Black on the other end. She placed her son on the couch, moved her long silky hair so she could hear better, placed the phone to her ear, and said, "Hello."

Once Ice responded, she was met with disappointment. She started to hang up, but she decided to entertain the call, especially since he hadn't called in months. "What do you want, Toussaint?" she asked sharply.

Although Nadeem's voice was anything but sweet, she still had a way to melt Ice's heart when she spoke.

"I was thinking about you and our son, wondering how y'all doing."

"You weren't wondering about us when you were fuckin' them

other bitches, so why worry now? And what the fuck took you so long to call, nigga?" She purposely called him a nigga to get him furious.

"Come on now, it ain't even like that. I thought that you needed time to cool off and time to forgive me. If I wasn't thinking about y'all, wouldn't I have put you outta my spot instead of me sleeping in my office?"

"Brother, please, you know better than to try and put me out. And you probably were with some bitch all this time. And why did it take you so long to call?"

"The way you left when we were on vacation, I thought you needed the time to calm down. Plus, I was afraid of the type of response I would get from you if I came home," Ice said trying to gain his woman's compassion.

"Well, you'll never know. Your son is fine. As far as me, you don't need to be concerned anymore," Nadeem said as she hung up the phone.

Ice pulled the phone away from his ear as the loud bang irritated him. He started to become furious, but he figured he deserved it with all the shit he did. Nadeem knew she could act like that because Ice would always be a father to his son and more powerful than that, she knew most of his dirt and could put him away for life, so her position was secure. As far as death, she wasn't worried. Ice would never leave his son motherless, because he still had nightmares from being motherless.

♦ ♦ ♦ ♦

Black sat on his bed thinking about Nadeem. His heart pounded as he thought about calling her. He knew he had to call her, especially since he made reservations at the Red Parrot Bar/Restaurant. He was so smooth when they first met, but he was wondering how he could keep a woman like her open. Most women came his way, even his first love, Kasha. Now he was open for someone, and the situation seemed to come with problems.

He pulled out Nadeem's number and stared at it for a while as he gained his courage to call her. Nadeem was just about to walk out the door to blow off some steam when her phone rang again. Without looking at the caller ID, she picked up the phone and yelled, "What the fuck do you want, Toussaint?"

Black pulled the phone from his head as his ear began to ring from the yelling.

"Whoa, I guess Toussaint is the complication you were trying to warn me about in the school parking lot?"

"Black? Is that you?" Nadeem asked, toning down her attitude.

"The one and only. Now what was that all about?"

"Oh, that was nothing that you need to worry about."

"I would ask you how your day is going, but from the sound of your voice, I can pretty much guess."

"Well, you don't need to worry. I'm in a much better mood now. How are you doing?"

"I'm good. I was just thinking about you."

"What were you thinking?"

"I was thinking that I'm hungry and didn't want to eat alone. So I was hoping you would join me," Black said, hoping she would join him this time.

"I would love to join you, but my situation hasn't changed from the last time we spoke."

"I think your situation is taking a turn for the worse, because if it wasn't, we wouldn't be on the phone right now. And I think you're just as curious about me, so why don't you just see me and see what happens? It's not like I'm asking for your hand in marriage." Black was a little surprised by his barrage of words since he wasn't so talkative when it came to females. He figured he had to approach this woman like he approached drugs—very serious and cocky.

Black's cockiness turned Nadeem on, but it also had her on the fence. Ice showed the same cockiness when they first started dating, and now their relationship was in a tailspin.

"You seem so sure of yourself, huh, Black?"

"Look, I know I saw a woman who looked like she has a good head on her shoulders and I was intrigued. Now I want to see if you have the ability to keep me intrigued. Besides, I know you're going through something stressful with ya' man, and you're close to finals at school, so I know you need to get out and relax. So how about it?" Black asked.

"That sounds nice. So where do you want to meet?"

"Is there something wrong with me picking you up?"

"I barely know you. Besides, I don't think now is a good time for you to know where I live, and I don't think that it's cool for us to be seen together." Nadeem wasn't too concerned about people recognizing her on the streets. Ice kept her pretty isolated from the outside world. He would take her on vacations far from the city of Elizabeth, and he kept her from the business and his associates. He wanted to make sure that no one knew his woman or child, except for some important individuals, of which weren't many. That way, no one could use them against him.

Black, on the other hand, had no idea about the woman he was about to get entangled with. So he had no reservations except he would protect her better than he did Kasha if things worked out. Making sure she wouldn't change her mind too soon, Black asked, "How 'bout we meet at the Red Parrot on Broad Street Uptown at 6 pm?" He was hoping she said yes since he made reservations a couple of days ago before he called her.

"I'll be there."

"See you soon," Black said, smiling from ear to ear. Knowing he had a few hours before his date, he figured he'd cruise the streets and check on his soldiers and money.

♦ ♦ ♦ ♦

Once again, Ice was in his office, meeting with a few men he tolerated rather than liked, but they helped and allowed his business to run and thrive. His mind really wasn't on the business at hand, though, especially since his conversation with Nadeem.

"Ice, are you listening?" Officer Swank asked, slamming his shotglass down hard on the desk. Ice just shot Swank a dirty look.

"So what about JD?" Ice asked.

"We have JD in county. I locked him up on some trumped-up charges so he could kill Prince so we wouldn't have to worry about a snitch."

"And what about it?" Dubois asked.

"I told him if he did the deed, he would do little to no time. I told him I would give him some names to drop so he could cut a deal with the DA."

"Well, that's your problem," Ice said sternly.

"No, it's *our* problem. JD has info on your black ass and your organization as well as the boys in blue. Killing him is not an option, because we need him and his little crew. Don't forget we're gonna have problems with Black and his people," Swank complained.

Ice stood on his feet and paced his office in silence. He wished that he had crushed Black months ago when he had a chance. Now things were spinning out of control.

Dubois, noticing Ice's frustration, spoke up. "How important to our cause is this young man, JD?" Dubois asked.

"He's important to this war that's about to go down real soon. His crew isn't large in numbers, but they're strong. Besides, JD and his crew pay rent money to this organization, and taking him out means losing millions in the long run, and none of us can afford that right now," Swank explained.

"Anybody can be replaced, Swank, including ya' white ass!" Ice yelled as his frustration built up. "This is going out of control! There are entirely too many ma'fuckas out there with too much info on all of us!" Ice continued to yell.

Swank thought to himself, *It was ya' nigger ass that got us into this shit, recording everything.* But he valued his life too much to say it out loud.

"Calm down, son," Dubois said in his calm manner. "Everything will be handled in time. We know just as much information on those who have information on us, so we're fine. No one wants to go to jail. Once we win this war, we burn those goddamn tapes and take out those who have too much information on us, especially those who aren't important to this organization.

"Now, Swank here's what you're going to do. You're going to have JD's lawyer set up a meeting with the DA. Ice and I are going to sacrifice a few men for the sake of this JD kid. We'll give the DA a few murderers in exchange for JD's freedom. The most he can get is probation and community service hours. If that doesn't work, than we'll take out JD and his crew. We'll give them Mo and Jean. Let the DA know they can find the bodies of Mark Jenkins, Tasha Wright, and Ronald Jones in the river on Front Street," Dubois explained.

"I'll get right on it," Swank said. He hoped that the deal would go through. He knew that JD was expendable, but he needed him to make sure that his own agenda would fall through. Swank left to hurry to JD's lawyer's office to set the deal in motion.

❧ ❧ ❧ ❧

Black was almost out the door when he heard a knock. Before he opened the door, he pulled his piece from his backside. As he opened the door, his tension began to ease once he saw Big Keith.

"What's up, Keith? You out of shit already?"

Big Keith greeted Black the way brothers in the hood would greet and answered, "I'm not out of shit yet. I have a proposition for you."

"I don't have a lot of time, so come in and make it quick." Black stepped aside to let Keith enter, and they took a seat.

"Listen, man, I know things are about to blow up with Ice and JD, and our crew don't want to be left out on the streets starving while y'all figure this shit out."

"As long as y'all keep doin' what ya' doin', ain't nobody gonna starve. The shit with Ice is my crew's business and mine. It ain't got nothing to do with you or JD," Black explained.

"Swank stepped to us the other day, and the shit he talkin' gonna affect all of us," Big Keith stated.

"Swank, Swank! What does that fat, white, cracker-ass cracker got to do with my shit?" Black asked in a small rage.

"Whoa, whoa, whoa, baby, calm down," Big Keith stood up, waving his hands up and down in an attempt to calm Black down with words and sign language. Black sighed, took a seat, and said, "Spit it out."

Keith took a seat and chose his words carefully. "Swank approached me and said he wanted to put a hit out on Ice. He said he has some men that were specialists in the Marines and that they were at his disposal, but he needs more men to do it."

"So?" Black said, not hiding the fact that he was pissed.

"So? So, that's where *we* come in. My crew, your crew, and Swank's men, we can pull this off."

"What's in it for Swank and your crew?"

"More money for Swank, and he gets rid of a lot of niggas."

"And you and your crew?"

"More money, more power, more respect."

"Once Ice is out of the picture, *I'm* going to take the reigns. Or did you think that I was just going to step off and let ya' crew take over?" Black asked.

"Black if it's anything that I know about you is that you're fair. JD and me know you would be the king, but you'd be a fair king. You'd unify everything so we wouldn't have to worry about separate crews or warring, and me and JD want in on that."

"You right. But we're going to do everything *without* the help of Swank. What's up with JD now?"

"Swank should be working some angles to get JD out."

"Well, once JD is out, I want you to call me so we can meet up and work out the details. Until then, try to avoid Swank like the plague."

"A'ight, I'ma go check on JD's status, and I'ma get right back to you."

Black and Keith embraced each other once again, and Keith left just as fast as he came.

❦ ❦ ❦ ❦

Big Keith walked in front of the county jail just in time to see JD walking out with Swank and his lawyer. Needless to say, they were all smiles and surprised. "Yo, Swank made it happen, baby!" JD said as he and Big Keith embraced.

"So what you get, son?"

"Three years probation and one-hundred hours of community service, baby! I just got to testify to some bullshit."

"Yo, let's go celebrate. The whip is in the parking lot."

"Don't celebrate too long. We got business to take care of. Ya' black asses still belong to me!" Swank yelled out at the two men speed walking away.

JD's lawyer was happy to get another client off. He didn't care that he was guilty, he just saw it as more income.

❦ ❦ ❦ ❦

Black made his rounds and noticed that he only had a few minutes to make it to the Red Parrot Bar/Restaurant on Broad Street. He knew he couldn't be late for a fine woman like Nadeem. His age was already a strike against him, so he didn't want to show his immaturity by being late. Besides, he wanted to see her make her grand entrance.

Black pulled up in his tricked-out Escalade and when he walked into the bar/restaurant, he was greeted with star treatment, especially since he kicked out a few thousand dollars to have the upper deck decorated with white roses and other paraphernalia prior to his visit.

"Black, come on in. Everything is waiting and perfect like you asked," a small Italian guy said, shaking Black's hand. They walked up the stairs and Black was almost caught breathless at the beauty Gino the owner had created. Each table was decorated with scented candles

will robbins

and satin cloth. White rose pedals covered the Italian oak wood floors while yellow roses decked the tables. Iced angels resembling Cupid glowed in the dimly lit room. Golden chandeliers hung above the tables and were covered with red roses. The chandeliers were also lit by candlelight.

Nadeem walked into the restaurant and all the men's heads turned, including the white and Chinese patrons of the bar. Her beauty had the ability to make any man's head turn, even if he were racist.

Gino walked down the stairs just in time to see Nadeem's coat being checked in. He couldn't help but stare at her radiating beauty, or chest, for a better word. She wore a tight V-shaped Prada top with no bra, and her breasts stood out like Mt. Everest. Her thick thighs and equally matched ass filled out her miniskirt to perfection. Her walk was hypnotizing in her knee-high boots. Her long flowing hair was as soft and beautiful as Egyptian silk, and her scent was even more intoxicating.

Gino walked up to Nadeem with his brightest smile and said, "You must be the lovely Nadeem."

Nadeem could only blush at the small, handsome Italian.

"How do you know who I am? I've never been here before."

"There is a young man upstairs who told me that the most beautiful woman in the world would be coming into my humble establishment. And as I look around, there is no competition compared to you," Gino said with a slight bow as he continued to smile.

"Thank you, um …" Nadeem was waiting for Gino to fill in the blank with his name.

"Oh, I'm very sorry, miss. My name is Gino," he replied extending his hand.

As she placed her lovely hand into his, he planted a soft kiss on it.

"Follow me, madam," Gino said as he held her hand and walked her up the stairs.

Nadeem reached the top of the stairs and had the same reaction as Black when she saw the setup. Ice had taken her to many resorts and exotic islands, but never did he put his own personal touch into a date. She was very impressed with the young man that was standing in front of her with a bright smile and dressed in Sean John casual wear. Nadeem walked like a model to the dinner table, and Black politely pulled out her chair. He then took his seat and sat across from her, where he couldn't stop smiling.

Ice and Dubois checked on their business just as Black had done. All was well, and they decided to head towards the mayor's campaign hall, knowing full well he won the election and it was time for Ice to celebrate. Celebrate the fact that he could now move on the Eastwick Hustlers without adversely affecting the mayor's campaign and ruining his own dictatorship over Elizabeth. Normally, Ice would hide the fact that he had ties with the mayor, but it was his last term and Ice wanted to show the people of Elizabeth who really held the power.

The campaign hall was louder than a Puerto Rican party after the polls showed that Mayor Cross was indeed the mayor of Elizabeth again. Champagne was popped, people congratulated one another on their hard work and success, but most importantly, they were able to exhale, especially since their jobs were secure for another term.

Mayor Cross, Chief Williams, and Swank were in a little huddle, all smiles, talking, while everyone else mingled. Suddenly, the music stopped and peoples' heads turned and got silent once Ice and Dubois walked into the hall. It was if they had walked into a racist country bar in the Deep South.

"Don't stop all the partying on our account," Dubois said.

"Give it up for Mayor Cross," Ice said, clapping. The attendees started to clap, and the music was cued back up, and Ice and Dubois were just as welcomed as the next man, so it seemed.

"What the fuck are you two doing here?" the mayor asked, fixing his tie, trying not to sweat.

"You weren't worried about that when you needed funding. We just want to share in your joy, baby," Ice said, shaking the mayor's hand to make things look legit.

"We figured we'd pick you up and go out to dinner to talk about some business strategies," Dubois said.

"What would it look like, the mayor, police chief, and a decorated officer fraternizing with known drug lords?" Swank asked.

"The same as it looks now. No one gives a fuck," Ice answered, looking around the room to show that no one was paying attention to the company that the mayor was keeping.

"Besides, you didn't have a problem fraternizing with us in public before the election, so what's the problem now?" Dubois asked.

will robbins

The chief cleared his voice and said, "Those public meetings were pretty private, and the rest were in the privacy of the mansion."

"Is that all you want, some privacy? We can go to the Red Parrot on Broad Street. I hear they have a pretty good private VIP section," Ice said.

"You have to make reservations for that place ahead of time," the mayor replied, hoping Ice would back off.

"Come on, now. You just got reelected, and I'm the 'King of Jersey.' How can we be turned down?"

"You're not going to stop until I say yes, are you?" the mayor asked.

"No, so you might as well come along and get it over with," Dubois said.

"Alright. I'll have my limo meet us out front to take us to the Red Parrot," the mayor told Ice. The men shook hands, and Ice and Dubois waited for the mayor and his two henchmen outside.

♥ ♥ ♥ ♥

Black and Nadeem continued to enjoy each other's company as well as the meal. Gino walked over to make sure everything was all right, but the young couple were so engulfed in their conversation that they didn't even hear or see Gino standing in their presence. Gino walked away and chalked it up to young infatuation.

"So what made you pick the Red Parrot out of all places, and how did you set this up?" Nadeem asked.

"I heard about how this place was *the* place to be, but I'd never been here before. So I figured now was as good a time as any. The setup was to show you that I have style and class, even though I'm young. I also wanted to impress you," Black said smiling.

"I'm definitely impressed, thank you."

"So what's your story?" Black asked.

"What do you mean 'what's my story'?"

"You know, where you been, where you come from, where you're going, do you have kids?"

"What makes you ask if I have kids?"

"That's not all I asked, but most people have some big story about themselves or some dark secret, so I figured I go fishing for info."

"If I have any dark secrets, they won't be brought out tonight, but here's a little taste of what you asked. I'm from India, but I moved to

220

the States with my father and my sister when I was nine."

"That explains the exotic beauty," Black said appreciatively.

"Thank you. I grew up in Pierce Manor. But now I live between the border of Elizabeth and Newark. You already know I'm in school, and I'm studying early childhood education. One day, I want to open and run my own daycare center."

"What about your man?"

"I'm getting there. Look at you, trying to get the good stuff."

"I'm just curious, girl," Black said as they smiled at each other.

Nadeem was getting caught up in Black's smile. She wasn't sure if she should go deep into her relationship with Ice or reveal the fact that her man was the biggest drug lord in Jersey or speak about the fact that she had a child. She didn't know how far she wanted to go with Black because she didn't want to turn him off or scare him away. Nadeem sat quietly for a few moments and Black started to wonder if she felt uncomfortable, so he asked, "Is everything all right?"

"I'm all right. I'm just wondering how much info I should tell you and if what I tell you is going to turn you off."

"There isn't too much that you can tell me that's going to turn me off. Just don't tell me that you were once a man," Black said laughing, making Nadeem relax a little.

"I've been with my man for about ten years, and we have a son together," Nadeem said as she looked to see if Black's facial expression would change. To her surprise, he didn't show any signs of being upset.

Once again she sat silently, and Black asked, "Was that suppose to turn me off?"

"So me having a child don't bother you?"

"I was raised by a single mother, so I can respect that. I love children. But after all these years, what's going on with you and ya' man that has you here with me?"

Nadeem sighed and replied, "There's been a lot going on in my life right now, and he isn't there for me like he used to be. That, and the fact that I caught him cheating a few times don't help."

Black sat there shocked that a man who was worthy enough to be in this beauty's presence was actually dumb enough to cheat.

"So what's wrong with *you*?" Nadeem asked as Black sat silently.

"Nothing. I just can't believe that someone would actually cheat on you."

"That's sweet."

"No, that's real. So, how old is your son?"

"He's about to be one soon."

Just at that moment, the mayor's limo pulled right in front of the Red Parrot Bar/Restaurant and the occupants exited the vehicle. The five-man entourage stepped into the restaurant like superstars, and technically, they were, in their own right. Some people in the restaurant began to clap at the appearance of the mayor, while others were appalled that he walked in with known drug dealers.

Gino stepped out of the kitchen when he heard the small raucous and saw the mayor, whom he recognized quite well. He also was aware of who Ice was, but Ice wasn't sure who Gino was. However, he would soon find out.

"Congratulations on your reelection, Mayor," Gino said, extending his hand. "What brings you to my humble restaurant, gentlemen?"

"We heard that this was the spot to be, so here we are," Ice answered.

"Well, you are certainly welcome here, gentlemen. How about I walk you guys over here to this table?"

"We were thinking we would take the VIP section upstairs for our first visit," Dubois said.

"I am so sorry to disappoint you, gentlemen, but the VIP section must be reserved in advanced. I will be more than willing to accommodate you and your party another time," Gino said, trying to sound apologetic when in actuality he could care less about disappointing a weak mayor and punk drug dealer.

The mayor cleared his throat and said, "I told you this would happen, now let's go." He was embarrassed and wanted to save face. Ice didn't hold his composure as well.

"Fuck another time! Do you know who the fuck I am?" Ice said as his voice raised a few octaves too loud.

"I know who you are, Mr. Ice, but I'm sorry I can't accommodate you and your associates upstairs today."

Ice pulled out a wad of money and asked real loud, "Can you fuckin' accommodate us *now*, bitch?"

Hearing the yelling downstairs, Black asked, "I wonder what's going on down there?"

"I don't know, but I think someone is very pissed off," Nadeem responded. She also thought that she recognized the voice but quickly dismissed the thought. She just knew that it had to be someone else that only sounded like Ice.

"I think I should check it out," Black said. Just as he was about to get out of his seat, Nadeem said, "Let the management handle it. That's what they're here for."

"You're right," Black said and sat back down.

"Your money doesn't matter. I have a young man up there right now that's entertaining a very beautiful woman, and he paid very well for it in advance. So you see I can't help you tonight," Gino said in his Italian accent.

"Get him the fuck outta there and let us up before I put him and his bitch out and take over myself," Ice said.

The mayor, police chief, Swank, as well as Dubois were getting embarrassed as the minutes passed. But to walk out without Ice would have been hurtful to them all, including Dubois.

Before Gino could answer, one of his waiters came from the kitchen and said, "Mr. Torelli ... Mr. Sanducci is on the phone for you."

At the mention of the names Torelli and Sanducci, Ice was taken aback and hoped that he hadn't gone too far with the disrespect.

"Mr. Torelli, like the Torelli and Sanducci *crime family?*" Ice asked a little worried.

"The media portrays us as a crime family while we just consider ourselves a family," Gino replied.

"Listen, I meant no disrespect, sir," Ice replied remorsefully once he found out whom he was speaking to.

"None taken, but just remember to whom you're talking before you open your mouth. Next time, I might not be as forgiving."

"I'm really sorry, sir. Maybe we can do business some other time," Ice humbly.

"That won't be necessary, but you and your crew have a nice night," Gino said with a smile.

Everyone in the hood would have paid handsomely to see Ice humbled and scared the way he was once Gino mentioned who he was.

After Ice left, Gino turned to the crowd and said, "Sorry about the

will robbins

commotion, everyone. Tonight, dinner is on the house. Everyone continue to enjoy yourselves." Then Gino walked upstairs to check on his special guests. This time, Black and Nadeem noticed the short, powerful Gino who apparently was more than a mere restaurant owner.

"What was all the noise downstairs, Gino?" Black asked.

"Don't worry about it. It was just some punk that bit off more than he could chew. Will there be anything else for you or the lady?"

"That's it, Gino, just the check will be fine," Black said.

"You've paid enough. Tonight your money is no good here. You and the lady enjoy the rest of your evening."

Gino walked Black and Nadeem out of the restaurant and bid them farewell. Black and Nadeem now faced the awkwardness of saying good-bye. She wondered if she kissed him would she be moving too fast. Or if he would think of her as a "jump off" because she said she had a man. Many thoughts were running through her mind, but she knew she wanted to taste his lips.

Black found it hard to kiss her because he didn't want to force himself upon her, knowing she had a man, and he didn't want to complicate her situation. But he also thought that if he didn't kiss her, she might think that he was a punk.

Both individuals threw caution to the wind and leaned towards one another and their kiss was so soft and so romantic that the only thing missing was light raindrops. Before they took it too far, Black walked her to her vehicle and both of them left floating on cloud nine.

However, Ice and his entourage were less fortunate. They ended up taking an hour's drive to Ice's mansion in Staten Island to work out their game plan in seclusion.

20

OFFICER DOWN

Broad Street was crowded as usual, and Danika and her girls were in the mix of anticipating shoppers. JD's release party was off the chain, and there were going to be many more parties to attend since his release. Danika missed the first party, but she damn sure wasn't going to miss any more, especially after what she heard chilling with her girls.

"Danika, you missed out on the party, girl. That shit was on point. All the niggas was out," Cookie, a short, light pecan-complexioned and very voluptuous girl, said.

"There was niggas from the Port Au Prince Posse there and from the Eastwick Hustlers, and no shit broke out either," Qiana, a tall basketball-type chocolate sister, added.

"Word?" Danika said.

"Word," Qiana and Cookie replied in unison.

"So what was my man doing?"

"You *really* want to know?" Qiana asked.

"I asked, didn't I?"

"I guess we better tell her," Cookie said a little hesitant.

"If you two bitches know something, y'all *better* tell me."

Cookie was happy that they were leaving out of Foot Action because she knew the info that they had on Big Keith would have Danika flipping.

"Talk!" Danika yelled while a few nosy people turned their heads.

"That bitch Pumpkin was all in Keith's face at the party," Cookie said.

"Next thing we knew, Keith took her to some back room at the party," Qiana filled in.

"A few minutes later, they came out of the room, fixing their clothes and shit," Cookie finished.

It seemed as if the two girls picked which part of the story they wanted to tell before they told Danika.

"And you two didn't stop them?" Danika asked in disbelief.

"Come on, now. Keith been cheating on you a lot, and you know it. We ain't gonna keep fightin' and cutting bitches 'cause you naïve," Qiana said.

"Shit, this the reason now why you need to let him go. Fuck his money. Ya heart and ya' feelings cost more than that nigga can afford," Cookie said.

Danika was in tears because she knew her girls were right. Eventually her tears turned to rage as she yelled, "Fuck that! We goin' to that nigga house!"

Big Keith lay in bed with Pumpkin, exhausted from their night of partying and sexing. Normally he took his women to a hotel to cut down his chances of being busted, but the alcohol, blunts, and Pumpkin's tight body had his mind in a haze. They both were deep in sleep when they were awakened by thunderous knocks on the door.

They both sprang out of bed like pop tarts, running around looking for their clothes. At first, they thought that it was the cops, but Danika's screaming voice on the opposite side of the door let them know exactly who it was. Once Keith realized it was Danika, he wished it *were* the police.

"Keith, open this door with ya' bitch ass!" Danika screamed while banging on the door.

"Yo, stay in the room and don't come out," Keith told Pumpkin with conviction.

"Fuck that bitch. You be scared of her? You don't think people at the party didn't see us? That's why she here now," Pumpkin replied as sassy as she wanted to be.

"I don't have time to argue. Just stay in this room."

Pumpkin folded her arms across her chest and sucked her teeth.

Keith reluctantly opened the door wearing a nervous smile. Danika pushed right past him and let herself in as her girls followed suit.

"What's up, baby?" he asked, giving Cookie and Qiana the evil eye for bringing Danika's wrath to his door.

"Don't 'what's up, baby' me. I heard you were fuckin' with that bitch Pumpkin last night!"

Pumpkin heard Danika calling her out of her name, and it burned her up inside to stay in the room when she wanted to fight. Keith couldn't deny what his woman was saying, knowing full well that Cookie and Qiana saw him and Pumpkin go into the room.

"I didn't fuck no Pumpkin. I don't know what you talking about, baby," Keith tried to lie.

"Don't lie, Keith, we saw you and Pumpkin coming out of the room all cozy and shit," Qiana countered.

"Fuck outta here, bitch! Get the fuck outta my spot!" Keith barked at Qiana. He opened his door and expected Qiana to walk out.

"I don't even need this shit," Qiana said as she headed for the door.

"Fuck him, Qiana! You don't have to go nowhere," Danika said.

Keith walked up and grabbed Qiana by her collar and tried to drag her out the door. He was almost successful until Danika ran over and caught him with a right cross, busting his lip. He let loose his grip on Qiana, touched his lip, and without thinking, he threw a harder blow, knocking Danika to the floor. Cookie and Qiana were in shock and frozen in time. Keith walked over and leaned down to pick Danika off the floor.

"I'm so sorry, baby, I, I, didn't mean to hit you, baby," Keith said, almost reduced to tears. Pumpkin was still in the room fighting the urge to come out and be nosy. But she didn't want to get jumped by the trio or worse, get her ass kicked by Keith.

"Get the fuck off of me, nigga," Danika yelled as she pushed Keith aside. Her girls helped her up from the floor. Danika collected herself and silently walked out of Keith's apartment. Keith knew that he would hear from Black later, but it wouldn't be so bad since they were going into deeper business together. But little did he know she had no intentions of bringing it to Black. She had a higher power to confer with.

will robbins

．．．．

Black and Nadeem looked perfect together sitting on a park bench under the glow of the moonlight. It was the second time around spending time together, and their chemistry was strong. Black held Nadeem's hand and asked, "How did you avoid the street life growing up in Pierce Manor?"

"Was I supposed to get caught up in the streets based on where I grew up?"

"I'm not saying that. It just seems like you're immune to all the bullshit, the drugs, money, violence. You don't even get involved in all the hood stories, like who shot whom or who's the biggest dealer. There aren't too many women like you. It's cool to be with someone from the hood, but not hood, you know what I mean?"

Nadeem knew exactly what he meant. Ice kept her shielded and very well protected. She didn't want to tell Black that she snuck out from under Earl, "The Bodyguard," and brought the baby to her sister's house for her to be with him. She still didn't have the heart to tell him that she was with Ice. She felt that Black was a dealer, but she didn't know that he was at war with her man.

"I'm not impressed with all of the hood stories," Nadeem replied, wondering how Black would feel if he knew who her man was.

"So what *are* you impressed with?" Black asked.

Nadeem looked deeply into Black's eyes and simply said, "You."

Black took his cue and leaned in and kissed Nadeem.

"Let's go. I have something to show you," Black said, taking Nadeem by her hand and leading her to the vehicle.

．．．．

Danika sat in her car across the street from the Lady Luck Club, waiting for a particular dancer to meet her outside. She was a little nervous, knowing she was sitting in the danger zone. She knew full well what could happen if Ice or someone else saw her and realized that she was Black's big sister. The National Guard would have to be brought in to maintain law and order in Eastwick if something were to happen to Danika. That's exactly why she kept a low profile.

Just as Danika's patience started to run low, Candy, one of Ice's dancers and one of Danika's high-school friends, came strutting out of the front door.

"What's up, girl?" Candy asked chewing gum.

"Nothin'. I just need a favor from you," Danika replied.

Candy folded her arms, sucked her teeth, rolled her eyes, and asked, "What kind of a favor you talkin' 'bout?"

The last favor Candy did for Danika, she ended up on a double date with one of Big Keith's boys, and to say he looked like a frog would have been a compliment. So now, Candy wasn't in the mood for one of Danika's "favors."

Looking at Candy's response to her question, Danika had to laugh and say, "Nothing like last time, girl. I just need you to get a message to Ice."

Candy let down her defenses and asked, "What is it?" She knew the situation between Black and Ice, so she didn't have a problem holding her girl down.

"Tell Ice that his boy Officer Swank, JD, and Big Keith plan on taking him out."

In shock, Candy's eyes flew wide open like saucers. She gathered her composure and asked, "How you know?"

"Girl, Keith is just like everyone else when he high and drunk. He told me the whole layout. I also overheard him talking to Black, but they didn't know I was home."

"But ain't Keith suppose to be ya' man? Why you want to tell on him, knowing what Ice gonna do when he find out?"

"First of all, Big Keith ain't my man no more. Second of all, he deserves everything he gets," Danika said as she removed the dark sunglasses from her eyes.

"Damn, girl, I was wondering why you had shades on at night. Keith did this shit to you? Oh, hell, no! That fat ma'fucka gots to pay! I'ma tell Ice so good of a story he'll think the Pope was telling it to him."

"That's what I'm talking about. I knew you would have a bitch back," Danika said as she gave her girl a pound.

"Let me get out of here before someone takes notice of me, girl," Danika said, starting up her engine.

"Don't worry, I got ya' back. I'ma handle this shit right now for you," Candy said, walking backwards, not paying attention to traffic. A car stopped just in time to avoid hitting Candy's bright future—her ass.

The driver stuck his head out the window and yelled, "Get the

will robbins

fuck outta the street, bitch!"

Candy fired right back and said, "Ya momma's a bitch, little dick ma'fucka!"

Danika just laughed and pulled off.

* * * *

Black headed down St. George Avenue into Rahway, where he bought a new house for the family. He made sure that no one knew of his new location. He was taking a risk by showing Nadeem, but he felt a deep connection with her, the kind he had felt with Kasha.

He pulled up in front of a brick-style duplex home on the corner of Hazelwood Avenue, opened the car door, and let an unsuspecting Nadeem out of the vehicle. She didn't expect to pull up in front of his house.

"What makes you think that I'm comfortable going into your house?"

"First of all, every woman wants a confident man, but not only that, all women like surprises," Black responded.

"So you have a surprise for me?" Nadeem asked with a teasing smile.

"You're surprised to be here, aren't you?"

"You best come better than that to get me to feel safe and comfortable with you," Nadeem said, still standing on the curb.

"I do have a surprise for you, but you have to come inside to get it. If you want, you can take my keys and go in by yourself and get it. I'll wait in the car for you," Black said, holding the keys out for her.

"Come on, boy," Nadeem, said ending the game.

She walked into Black's home and was thoroughly surprised at the décor. It was as if Black hired his own personal interior designer, but the most surprising piece was a painting that hung above a Moorish-style fireplace. Nadeem slowly walked up to the display in disbelief. "Oh ... my ... god. How ... when ... where, I mean, how did you get this? Who did this?" Nadeem asked.

Black walked up to her, grabbed her around the waist, and said, "Gino saw our chemistry and beauty on our first date, and he wanted to capture it forever. So he gave me this painting, and I couldn't be selfish and keep it to myself."

Nadeem turned around, looked Black in his eyes, and said, "It's beautiful ... thank you." They were both inspired by the moment to embrace in a passionate kiss. Not only was Gino a restaurant owner and gangster, but also he was a talented artist. He had painted Black and Nadeem sitting together at a candlelight dinner surrounded by black angels in flight. The background had a peaceful, heavenly appeal to it.

Then Black led Nadeem upstairs, and she put aside all of her reservations. The painting, kiss, ambiance, and his gentle touch made her panties wet and her body quiver in anticipation. And if the upstairs looked anything like the downstairs, she felt like she would finish before Black started, if he chose to.

Nadeem was equally impressed as she had been downstairs when she stepped into Black's room. The style was also exquisite, but she was more enthusiastic about his small library. He had everything from history books to cookbooks. One of the books that quickly caught her eye was a book on Hinduism.

She picked up the book from the shelf and asked, "So you believe in Hinduism? Why didn't you tell me when we first spoke about religion?"

"I didn't tell you, because I didn't want you to think that I would use your beliefs to get in ya pants," Black said smiling.

"Wasn't that your goal in the first place?"

"My goal is to know you spiritually and mentally first. And to know you spiritually and mentally, I'll also need to know you physically."

"Whatever, Mr. Smooth. What made you interested in the religion?"

"I like the philosophy of obtaining satisfaction by any means necessary basically. I also like the belief that you can obtain anything you want. I don't buy into any one religion though. I'm fascinated by many religious philosophies. What are you interested in?"

Nadeem put the book down, walked over to Black, and said, "I'm interested in you." Then she pushed Black on his soft, plush bed, straddled him, and let months of celibacy run wild.

Black lay back and accepted whatever pleasure Nadeem was willing to give. She tugged at his shirt, and he sat up and removed it. She was even more excited as she saw Black's bulging chest and six-pack abs. She licked his body like it was ice cream melting down a cone. Black's mind was in overdrive in anticipation of receiving head. He heard about it, saw it on porn, but his experience was extremely limited. His first love was killed long before he experienced the freaky side of sex.

Nadeem unbuckled Black's pants, unbuttoned the button, and pulled down his zipper, and just like Kasha, Nadeem was more than surprised. But she acted her age and was more than professional when she saw his dick erect and in full view.

She gripped his manhood with both hands and took in more than half of it with her hot, wet, moist mouth. Black started to grab her head and push her down further, but he didn't want to choke her and appear to be inexperienced.

After tasting Black, Nadeem stood up and undressed for him. Black stood up as well and removed his clothes, leaving both of them naked in front of one another.

He lifted Nadeem in his arms and gently laid her on the bed. Black wanted to return the favor for her, so he fell to his knees, opened her legs, and dove tongue deep into her pussy. He couldn't believe the response he was getting. She was moaning, grabbing his head, and gyrating uncontrollably. He knew for his first time he was doing a damn good job or she was a great actress full of shit.

"Eat this pussy, Black, oh shit, ooh, ooh, *damn*," Nadeem said, feeling Black's tongue attack her sugar walls. She tightened her grip on Black's neck, squeezed her legs together, and exploded in his mouth and all over his face.

Black stood up and watched her shiver in ecstasy on his bed. Seeing the way she was shivering, Black's thought was confirmed—he was doing a damn good job. He walked over to his drawer and removed a condom. Nadeem was still shaking as he pulled the Magnum over his rod. Then he slid into her smoothly and gently. He cupped both of Nadeem's breasts into his hands and began to suck on her hard nipples as he stroked her passionately.

Nadeem wanted to show Black that she could handle more dick than what he was giving her so she turned him on his back and placed his dick in her and rode him like a stallion.

"Give me this big dick. Make this pussy come, Black. Push that dick in me. I ain't no little bitch. Fuck this pussy!"

"Damn, girl, you gonna make this dick come," Black said, pushing his manhood deeper inside her like she asked. Nadeem rode Black until she felt his dick throbbing, about to unload.

"I'm coming, I'm coming," was all Black could say with each passionate animal-like stroke that Nadeem gave. As each lover exploded, Nadeem collapsed on Black's chest and lay still to gather her composure and breath.

❧ ❧ ❧ ❧

Candy walked back into the club and stepped to Ice, who was sitting at the bar enjoying the close-up view of his new dancer.

"Excuse me, Ice, I need to talk to you in private. It's very important," Candy said, panting like she finished the hundred-yard dash.

Ice was a little irritated, but he knew it must have been urgent for one of his dancers to step to him. He turned to Candy and said, "Follow me. This better be good."

The two of them took the private elevator to his office. Ice walked over to his bar and poured a straight shot of Grey Goose. He politely poured Candy a glass, who declined.

"So what's so important that you interrupt my free time?"

"Normally, I wouldn't, but this is a matter of life and death," Candy said, putting on her best act.

"Well, let's hear it."

"You know that party that JD and Big Keith were throwing the other night? I heard those two and a couple of their boys talking about some dude named Swank and they were going to help them take you out."

Ice knew many people wanted to take him out, so her news wasn't a surprise. But he knew that she had to be telling the truth because he knew for certain that she didn't know Swank.

"What else did you hear?" he asked, taking the bait.

"They're supposed to be inviting you to dinner in a few days to discuss business, but it's only a setup."

Ice was a little hesitant, but he pulled a few bills out of his pockets for her trouble. Candy gladly took the easy money and said, "Sorry I had to be the one to tell you the bad news, Ice. I see the look of doubt on your face, but Big Keith ran his mouth to his girl, Danika, about their plans, and my girl confirmed what I heard. You know drugs and alcohol leads to loose lips."

Ice looked at Candy and said, "Thank you, I'll handle it."

Candy left from Ice's presence wearing a huge smile on her face.

will robbins

♦ ♦ ♦ ♦

Annex, Donald, and Raymond were hanging in the Brown Derby, a small strip club that featured the usual dancers that had stretch marks, bullet wounds, and cigarette burns. The only reason they landed there was because it was the only place where they could get their freak on and be close to business. They could have gone to the Lady Luck Club, but they didn't want to be that close to Ice and Dubois.

All three men sat in a corner, nursing their Coronas while a fair stripper shook her ass for them. Donald kept slapping her ass to see it jiggle while Annex and Raymond were trying to see if it jiggled enough to come up off their ends. Annex's phone interrupted their thought process once it rang. He stood up and walked to the bathroom to answer it since the music was too loud where they were sitting.

"Hello," Annex answered once he stepped into the pissy-smelly bathroom.

"It's Ice ... now listen carefully. I have a job for you and ya crew."

"What is it?"

"It seems our friends Officer Swank, JD, and Big Keith are unhappy with the powers that be and wish to take me out. Big Keith ran his mouth to his bitch as well as to others, and the news got back to me. So I need for you to find Officer Swank and get rid of him quick."

"Ice, you know how much heat that's gonna bring? I mean, we talking about a cop here. A dirty one, but he still a cop."

"Annex, you one of my top people because you're smart and follow directions. Don't start to disappoint me now. Understand?" Ice's tone and octaves were very threatening. Annex knew his life was in jeopardy if he didn't continue to follow orders.

"How do you want this handled? Silent or loud?"

"I want it loud so people will know that the Port Au Prince Posse still holding power," Ice said, hanging up the phone.

Annex left the bathroom and informed his boys of the task that they had to handle. Donald was a little disappointed because he was seconds away from going to a backroom to get his dick sucked by the jiggly-ass sister. All three men exited with murder on their minds.

♦ ♦ ♦ ♦

Once again, it was late night and Officer Swank was on the prowl for some plantation pussy, and there was no better place to find it than at the bar on First Street. The atmosphere was usual. Players, hustlers, and bitches in search of a dream all dwelled in the bar. Officer Swank sat on a barstool while a pretty young thing was nestled under his arm. Most of the hustlers were trying to ignore the fact that Swank was in their presence, but he made it difficult every time he yelled, "You nigga fucks better have my money right, or I'm going to bust a whole lot of your shiftless asses."

The young black woman spending time with Swank should have been offended by the nigga comment, but the money Swank was willing to pay bought off her pride.

"I hope somebody shoot that ma'fucka some day wit' his bitch ass," a young hustler playing pool said to no one in particular. Little did he know he was going to get his wish.

Annex, Donald, and Raymond pulled up in front of the bar with their hearts pumping more than usual for the task at hand. Swank was a connected man, and Ice wanted this killing to be loud so the men knew that this deed would come back to bite them in the ass. But the situation was do-or-die. All three men checked their weapons of assault and entered the bar.

"Let's hope this ma'fucka here," Annex said as they stepped into the dark bar. They looked left to right but couldn't see the fat man with the slew of people and heavy cloud of smoke.

"Yo, what's up, Annex, Donald, Raymond?" a dude said as he exited the bar. Annex started to probe the bar to look for Swank, but it was unnecessary once he heard the big man laughing at the end of the bar. Donald tapped him on his shoulder and pointed in the big man's direction.

All three men approached Swank as Annex yelled, "Hey, yo, Swank." Swank turned in the men's direction and smiled at the familiar faces. But Swank's smile was turned upside down and he reached for his sidearm once he saw the three men pointing death in his direction. Once the guns were pulled, people started to scream and run for the exit.

Before Swank could get out the word "nigger," he saw white flashes and his body was hotter than a grill at a cookout. Annex and his crew just walked out of the bar as if nothing happened. They knew they had plenty of time before the Boys in Blue would respond in the hood.

Annex dialed Ice and said, "Swank is done."

will robbins

"Good, we'll take care of JD and Keith later," Ice responded.

♥ ♥ ♥ ♥

Big Keith lay on JD's couch with the glare of the TV flashing across his pudgy face. JD woke up with the morning sun shining upon his face, which caused him to get up earlier than usual. He walked out of his bedroom to hear Keith snoring on the couch. JD tried to ignore the bearlike sounds, but it was too unbearable, so he kicked the couch, which caused Keith to wake from his deep sleep.

"What the hell is wrong with you, nigga?" Keith asked annoyed, waking from his sleep.

"Ya' damn snoring, nigga, that's what's wrong with me." JD walked into the kitchen to make his usual breakfast of scrambled eggs and cheese.

"Yo, hook me up, nigga," Keith yelled from the couch. He didn't have to yell too loudly because no doors divided the front room and kitchen.

"I got you. Yo, where has Danika been, nigga? I didn't even see her at the party last night," JD said.

"I ain't fuckin with her no more, my dude. Her girls outted me, and we got into this fight."

"A fistfight?" JD asked surprised.

"She punched me, and I socked the shit out of her."

"Nigga, is you crazy?"

"What?"

"You know Black gonna be all on our shit now! You always fuckin' up!" JD yelled, knowing that he was going to have to deal with some type of heat with Black. If he only knew that Ice was on his tail, he would have worried less about Black.

"Man, that shit happened days ago. If Black was going to do something, he'd a done it already," Keith responded being arrogant.

JD and Keith were about to engage in a full-scale argument until a voice caught their attention on the TV.

"I'm Latoya Wright, reporting to you live for Fox Five News. I'm standing in front of a popular bar on First Street, where one of Elizabeth's finest was gunned down last night like an animal."

"Yo, you see this shit, kid?" Keith asked in total surprise and disbelief. JD took a seat on the couch to make sure that his eyes weren't lying to him.

Police and people were seen swarming in the background of the reporter as JD and Keith looked on in awe.

"Keep these fuckin' people back behind the yellow line," a short officer could be heard in the background.

Chief Williams stepped on the scene and was too slow to escape the barrage of questions that the reporter asked.

"Chief Williams, how could something like this happen? What does the department plan on doing about this?"

Chief Williams continued to move about and ignore the reporter's questions.

"Just like everyone else, the chief is clueless as to what's going down in this city."

The chief turned around and gave the reporter the response that she was looking for. He grabbed the microphone and said, *"Listen here, lady, the man or men who did this will pay and pay severely. No one takes down one of my officers and gets away with it."*

"Do you have any idea who would be so psychotic enough to take an officer down like this?"

"If I knew that, I wouldn't be here wasting my time with you now, would I?" Chief Williams asked with undisguised sarcasm and walked off.

"This is Latoya Wright for Fox Five News, and I will be reporting back to you with any new developments in this story."

Before the reporter could close out, she saw an old man that looked like he hung out at the bar all his life, so she decided to grab on to one more lifeline.

"Excuse me, sir. Do you happen to know anything about last night's shooting?"

"My name is Bennet, and I ain't in it," the old man said and walked out of view of the camera.

"Yo, I bet you it was that bitch-ass Swank that got hit up," Keith said.

"How you figure?"

"What other cop you know hang out at the bar?"

"You right. Good one. Last cracker we got to worry about," JD said bluntly.

"Yo, who you think hit him up?" Keith asked.

"Black, who else, nigga?" JD said without an ounce of doubt.

will robbins

"So you think Ice is next or what?"

"I don't know what's on that nigga's mind, but we'll find out tonight when we meet with him."

❢ ❢ ❢ ❢

Annex, Donald, and Raymond pulled up in front of JD's building in Midtown early to make sure things would be quiet, as well as to catch JD alone. Little did they know they were about to kill two birds with one stone. All three men walked through the dilapidated door and walked up the squeaky steps to the second floor where JD resided.

"Shit, with all the money this nigga make out here, you'd think he'd move to a better place," Annex said disgusted with the filth he was surrounded by.

"You know how niggas is. They need to be close to the fiends and money, baby," Donald replied.

Once they had reached JD's door, Annex had hushed everyone and placed his ear to the door to be cautious. He heard two voices behind the door, which made him more alarmed.

"Yo, it's at least two people in there," Annex warned.

Both men gave him a nod to show they acknowledged his statement. Then Donald knocked on the door as the rest of the men stood out of sight of the peephole.

"Nigga, what are you doing?" Raymond whispered.

"Watch," Donald replied.

Annex just remained cool and stood off to the side.

"Yo, who is it this fuckin' early? Karen, it better not be ya' stank ass 'cause I ain't got shit for you," JD said with much attitude. Karen was JD's fiend-ass neighbor who would knock on his door all times of day and night to get served.

All three men outside remained silent, which made JD more annoyed. "I said, who the fuck is it?!" JD yelled.

Just as JD was about to open the door, Keith jumped up, cut him off, and said, "I got it, my nigga. It's probably Karen, and if it is, I'ma get my dick sucked. You know she can suck a golf ball through a garden hose," Keith said jokingly.

He opened the door, stuck his head out, and asked, "Who the fuck is it?"

Keith couldn't believe that he was staring down the barrel of a gun when he opened the door. Before he could react, Donald squeezed the trigger and blew half of his face off. Keith died before he hit the floor.

Annex and Raymond jumped back as Keith's face and brain matter splattered all over their clothes. The gunshot put JD on notice as he ran to his room to retrieve his gun.

Quickly, Annex, Donald, and Raymond stormed into the apartment and took cover behind the couch, waiting for JD to strike. Meanwhile, JD stood in his bedroom sweating bullets, wondering who was attacking him. He knew he was outnumbered, outgunned, and without a plan.

"Fuck it, balls to the wall," JD whispered to himself as he exited his room with his gun drawn.

Annex tapped Raymond and gave him the gesture to look for JD. Raymond was halfway out of a crouch when JD saw his head emerging from behind the couch. With high adrenaline and accuracy, JD pulled the trigger and the bullet zipped through the air and crashed right into Raymond's skull. The impact caused his body to fly in the air, only to crash hard on the hardwood floor.

Once Annex and Donald saw Raymond's body hit the floor, they sprang into action without fear. They both jumped from behind the couch and let off their weapons of assault. JD, like a true soldier, shot back at his assailants as he tried to make it to his kitchen for cover but he was unsuccessful.

Annex's first shot hit JD in his leg, which caused him to stumble. With the lost second in his pace, Donald's shot hit him in the shoulder and JD fell like a ton of bricks. He hit the floor, and his gun slid across it, leaving him defenseless. Annex and Donald walked over and stood towering over JD's body. JD tried to get up, but a quick kick delivered to his face by Annex killed his ambition.

"Stupid-ass nigga. How you gonna try to take out the king and live?" Annex asked. JD had a confused look on his face. He couldn't figure out who ran their mouth. Donald decided to take the look of confusion from his face.

"Don't play dumb, nigga. Ya' man bitch told us the whole story about how y'all was gonna take out Ice with the help of that bitch-ass Swank."

JD shook his head and simply replied, "Ma'fucka."

"Yeah, ma'fucka," Annex replied as he shot JD in the face, making sure that it would be another closed casket funeral in the hood.

Once again, Annex hit Ice up to let him know the deed was handled. Ice gave them instructions to stay at the mansion until further notice. It was something that the men had no problems doing. They needed a break from the streets after the bloody work they committed.

21

SHOCK TO THE HEART

Sandra woke rejuvenated each passing day in the rehab center in Colorado. She started to gain her weight back in all of the right places, and her features took on a healthy glow. She started to blossom into the beautiful butterfly that she once was. Each passing day brought her closer to return to the devil's playground, which is Elizabeth N.J. She couldn't wait to return and face the devil with her newfound strength and make her remaining children proud of her.

She had grown to love the center and the staff as time went by, but it wasn't like that at first. Her first few days had her mind and body in a total tailspin. The vomiting seemed to never end, and her mind had hot flashes just like her body. The violent shakes made her feel like her bones were going to crack and her bowels were looser than a hooker on Saturday night.

Any- and everyone were subject to get physically or verbally abused when they entered her room. The females were "dirty, stinking-ass bitches," and the men were all a bunch of "pussies." Today, Sandra woke up happy that those days were behind her and that the rehab center was only a few days from being a distant memory, just like her habit.

Ben, one of the few black men who worked at the rehab center, knocked on Sandra's door and waited for a response before he entered. Then he walked in and saw Sandra standing wearing her tight-fitted

will robbins

jeans, which complimented her lovely curves, and a plain T-shirt. Her hair was flowing loosely.

"Good morning, Ben," Sandra said with a flirtatious smile, teasing.

"Good morning to you, too, miss thing." Ben had a thing for Sandra, and he made her aware of it a time or two. The only problem was Ben was married with children and Sandra wasn't going to play second best to no one. She also didn't want to complicate her life any more than she had to. She couldn't kick her habit in the ass as well as kick a bitch in her ass. So she let Ben know, "Thanks, but no thanks."

"You have a telephone call," Ben informed her.

"Who is it?" Sandra asked getting excited. She received a few calls from Nate and Danika with concerns about her well-being, but none from her son or other important family members. She was hoping that Ben would tell her that it was Black, but he simply answered, "They didn't say."

Sandra walked out to get the phone, picked up the receiver, and said, "Hello."

"You sound good, Mama," Black said, totally surprising his mother.

"Oh my god, baby, how are you?" her voice was squeaky with surprise.

"I'm good, Ma."

"What took you so long to call, baby?"

"I figured you needed to concentrate on the task at hand and not worry about what was going on with us and the world."

"I know, but it would have made it a little easier hearing from you."

"I'm sorry, Ma, but I'll make it up to you. I also have a surprise for you when you come home."

"Really, what is it?"

"If I told you, it wouldn't be a surprise, now, would it?"

"No. You know I'll be home in a few days, baby," Sandra replied almost reduced to tears of joy.

"I know, Ma, and I'll be at the airport to pick you up. Are ya' flight plans still the same?"

"Yes."

"Then I'll see you soon, Ma."

"I love you, baby."

"I love you, too, Ma."

"Wait, I know you not hanging up on me that fast, son."

"I don't want to keep you from ya daily routine, Ma."

"Boy, *pleezzz*, you mean you don't want me to keep *you* from ya' daily routine. You lucky I have one last meeting to attend or I would let you know a thing or two," Sandra said playfully.

"I'll see you, Ma. I love you."

"I love you more. I'll see you in a few days," Sandra replied as she hung up the phone.

Black stared at the portrait of himself and Nadeem and was lost in its beauty. The sound of his doorbell ringing was indistinct as he was off in "La-La Land." The hard knocks brought Black back into reality, and he walked over to his door. He had his hand on his weapon that was placed in the small of his back because he wasn't used to visitors, especially since no one knew where he lived. He cautiously opened the door and was thoroughly surprised to see Nadeem standing there unannounced.

"Surprised to see me, baby?" Nadeem asked.

"Hell, yeah, but it's a nice surprise," he responded, holding his arms open to embrace her.

She hugged him and said, "I'm not staying. I want to show you something for a change."

The ride from Rahway to Nadeem's place was just long enough for Black to get curious about where they were headed. She pulled in front of a beautiful towering building on the borderline of Elizabeth and Newark. A valet greeted them and took the car into a private parking lot. As they stepped into the elevator, Black finally asked, "Where are we?"

Nadeem looked at Black smiling and said, "My place."

The look of surprise on Black's face was priceless. They stepped in the spacious penthouse and all Black could think about is how this woman afforded a place like this. His next thought was that her man was really paid.

"*Damn*, I got to step my game up," Black said out loud.

"What's that, baby?"

"Nothing."

Black and Nadeem walked into the front room area where

will robbins

Samantha, Nadeem's sister, was holding baby Toussaint. Nadeem was just about to get into the introductions, but Samantha put the baby down, stood up, and asked, "Black, what are you doing here?"

"You two know each other?" Nadeem asked fully surprised.

"We seen each other around a few times," Black said, trying to downplay the situation.

"Girl, don't you know who this is?" Samantha asked, getting on Black's nerves. Samantha talked too much and was always looking for a handout or chasing a nigga's nut sack. She made a play for him once, but when he turned her down, she went straight for E-Double, who had no problem laying pipe to her.

"How do you two know each other?" Nadeem asked, looking at her sister smile from ear to ear. She also didn't miss the look of disappointment on Black's face when he saw her sister.

"We know each other from the hood. Don't trip, big sis," Samantha said, walking away. She also read Black's body language and knew to leave well enough alone.

Just as Samantha walked out, Earl walked in. "Nice to see you're safe and secure, Miss Daru," Earl said sarcastically.

"I'm fine, Earl, thank you."

Earl was upset that Nadeem kept sneaking off and not utilizing him. Ice was also putting pressure on him to know her whereabouts and to make sure she was safe at all times. Her disappearing acts made his job very difficult.

"Who are you?" Earl asked, looking at Black.

"I'm Black," Black said extending his hand.

Earl just shook his head and walked off.

"Who was that?" Black asked, watching Earl exit.

"That's my personal bodyguard, but mostly he watches over the place."

"So I guess this is your son?" Black asked, watching the baby sleep inside of the playpen.

Nadeem smiled and said, "Yeah that's my prince. And you already know my sister. Later, we're going to get into that, but for now, make yourself at home and I'll be right back."

Black watched Nadeem disappear and started to pace around the front room area, looking at hanging portraits. He saw one of Nadeem holding her son with a sky blue background. He saw another with

Samantha and Nadeem, but the one that caught his attention was the one with her father standing in front of a beat-up Oldsmobile that sat in front of the 400 Building of Pierce Manor. That picture brought Black back to the videotape he watched that he stole from Ice a few months back.

"Please, Ice, don't kill me. I'm all my daughters have," Mr. Daru pleaded as he sat duct taped to a chair in a basement.

"No. Your daughters are all YOU have, you degenerate fuck," Ice spat.

"I swear I can get you your money. I just need a little more time," Mr. Daru continued telling the lie that is the anthem for degenerate gamblers.

"You're all out of time."

"Come on, man, what about my daughters and grandson? They need me."

"They don't need you, they got me. And it's because of them that I'm not torturing you. Shoot this piece of shit, Annex, and get rid of the body," Ice said and headed for the steps.

"Noooooo," Mr. Daru yelled as Annex squeezed the trigger, making his chest look like a smiling face.

Black stared at the picture, wondering what type of connection Nadeem had to Ice, if any. He also wondered if Nadeem even knew that her father was dead. They spoke about him being missing a while ago, but he had no idea who her father was at the time. Now he knew exactly who her father was, and he knew Ice killed him. Black figured Nadeem and her father were just other lives that Ice had fucked up. Black knew that he wouldn't tell this beautiful woman that the biggest dealer in Elizabeth killed her father; she would have to find out on her own.

"You know him, too?" Nadeem asked as she saw Black staring at the photo of her father.

"No, no, no," Black said coming back from his trance. "I just was looking to see where you got your beauty from."

"I get it from my mama," Nadeem said playfully.

"I don't see any pictures of your mother or Toussaint," Black said getting curious. He wanted to see the man that made the mistake of breaking Nadeem's heart.

"Well, in a fit of rage, I threw all the pictures of him away. As far

will robbins

as my mother, all I have to do is just look in a mirror. At my father's place there are a lot of pictures of her," Nadeem said.

"You miss her a lot, huh?"

"Every day."

Black and Nadeem sat silently for a few seconds until she broke the silence by asking, "So what do you think?"

"About what?"

"I brought you here to see my place and to meet my son. So what do you think?"

"I think your son is just as beautiful as you are. Did Toussaint hook you up with this place? What does he do?"

"He's an entrepreneur," Nadeem said halfway lying. She didn't have the heart to say that her man was one of the biggest dealers in Jersey.

"I need to get in his line of business."

"So what do you do?" Nadeem asked for the first time after weeks of knowing Black.

"I'm living," Black responded, trying to avoid the question. He didn't want to lie, but he didn't want to be truthful and lose her.

"I see you're living. I mean, there aren't too many nineteen year olds from the hood that ain't a rapper with their own house, car, and obviously, you got money."

Thinking fast on his feet, Black replied, "My father runs a magazine company in L.A., and since he wasn't in my life when I was young, he tried to compensate me with that house and car you see me with. He also gave me a healthy bank account." Black felt bad lying. He couldn't bring himself to tell her he was a dealer. He didn't even tell her the story of E-Double, his mom, or sister. He knew he was falling for this woman, but he felt she was too fragile to know the true person he was at this point. He was going to continue his façade until the proper time.

Black and Nadeem spent their afternoon getting intimate and continued to hide their true identities.

❀ ❀ ❀ ❀

"I want the men who are responsible for the deaths of Officer Swank and those two young men, and I want them *now*!" Chief Williams yelled at Ice.

Ice reclined in his seat and coolly responded, "I ain't giving you shit, Chief. I kept my promise. The city was quiet for months, Mayor Cross was reelected, and you kept your job. Now that all is said and done, and the city is about to be hot like fire until the competition is dealt with. Besides, don't have a bleeding heart for Swank. He was going to kill me as well as you."

The chief's eyebrows narrowed at the mention of Swank killing him. Ice, picking up on it, said, "Don't look so surprised. Swank was going to take you out so one of the white boys could become chief and move him up the ranks faster than ya' black ass could," Ice said lying.

"I don't give a fuck! Swank was a racist, dirty ma'fucka, but he was still a cop, and you're going to give me what I want or else—"

Chief Williams was going to continue his threat until Ice stood up and yelled, "Or else *what?* You going to put me away? I got shit on you, too, and you know it. Now if you play ya' cards right, I might give you what you want and make you look like a hero, but for now, get the fuck out of my office."

"Fuck you, Ice. Your time is limited," he said turning to walk away.

"Is that a threat?"

"No, it's a fuckin' promise," Chief Williams retorted, slamming the door behind him.

❦ ❦ ❦ ❦

Silk's pool hall was unusually packed for a Friday night, but it wasn't filled with the usual customers. Black and his Eastwick Hustlers were there planning their attack on Ice. Woo and his boys were present as well. Black had his capos and generals in attendance and planned on having the info passed down accordingly. He stood on a pool table to make sure that everyone saw him as well as heard what he was saying. It also made him feel a little more powerful to tower over everyone.

"I'm glad to see we all here and we all know why we here. Ice been killin' our peoples and hurtin' our business left and right. The other night, he killed that bitch ass Swank for whatever reason." Black tried to continue his speech, but the crowd yelled with elation at the mention of Swank's death. He gave them a moment to celebrate before he continued.

Finally, Black cleared his throat and said, "A'ight, a'ight, hold it down." All the men complied and he continued. "He also killed Big

will robbins

Keith and JD, who was down with us. We not gonna sit down and lay low and take this shit anymore."

"Yeah, yeah, that's what we talkin' 'bout," the crowd yelled in anticipation.

"Woo got word that Ice is having a party at his mansion in Staten Island, and we there tomorrow at 9 pm sharp. Anybody scared and not down with that, there's the door like always. Woo, once you and ya' boys start, there ain't no turnin' back," Black said sincerely.

"After all the plannin' we did, you think I'ma step off?" Woo asked as if Black were crazy.

"Taye, Man, Damien, Calvin, y'all sure y'all want a part in this shit? I mean, everyone in this room ain't coming back alive, so I understand if y'all walk," Black said.

Taye stood up and spoke for everyone and said, "We good."

"A'ight, cool, any questions?" Black asked.

Agent Simms—a.k.a. Bobby—stood up and asked, "So what's the plan? Seems to me like it's still a suicide mission." Bobby was trying to sound negative, but he really wanted to know all the info to report back to Dawkins.

"Tomorrow we meet back here at 8 pm. There'll be four rental trucks that me, Naim, Flex, and Woo gonna drive. We already picked who gonna ride with us, but we'll square that away later. Everyone else is going to follow us. When we get there, Booga gonna cut the alarm system down, and we gonna take out the front guards. From there, we are going to quietly take out as many of Ice's men as possible before all hell breaks loose," Black said.

"You make it sound so easy," one of Black's men said.

"This shit is going to be the hardest thing we ever did, but it's necessary to make sure we live. It's do-or-die, baby. Anything worth living for is worth dying for, and respect and revenge is definitely worth dying for," Black said.

"*That's* what's up, baby," Bobby said.

"A'ight, everyone, get out of here and handle ya' business. We got a long night ahead of us tomorrow," Black said.

Black wanted his men to say good-bye to their loved ones and tie up any loose ends. He knew it was a possibility that he wouldn't return as well as the rest of his crew. He felt strong and secure, but nothing was concrete. Ice wasn't a person to take lightly, and they were bringing the pain to his front yard, which gave him home field advantage. Black made his plans on the blueprints of Ice's place that Woo gave him, and those blueprints were from years ago. He was praying that he wouldn't be blindsided by any major changes to the mansion.

Woo was almost out the door with the rest of the crew when Black called out, "Woo, wait up." Woo turned around and waited for Black to get closer. "I need you to take a ride with me."

"A'ight, you alright?" Woo asked, seeing the concern in Black's eyes.

"Yeah, I'm good."

Silk walked over to the two gentlemen and addressed them. "Black, I know there's nothing I can say or do to change ya' mind, so let me show you something."

Black and Woo followed Silk to a back room where he removed a long, mounted wall mirror. The men were surprised to see a door. Silk pressed a few buttons, and the door opened. As they walked down the steps, their eyes popped open as wide as saucers when they saw all the weaponry the room contained. Silk had all manner of assault weapons, handguns, grenades, explosives, knives, and other warlike paraphernalia. He was ready for World War III.

"Silk, where the hell did you get all this?" Black asked, amazed.

"Yeah, man, I thought y'all lived by a strict moral code of rules back in the day," Woo said.

"Yeah, we did, but that didn't mean everyone respected it because if they did, my brother would be here and I wouldn't be limping. Sometimes when people got out of line, they were dealt with. And most people understand the power of the gun, so here we are," Silk said, giving Woo and Black a tour.

"Your plan sounds okay, but tomorrow, come back here and take what you and ya' boys need to get the job done. I know your little handguns ain't gonna cut the mustard. Get people here early and get some practice in the range I got in the next room," Silk said, being helpful to the suicidal cause.

"Bet," Black said excited, feeling like the Lord was on his side.

"*That's* what's up," Woo concluded.

All three men exited the basement, and Silk bid the boys peace.

Once again, Black headed up St. George Avenue to his home in Rahway. This was the first time that Black had Woo ride with him to

will robbins

Rahway. He didn't even tell Woo where he lived, so naturally, Woo was kind of curious.

"Hey, man, this don't look like Elizabeth, so where are we going?"

"My house," Black simply answered.

Woo looked over at Black to make sure he wasn't joking. He knew Black was hiding things, but he didn't think that he was hiding his residence.

"You're serious, huh?" Woo asked.

"After the funeral, someone fucked my spot up. I figured it was a message from Ice, so I found a nice quiet spot out here and didn't tell anybody. I mean, Danika knows, but I made her promise not to tell anyone because of our situation. My mother will know when she comes home in a few days. Oh, and my girl," Black said proudly.

"Ya' girl? When did this happen, Virgin?" Woo asked, clowning Black.

"First of all, I ain't been no virgin since Kasha, nigga. Second of all, my girl is actually a grown-ass woman," Black said, boasting.

"So what's her name?"

"Nadeem."

The name rang a bell to Woo, but he couldn't place the name with a face. Before Woo thought further about it, Black pulled up in front of his house.

"Here we are, baby boy," Black said stepping out of the truck. Woo followed suit.

They stepped into the house, and Woo was impressed the same way Nadeem was, but he wasn't turned on. Danika came downstairs when she heard voices. She saw Woo and said, "What's up, Zebra?"

"Nothing much, Soup Coolers," Woo said referring to her big lips and returning the clowning insult.

"Whatever, there's some food in the kitchen if y'all are hungry," Danika said, walking back up the stairs.

Woo continued to look around and his heart stopped for a second when his eyes met the painting that hung above the fireplace.

"Black, tell me this isn't ya' new woman, man," Woo said serious as a heart attack.

"Yeah, man, what's up?"

"Do you know *who* this woman is?"

"Yeah, her name is Nadeem, she grew up in Pierce Manor, she has a son, she lives in a penthouse close to Newark, and she's my woman."

"I'm fuckin' serious!" Woo said, raising his voice.

"What?" Black said, matching his tone.

"That's Ice's woman, and Ice is the father of her baby."

"Get the fuck outta here. I'm not tryna hear that shit," Black said agitated. He knew Woo wouldn't lie to him, but he was hoping that he was mistaken.

"Look, you know I wouldn't lie to you. Ice trusted me a lot back in the day, and with that trust, I met his woman and *that's* her," Woo said calming down, pointing at the painting.

Black pulled out his cell phone and quickly dialed Nadeem.

Nadeem stood in her mirror, brushing her long, silky hair when the phone rang. She pranced happily to get the phone, hoping that it would be Black.

"Hello," Nadeem said.

"Baby, it's Black ... I need to ask you something and please don't lie to me," he said with desperation in his voice. He was almost reduced to tears.

"Okay, baby, what's wrong?" Nadeem asked, alarmed.

"Is Toussaint a.k.a *Ice* the complication you were warning me about before we got together, and is he the father of your child?" Black asked with much emotion.

The question threw Nadeem off more than a little, and she was tempted to lie, but she loved this man and wanted to be upfront.

"*Is he?*" Black yelled, choking on his spit.

"Yes, yes, yes," Nadeem responded, crying over the phone.

"Why didn't you tell me this shit before?" Black asked, crying. He didn't care that Woo was watching.

"Because I didn't want to scare you off. I know people are afraid of Ice, and you were so persistent in trying to get with me and I needed that at the time. I didn't know I was going to fall in love with you, and if I told you, I knew this would happen," Nadeem said referring to the fact that Black was hurt and angry.

Black was so disgusted, hurt, and angry that he just hung up the phone.

"Black, Black, Black," Nadeem called out until she heard a dial tone. She lay down on her bed and cried uncontrollably.

Black threw his phone against the wall, sat on the couch, and cried. The woman he loved belonged to the enemy. He didn't know if he wanted to kill her to pay Ice back for taking Kasha and his brother or simply leave her alone. Black was a torn man in love. Woo saw the hurt in his cousin's eyes and said, "Sorry. I guess it's better you found out no'., than later. So what do you want to do now?"

Black wiped his eyes, sniffed up his snot, and said with a cold stare, "We go along as planned."

22

MANSION MASSACRE

A gent Simms—a.k.a. Bobby—walked into Dawkins' office, but this
time, he was really pleased to walk in more than any other time.
Bobby had invaluable information that would soon close the case and
return him back to Atlanta. The time that he spent on the case was
finally about to pay off, and he'd be able to write his own ticket like
Dawkins promised.

"It's going down tonight," Bobby said with a smile nearly close to
laughing as he saw Dawkins sitting behind his desk.

"Are you sure?" Dawkins asked, standing up.

"Tonight we attack Ice's mansion in Staten Island at 9 pm sharp."

"No bullshit."

"No bullshit," Bobby said.

"Do you know what this means?" Dawkins asked, unable to control his enthusiasm. He picked Bobby up in his massive arms and
hugged him so tightly that he had cut the smaller man's air off.

"I can't breathe," Bobby, said with the little breath that he had.

Dawkins put him down and said, "Sorry. But do you know what
this means?"

"Yeah, it means that we can finally arrest Ice and his crew as well
as Black and his boys. But more importantly, I get to go back home."

"You're absolutely right, son. I get what I want, and you finally get
to go home. I can say this much, I will damn sure miss you. You did a

great job in front of many obstacles and still came out on top. There aren't many agents like you. Are you sure I can't do anything to make you stay?" Dawkins asked sincerely.

Simms took a deep breath and responded, "Sorry, but my people in the ATL need me there. I do appreciate the offer."

Dawkins put his hand on Simms' shoulder and looked him directly in the eyes. "Tonight is going to be very dangerous. I want you to be careful out there. Don't take any unnecessary risks. Cruz and his men as well as I will have your back tonight. Before things get too out of hand, we'll be there. So lay low and be careful. Do you understand?"

"I understand, baby."

The two men stared at one another for a few seconds, realizing that the case was really almost over with. Finally, Bobby broke the silence and said, "I got to go meet up with Black to go over some last-minute details. I'll keep you posted, sir." He headed towards the door to exit, but he turned around and said, "Thank you, sir," and exited.

Dawkins watched Bobby leave and thought about the son he never had. He spent his career chasing Ice, and now it was almost all over. It felt bittersweet to him. He wondered what life would be like without Ice. He was certainly going to find out.

❦ ❦ ❦ ❦

Cruz and his men sat idly in their quarters. They were all contemplating going out in the streets to rouse things up. They figured Gregg, T-Money, or Bird should have more info by now. Cruz, growing tired, said, "Fuck this. Let's go see if the three stooges, Gregg, T-Money, or that bitch-ass Bird, have any info for us."

They all stood up, and Mendes said, "Don't you threaten us with a good time."

Just as the men thought that their boredom was about to break, the phone rang. Cruz raced to get it in hopes of picking up some real action. "Hit Squad," he said, "and make it quick, I got streets to clean and suspects to arrest."

"It's Dawkins ... sit tight. I got something real for us all tonight."

Cruz started to salivate at Dawkins' words and said, "Well ... don't keep me in suspense."

"I got good word that the Eastwick Hustlers are going to attack Ice's mansion tonight at 9 pm sharp. So get your men together, along with some others that you can trust. I'll have some men with me that can be trusted as well. I have a judge friend that's going to sign a warrant to search Ice's mansion, club, and penthouse suite. Meet me and my men at 8 pm at the Bayway Center, and we'll go over the rest of the details," Dawkins said and hung up.

❦ ❦ ❦ ❦

While Black was busy planning the next "St. Valentine's Day Massacre," Danika was planning a coming home party for her mother. She didn't want it real big, so the new house would do just fine. The house would serve as her party and gift. Danika figured she'd kill two birds with one stone as well as save money. She had Cookie out food shopping and Qiana out buying decorations and other miscellaneous things. Danika busied herself calling family members and friends. Her heart jumped a beat as she thought of the person she had to call next. She dialed the number and almost hung up the phone when the masculine voice on the other line said, "Hello."

"Daddy," Danika replied, gaining her courage. She was nervous because she didn't exactly accept him willingly the last time he came to visit. She didn't spend time with him like Black had done, so she was nervous.

"Danika ... baby, is that you?" Nate asked, happy to hear from his daughter.

"Yeah, Daddy, it's me," she said, lighting her Newport to calm down.

"What's going on, baby girl?" Nate asked as he picked the layout for the front cover of his magazine.

"I'm throwing a coming home party for Mom, and I figured since you got her to go to rehab, you might want to be here to congratulate her."

"When is it, baby?"

"Tomorrow at 6 p.m."

"I already have my plane tickets, baby."

"You do?" Danika asked, totally surprised. She thought her father was going to say that he was too busy with work to show up. This time, she would be willing to let her guard down and be more receptive to him.

"I was in constant contact with your mother, and I let her know that I would be there when she returned. I just didn't know you guys were throwing her a surprise party is all."

will robbins

"So we'll see you tomorrow then, Daddy," Danika said and hung up the phone. She was smiling ear to ear and was more enthusiastic than ever to throw the party.

❧ ❧ ❧ ❧

Black was chilling in Bobby's crib for the first time, trying to gather all his thoughts before the big night. Bobby was one of the few members of the Eastwick Hustlers that rarely took a drink or smoked, but most importantly, he thought almost like Black. Black sat on the couch rubbing his temples, looking more worried than ever. Bobby sat opposite of him having the same worried thoughts. Both of them were wondering if they were going to make it to see tomorrow. Both of their thoughts were broken up by the sound of a cell phone.

"Eastwick," Black said into the phone.

"It's Danika."

"What's up?"

"I'm calling to let you know that Daddy is coming to the party tomorrow."

"For real?" Black asked, perking up.

"Yeah, he said he got his tickets already. Uncle Tyson and some of Mommy's friends are coming too. I didn't invite none of her fiend friends 'cause she don't need no negativity around her yet," Danika said.

"Yeah, you right. So you don't need anything else? I mean, you got the food and stuff?"

"I got everything under control. I just need you to pick up Mommy, playboy."

"I got you. I'm out." They both hung up the phone and thought about how nice it would be to be a normal family.

"So ya' mom coming home tomorrow, huh?" Bobby asked.

"Yup," Black said, standing up and stretching his legs.

"You sure you want to go through with this tonight? I mean with ya mom coming home and all?"

"It's tonight or never, baby."

"You know once we do this, it ain't no going back, right?" Bobby was letting his officer mentality take over. He knew Black was a decent kid and he didn't want to see the young man go down. He wanted to tell Black that he was an agent before things went too far, but he couldn't allow his personal feelings to get involved. He also didn't know if Black would try to kill him if he let the truth be known.

Black sat back down and said, "I know you're not trying to talk me out of this shit 'cause it ain't gonna work."

"Come on, man. The money is still rolling in. Ya' mom coming home, you got a new girl I keep hearing about—"

Black cut Bobby short and said, "That new girl is Ice's girl."

Bobby stood up and said "What?!"

"Calm down, man. I ain't messing with her no more. Ice got to pay for my brother, Kasha, Slim, and everyone else he done fucked over. Now if you scared, let me know now and I won't hold it against you, but if you with me, I don't want to hear shit else," Black said demandingly.

"I'm down," Bobby said, defeated.

❣ ❣ ❣ ❣

Ice sat behind his desk thinking about all the people he had killed and the families he destroyed. He wondered had his parents not been so senselessly killed if he would have become the man he is today. He took because people took from him. He destroyed before he was destroyed. People took from him and his people, so he figured no one was going to give them a damn thing, especially not the "American Dream."

His thoughts turned to Black. Once he was out of the game, he would take a long vacation from it. He would marry Nadeem and focus on his son. He would go legit and straighten some of his issues out. He even thought about therapy.

Dubois walked in interrupting Ice's epiphany saying, "It's time to roll. We got a party to get ready for."

Ice was throwing a huge party to celebrate life. It was ironic, given the fact that he and his men were getting ready for war. He knew he was going to lose a lot of men, so he wanted to make sure that they had one last hoorah before they died. He gathered up his things and headed out the door with Dubois.

Time seemed to fly, but no one was having fun. All the members of the Eastwick Hustlers were nervous as the time drew near. Each man had to face his own demons and fears. They all knew this could be their last night on earth and any advice that they had received from their parents or other community leaders seemed to linger in their minds. Every time that they had said they didn't give a fuck crossed

will robbins

their minds. No one wanted to admit that they were scared, and no one was going to back out and be labeled a punk. Now was the time to put up or shut up.

Silk emptied his pool hall in anticipation of Black and the Eastwick Hustlers' arrival. He prepared his shooting range to let the youngsters get some target practice in before going off to war. He was going to give them a quick introduction to boot camp.

Cars of all makes and models started to occupy Third Street near Silk's pool hall. The most noticeable vehicles were the four vans that Black had rented. Black stepped out of one van, and it was nearly impossible to greet all the loyal men that stood before him. The street looked like a block party, absent of women, except for the few women that were hard enough to be down with the Hustlers.

With a crowd this big, you'd think that the cops would be out in full force, but a little money goes a long way. Besides the mayor and the chief of police knew exactly what was going down, and they hoped that Black and his men would rid them of Ice altogether. They also made sure that Ice wouldn't be warned. Little did they know Black was going to have a surprise in the form of Dawkins and company.

"What's up?" Black asked, approaching Silk, who stood in front of his building smoking a Newport as Black stepped up.

"Nothing much. Send some of ya' boys downstairs. I got some-body down there already waiting to show them some shit with those guns," Silk said, blowing smoke from his nose. He didn't say it, but he was fond of Black and many of the young men that crossed his path. He also didn't want Black to know that he was worried about him.

Black sent in Flex, Naim, Noah, Woo, Jab, and a few others to practice with the weapons of destruction as he talked with Silk.

"Hey, Silk, you think I'm doing the right thing, man?" Black asked, anxious to see what the wise man had to say.

"Don't you think it's too late to worry about that now, youngster? I mean, these boys are ready to give their life for what you believe in, for what they believe in. I've been in this game for a long time, and I don't have any right or wrong answer for you. All I can say is man has always been plagued with the 'Fight or Flight' syndrome, self-preser-vation, you know what I mean?"

"I think so," Black said, unaware where Silk was going with the conversation.

"See, I know you boys ain't got nowhere to run," Silk said pointing at all the various young men milling around. "So naturally, y'all gonna fight to preserve ya way of life. So who am I to judge? All I can say is y'all need to place a value on life and not material things. Fight to preserve ya life, not the things you get out of life. That's where you boys lose focus. Ya way of life can't just be about cars, money, jewelry, girls. All that shit comes with time and hard work."

"Yeah, but this ain't about no cars, money, or any other bullshit. This is about revenge and making Ice pay his debt," Black said.

"Vengeance is for the Lord," Silk simply said.

"Don't get spiritual on me now, Silk. If you think I shouldn't be doing this, why you helping me?" Black asked confused.

"'Cause I figured if I can't stop you, I might as well help you. If I keep you around long enough, some of my wisdom and spirituality will wear off on you," he said sincerely. "Let's go downstairs and see how ya boys are doing." Silk walked back into the pool hall with Black heading up the rear.

♦ ♦ ♦ ♦

Dawkins, Cruz, and several other officers were in the recreational room in the center at 8 pm as planned. Every man's heart beat with anticipation of taking down Ice and his men once and for all. Everyone felt like Rambo as they checked their gear. They all wore black army fatigue pants and shirts. Their Kevlar vests were tight and snug for extra protection. Their black combat boots were tight fitted for extra speed, and they even wore war paint for the intimidation factor. Each man had his own specialty weapon. Spa shotguns, assault rifles, sniper rifles, and small handguns were on deck. The only thing that made them look different from the common street thug was their jacket that had Police, DEA, or the Sheriff logo on the back.

Dawkins put the magazine in his gun, checked it one last time, stood up, and began to speak. "Tonight, we have the opportunity to rid our streets of the biggest dealer Elizabeth has known, and that's Ice," Dawkins said with conviction in his voice. He waited for the men to stop shouting before he began again.

"Ice has been slipping away from justice far too long, but tonight, we end his treacherous reign. Tonight, we go into hell and face the devil head-on. Tonight, all our hard work will pay off. All the times you couldn't fuck your wives, all the baseball, basketball, football games

will robbins

you missed with your kids, all the personal shit you put off will be paid back tonight when we arrest that son of a bitch Ice.

"But before we go, let us say a prayer," Dawkins said. Everyone bowed their head and waited for Dawkins to send up a prayer. "Heavenly Father, we ask that You watch over us men as we go to do what we think is Your will. Send an angel to guide us and protect us in the Valley of the Shadow of Death. Bring us back home to our families and give us the strength and the courage to endure this journey. Lay our enemies down before us. Give us the armor of David, the strength of Sampson, and the wisdom of Solomon to wipe out the evil that shall come upon us. We ask for all things in Jesus' name, and everyone say Amen," Dawkins concluded.

As one voice, every man said, "Amen."

"Now, let's go!" Dawkins yelled at the top of his lungs and ran for the door. Each man followed as if they were about to hit a football field.

♦ ♦ ♦ ♦

Boot camp was over for the Eastwick Hustlers, and they were ready for war. People picked out his or her weapon to their liking. They all felt like some sort of god after shooting off a few rounds. They knew they had the power to take life like God, and they all felt more powerful than ever. And they were ready to exploit and abuse their power.

Woo ran up to Silk and Black who were talking and asked, "Black, you ready?"

Everyone else was busy filling up the vans and various cars that occupied the streets.

Black looked at Woo and said, "Give me a minute." Woo stepped off and got behind the wheel of the van. He turned the ignition, and the engine began to sing. Everyone had to follow Woo to the mansion. He had been the only one privileged and trusted enough out of the Eastwick Hustlers to once get a grand tour. Woo continued to wait for Black.

"Silk, I need you to do me one more solid."

"No problem, what is it?"

Black walked over to the van, and Silk followed behind him. Then Black opened the trunk and pulled a bag towards him. He unzipped it, pulled out a VHS tape, and handed it to Silk. Silk observed the tape and asked, confused, "What am I suppose to do with this, youngster?" Black looked at him pleadingly and said, "I need you to drop this tape off to a woman named Nadeem. She lives in the Towers. You know where that is?" he asked, hoping that Silk would say yes. Black was in luck as he heard Silk say, "Yes." He continued. "I need you to get this to her tonight. Her door number is 1414, you got me? Oh, I almost forgot. Take this to her, too," Black concluded as he handed Silk a sealed envelope.

"Yeah, I got you. Don't worry about it."

Black jumped in the vehicle feeling a little more secure that the tape would be delivered. He knew that he could count on Silk. Silk knew exactly what Black was asking of him. Silk knew that Ice lived in the Towers and Nadeem was his woman. He also knew that whatever was on the tape was going to set Ice up lovely if he lived through the night. Normally getting close to the Towers or getting in to drop off a tape was damn near impossible, but Silk was still cool with Earl, "The Bodyguard." They were close back in the day, but since Earl started working for Ice, their relationship strained. But he knew Earl would allow him to complete his task for old times' sake.

♥ ♥ ♥ ♥

Music was blasting through the speakers inside the mansion as everyone was dancing and enjoying the festivities. People were sipping on the most expensive champagne and getting high on the purest of coke and dope. Ice spared no expense when it came to selecting all manner of weed, pills, or any other favored addiction. Some people were even mixing to get that galaxy high. Ice thought they might as well get fucked up now because they damn sure was going to get fucked up later when the war started.

Women were dressed scantily, practically wearing only their birthday suits. It was almost like a party at Hugh Hefner's Playboy Mansion. For the first time in months, Ice allowed himself to get loose and indulge in his own pleasures. He didn't bother with the security check, nor did he have extra security on board for the night. He even began to drink, get high on coke, as well as receive head from various women at the party. It wasn't that he was really loose; he was trying to drown out the pain that he was feeling for Nadeem. She continued to hang up on him and be disrespectful. He also found out from Earl that she was keeping strange hours. Earl didn't have the heart to tell

will robbins

him that she was seeing someone else. Ice felt like he had really messed things up for himself with Nadeem.

Dubois was the exact opposite of Ice. He was pure of mind and body. He continuously checked with the outside guards and screened the monitors. He was so on edge that he began to make Annex and his boys uncomfortable. Dubois' behavior stuck out like a sore thumb compared to everyone else's behavior. He paced the marbled floor and spoke into a headset and kept asking, "Is everything quiet out there?"

A Haitian brandishing an AK-47 answered, "Everything is quiet out here, boss." He looked around to assure himself that everything was quiet. As he saw his fellow guard across the yard, he simply nodded in a way to convey that everything was all right. Just as Dubois was going back to the monitoring room, Annex approached him in a disrespectful manner.

"Man, what the hell is you so jumpy and nervous for, nigga?" Annex asked in a drunken slur. Dubois turned around and just smiled at the young man.

"Nigga, I look funny to you?" Annex asked with fire burning in his stomach. He couldn't let go of the way Dubois killed Mark.

Dubois only let out an eerie laugh and turned his back on the younger man. Annex felt real disrespected. He knew the older man had great power and authority. He also knew that he was Ice's advisor, but Annex felt like he had no right to disrespect him. He reached out his arm and turned Dubois violently around by the shoulder. As Annex turned Dubois, he tried to say, "Nigga, don't you *ever* turn ya' bac—"

Dubois turned around and hit Annex with a left punch to the gut, which caused him to buckle. As Annex crumbled, Dubois came hurling down with a vicious right hand that made Annex hit the floor. He stumbled to get to his feet. As he stood upright, he looked Dubois in the eyes who said, "You got that?"

Annex said his few words and returned to the party. Dubois continued to watch the monitors.

♥ ♥ ♥ ♥

Donald and Raymond were getting their freak on with two lovely, shapely Haitian women. At the moment, they were pouring champagne on the women's naked bodies and sucking it off of their ebony breasts. Raymond took it a step further and slid his hand down south and played with her pubic hair before his fingers entered into her love canal. The young Haitian woman let out a sigh of ecstasy as she watched Raymond's big dick bulge through his RocaWear jeans with eyes full of lust.

Donald took a second to look at his surroundings and saw Annex stumbling, wiping blood from his mouth. He tapped Raymond and pointed in Annex's direction. Raymond waved him off and kept up his sex play. Donald stepped off, and his freak asked with disappointment, "Where are you going, baby?" He ignored the question and rushed over to his man.

"What the hell happened to you, nigga?" Donald asked, surprised.

"That bitch-ass half-breed Dubois snuck me," Annex said after he wiped blood from his mouth.

"For what? What happened?"

Annex sucked his teeth and said, "His ass was looking all nervous and jumpy, like he knew something we didn't, so I checked him. He laughed at me and turned his back on me like I'm pussy. I turned him around and out of nowhere, he starts throwing punches. But I'ma get his ass," Annex finished telling his story, his eyes filled with fury.

Donald took a step back and studied Annex. "Fuck that! We gonna pay his ass back tonight for what he did to Mark … and you. Besides, it's time for you to be Ice's right-hand man. Fuck Dubois' bitch ass."

"Yeah, it is time for me to step my game up," Annex said once he knew Donald was serious.

♦ ♦ ♦ ♦

The ride over the Goethals Bridge into Staten Island went off without a hitch. The Eastwick Hustlers were only moments away from their destination. The closer they got, the more their heart rate sped up. A few men were actually hoping that all their cars would arouse suspicion from the cops and they would be stopped and detained from the mission. They had no such luck.

Woo stopped the van a few paces from the mansion. He made sure that no one would be able to see them from the house. He knew the men walking the balconies rarely used their binoculars or scopes from their guns to see from afar.

All the men silently stepped out from their vehicles. Booga pulled out his laptop and placed it on the trunk of the car. Black walked over and asked, "You sure this shit is gonna work?"

"Is a pig's pussy pork?" Booga asked as he laughed.

will robbins

"Whatever, nigga, make it happen."

Everyone waited for the signal to move. Woo walked over to where Man, Calvin, Damien, and Taye were standing. Man was smoking a 'Port, hoping that it would calm his nerves. He wanted a piece of Ice for not taking care of his nephew that he fathered. He didn't even claim the baby. Ice took his sister's virginity and played her out like she was a smut.

Calvin wanted a chunk of Ice's ass for turning his mom onto drugs and wrecking his family's stability.

Taye was there for payback for his cousin, and Damien was there for the ride.

"Y'all all right?" Woo asked with genuine concern.

Man blew the smoke out and said, "You know how you said at those karate tournaments ya' stomach be doing flips, and you wish it was over before it started? That you pictured yourself riding back home with the winning trophy?"

"Yeah."

"Well, that's how I feel. I wish this was all over with and we were riding down the highway with Ice's head as a trophy," Man said as he stubbed his cigarette out.

"It ain't too late to take one of these whips and take off," Woo said. They all sucked their teeth and in unison said, "Nigga, *pleeezz*."

"That's why I fucks wit' y'all," Woo said as he gave all of his boys a hug. Then he stepped back and looked at them one more time. He started to say something, but Calvin waved him off and said, "Save it for later, baby."

Booga played around on his laptop for a few moments. Inside the mansion, the monitors went blank, and Dubois was more than concerned when he saw this happen.

"It's done," Booga said, proud of his work.

"Good, let's move on in," Black announced.

Dubois spoke into his headset again, but once more, he was assured that everything was all right. He still instructed the guards to be on high alert and told them to check on the fuse box.

Black waved for Noah to step up. Noah complied, knowing exactly what Black wanted. He dropped to one knee, lifted his rifle, squinted his right eye, and placed his left eye into the scope. Noah played this scenario out in his head plenty of times as he played the video

264

game Silent Scope, but the real thing was much more exhilarating. He had practiced with this weapon for months in anticipation of this very moment.

After taking a few deep breaths, he locked onto his target walking the balcony. He took one last breath, held it in, and squeezed the trigger. The bullet exploded from the muzzle silently and zipped through the air with precision. It slammed into the chest of the unsuspecting guard as the powerful force caused him to fall from the balcony, causing a loud thud. Noah changed position, took aim on the guard holding post on the west wing of the mansion, and had the same result.

Dubois knew in his heart and soul that something was terribly wrong. He felt the negative energy. The bad mojo. He smelt death lurking around the corner, and the voodoo priest in him welcomed it. He needed to warn his business partner and friend of his suspicions before it was too late, because unlike him, Ice was secretly afraid to die. Dubois hoped that his friend was smart enough to remove his dick from the young women's mouths long enough to listen.

Just as Dubois was set to leave the room to look for Ice, Annex, Raymond, and Donald walked in. Once Dubois set eyes on the three thugs, he knew the Death Angel was in front of him in the form of Annex. He had no problem dying, knowing he led a full and very eventful life. His only regret was that he knew he wouldn't be able to warn and guide Ice any longer.

Once again, Dubois smiled at the young men, only agitating Annex more. Dubois didn't give the young men the satisfaction of seeing fear or defeat in his eyes. His smile was wicked, like he knew something that they didn't.

"What the fuck you laughing at, old man? You think this shit is a game?" Annex asked as he pulled his gun out and pointed at Dubois' head. Dubois continued to smile, fueling Annex's rage.

"This nigga think I'ma joke!" Annex said, looking at Donald.

The brief second that Annex took his eyes off of Dubois was all the old man needed. He sidestepped and grabbed Annex's wrist and twisted it until he dropped the gun and heard bones snap. Annex fell to the ground, screaming out in excruciating pain. Donald had advanced on Dubois, who turned around and spit green fluid out of his mouth, blinding Donald. Donald ran around the room, shouting and wiping his eyes with the sleeve of his hooded shirt. Raymond's speed was a bit much for Dubois to handle. The numbers game finally caught up to him.

Raymond pulled out his death deliverer and let off three nervous shots. The first shot hit Dubois in his right leg, causing him to buckle. He caught his feet in time to lunge at Raymond as the second shot ripped through his shoulder. The last shot hit Dubois directly in his heart, but before he took his last breath, he reached out to put his hands around Raymond's neck to choke him. Dubois tightened his grip with all the strength that he could muster. Raymond stupidly dropped his gun and tried to ply Dubois' grip loose before he was choked to death. The old man had a pit-bull lock around the young man's neck that seemed unbreakable. Raymond was losing his breath to the point he thought he was going to die.

Donald finally stopped screaming as he gained partial sight and the burning in his eyes cooled down. He picked up the gun that Annex dropped, aimed it in Dubois' direction, and pulled the trigger. Dubois felt fire in his back, spit a massive amount of blood from his mouth, and wetted Raymond's shirt a bright crimson red, which made it look as if he'd been shot. Then Dubois lost his grip and his life simultaneously.

Annex walked over, holding his wrist, fighting back tears. As he stood over Dubois' body, he kicked him and said, "That's for Mark, bitch-ass nigga."

All three men spat on the body, feeling triumphant. They didn't care how Ice felt about it. They would deal with it later, or so they thought.

Noah successfully picked off each man holding post on the balconies as if he were playing Silent Scope. The guards walking the yard didn't notice any particular changes in the atmosphere, nor did they see their fallen soldiers lying dead on the ground.

Black and Woo moved toward the front gate, crouching down in stealth mode so they wouldn't alarm the two guards that were holding post there. Once Black and Woo advanced on the guards undetected, they pulled out their silenced .22-caliber guns and took aim. Both guards took shots to the chest and died without knowing what had hit them.

Then Black waved his hand, and all of his men pushed opened the large, black metal gate that was supposed to keep intruders out.

Booga's genius also broke the locks and all security codes. Once Black and his men advanced into the yard, all hell broke loose.

❦ ❦ ❦ ❦

Silk pulled up in front of the Towers in his F150 truck, excited to see his longtime friend Earl. He also was happy that Ice was finally going to get fucked after all he did, and he was going to be a part of it. Silk walked with his cane that looked just as prestigious as the building he was going to enter. His cane was studded with real diamonds and rubies. It was oak, and the handle was ivory carved into a lion's head. The lion's eyes were black rubies, and the teeth were brillant diamonds. The base and the shaft were filled with various color diamonds and rubies. Everyone respected and feared Silk too much to rob him of his precious artifact.

Silk stepped into the outer doors of the lobby and quickly pressed the button 1414. Nadeem was deep in thought over Ice as well as Black. She had just put the baby to sleep and all her focus was set on the two men she loved. She wished that she had told Black about Ice long before their feelings got involved, but now it was too late. She was happy about moving on without Ice, but Black was someone she couldn't do without, and if she had it her way, she wouldn't be without him. Her thoughts were invaded as she heard the phone ringing, indicating that someone required her attention.

Just as she was about to answer the phone, Earl stepped in and said, "Relax, I'll get it." Little did Earl know Nadeem was happy that he was answering the phone because she didn't want to be bothered.

"Hello," Earl said as he picked up the receiver.

"Long time no hear from Earl," Silk replied.

Earl stood silent for a few seconds, trying to catch on to the voice, but it was too unrecognizable. It had been too long since he heard that voice.

"Who is this, and how may I help you?" Earl replied, trying to be professional.

"It's Silk, baby. I guess you wouldn't recognize my voice, seeing how you living the high life and shit."

"Oh, shit. This Silk for real?"

"The one and only, baby."

Earl was happy to hear from his old friend, but he quickly jumped into defense mode. He knew Silk didn't show up just to shoot the breeze. He knew something was definitely up.

"Hold on, hold on. Why the hell you showing up outta the blue and shit?" Earl asked.

"I have some important business. Buzz me in and I'll meet you in the lobby," Silk said with serious conviction in his voice. Earl pressed the button to buzz his friend in and addressed Nadeem.

"I have to see someone downstairs. I'll be right back up." She just waved her hand to let Earl know that she had heard him and could care less.

Silk walked into the lobby and checked his surroundings. The lobby looked more like a club. A bar was set up, and the furniture was lavish enough to satisfy any celebrity that may have walked in. French mirrors decorated the walls, as well as expensive artwork. Silk walked over to the bar and took a seat as he waited for Earl. A thin white man that looked like a college student walked over to Silk and said, "What will it be, partner?"

"Just orange juice," Silk said as he placed a five-dollar bill on the counter. The man walked over to retrieve Silk's drink as Earl stepped up.

"I see you still can't get enough orange juice," Earl said.

"And I see you still have a big-ass head."

Both men embraced each other as they laughed. Just as they sat down, the young bartender brought Silk's drink.

"Would you like anything, sir," the bartender asked.

"No, thank you," Earl said turning his attention back to Silk.

"Now what was so urgent that you came to my place of business, risking your life with Ice," Earl asked concerned. He knew the full history between Ice and Silk. Silk pushed the tape and letter in Earl's direction. Earl looked at the items and asked, "What the hell is this, and what am I suppose to do with it?"

"Earl ... I know I'm asking a lot, but see to it that Miss Nadeem gets this tape and letter soon as you get back up to the suite," Silk said, pleadingly. Earl picked up the tape and letter and looked at them suspiciously.

"What's on the tape?" Earl asked, itchy with curiosity.

"I'm not exactly sure. I just know that those things need to get to Nadeem," Silk said, being truthful. Earl started to turn his friend down, but Silk gave him a look that stated, "You *owe* me this one."

Seeing the look on Silk's face, Earl quickly said, "After this, we even."

"No problem," Silk said, as he downed his orange juice. He jumped from the barstool as if it were hot and headed towards the door.

"What are you in a rush for?" Earl asked as he saw his friend quickly jump from the stool.

"I got somewhere to be, and I'm already late!" Silk yelled as he bolted out the door.

Earl shook his head as he saw his friend leaving and couldn't help but to remember why he owed Silk. Earl worked for Ice, but that didn't keep Ice from trying to seduce Earl's fifteen-year-old sister. Although she was fifteen, like most girls her age, she was fully developed like a grown woman. Ice didn't see a young girl. All he saw was a fat ass and perky breasts. He didn't even care that she was Earl's sister. That made Ice even more drawn to the young girl.

Knowing that he couldn't protect his sister from Ice too much longer, Earl approached Silk. Silk understood and immediately set the young girl up with his mother in South Carolina, no questions asked. Ice asked about the young girl from time to time, but eventually she became one of the numbers out of sight, out of mind.

Earl's sister grew up to be a beautiful young woman who attended Spellman College under Silk's mother's guidance. Earl would send money and visit his sister from time to time. She was one of the few people that wasn't affected by Ice's cruel intentions, and for that, Earl was indebted to Silk.

Silk had finally cashed in.

♦ ♦ ♦ ♦

Black and his crew rushed the mansion and killed more than a dozen men. The music inside the mansion was far too loud to hear the AK-47s, MAC-10s, and various other weapons that were being fired. The security outside the mansion was overwhelmed, outnumbered, outgunned, and definitely outsmarted. Before they were able to mount a defense, they were all taken out. No one even survived to warn the men on the inside that there was a small army advancing on them.

Black looked around for Woo on the compound once the gunfire had ceased. He was elated when he saw Woo, as well as most of his men bringing up the rear, drawing closer towards the mansion's vari-

will robbins

ous entrances. Black, like an army general, assembled his men and planned the next wave of attacks.

"Woo, take ya' boys and go to the kitchen entrance and kill anything that's a threat. We got a lot of civilians in there, and we ain't a bunch of heartless ma'fuckas so be careful," Black warned.

"Flex, Noah, Naim, take the back with some more brothas. Greg, T-Money, Bird, y'all take ya' boys and hit the garage entrance. Booga, Bobby, Jab, and the rest of y'all niggas, y'all wit' me. We gonna be bold and go right through the front door. Jab ... where's Jab?" Black asked, looking for one of his closest boys who didn't respond when his name was called.

"Jab got cut down back there by one of them dreadhead ma'-fuckas," Bobby said, as he witnessed Jab's murder.

"Fuck it ... just do what the fuck I said and everything should be a'ight." Black finished with his instructions, knowing that he was going to suffer some more casualties. He just hoped that it wouldn't be anyone that he was too close with.

Each crew ran to their destinations with murder and payback on their minds.

Woo walked down the steps slowly with his "Street Sweeper" in tow. Man, Taye, Calvin, Damien, and various other young men were right behind him, ready to give their trigger finger some extensive exercise.

Woo put his ear to the door to try and hear anything out of the ordinary, or to a least have an idea of how many people were behind the door. But, once again, the music threw all sound off. He looked back and said, "Yo fellas, I don't know what's behind the door, but once I kick it in, be ready for anything and be careful." Then Woo stood in front of the door, took a deep breath, and threw a vicious front kick that snapped the door off the hinges.

The explosion had put the men that were milling around in the kitchen on instant notice. At the sight of Woo aiming his machine gun, the men pulled out their handguns, which were no match for the "Street Sweeper."

Woo ran to the right of the room, leaving the door clear for the rest of the men to enter and flood the kitchen area. He squeezed the trigger, giving cover for his boys to enter safely.

"Yeah, ma'fuckas!" Woo yelled, as the bullets ripped through the cedar countertop and cabinets. Glass shattered, expensive china was ruined, and the hanging pots and pans were riddled with bullets. One soldier was too slow to take cover, and his body resembled Swiss cheese.

The gunfire made the occupants in the mansion aware that the party was definitely over. Many soldiers of the Port Au Prince Posse advanced towards the kitchen area ready for combat.

"Take cover!" Woo yelled as he saw many men running towards the kitchen, ready for war.

Man and Calvin took cover on the opposite side of the countertop. Taye and Woo both pushed the huge metal refrigerator over and hid behind its massive frame for cover. Damien sought refuge behind a thick cherrywood table that he had turned over. The rest of the crew stood outside the door, waiting for their chance to enter.

Roc, one of Ice's capos, ran into the kitchen with four men heading up the rear. All the men took cover as well before they let off any shots. Roc poked his head out from behind the wall to see where each man was located. The kitchen seemed to be empty as each man's body was hidden behind some kind of structure.

"Who the fuck is in here?" Roc asked, as he was ready to take a few lives.

"Eastwick, bitch!" Woo answered.

At the mention of Eastwick, Roc and his men went crazy. They abandoned their cover as they jumped out from behind the wall, spraying bullets in the direction where the voice came from.

"Die, ma'fuckas!" Roc yelled as he let his pump handle shotgun speak volumes of seriousness. The rest of his men followed suit and cursed in their native tongue. Woo, Taye, Man, and Calvin all braced themselves as bullets zipped past them and tore everything up around them.

Damien, noticing that no one was shooting in his direction, jumped up with his eyes closed and let loose his twin 45s. He was shocked when he opened his eyes and saw that he had hit his target. He had never killed anyone before, let alone fired a weapon. Before Roc knew what hit him, he was laying on the floor leaking heavily in a pool of blood.

Roc's men looked on in shock as they saw their capo fall to his death. Each man turned his weapon in Damien's direction, firing, hoping to make him join Roc in hell. That was all that Woo and his boys needed to get the upper hand. They stood up and took aim at the four men that tried to take out their boy.

The men who waited outside also took the distraction as a way to enter the kitchen. Taye squeezed the trigger on the Mac-10 and was surprised by the kickback as it was his first time firing a weapon as well. Calvin, Man, and Woo had no such trouble with their weapons as they had practiced plenty of times with various guns.

Damien ducked back down as bullets threatened his young life. Woo and his crew turned to the men that were firing at him. They squeezed the triggers on their weapons and threw caution to the wind. Woo, Man, Taye, and Calvin had missed, as the four men were able to dodge the bullets as they fired back, running for cover. The few men that waited outside for safe entrance ran into the kitchen and were killed by the powerful bullets that shot through the air. Woo, Taye, Man, and Calvin once again took cover as they saw their Eastwick soldiers fall victim to the cold, calculating Port Au Prince Posse.

"You ma'fuckas is gonna pay!" Woo yelled as he reloaded his weapon.

"Damien, you a'ight?" Man asked, knowing that Damien took cover alone.

"Yeah," Damien said, as his voice cracked. He was almost reduced to tears as he realized he could get killed. He wished that he had taken the car back when he had a chance instead of taking a life.

"Fuck you," Baptise said. He was one of the men that ran in the kitchen with Roc.

"Fuck *you*. We sendin' y'all asses back on the banana boat where y'all came from!" Taye yelled, losing his patience as fear and adrenaline took over his body. The racist comment had set the men off as they lost their cool and common sense. Once again, all four Haitians took aim and fired senselessly in Woo and Taye's direction.

Man, Calvin, and Damien jumped up and took aim at the four-man crew. Damien dumped his 45s as fast as his finger could squeeze. His first shot hit Baptise in his abdomen. Baptise's adrenaline kept him standing long enough to let off a few wild shots. The second shot blew out Baptise's left eye, and as his head hit the ground, the bullet traveled to his brain killing him instantly.

Man pulled the trigger of his M40 assault rifle and killed two of

the assailants as Calvin layed to rest the last Port Au Posse member
that was left in the kitchen. Then Woo, Taye, Man, Calvin, and Damien
walked around, looking at their boys lying dead on the ground.

"The rest of y'all okay?" Woo asked.

"Yeah," all the men answered in unison.

"Let's go help the rest," Woo said as they all walked off.

Gregg, T-Money, Bird, and a few others had reached the garage.
Once they were there, they were all sidetracked by the various parked
luxury cars. Bird stopped in front of an eggshell-white Mercedes Benz.
He put both hands up to block the shade as he looked inside of it. The
seats were a burgundy-colored velvet. The dashboard was oak, and
everything was digital. The headrests facing the back boasted TV
screens with a PlayStation and Xbox.

"Damn, y'all see this shit?" Bird asked as he admired the vehicle
in front of him. Gregg and T-Money were too busy focused on a '66
money-green Camaro while the other men were touching the Aston
Martin, Bentleys, and old-school Caddies. Ice even had a few custom-
made motorcycles that were impressive. The men were so engulfed in
the vehicles that they forgot why they were there in the first place. No
one even covered the entrance door to the mansion.

A few soldiers were listening on the opposite side of the door as
Bird and the rest of the men made a lot of noise as they admired the
vehicles like a bunch of kids in a candy shop.

"Let's kill these ma'fuckas," Joc said to the men that were eavesdropping. He opened the door as his men ran to take out Gregg and
his team. Unfortunately, Gregg and his boys were too wrapped up in
fantasyland that they didn't hear the door open, nor did they realize
that they had company.

"What's up now, ma'fuckas?" a short Haitian yelled as he opened
fire with his Uzi. The rest of the men started to shoot as well.

The Eastwick Hustlers were caught off guard, and it was too late
to make a full recovery. The Uzi and the rest of the men's weapons had
taken out more than half of the men that were with Gregg. A bullet
struck T-Money in his throat, and he hit the floor, destined to choke
on his own blood. After seeing T-Money go down, Gregg took cover
behind the money-green Camaro.

Bird found luck behind the Mercedes Benz. He pulled the hammer back on his .357, ready to let the shit hit the fan. Cautiously,

Gregg stuck his head out to look at T-Money's status. T-Money held both of his hands around his throat, trying to stop the blood from leaking, but to no avail. His legs kicked around like a fish out of water.

"Y'all killed my nigga; y'all gotta die!" Gregg yelled. He jumped out from behind the Camaro and let his "Chopper" sing. Joc and a few of his men were smart enough to jump behind the black Escalade and Ford Explorer. The rest of the men were riddled with lead as Gregg pulled the trigger, sweeping left to right.

"Yeah, die you Haitian ma'fuckas, *die*," Gregg yelled. With all the excitement, Gregg didn't even realize that he was out of ammo. Joc and the short Haitian with the Uzi wasted no time in taking him out. Joc raised his assault rifle and let loose, right along with his fellow Haitians.

"Fuck you!" Joc yelled, as his men squeezed their triggers.

Gregg's body shook from left to right as if he were having a seizure. Blood seemed to shoot out from every artery in his body. Bird looked on in horror as Gregg's body seemed to levitate with every shot he took. He was wondering when the body was going to drop.

Bird, realizing he was going to be next if he didn't react, stood up, aimed his .357, and pulled the trigger several times. The bullet took a life of its own as it zipped through the air faster than Superman.

The short Haitian still had his aim on Gregg, shooting away. Without warning, the bullet made direct contact and struck the short Haitian in the head. The impact lifted him off his feet, and he crashed into the Ford Explorer, leaving a big dent.

Joc turned to let another round off and to his surprise, a bullet impacted right in his chest, making him lose his feet. He lay hurt on the floor, barking orders. "Kill that bitch." His men let loose with everything they had. Once again, Bird took refuge behind the Benz.

Bird was afraid and knew he had to do something quick. He knew he couldn't hold off all the men with their assault rifles with only his .357. Thinking quickly on his feet and longing to have a hood story to tell, Bird aimed his .357 at the gas tank on the Escalade. As the bullet was heading toward the tank, Bird kept his head down and ran out of the garage to avoid the inevitable. *"Boom! Boom! Boom!"* was all that Bird heard as he was lifted into the air by the explosion. He hit the ground hard, and as he turned around, he saw the flames and destruction.

Slowly, Bird stood up and laughed as he beat the odds. He looked down to dust himself off and heard one more explosion from the garage. As he looked up, he saw a flaming car door flying his way. Bird was a deer stuck in headlights as the car door spiraled through the air and took his head off. Instantly, he became another has-been that never was. He wouldn't be the first or the last to chase hood legend status and fail.

Inside the mansion was pandemonium as Woo and his team advanced in the house with many other soldiers. Each man was looking for Ice to exact revenge. There was no telling Ice's whereabouts inside the huge mansion. A lot of soldiers lost their lives inside the mansion by losing focus. They looked past the men with weapons in front of them searching for Ice, and that mistake was costly for many.

Flex, Naim, Noah, and the rest of the crew had a rough time getting to the back as many men advanced on their position. Flex and his boys fought hard like a bunch of savage Romans to make it to the back entrance. They knew that their attack on the back was vital to the overall success of the mission.

As they reached the back, they were totally surprised to see a beautiful female standing out back, laughing as if nothing was happening. They stood still wondering if they should shoot her or try to get her number. The woman turned her back on the men and opened the large white double doors. With her back turned, the men were thoroughly mesmerized by her backside. However, they all snapped back to reality instantly when they saw a horde of pit bulls and Rottweilers racing toward them savagely barking with fangs exposed. The men quickly opened fire on the savage beasts taking a few of them down. Knowing that her distraction worked, the beautiful woman pulled out a light SMG and opened fire on the men.

Seeing another threat, Flex ran and took a dive into the pool to avoid the gunshots as well as the dogs. Naim was fast enough to dodge behind a gargantuan waterfall statue. Noah was too slow when it came to firing on the dogs. He had a genuine love for animals and hesitated when the pit bull ran his way. He was tangling with the pit bull that was locked onto his arm when the woman took aim on him. Naim, seeing that his boy was going to be taken out, leaped from behind the statue and shot the woman.

His shots hit her in her legs, incapacitating her. She quickly

will robbins

dropped her weapon and fell on the ground, writhing in pain. Flex emerged from the pool, knowing that the immediate threat was taken out. Noah was still struggling with the dog when Flex ran over and shot the beast in his head. The three men looked around to see how many of their associates and boys were dead. The beautiful woman definitely proved that death came in all forms because she took out many men. She also proved that women could be more dangerous than men.

Once the dogs and the woman were taken down, some men emerge from behind the various trees that were out back. Flex took an inventory of the men. "Everybody good?" he asked, ready to continue the fight.

"Everybody but those niggas," Naim said, pointing at the dead bodies.

"Thanks for that save back there, you two," Noah said to Naim and Flex in reference to the dog and woman.

"No problem, my nigga," Flex said.

The rest of the men ran into the mansion, seeing that the coast was clear. Naim and Noah followed suit with Flex bringing up the rear. He stopped as he felt a hand touch his ankle. Flex looked down, and it was the beautiful woman.

"What a waste," Flex said as he aimed his .38 and shot her in the head.

Black was at the front door with his crew. "Everybody ready?" he asked, making sure his people were on point.

"Yeah," everyone replied.

Black looked over at Booga and noticed that he didn't have a gun. He reached in the small of his back and pulled out a 9mm. "Take this Booga," Black said, trying to hand him the gun.

"You know how I get down," Booga said as he pushed Black's hand away.

"Just take it. It'll make me feel better."

"That shit just slows me down."

Before they could finish the argument, Bobby had kicked in the front door and threw a flash bang grenade, blinding the occupants inside momentarily.

"Let's roll!" Bobby yelled.

Black and his boys entered, guns blazing. Bobby stood off to the side out of sight, knelt down, and pulled out his cell phone.

Dawkins, Cruz, the rest of the Hit Squad, and a few trusted officers were heading toward the mansion when Dawkins' cell phone rang.

"Yeah," Dawkins said, his voice tense.

"It's me, Simms. Where the fuck y'all at? The shit is going down *now*!" Bobby yelled over the massive gunfire.

"We're only a few minutes away. Hang in there, son," Dawkins said as Bobby's phone went dead.

"Push this ma'fuckin' van, Cruz," Dawkins demanded.

A few Haitians were running down the stairs on the west wing, ready to join the party. Booga, seeing the men on the stairs, took his opportunity. He started throwing Chinese stars with great precision. Each man dropped, rolling down the stairs with a star planted in his forehead. Black looked at Booga's work and realized that the young man moved faster without a gun. He only wondered what Booga would do when he ran out of stars.

Bobby ran in the front door just in time to see a few weapons locked on in Black's direction. Black had his head turned away from the east wing of the stairs, looking at Booga in amazement. He had never seen anyone use that type of weapon with such skill. Black didn't notice the danger. Just as the men were about to take his life, Bobby squeezed the trigger on his assault rifle taking out the danger.

"Thanks!" Black yelled as he put his full attention back to the task at hand.

The Eastwick Hustlers had moved the fight to the upper decks of the mansion. Woo was in stealth mode looking for Ice. He felt he had a better chance of finding Ice on his own, so he broke away from everyone else. He opened a door and found himself in a workout room. As he walked in, he felt a sharp pain in the back of his head. The pain caused him to drop and almost blackout. Woo looked up and his vision was a little blurred. As he regained focus, he saw a tall, massive Haitian that resembled Six-ten holding a .45 pistol. The big man was actually Six-ten's cousin. He easily towered over Woo. Seeing Woo as an easy target the big man got cocky.

"I'ma give you a fighting chance," the big man said, throwing his gun to the side.

Woo, with fear in his heart, stood up ready to fight. He didn't

will robbins

know how he was going to take out the big fellow.

Fear and adrenaline pumped through Woo's body at breakneck speed. The big man was far too cocky to be intimidated by the smaller man. He quickly threw a flurry of punches that Woo easily evaded.

"Stop running, lil' bitch," the big man said, losing patience with his adversary.

Woo figured he let the big man tire himself out and then he would make his attack. Once again, the Six-ten look-alike threw another flurry of punches. Just as Woo suspected, he wore himself out. By now, he could barely hold his guard up.

Seeing his chance to win, Woo launched his attack. He threw a right heel kick connecting to the big man's chin. He then followed with a spinning left heel kick that staggered the Haitian. Woo tried to advance but was stopped when the man threw a front kick to his stomach. Before he fell, the big man grabbed Woo by his shirt and hit him with a right cross that spilt his lip. Woo fell to the ground and tasted his blood.

"Get up, lil' bitch," the Haitian demanded.

Woo stood up ready for round two. The big man threw a right haymaker, and Woo quickly blocked it with his left hand. He then stepped forward and gripped the big man by his waist and hip-tossed him to the ground. Woo held on to his left arm as he hit the floor, then he lay down and placed the big man's arm between his legs, squeezed his knees together, and pulled with all his might, snapping the big man's arm. Scrambling to his feet, Woo stood up and looked at the screaming man holding his broken arm.

Woo mounted the defenseless big man and asked, "Where's Ice?"

"Fuck you, lil' bitch," the big man said. He actually respected Woo for what he did, but he wasn't going to give him any info. Woo knew that the man wouldn't give up Ice, so he delivered a knockout head bunt. Woo broke the Haitian's nose and busted his mouth along with a few teeth. Because Woo respected the man as a warrior, he refused to kill the unarmed and unconscious man. He also knew that there was no honor in it.

Black searched around the compound looking for Ice. He opened a door and as his eyes scanned the area, he noticed he was in a bar-style room. Everything seemed quiet and empty—until Donald and Raymond jumped out from behind the bar, firing their 9mms. Black ran towards a table, rolled over it, and pulled it down to take cover from the bullets.

Booga, not too far behind Black, ran in the bar and simultaneously hurled two stars in the air like a ninja. One star hit Donald in his right arm, causing him to drop his 9mm. The other star hit its mark when it crashed into Raymond's skull, knocking him backwards, instantly killing him.

Donald bent down to retrieve his 9mm. As he stood up to fire on Booga, Black raised his gun and cut him down.

"Good lookin' out," Booga said, knowing he would have died had Black not moved as fast as he did.

"Just returning the favor, baby boy. Any luck finding Ice?"

"Hell, no," Booga said as he sucked his teeth in disappointment.

"It looks like nobody else did either."

As they were talking, Annex ran out of the bathroom, catching Black and Booga off guard. He fired his weapon, and the bullet flew through the air, catching Booga in the chest. He fell to the ground, clutching his chest. Black dropped to one knee and fired twice in Annex's direction before Annex could get off another shot. The first shot hit Annex in his left thigh, causing him to jerk, and the second shot took his manhood away. Annex fell to the ground screaming like a woman. He grabbed what used to be his dick, hoping that he could save himself. Black walked over and put a bullet in his head so he could die with dignity.

Then Black knelt down to check on Booga's status. "Damn, Booga, you a'ight?" Black asked, removing Booga's hand to see how bad he was.

"Shit, shit, shit, it burns," Booga said as tears fell from his eyes.

"I'm sorry, man ... this shit wasn't suppose to go down like this," Black said, fighting his own tears as he saw his boy close to death. As Black looked upon Booga's face, Booga's facial expression changed. Before Booga could say anything or warn Black, another shot hit him in the chest, immediately killing him.

Black turned his head to look up and was face to face with the barrel of a .357. The man that held the weapon in Black's face was none other than the notorious Ice.

"Looks like I caught you slippin', lil bitch," Ice said.

Black started to stand up but quickly stopped when Ice pulled the

will robbins

hammer back and yelled, "Stay where you are, lil' bitch."

Black just looked at Ice with fury in his eyes. He hoped that some-one would come in and save him again like Booga had previously done.

"All this trouble you and ya' boys went through to kill me, and now look at you. Staring down the barrel of my gun. Everything was so sweet. You had the cars, money, bitches, protection, and then you and ya' brother had to fuck it up by being so goddamn impetuous. You know how much trouble and money you cost me, lil' nigga?"

"Not enough, ma'fucka. You had Bricks, Banks, Slim, and my ma'fuckin' brother killed, nigga. You strung my mother out on that shit. I can't pay ya' bitch ass enough for that shit, nigga."

"And now I'm going to add you to my list," Ice said.

A shot rang past Ice's ear, distracting him. He turned to see where the shot had come from, and as he turned, another shot rang out, striking his hand, causing him to drop his weapon.

Black reached down for the gun ready to finally take his revenge. Unarmed and outnumbered, Ice ran towards another exit door. Black and the mysterious shooter both fired upon Ice, missing every shot. Ice was like a track star dodging bullets, making it toward safety. Black gave chase but quickly stopped when he couldn't get the door open.

He turned around and addressed his savior. "Silk, what the fuck is you doing here?"

"Remember I told you that someone had killed my brother and made me walk with this cane?" Silk asked, raising the cane a little.

"Yeah," Black said, confused.

"Ice was that person. Just like every man here, I'm looking for my revenge. Besides, I knew you young brothas was going to need my help."

"What happened to 'vengeance is for the Lord' and shit?" Black asked, amazed.

"Sometimes the Lord uses people to carry out His vengeance. I felt like I was that person," Silk said.

"I ain't mad at cha'. Just surprised is all. Hey, you drop those things off?" Black asked, remembering the favor he had asked of Silk.

"Easy as saving your black ass," Silk said, laughing.

"Thanks for the hookup, and thanks for saving my ass too ... I won't forget it," Black said sincerely. In the background, Silk and

Black heard police sirens breaking up their moment.

"Damn police. They're always around when you don't need them and never around when you do need them."

"Shit. What the hell we gonna do?" Black asked a little panicked. He didn't have a plan in case the police showed up. He knew the mansion was secluded and figured no one would have called the police. He didn't know he had a mole in his camp.

Dawkins and his crew of men pulled up in front, back, sides, and various other exits near the mansion. All the men jumped out with their weapons drawn waiting for action. Dawkins jumped on the loudspeaker and said, "Everyone come out with your hands up. We got the place surrounded, and there's no way out except through us. And we're just hoping you give us a reason."

Before Dawkins knew it, a few remaining Haitians that would rather die than be deported came out shooting. Cruz and his men immediately fired back, dropping the men like dominos. Black and Silk heard the firing and knew that the police weren't joking. Black only hoped that it wasn't any of his crew that was stupid enough to war with the police.

Silk looked over at Black and said, "We gotta give it up, young blood. We can fight in court."

"I know, let's go," Black said as he dropped his gun. The two men slowly walked down the stairs and saw a few of their people walking towards the door ready to give up. Black and Silk walked out of the mansion with their hands locked on top of their heads. Black looked to his left and smiled as he saw Woo, Naim, Flex, Noah, Man, Calvin, Damien, Taye, and a few other close friends standing in the lineup.

"Where's Booga? Anybody see Booga?" Woo asked. Black looked over and shook his head. Woo knew by the look on Black's face and the way he shook his head that Booga was dead.

"Shut the fuck up. No one told you to speak, and keep ya' fuckin' smiles to yourselves," one officer said. Dawkins called for the coroner's office, a number ambulances, and everyone else he needed to clean the huge mess up. They put the remaining Eastwick Hustlers in the squad cars and headed Uptown to the Elizabeth Police Dept.

Ice smiled as he knew he escaped death and the police. The fact that his hand was shot didn't even bother him. He wrapped it and escaped through an underground tunnel that led to his secret garage

will robbins

that housed his fully loaded Jaguar and other vehicles. Ice didn't kill the leader of the Eastwick Hustlers, but he didn't get killed either. He knew that he could get at Black another time. His main concern was to get his woman and child and get out of Dodge before the police caught up with him. Everything else could wait.

Black rode in the squad car, knowing that he didn't get to kill Ice, but he knew it wasn't all in vain. He also knew Ice was going to pay real soon. He would let his boys know that what they did wasn't in vain. Black planned on ruining Ice's life as well as the people who associated with him.

23

POLITICAL BREAKDOWN

Earl finally returned from the lobby bar after fraternizing with a young female that was hanging out there. Nadeem was sitting on the couch with her smooth legs crossed, reading, when Earl entered. He walked over and said, "This came for you."

Nadeem looked up from her book, and Earl handed her the tape with an envelope.

"What's this?" Nadeem asked as she took the contents from Earl.

"I don't know. A friend of mine said that you needed to have these things."

Nadeem put the tape down and focused on the envelope. She hoped that these things were from Black. She knew he was hurt and upset to find out that Ice was her man, and the way he hung up on her, she thought that she would never see or hear from him again. She opened the envelope, pulled out the letter, and began to read.

> *Dear Nadeem,*
> *I wish I could say that I hate you for the tremendous pain you caused me, but I would be lying to myself. I know what I sent you is going to hurt you to the core, but know that it isn't a cheap payback to regain my pride. I really don't want to hurt you, but I need for you to realize what type of man you fell for. I wasn't hurt that you had a man,*

*because I knew that coming in. I was hurt, however, to find
out that it was Ice, and after you watch the tape I sent, you
will realize why. After you watch the tape, you will feel the
same type of hurt and anguish that Ice has spread all over
the community. You will also understand why I must take
him out, and if I don't, someone else will. I apologize for
your loss and your son's loss ahead of time, but maybe I'm
doing y'all a favor. Please forgive me. I really do love you,
and if I live through this night, in time, my heart will heal
and so will yours. Maybe in time we can really forgive each
other and maybe have a fresh start together. Once again, I
am truly sorry.*

Love, Black

Nadeem put the letter down and buried her face in her hands and
cried. The two men she loved most in her life next to her father and
son were at war with each other. Seeing the letter that Black wrote
made her worst fears a reality. Ice was going to have to pay for his
indiscretions and cruelty. She tried to tell herself for months that she
despised Ice, but knowing that someone was going to kill him made
her realize that she still loved him. She didn't want to be with him,
but she damn sure wanted him around for his son. The fact that Black
was the one who was gunning for Ice really broke her heart.

Nadeem looked down at the tape and pulled herself together. She
walked toward the entertainment center and placed the tape inside
the dual VCR/CD player.

For a few moments the flat screen TV that was mounted on the
wall only showed static. Nadeem thought that it was a joke being
played on her until the tape came into focus. Her face was horror-
stricken when she saw her father strapped into a chair, busted up,
pleading for his life. Nadeem couldn't believe what her eyes were seeing. She damn sure couldn't believe what she was hearing.

Ice was giving the order for her father to be killed. Nadeem put
one hand over her mouth, reached out to the TV, and screamed,
"Nooooooo," as if she could stop what was about to happen.

In the next second, she watched her father's brains splatter as Ice
looked on in satisfaction. Tears flowed from Nadeem as anger and
hatred filled her every emotion. She grabbed both ends of the TV,

284

yanked it, and threw it against the wall. Nadeem screamed and cried uncontrollably as the TV crashed into the wall.

Earl, hearing all the noise, ran into the front room area with his gun drawn. He saw Nadeem lying on the floor in the fetal position crying. He put his gun away, bent over her, placed his firm hand on Nadeem's shoulder, and asked, "What's going on? What happened?"

"That motherfucker Ice killed my father," Nadeem managed to say between sobs.

"What?" Earl said, confused.

Nadeem sat up, grabbed Earl by his shirt with both hands, and yelled as she shook him. "On the tape. Ice … Ice had my father killed."

Earl just embraced Nadeem as she cried. He knew that there was nothing he could say or do to make her feel better. He knew his employer was ruthless, but surely not as ruthless to kill his own woman's father. All Earl could think was *damn*.

♥ ♥ ♥ ♥

Back at the EPD, not a few crooked officers nearly shit their pants to see Black and many of the Eastwick Hustlers in the custody of Dawkins and Cruz. One particular officer made eye contact with Black, and they both winked at one another. The rest of the crooked officers knew their careers and life on easy street would halt if anyone sang like a canary. Most of the young men were placed in the holding cells, while Black and Woo were brought into separate interrogation rooms.

Black sat chained to a metal chair. In front of him was a yellow pad and a pen. Dawkins hoped that the young man would get nervous and start to write a statement. Black put his head down on the table, exhausted but happy to be alive. He nearly fell asleep until he heard someone enter the room.

"What's up, Black?" Officer Reed asked. Black just looked at Officer Reed with disgust. He knew Reed was on Ice's payroll and was Officer Swank's "Go-to Guy." Officer Reed really fit the description of KRS-One's song "Black Cop," but just a little worse.

"Well, let's get a few things straight before Dawkins and his crew get at you. I don't know you, and you don't know me. My name or my fellow officers' names better not leak outta ya' mouth, lil' nigga. You goin' down, so make sure no one else goes down with you that ain't suppose to. You feel me? I know you'll live by the code of the street and the way you niggas rockin' them 'NO SNITCHING' shirts, I'm pretty sure I don't have nothin' to worry about—*right?*" Officer Reed said, patting Black on his cheek.

Black kept his mouth shut and didn't even acknowledge Reed's words, which made Reed uncomfortable. Reed knew that he didn't have much time, so he looked Black in his eyes and said, "Whatever, nigga." Then he walked out of the room leaving Black to his thoughts.

When Officer Reed walked out of the room, he bumped into Dawkins. "Excuse me, Dawkins," Reed said with a smile.

"What the fuck is you doing coming out of this room with my suspect?" Dawkins asked as he fixed himself. Dawkins was already skeptical about doing the interrogations in the EPD, but it was his closest, and only, choice.

"Well, the young brotha was in there a long time, so I went to check on him, you know? See if he needed anything to drink or something to eat. Just looking out for a brotha. You can understand that, right?" Reed asked, clearing his throat.

Dawkins knew that Reed was pulling the race card, and he also knew that he was lying through his teeth. He stared at Reed with his piercing eyes but didn't utter a word. Reed, getting the point, just threw his arms up defeated and walked off.

Then Dawkins and Cruz walked in the room, once again disturbing Black's rest.

Dawkins walked over and took a seat in front of Black while Cruz held up the walls in observation. Dawkins took a sigh of relief knowing he was close to nailing the case.

"Hello, Black … I'm Darius Dawkins, director of Operations for the DEA," Dawkins said as he held out his hand.

Black wasn't sure if Dawkins was filthy or not, but he knew he wasn't going to shake the man's hand.

"You look real comfortable for a young man who could be facing life as an adult. So what do you want to tell us?" Dawkins continued with a smirk. He wasn't happy that Black left his hand hanging.

"Nothing," Black simply said.

"Come on … Black. We don't even want you. We want that son of a bitch Ice, and we know you can hand him to us."

"Like I said, I ain't got nothing, and y'all ain't got nothing on me," Black said, strong in his conviction.

"We don't have anything on you? How about a lot of dead bodies at that mansion back there? How about a lot of people strung out on that shit you sell to them, huh?" Dawkins asked, getting furious as the moments passed.

"First of all, Ice and I are real cool, and he invited me to that mansion back there," Black said in a mock tone. "Second of all, people start shootin', and I'm running around trying to save my life. Next thing I know, you guys show up and rescue me. Elizabeth's finest," Black continued to mock.

"And as for the people I've strung out, I never sold drugs in my life." Black knew that they couldn't prove that he had killed anybody in that mansion and last he checked, it wasn't a crime to attend a party. He also knew that they couldn't make any drug charges stick. He wasn't worried about Woo or the rest of his boys, because they were sitting pretty just like him.

Cruz grew tired of Black's cute attitude and yelled, "Cut the bullshit, Raheem! We know you and ya people planned that hit on the mansion, and everybody knows next to Ice, you're the biggest drug peddler in Jersey!"

"Prove it!" Black yelled, feeling too confident.

Dawkins waved Cruz down and tried an even-tone approach.

"You know we spoke to your cousin, Woo, in the next room, and he had a different story to tell."

Black knew that Dawkins was lying. He didn't take the bait that Dawkins was trying to dish out.

"I bet he did."

"He sure did, asshole. How did we know that you two shit stains were cousins?" Cruz asked.

"Common knowledge," Black stated matter-of-factly.

"You know, once I talk to the rest of your clan out there, someone is going to break and give me what I want. I'm giving you the opportunity to talk first. Cut you a deal. If you don't want it, I'll give the first man who wants to talk a sweeter deal than Karrine 'Superhead' Stephens giving you head," Dawkins said.

"Try ya luck. My niggas would die first before they give you shit. You can't prove they did shit, just like you can't prove I did shit. They know we all walking outta here when my lawyer comes, baby," Black said, still overly confidant.

Dawkins knew that Black was right about his boys not giving him shit, because he tried it long before he spoke with Black. That's why Black was left unattended for so long. He grew tired of the back and forth game with Black, so he decided to end it. He motioned his head towards the door, and Cruz left the room.

Dawkins sat silently, and Black wondered where Cruz had stepped off to. He didn't have to wonder too long because Cruz returned immediately with company. Once Black saw who Cruz brought in the room with him, his face went from confident to worry. Black wasn't sure why Cruz brought Bobby—a.k.a. Agent Simms—into the room with him. Black knew Bobby was a soldier, so he couldn't be in the room to be a snitch, or so he thought.

"By the look on your face, I'd say you're surprised to see Agent Simms in here," Dawkins said, pleased to see the new look on Black's face when he introduced Bobby as an agent.

Black jumped up from the table and yelled, "You a fuckin cop?"

Agent Simms held his head down for a few moments feeling guilty that he betrayed Black's trust. He thought to himself for a second, then he looked up feeling less guilty and said, "Yes, I'm a cop. Black, you're a good kid. Why throw your life away for a piece of shit like Ice? He had your brother killed, strung your mother out, and God knows what else. Help us take him off the streets, please."

Black sat back in his chair and decided to speak. "I should've known you were a cop. All the personal questions, asking what was on the tapes and where they were, I *should've* known. See, Ice has done too much to sit in someone's jail cell. He gots to die."

"Not by your hands. Let us help you," Simms said.

"Fuck that!"

"Fuck you, then you go *down!*" Simms yelled back.

"So what? You seen me sell drugs? It's my word against yours, and everyone knows that you toy cops in Elizabeth is as dirty as a pigpen."

"First of all, I'm not an Elizabeth cop; I'm from the ATL, shorty. Second of all, half the time that I was with you, I was wearing a wire. Third of all, you forget that I saw you pull the trigger a few times back at that mansion as well as a few other times. Don't forget about Brick's head either. Now you can take your chance in front of a jury, but once they hear what I got on those tapes, you going down," Simms said.

Black knew that Simms wasn't bluffing about wearing a wire or what he saw and he didn't have anything on Simms to back him down, and he damn sure didn't have anything on Dawkins, Cruz, or the Hit Squad. Black knew he had to make a deal for the sake of his crew and himself, which was his plan in the first place.

He sat for a few weighing his options. He knew this day would come, he just didn't know that it would come so fast. He also thought that Ice would be dead and gone before the law caught up with him.

Dawkins saw Black's facial expression and figured he'd interrupt the young man's thoughts. "Now that you know we got you and your boys by the balls, what about those tapes?"

Before Black could answer, a tall, slim, white man with salt-and-pepper hair walked in. "Is my client under arrest?" the tall man asked.

Dawkins stood up and said, "He can be if you want to push the issue, Mr. Epstein."

Epstein was well-known in the courts and the criminal world as a no-nonsense attorney. Upon advice from Ice, Black prepaid a lot of money over the years that he was hustling and now it was going to pay off. It was the best advice that he had ever taken from Ice.

"Did you answer any questions, Black?"

"NO."

"What do you have on my client that makes you think that you can charge him?"

"Well, for starters, we have a lot of dead men back in a mansion in Staten Island that your client is responsible for. We also know that he is the leader of the infamous Eastwick Hustlers Inc. One of my agents here has a lot of pictures and audiotape against your client. He also can testify that Black killed a few men in that mansion as well as a few others," Dawkins said, pointing his finger towards Agent Simms.

Mr. Epstein looked down at Black who was still seated, and Black shrugged his shoulders.

Epstein took a seat next to Black and asked, "What do you want to do?"

"I want complete immunity for myself and my boys in exchange for those tapes you are desperately seeking to get ya' hands on," Black said as he looked directly at Dawkins.

"Fuck that. You have got to do some time and your boys—forget about it," Dawkins said.

"What I got on those tapes is much larger than myself and Ice combined. Those tapes will be the biggest bust this city has *ever* seen, and *you'd* be responsible for it. Ice and me is pennies compared to what you'll uncover with those tapes. So if I don't get full immunity for my boys and me, then there's no deal, and to sweeten the pot, I'll even give you Ice. You're not the only dealmaker in this city. I'm trying to help you further your career, brother, and give you what you want at the same time. You just have to swallow ya' pride and give me what I want in return."

Dawkins sat for a few wondering if Black was bullshitting. He wanted Ice so bad that he could taste it, and if he had something bigger than Ice, he damn sure wanted in on it too. Dawkins was too intrigued to let the opportunity pass him by so he asked, "What's on the tapes?"

"First, my client needs to know if he has a deal, and if so, you need to call the district attorney and confirm the deal. After my client has given you what you want, then you start the process for his release as well as his associates. Got it?" Epstein said with full authority.

"I don't need to call the DA on this one; I have full authority to do what I have to do to make an arrest on Ice. Now, once again, what's on those tapes?"

"Once again, does my client have a deal?"

"Let's stop the ping-pong game. Tell me what's on those tapes, and if it's good enough, your client has a deal," Dawkins said, getting fed up.

Black looked over at his lawyer and then focused on Dawkins. He wiped his tired face, sighed, and said, "How about the mayor engaged in a conversation with Ice? The mayor agreed to take care of some immigration problems, and in return, Ice would take care of the men who raped his daughter. How about the chief of police being recorded killing a witness against Ice? Or how about information on the officers that are on Ice's payroll? How about the mayor and some of your local officers being recorded having sex with underage refugees from Haiti? The list goes on."

Dawkins sat with his mouth dropped open, big enough for a truck to drive through. He couldn't believe everything he was hearing, and by the look on the rest of the men's faces that were in the room, they couldn't believe it either.

Black looked around and smiled, knowing that Dawkins wouldn't let something like this pass. He knew he would get his deal and be home in time to pick his mother up from the airport. Dawkins, still shocked, asked, "You have all that?"

The rest of the men in the room also asked in unison, "You have all that?"

"Damn right, I have all that, and then some," Black replied with a confident smile.

"Where is it?" Dawkins asked, unable to hide his excitement.

"Do we have a deal?"

"Hell, yeah … if you got all that."

"Put it in writing," Epstein demanded.

"No problem, just tell me where the evidence is."

"Bring the paperwork, and I'm sure Black will tell you what you want to know."

Dawkins and his team cleared the room to get on the paperwork. Dawkins was salivating at the thought of busting heavy police corruption as well as exposing the mayor. Not only would he be able to write his own ticket on this one, but also his pay raise would skyrocket.

After half an hour went by, Dawkins walked back into the interrogation room with Cruz and Simms heading up the rear. Dawkins slid the paperwork across the table for Epstein to examine. Epstein was happy with what he saw and directed Black to proceed with the deal.

"Bring Officer Jones in here," Black demanded.

Officer Jones was the man that winked at Black on his way in.

With a confused look on his face, Dawkins asked, "What does he have to do with this?"

"Just bring him in here and you'll see."

Dawkins once again looked at Cruz, who immediately left to do Dawkins' bidding. Cruz came back just as fast as he left with Jones in tow.

"You got me, Jones?" Black asked as Jones walked into the room.

"I got you like we planned," Jones said, smiling. Allen Jones was only a few months out of the academy, but he grew up in Bayway and he was a family friend, so Black knew he could trust him.

Allen walked back to his locker and retrieved a few audiotapes and videotapes. He returned to the interrogation room and handed Dawkins the tapes. Dawkins immediately requested a TV/VCR and a

will robbins

cassette tape player. Officer Jones went to retrieve what was needed so Black and his crew would be released.

Jones returned, rolling in a TV and VCR with a cassette player as well. After setting everything up, each man sat silently in anticipation to watch and listen to the tapes. Dawkins chose the visuals first and popped a tape into the VCR.

Once the tape came into focus, everyone in the room was shocked at what they saw except Black. He sat there laughing out loud at the raunchy things that they were seeing.

"Yeah, suck this cock, baby. I love those young, black, luscious lips," the mayor said as he stood with his pants around his ankles, *grabbing the back of a girl's head that couldn't be more than fifteen years old. Another girl was there, licking his ass, pleasing his freaky fantasy.*

"Look at the mayor gettin' his R. Kelly on," Black said laughing as the men looked on in disgust.

"Shut the fuck up," Dawkins said. Simms bit his bottom lip to keep from laughing during this serious situation. Seeing enough, Dawkins shut the tape off, took it out, and put another one in.

The VCR did its tracking thing, and the screen came into focus. Ice sat behind his desk with the mayor sitting on the opposite side of the couch. Chief Williams walked in and immediately started interrogating.

"What the fuck is going on here and why is this man tied up and beaten?" Chief Williams asked, pointing towards the victim.

Ice stood up, and Williams locked his weapon in Ice's direction. *"Calm down and put the gun away, Williams,"* the mayor demanded.

"Do what the boss says, Chief. You're not in any danger here," Ice reassured him. Ice stood next to the victim and started to explain why the chief was in his office. *"This man here is a potential witness against me and must be dealt with properly for the safety of all our careers."*

"Fuck you talking about? My future and my career are just fine. Tell me why I shouldn't arrest your Haitian ass right now?"

"Because if you arrest me, then the mayor, in turn, gets arrested, and then you get arrested. Don't think that I don't know about you and the mayor's embezzlement of city funds. See, I'm the silent partner that the mayor talks to you about. I know everything. Now ... I

brought you here to make sure that you stay loyal to our business, and you're going to prove it by killing this witness." The chief looked at the mayor and then at Ice to see how serious they were.

"What makes you think that I won't arrest you and take whatever consequences I get?"

"Because of your beautiful wife, kids, new mortgage, college tuition. You can't take care of all of that in jail or dead. Now, I can kill this man, and you'd still get just as much time if you did it yourself. We both know you aren't going to turn me in. That's not going to happen."

Williams knew that Ice was right and there was no way that his wife and kids would make it without him, and he damn sure wasn't going to jail. He reasoned with himself that the man he was going to kill would kill him in a heartbeat if they were in the streets. Williams took out his service revolver, pointed at the victim's head, and fired a fatal shot.

After the man was killed by Williams' hand, Ice said, *"Smile, you're on* Candid Camera*."* Williams turned around and looked into the camera. The screen went fuzzy, and Dawkins removed that tape.

Dawkins, Cruz, Simms, Black, and Epstein watched every tape and listened to every audiotape that was provided. It was a slow, tedious, and interesting process. Each tape was more mind-blowing than the last. Dawkins couldn't believe how corrupt the community leaders were.

Epstein, growing tired, decided to speak up. "Now that you have sufficient evidence, you and your people can start the process of letting my client and his people go."

"Raheem, what you gave us here is incredible as well as brave. I have a new respect for you. I'm going to let you and your boys go, but don't go too far because I'll need your testimony. For the sake of your family, community, and yourself, I hope you take this second chance and clean yourself up."

"You talk to your people, and I'll talk to mine. We'll see what happens," Black said.

"Let's get out of here. My old ass is tired," Epstein complained.

Black and Epstein waited for the rest of the crew to be processed out before leaving. Dawkins, Simms, and Cruz embraced each other, happy that they finally had enough evidence against Ice. They also

will robbins

knew that they all landed their career bust in terms of the chief of police, mayor, and several other officers. They were now in the position to really clean up Elizabeth.

"Cruz, get the warrants for the mayor, chief of police, Ice, and every officer that's on those tapes. Hurry up and get the judge's signature before anyone gets wise to what's going on," Dawkins said.

Woo, Taye, Man, Calvin, Damien, Flex, Noah, Silk, and many others were released from the holding cells. Black and Epstein were both there ready to greet them. Each man was smiling broadly as he saw Black waiting for him.

"I'm glad none of y'all had loose lips, otherwise all of our asses would have been done," Black said.

"How the hell you get them to let us all loose?" Silk asked, curious.

"Let's just say that the tape I gave you wasn't the only one that I had. Now all of us can forget that this night happened and move on with our lives."

"What about Booga and Jab?" Woo asked.

Black put his head down and said, "I'll tell their mothers. They'll have the biggest and most memorable funeral next to my brother's."

"All right, hit the bricks, you fucking degenerates, before we change our minds," an officer responded, growing tired of the men throwing their freedom in his face as well as his fellow officers'.

"No problem, Officer Friendly," Black said sarcastically as he and his crew hit the front door.

♦ ♦ ♦ ♦

Hours had passed since the Eastwick Hustlers were released from the EPD. The sun shined down over Elizabeth as the morning squares were getting ready for work. Black as well as the rest of the Eastwick Hustlers retired to the comforts of their beds. Black had some hours before he had to pick his mother up and get ready for the party. Dawkins had received his warrants and was preparing to make some arrests. Officer Reed found himself making his way over to City Hall to warn the mayor of last night's actions. The mayor was sitting behind his desk shuffling papers as Reed barged into his office.

"What the hell?" the mayor said, jumping to his feet as Reed scared the bejesus out of him.

"I'm sorry, sir, I tried to stop him, but he said it was urgent and barged right in," the skinny white stick figure of a secretary said.

"It's okay, thank you, Rose," the mayor politely said, straightening his suit.

"What's so important that you barge in my office and embarrass me, Reed?"

"Last night, Dawkins, Sgt. Cruz, and their men arrested Black and a whole lot of the Eastwick Hustlers."

"So, good. Less worries I have with the drugs and shit."

"No sir, you don't understand. They let them all go this morning."

"*All* of them? How could this happen?" the mayor asked suddenly cold with fear.

"Black or one of those clown-ass niggaz must have given them some heavy info to be released. Damn those snitch-ass niggaz!"

The mayor sat back down feeling like his knees were going to crumble. He said, "They must have given Dawkins the tapes that they stole from Ice. We're all done for," the mayor said, defeated.

Dawkins and the Hit Squad dressed in full gear before they headed to City Hall to arrest the mayor. They wanted to embarrass him for being disloyal to the city. They wanted him to feel the shame as they put the cuffs on him and hauled him out in front of the news cameras and his peers, as well as the people of the city. Mayor Cross and Officer Reed heard the sirens as Dawkins and his people pulled in front of the building.

"Good luck, sir," Officer Reed said as he ran out the door in an attempt to escape justice. Mayor Cross opened his desk drawer and pulled out a small .22 caliber. He fondled the piece as he cried, thinking about his wife and children. Resigned, he put the piece to his temple and whispered the words, "I'm sorry," then he pulled the trigger and brain matter and blood shot out everywhere as he fell limp in his reclining chair.

"Aaah, aahh, ohmygod!" the stick figure secretary yelled as she walked into the mayor's office to see what the loud bang was.

Dawkins and the Hit Squad followed the sounds of the woman's voice and ran into the office.

"Damn!" Dawkins yelled as he saw the mayor dead in his chair, minus a huge portion of his skull and brainless.

"Mateo, take care of the woman and everything else. Handle the media and contact the coroner's office. Help clean this mess up. The

will robbins

rest of you, let's go get our star prick, Ice," Dawkins said.

• • • •

Ice tied up some loose ends and decided to get his woman and child and get out of Dodge before the law caught up with him. He sped through Uptown traffic lights and weaved in and out of the light traffic since it was still early in the morning. Within moments, he pulled up in front of the Tower and rushed to his suite. After he entered, he saw Nadeem sitting on the couch, so he started frantically barking orders at her.

"Nadeem ... baby, pack your shit and get the baby ready. We have to get out of here." Ice was running around, trying to gather important papers. He didn't even notice that the TV was broken and everything else in the front area was destroyed. He continued to pace and bark orders as Nadeem continued to sit still on the couch.

"Nadeem, baby, don't you hear me talking to you?" Ice asked, standing in front of her.

She continued to ignore him, and he finally started to notice the damage around him. "Nadeem, what the fuck happened in here? Where's the baby? Where's Earl?"

"I sent Earl to the store. The baby is with my sister, and the mess I did," she calmly said.

"Why? Look, we don't have time for this. We need to get out of here. We'll pick up the baby from your sister's house on the way out." Ice pulled at her as she continued to sit.

"Get the fuck off of me!" Nadeem screamed as she finally stood up and pushed Ice back.

"Baby, we don't have time for this! Right now, the cops could be on their way here or some other niggaz, but either way, we need to get out of here."

"You killed my father, you sick, twisted, egotistical, greedy, heartless bastard motherfucker. I hate you! I hate you!" Nadeem yelled, sobbing.

"Baby, what the fuck are you talking about?" Ice asked, playing dumb.

"I saw it on tape!"

Ice stood in the middle of the floor, stunned. He didn't know what to say except, "Baby, it wasn't me. Someone is playing a sick joke."

"No ... *you're* the sick joke if you think I'm gonna fall for that shit!"

Ice grabbed her by her shoulders and started to shake her vigor-ously as he yelled, "I didn't kill ya' fuckin' father, now get ya' shit and let's go. We can straighten this shit out later."

Nadeem pushed him off her once again and continued to yell, "Later! Later! There ain't gonna be no later."

Ice tried to grab Nadeem once again, but this time she backed up and pulled out a small .38 snub-nosed six-shooter. "Back up, mother-fucker. You think you can kill my father and walk away from that shit? I told you someday you would have to pay for all the shit you did, and today is that day."

Ice walked towards her with his arms stretched out, thinking she was bluffing. "Baby, please come—" was as far as he got before she closed her tear-filled eyes and squeezed the trigger. The shot stopped Ice dead in his tracks as the bullet went straight to his forehead and out the back of his skull.

Just as Ice's dead body hit the floor, Dawkins and his men kicked in the front door with their guns drawn. Nadeem jumped, dropped the gun, and put her hands up as she saw the officers with their guns drawn ready to kill. Dawkins walked over and inspected the body and realized that it was Ice. He wiped his fingers across his throat to indi-cate that Ice was dead.

Dawkins looked at Nadeem and asked, "Did you do this?"

"Yes, yes, yes," Nadeem answered, crying uncontrollably. Dawkins snapped his finger and placed his hand out towards Cruz. Cruz knelt down and pulled out a small gun from his ankle and placed it in Dawkins' outstretched hand. Dawkins wiped it off and placed it in Ice's hand.

"The story goes like this. He came home and tried to kill you. He thought that you were going to testify against him so you killed him in self-defense. Everybody got that?" Dawkins asked.

Nadeem nodded her head, still crying.

"Call the coroner and get this shit cleaned up," Dawkins demand-ed. He walked out of the house, disappointed. He wanted Ice to own up to what he did and take responsibility for all his dirty actions. He wanted to show Ice that he had finally nailed him, and take that smug look off his face permanently. As far as Dawkins was concerned, Ice was given the easy way out. He didn't know why he protected the

will robbins

young lady, but as far as he was concerned, she was a justified rene-gade.

Dawkins and his men were able to arrest the crooked officers that were in bed with Ice as well as the other individuals that starred on the tapes. Back at the station, Captain Blake Johnson had Chief Williams, Officer Reed, and several other officers lined up side by side giving them a small speech before stripping them of their badges and freedom.

"You men are a disgrace to this city, yourselves, and to your badges and uniform. It is a privilege to serve this city and wear these uniforms, and you pissed on it for a few funky dollars. How dare you! Get these men out of my sight now!" Captain Johnson, soon-to-be chief of police, barked.

"Good job, Dawkins. I hope now that Ice is out of your life, you can rest more easily at night," Johnson said.

"I hope now that you have your station cleaned out, *you* can rest at night."

"Well, let's just say both of us will be getting some well deserved pussy and rest," Johnson said, as he and Dawkins began to laugh.

"Now that I'm going back to the ATL, I can also get some well deserved rest," Simms put in.

Dawkins shot Simms a look after his statement. Catching on to what the look meant, Simms quickly responded, "Don't worry, Dawkins, I'll be back for the Grand Jury and the trial."

"I expect nothing less, son. Good job, men, until the next case," Dawkins said as he walked out of the precinct.

24

Returnin' Home Party

Sandra rested her head on the comfortable seat, gazing out of the small window of the plane. Like most people, she played the game of trying to see what the clouds resembled. Growing tired of the game, she simply closed her eyes, and thought how her homecoming was going to be. She knew she had to first and foremost apologize to her children for all the mistakes she made. She also knew she had to make amends to the people she lied to, cheated, and stole from chasing that almighty high. Then she would find a sponsor, hit some meetings, and take things one day at a time. Her mind was racing with excitement and anticipation.

❦ ❦ ❦ ❦

Danika woke up and pulled the comforters off her smooth, golden-brown body. She always loved sleeping in the nude. She was more excited than usual, knowing her mother was finally coming home and that her father would be in town shortly. She knew her mother would be more beautiful than ever before and that she would be a changed woman, especially if the place had the same effect on her as it did on her father.

Excited, she put her pajamas on and pulled her hair back into a ponytail. After making a bathroom stop, she headed downstairs, opened the front door to check out the weather, and noticed a newspaper on the porch. She bent over and picked up the paper and read the headline:

DRUG KINGPIN KILLED IN HIS PENTHOUSE SUITE

The news of Ice's death eclipsed the news of the mayor committing suicide and the arrest of the police chief and several other high-profile officers. They were also in the paper, but Ice's murder took precedence when it came to the headlines.

Danika read and reread the article and couldn't believe what she was reading. Ice was finally dead. The paper said that his woman killed him in self-defense and that no charges were going to be brought against her. Danika ran upstairs and burst into Black's room. He had fallen asleep only two hours ago.

"Black! Wake up! Wake up!" Danika yelled excitedly, shaking him awake.

"What's up?" he asked.

She handed him the paper. Groggily, he wiped his eyes and read the headline. Absorbing the words, he was fully awake. It took him a few minutes to read the article. He wasn't surprised. It was exactly what he expected to happen if he didn't get to Ice first. He knew Nadeem well enough to know that she wouldn't allow Ice to live, knowing that he murdered her father. She wasn't a hood chick, but she was from the hood, and he knew that she wouldn't let Ice think that she was that sweet to let that shit ride.

After he was finished reading, Danika asked, "Can you believe that shit?"

"Yeah, I can believe it. Now get out. I have to get some sleep."

Once Danika left, Black lay back down and smiled, knowing that his plan had worked.

❦ ❦ ❦ ❦

Everyone in Elizabeth bought a paper or watched the news. The news of Ice's death spread like wildfire. The hardworking people of the community were happier than the Munchkins when the Wicked Witch of the West was killed. But even with Ice removed, there are ten more waiting to take his place. The news of the mayor killing himself and the arrest of several crooked cops rocked the community. The media was all over the stories like flies on shit. Most of the reporters were looking to boost their careers through the ratings and scandals. They even tried to get an exclusive from Nadeem, who turned them down instantly, preferring to grieve alone.

They offered her money for her story, but like Ice said, she wouldn't have to worry about money once he was dead and gone. The media, however, wasn't totally left out in the cold. They had exclusives from Dawkins, Agent Simms, Sgt. Cruz, and surprisingly, a few members of the Port Au Prince Posse.

❧ ❧ ❧ ❧

Danika looked at the antique wall clock and realized that it was time for Black to pick their mother up from the airport. She turned the flames on the stove low and turned the heat down on the oven. Then she walked back into Black's room. The room was empty to her surprise. She heard the shower running and opened the bathroom door. As she did so, she was hit with a blast of steam. "Damn ... hey, Black, it's almost time to pick Mommy up," she said, waving her hand through the steam, trying to clear the air.

"I know. I'm almost done."

She closed the door and left her brother to his business. Just as Danika made her way downstairs, the doorbell rang. As she opened the door, she was happy to see her Uncle Tyson, Woo, Dee Dee, and Dee Dee's baby standing there.

"Hey, Uncle Tyson, Dee Dee, come in," Danika said, giving her uncle a hug.

"Hey, to you, too, Woo," Danika said as Woo walked in right past her. She took the baby from her cousin Dee Dee. She could never resist a baby.

"Come on, girl, you know I love you," Woo said wearing a big smile.

Black made his way down the stairs, dressed in beige khakis and a button-down, long sleeve Jean John shirt with new Timberland boots. "What's up, everybody?"

"Nothing much. Just happy to know your mother's coming home clean and sober. I'm ready to celebrate," Tyson said.

"What's up with you, Woo?"

"Here for the same thing."

"Well, I'm on my way to pick my mother up. Why don't you roll with me, Woo?"

"I'm down with that."

"I'll be back with the guest of honor soon. Hey, what's up, Dee Dee? Long time no see," Black said as he reached out to hug his

will robbins

cousin.

"I know ... I just been busy with the baby and all," she replied, embracing her cousin.

Black and Woo headed out the door. Just as soon as they left, a lot of the invited guests started to show up. Danika was more than pleased when she opened the door and saw her father standing there looking handsome.

"Hey, baby girl, how's everything?"

"Everything's going according to plan. The food is almost ready, some of the guests are here, you're here, and Raheem just went to go pick Mommy up."

"Good ... this is going to be real good," Nate said, entering the house. He introduced himself to the people he didn't know and got reacquainted with the ones he did know.

● ● ● ●

Sandra's plane landed at the same time that Black and Woo pulled in front of the terminal from where she was going to exit.

"Stay in the car just in case someone tells you to move it," Black said, exiting the car.

Sandra stood by the baggage claim belt waiting for her luggage. She had her back turned to Black, who didn't even recognize her because of the healthy weight she had put on. She also let her hair flow down to her shoulders now.

Black was just about to admire his mother's backside when she turned around and immediately ended his thoughts. Her eyes connected with Black's, and she ran to him as if he were the Second Coming of Christ.

"Baby ... baby, I missed you soooo much," Sandra said, embracing her son for the first time in months.

"I missed you, too. You look different; I mean, you look *good*."

"Don't I know it," Sandra said smiling, slowly turning around so Black could get a good look.

"I'm parked illegally. Let's get ya' bags and go."

Woo stood outside the Escalade and smiled as he saw his aunt exiting the terminal with Black.

"That place really agreed with you, Aunt Sandra; you look good."

"Thank you. Now shut up and give me a hug."

Everyone finished with their formalities and entered the vehicle, and Black pulled into traffic and headed toward his mother's surprise.

Sandra spoke about her experience in the rehab center long enough to realize that she wasn't heading toward Elizabeth. "Black, where are we going, baby?"

"It's a surprise, Ma."

"Baby, all I need is to be around my family in my own home and around things that are familiar to me."

"Aunt Sandra, you gonna get that, *plus* more. I think you're gonna like the surprise."

"What's he talkin' 'bout?"

"Just relax, Ma. Woo, put the blindfold over her."

"Blindfold? I just got out of rehab, not the mental institute. Ain't nobody blindfolding me," Sandra protested.

"Don't they teach you how to cooperate in rehab? Come on, Ma, do it for me."

Sandra thought for a few moments and then figured she'd let her son take care of her.

"All right, all right, put the blindfold on. This better be worth it," Sandra said, smiling.

It was only minutes after that small debate that Black pulled up in front of his home. Danika saw the vehicle pull up and yelled, "They're here! They're here! Get ready!"

Black opened the car door for his mother and took her by the hand.

"I got you, Ma," he said as he walked her up the brick stairs.

Woo opened the door, and Black and Sandra walked through. Then Black pulled the blindfold off his mother's eyes, and everyone yelled, "Surprise!!"

"Oh my god, oh my god," Sandra said, crying.

"Welcome home!" many people said at once, smothering Sandra as she tried to hug everyone.

Once all the hugs and kisses settled down, she saw Nate standing in the middle of the floor. She walked over to him with her arms outstretched, and he quickly embraced her in his massive arms. They both were shedding tears knowing what they had both been through. Danika, Black, Dee Dee, and Woo all exchanged glances and smiles as they witnessed Nate and Sandra sharing a moment.

Sandra let Nate go, wiped her tears, and asked, "Who put this

will robbins

together, and whose house are we invading?"

"Well ... Danika put this together, and the house we're invading is yours, Ma," Black said, smiling, knowing that he accomplished something special. His only regret was he bought the house from the ill-gotten wealth off of other people's misery.

Sandra's eyes flew open in amazement as she began to cry again. Once more, she hugged her son. She knew that she was living in a home bought off the pain and despair of many fiends, but this would be the last time that she'd accept anything that wasn't bought with hard work and dedication. She was going to get her family back together and on track, even if it killed her.

Breaking the moment, Tyson yelled, "Let's eat!"

"I know *that's* right," Sandra said as Nate took her by the hand and led her to the huge, king-sized table.

Dinner was over and done with when Black decided to show his mother the rest of the house. First, he took her into the master bed-room, which was decked out MTV *Cribs Style*.

Sandra decided it was time to have a personal talk with her son. She placed both of her hands on Black's shoulders and said, "Son ... I love you and this house. It's beautiful and I know you have nothing but good intentions. But just remember that the road to hell is paved with good intentions.

"This house, that truck, all the money, it's all acquired by the suffering of our own people. Suffering that I went through myself. This house is the last gift that I will accept with drug money. I know it sounds like I'm being hypocritical, being clean for only a matter of months, but, son, I know what I'm talking about.

"I will never touch another drug again, and that's the truth. I'm sorry for the embarrassment I caused this family. I'm sorry that I wasn't strong enough to protect you and your brother from those streets. I lost your brother, and I damn sure ain't gonna lose you. I have a clear mind, a stronger spirit, and a will to see you and your sister become better than what you are. We are one black family that's gonna make it, I promise you," Sandra finished, reduced to tears.

Danika walked in the room and saw her mother embracing Black as she cried. Danika walked closer, and her mother put her arms around her as they all embraced in a group hug.

"I'm sooo sorry, babies. This is the last time we are going through this."

"We believe you, Ma," Danika said, as she began to cry. They were all still missing E-Double, but this was a joyous occasion for them as a family.

Nate began to wonder where the guest of honor had disappeared to with his children. Then he saw his family embracing and remembered when they all were close back in the day. He cleared his throat to let Sandra know he was in the room.

"It's nice seeing everyone back together and happy again," Nate said.

"So now that Mommy's back and there ain't no funerals, I guess we ain't gonna hear from you after this," Black said apprehensively.

"I'll be around a lot more than you think, baby boy," Nate said with a reassuring smile.

"Does that mean you're moving back to town?" Danika questioned.

"Yes. I can open up an office out here with no problem," Nate answered.

Sandra looked at her children and said, "That ain't even the cool part."

Black and Danika looked at their father and then mother, trying to figure out what they were so giddy about.

"Stop playing and tell us what's going on," Black said filled with curiosity.

"Yeah," Danika said, cosigning.

"Your father and I, over the past few months, discovered that we never stopped loving each other. It was only the drugs that kept us apart. The cleaner I got, the more I could see and focus. I realized that I hated your father for having the strength to kick his addiction. I was jealous and hurt back then. I hated myself and everyone else. I've learned to love myself and realized my self-worth as a woman. I'm now ready to be the woman the Most High created me to be. Now that I've learned to love myself, I can love others around me."

"Ma ... I'm happy and all, but what does all this mean?" Black asked, interrupting his mother.

Nate, growing tired of all the waiting, said, "What she's trying to say is that we want to see if we're compatible again."

"Get the fuck outta here!" Danika yelled happily.

will robbins

Sandra and Nate's mouths dropped as they heard their daughter curse.

Black started to laugh and said, "It's cool, Dad, real cool."

Once again, the family was reconnected and stronger than ever this time. They all embraced each other, as they all realized that the Most High had created another miracle and blessing for them.

"Let's go downstairs and tell everyone the good news," Sandra said. They were more than willing to share the news.

The few people that stayed after dinner were dancing when Nate, Sandra, Black, and Danika came rushing down the stairs.

"Guess what? Guess what?" Danika yelled like an enthusiastic little schoolgirl jumping up and down.

"Chicken but," Woo said in response to Danika.

Tyson walked over to the stereo and turned it off. Everyone stopped dancing and gave them their undivided attention. Sandra and Nate held hands and stood in the middle of the floor, smiling.

"What's this news that got all of y'all running down the stairs about to break ya' necks?" Tyson asked.

"We're gonna give love another shot," Nate and Sandra said.

Tyson walked up to his sister and gave her a hug. "Thanks for what you did for my sister. I won't forget it. Congratulations," Tyson said as he shook Nate's hand.

"Thank you. I love her," Nate said, sincerely.

Woo saw how happy everyone was and decided to keep the party going.

"Excuse me, excuse me. I was going to wait till later, but I figured I'd tell everyone now." He waited until he had everyone's attention before speaking again.

"Well, go ahead, son, we don't have all night," Tyson said, smiling, messing with his son.

"Well, Pop, ya' son is going to be living in D.C., because my acceptance letter to Howard U. came in the mail today."

Tyson ran over and bear-hugged his son.

"I *knew* you could do it; I'm so proud of you."

Sandra hugged her nephew and said, "I knew you would be the one, baby."

"They let anybody in there nowadays, I see," Danika said, teasing. "PSYCH! I'm just clowning. I'm happy for you," she said.

"Excuse me, excuse me," Black said, trying to calm everyone down. All eyes turned in Black's direction, and everyone now gave him their undivided attention.

"We've had a lot of surprises here today, and I have one last one. I, too, will be living in D.C., because *my* acceptance letter from Howard U. also came in the mail today."

Everyone said in unison, "What?"

Laughing, Black covered his ears to escape the noise. Everyone continued to look at him for an explanation.

"Woo ... remember I would disappear at the same time every day?"

"Yeah ..."

"I was studying for my GED, and when I passed it, I started to take classes at Union County College. I applied to several other colleges, but I really wanted to attend Howard. That's why I told you to apply there. The day you took your SAT test, I was also there taking mine, too, but I didn't allow you or Taye to see me. I got a qualifying score, so I will see you on campus, baby boy," Black said, laughing.

Hearing Black's news made Sandra cry once again as she asked her son, "Are you serious, baby?"

"As a heart attack, Mama."

"My baby is going to college!" Sandra yelled as she embraced her son with tear-filled eyes.

"Damn, baby, can a father get a chance to congratulate his son?" Nate asked.

He wrapped his arms around Sandra and Black. Sandra couldn't seem to let Black loose.

Tyson was happy that his son and nephew were going to a school of higher learning, but one thing was stuck in his mind, so he had to ask, "Woo, Black, did they give you guys any scholarships for athletics or academics?"

"No," the young men both answered.

Tyson asked one more question, "Do you two have it figured out on how your tuition is going to be paid? I know this seems like a bad time to ask something like this, but I need to know what type of plans we need to make to make sure you boys get there."

"Well, Uncle Tyson ... we all know that I'm one of the biggest dealers in Jersey."

"*Ex*-dealer," Sandra said, interrupting her son.

"*Ex*-dealer, excuse me. I knew I wanted something better than being a dealer, so when I figured I wanted to go to college, I put a lot of money aside for it. I was wise with my money. You don't have to worry about Woo, 'cause I got enough money for him as well."

Woo looked over at Black in shock and said, "You don't—" That was as far as he got before Black cut him off.

"I wanted Double to take this ride with me, and since he ain't here, there ain't another person I'd rather do this with. If Double was here, he'd *want* you to go."

Sandra and most of the people in the room started to cry.

"If Double was here, *he'd* be going, bruh'," Woo said, trying to make people laugh.

Nate wiped his eyes and stepped up and said, "Neither one of you need to worry about paying for school. My company will handle it. Keep your money, boys. I'm also going to start a scholarship fund in your brother's name."

"This is too much," Sandra said. She was living a real-life hood fairy tale come true. She was clean, owned her home, her son was going to college, and her man stepped back into her life. Never did she dream that her prayers would be answered. She would die if Danika gave her some positive news. She knew eventually her daughter would get something going for herself. She'd just keep the faith until it happened. The party lasted until every morsel of food was gone and the neighbors started to complain.

❧ ❧ ❧ ❧

A FEW MONTHS LATER

B lack was running top speed up the hill to make it to his statistics class. He ran through the gate into the courtyard and was nearly at the building where his class was held when he bumped into someone. His books fell on the ground, and other books fell on top of them. Black bent over to help pick up the books. Neither person looked up as they tried to gather their books.

"I'm sorry about this; I wasn't even looking. It's just that I'm late for class."

"It's all right, I understand," a feminine voice answered.

Black looked up. The voice seemed familiar.

"Nadeem?" Black said.

"Black?" Nadeem asked as she looked up.

They both stood up, and Black asked, "What are you doing here?"

"I go here. What are *you* doing here?"

"I go here too."

Once their eyes connected, it seemed as if their souls connected as well. All the things that they had gone through prior to running into each other didn't matter any more. It was like ancient history.

Black and Nadeem looked into each other's eyes quietly as if they were studying each other's heart.

"Nadeem, all that shit that happened a while ago, I'm—"

Nadeem shut Black's mouth by passionately kissing him on those luscious lips.

She looked Black in his eyes and said, "In your letter, you said that if you lived through the night, that in time, your heart would heal, and mine would, too. You also said that you were doing my son and me a favor. Well, you were right. This is a new place and a fresh start for both of us. I never stopped loving you, and I know you still love me. So can we make this our fresh start?"

Black shed a tear as he saw the sincere look in Nadeem's eyes.

"Yes," was all Black could say as they embraced each other.

will robbins

Epilogue

Flex, Noah, and Naim ran the Eastwick Hustlers with an iron fist, only to be taken down by Cruz and his Hit Squad. But for every one drug dealer taken off the corner, there are many more eager to replace them. As long as there is poverty, disenfranchisement, oppression, and suppression, dealers will be like roaches and multiply.

Dawkins retired after Ice was dead and gone. There wasn't any more glory in the job for him. Agent Simms left the ATL with a little persuasion from Dawkins. He rightfully took over where Dawkins left off. Sandra remained clean, but years of abusing drugs and letting men abuse her body left her with a diagnosis of HIV. Nate, upset by Sandra's plight, moved back to L.A. and only kept minimum contact with his kids. Tyson inherited his brother's bar and apartment complex after his brother's early demise.

Black and Nadeem's relationship was just as strong as their grades. Woo focused and studied his ass off to make the grades. He didn't have time to bullshit, knowing Anasia was pregnant back home. Taye ran track for Rutgers University and was training for the Olympics. Calvin went on to receive his CDL license driving trucks, and he found that the world was much bigger than the projects in Elizabeth. Man decided that he would study the art of cutting hair and worked as a barber. He also dabbled in comedy, waiting for his chance to debut on *ComicView*. Damien stayed in Elizabeth and chose to go to Kean College, but things got rough when his parents divorced.

Vicky continued to strip and allowed herself to be smutted. Lisa followed her man Taye to Rutgers University, where they still found a cozy spot beneath the stairs to fuck. Danika continued to be used and abused by men, even after learning of her mother's condition.

With Ice dead and gone, Black out of the game, and the crooked officers and politicians removed, Elizabeth had an opportunity to thrive. But it wouldn't be long before all the positions would be filled with someone more greedy and more treacherous than the last. Enter Fat King!